RAW
DEAL

ALSO BY LES STANDIFORD

Done Deal

Spill

RAW DEAL

A NOVEL

LES STANDIFORD

HarperCollins*Publishers*

AUTHOR'S NOTE

Though I love South Florida just as it really and truly is, this is a work of fiction, and I have taken occasional liberties with the landscape and place names involved. May they please the innocent and guilty alike.

HarperCollins books may be purchased for educational, business, or sales promotional use. For information, please write: Special Markets Department, Harper-Collins Publishers, Inc., 10 East 53rd Street, New York, NY 10022.

FIRST EDITION

Designed by R. Caitlin Daniels

Library of Congress Cataloguing-in-Publication Data

Standiford, Les.
    Raw deal / by Les Standiford. — 1st ed.
        p.   cm.
    ISBN 0-06-017732-2
    I. Title.
PS3569.T331528R38   1994
813'.54—dc20   94-18396

94 95 96 97 98 ❖/HC 10 9 8 7 6 5 4 3 2 1

It might be possible to live in the valley,
To bury oneself among flowers,
If one could forget the mountain,
How, setting out before dawn,
Blinded with snow,
One knew what to do.
　　　　　　　　　—Donald Justice,
　　　　　　　　　　"Here in Katmandu"

What matters is not the idea that a man holds
　　but the depth at which he holds it.
　　　　　　　　　—Ezra Pound

This one's for Charlie W., Dean of the Miami School,
and for Ressie Patterson, sweet lady of Cambridge
—may they waltz forever in the great dance hall.

And, as always, for Kimberly, and the Three Muskatoots.

Deal and I would like to extend special thanks to Captain Buzz
O'Sullivan, Ron Magill, Nat Sobel, Dr. Eric Kurzweil, Rhoda
Kurzweil, and James "Independence" Hall for their invaluable help
in the preparation of this manuscript.

 Tha-*wing*, tha-*wing*, tha-*wing* . . . the sound echoed in Coco Morales's ears as he swung the heavy blade again and again into the endless stand of cane before him. He was groggy from the unaccustomed exertion, from the afternoon heat, from the hypnotic sweep of the steel before his eyes. Tha-*wing*, tha-*wing*, the brittle rush of stalks falling one after the other, his feet shuffling forward between the jutting cobs, the steel in his hand so sharp he could hardly hear the pinging at the end of his arm, sugar's last scream before it died.

"Fock, man." A voice behind and to the left of him. "Fock this shit."

"Yeah, we might as well be in Camagüey." Another voice, also in Spanish, this one on Coco's right.

Coco stood, wiped sweat from his brow with a swipe of his already soaked shirtsleeve, glowered back at the two who'd spoken. "Shut up," Coco said. "Someone hears you, then what?"

"I'm no focking cane cutter," the small one from Camagüey said. Edgar. He was a mulatto, had his head shaved, had what looked like a jailhouse tattoo peeking through the blue stubble up there. He'd stripped his shirt off, tucked it into the waistband of his canvas pants. Wiry arms, shoulders puffed with muscle. He'd sheathed his machete and was rubbing his sore arm.

The other one, Manrique, a hulking creature with tiny eyes in his big, broad face, had also given up the pretense of work. His eyes flickered back and forth between Coco and little Edgar, the hint of a grin on his puffy lips.

Coco nodded thoughtfully. "It's true, you're no cutter." He sighted in on the little one's tattoo. What was it? A rose? A gnarled heart? Maybe something Edgar had hacked in there himself.

Coco heard a motor somewhere far off, glanced toward the sound. What strange things could happen in this life. Here he was, out in the middle of the Florida nowhere, with two Marielitos, all of them pretending to be cane cutters. Not exactly what he had bargained for the day his employer had taken him on.

The sky was leaden, the underside of a barge. Not even clouds, really. Just a barge full of rain up there, so heavy it could hardly move, a barge full of water steamed up from the Everglades, sliding over toward the coast a few miles, never to make it to the beaches, about to dump itself down on Coco and his men, on all this big sugar land.

Lot of money in sugar, all right, Coco thought. And this was the place to grow it if you couldn't be in Cuba. All this flat land and rain when you needed it, and big Lake Okeechobee up there to drain onto your land if the clouds forgot to come.

"Edgar, he is tired," Manrique offered.

Edgar nodded agreement. "How long we going to fock around this way?"

Coco had the tip of his blade at his lips, tasted sweet stickiness on the point with his tongue. Spend enough time with creatures like these, you would understand how a caste system had developed.

He noticed a tiny vein pulsing like a crooked river down Edgar's scalp. The vein reached the odd tattoo and disappeared. Maybe it wasn't a tattoo after all. Maybe it was some strange type of birthmark, maybe the little vein fed it. Coco was also wondering if he could accomplish what he had been sent to do with only one helper.

Edgar stared back, barely widening his eyes in question. Bored. Or was this going to come to something?

The sound of the motor was growing louder. Coco jerked his head toward the sound. "Perhaps it is him. You want to get paid, you start the cutting."

Edgar looked away, then back at Coco. Coco watched him,

watched Manrique from the corner of his eye. He listened to the motor, a sudden whine. That was surely it, the Jeep, making the sudden turn off the main levee road, climbing over the narrow arched bridge . . . yes, a Jeep in low gear.

Coco knew how much time before the Jeep arrived. Knew how deep was the water in the canal that ran beside them. Knew what he could do to Edgar and Manrique. But couldn't know for certain who was coming. Just the foreman, riding by to check again on the new crew's progress? Or maybe *el jefe* too, the opportunity they had been waiting for. In which case he would need help.

He felt a stiffness growing in his shoulders. He was tired too.

"Perhaps it is him," Coco repeated. "Let us do the job, okay?"

"Fock, man." Edgar shook his head. "I'm sick of this shit." But he appreciated being *asked*. He dropped his gaze, went back to the cane.

They were all back to work by the time the Jeep arrived, throwing up a screen of dust from the dirt track along the canal. Coco glanced between his legs, felt his pulse quicken as the dust subsided.

All this he saw upside down: the foreman at the wheel, a beefy Anglo in stiff khaki shirt and pants, mirrored sunglasses in the middle of his fried pink face. A second man in khakis rode the jumpseat in back, a shotgun cradled between his legs. But what excited him was the third one, the white-haired man in the passenger seat.

"*El jefe*," Coco said, as if crooning to himself, and stood to turn. He waved and grinned and walked toward the idling Jeep, and Edgar and Manrique followed after.

Coco had his cap off, held it crossed over his chest as if he were a ballplayer waiting for the game to begin. Edgar and Manrique, on his heels, bowing and scraping too. Weren't they all happy to be out here, slaving for *el jefe de azúcar*, king of the endless sugar fields?

The foreman leaned to say something in *el jefe*'s ear as they approached. *El jefe* nodded and turned to Coco, who had come to a stop near the open-sided Jeep.

"You are recently arrived from our country," *el jefe* said. Snowy-white hair, clear blue eyes, a starched white shirt with a tiny horse and rider embroidered on the breast, cotton slacks, and moccasins without socks. You might mistake him for any of the wealthy Anglos treading the sidewalks of West Palm Beach, not thirty miles from where Coco stood. But *el jefe* spoke flawless Spanish, with a Castilian accent drilled into him by relentless Jesuits in Havana and polished at a university in Madrid.

Coco knew of *el jefe*, as anyone from his tiny village did. The father of *el jefe* and his father and his father before had held sugar plantations in Santiago de Cuba, and their bloodline was said to have found its origins in that of Queen Isabella herself. Now he sat in a Jeep in a Florida field and wore a pistol in a capped leather holster at his hip and spoke familiarly to Coco Morales, who traced his own bloodlines back to shit.

"I am." Coco nodded. He indicated his companions with a sweep of his cap. "We are."

El jefe regarded them as if what had washed up to Florida from his homeland was a great disappointment. In the mirrored reflection of the foreman's glasses, Coco saw what *el jefe* saw: a fat clown and a thin fool led by a cadaver with his cap in his hand. A pathetic trio, no doubt about it.

"I will give you some advice," *el jefe* said, using the tone of an impatient schoolmaster. "First, you will have to forget all those stories about the streets of gold." Coco nodded. He was thinking about his father, who had died drunk and asleep in the middle of a muddy road outside Salazar, his head crushed beneath the wheels of a propane truck.

"You will work hard for the privilege of being here," *el jefe* continued, his nostrils flaring. "It is your duty and your privilege." Coco saw that the guard with the shotgun had noticed his cap, bearing the likeness of a seal-like creature and the name of a professional baseball team. The identical cap was perched atop the head of the guard who stared down at him. The look on the guard's face did not suggest that they would enjoy baseball games together.

"Save your money, learn English," *el jefe* said. "Try to make something of yourselves."

Coco nodded. *El jefe* gave him a last admonishing glare, then seemed to remember that he was paying the three of them nearly four dollars an hour to stand in the broiling heat and listen to his advice. He dismissed Coco with a nod and turned to order the foreman away.

Coco gestured to Edgar and Manrique with his chin. "Now," he said, in case they doubted him.

Edgar had edged toward the front of the Jeep during *el jefe*'s speech. At Coco's gesture, he spidered his way back to the opposite door, raised his knife, and swung.

The foreman, who'd been wrestling with the wheel of the Jeep, glanced up in time to see the sky, reflected in a flash of steel, fall upon him. He tried to shield himself with his arm, but he was too late. The blade took him high, his mirrored sunglasses flying off in two pieces.

The guard in the jumpseat was still fumbling for his shotgun when Manrique reached him. Big Manrique braced himself against the frame of the Jeep with one hand and sent his blade at the guard in a backhanded arc. It caught the guard just beneath the chin and sent his head flying backward, lolling across his shoulders on an impossible hinge.

Coco had cautioned the others that *el jefe* was his, his alone, but the foreman had fallen sideways across the seat, spraying blood, blocking Coco's aim. *El jefe* clawed at the covered holster on his hip, trying to escape the clutch of the dying man. The foreman's foot jammed against the accelerator, his arm tangled in the wheel. The Jeep began to slew in a tight circle, its motor screaming, its rear wheels spewing sand.

Then the wheels caught and the vehicle shot forward. It sped fifty feet down the narrow track, slewing back and forth, finally crashed into the framework of an irrigation gate jutting from the canal bank. The impact tossed the bodies of the guard and the foreman out into the murky water. The Jeep teetered at the edge, then plunged in after them with a roar.

Coco stared for a moment, watching the steam rise from the roiling water, trying to collect his thoughts. Jeep, foreman, guard—none of that mattered in the slightest. For what he realized was that *el jefe* had escaped. The white-haired man was tumbling through the dust— shoulders, knees, shoulders again—now staggering upright, running, disappearing into the waving stalks of cane.

It had happened so quickly that Coco felt as if he were awakening from a dream. He turned and motioned the others forward. "Go!" he shouted, waving his machete toward the crackling cane.

Coco led the way, pushing the rough stalks aside, pausing now and then to listen to the path of *el jefe*. Edgar moved more quickly, slipping sideways through the tangle like a greyhound bred for thickets, while Manrique crashed along without bothering to clear a path, flattening the cane stalks as if they were grass. A buffalo, Coco thought. A human rhinoceros.

Coco stopped again, held up his arms to halt the others. He listened, but heard nothing. *El jefe*'s thrashing had stopped. Coco remembered the polished leather holster that hung at the old man's hip, imagined the soft clasp sliding open, a trembling hand on the pistol's steel.

Still, what could he do? Run away? Assuming he'd ever get out of these fields, where would he go? Slink back to Miami and explain to his employer that there had been an error, he had lost their prey in a cane thicket? He would prefer the bullet of *el jefe*'s pistol to what would happen to him then.

Coco's eyes were fixed on a dense clump of cane and stray pepperbush a few feet ahead. He stared hard at it, willing his eyes to disregard the green patchwork of leaves, to penetrate the tiny latticework of shadows. A mosquito whined through the silence near his ear. Was that a fleck of white behind a fluttering leaf? The heat seemed to urge itself up a notch and Coco felt sweat rolling down his brow. He didn't try to wipe it away.

A vision overlaid itself on Coco's sight, a boy standing on a crate, peering through the shutters of a shack into a tiny bedroom, a sheet ripping away inside like a sail shorn in a windstorm. Coco watches a man's glistening buttocks rising and falling, his mother's bare legs waving skyward. Her sounds sharp, shrill, as if she was being hurt, as if this strange man was hurting her. "*Mami,*" the boy calls, and the woman lunges up on her elbow, outraged.

"Get away," she shrieks, though the man is pumping still. "I am working. Get away." And Coco does.

Coco felt a mosquito pierce the flesh of his cheek, felt another settle on the sweaty nape of his neck—fat, healthy mosquitoes, nourished on the dark blood of cane workers—but he had not moved his gaze from the tangle of brush in front of him. He saw another fluttering movement there, thought he caught a glimpse of dull steel. But it might have been a trick of his eyes. If he could see the past in a tangle of brush, he might see anything.

He turned to Manrique, who was standing nearer the spot, and motioned the big man forward with the slightest motion of his chin. Manrique hesitated, then started forward.

Manrique reached out to part the brush, his machete raised.

6

Coco tightened his grip on his own blade. Manrique took another step . . .

. . . and staggered backward as a gunshot blew away the silence. Manrique tottered, gave a spinning little half-step, a black dot sprung up on one of his doughy cheeks, a patch of bone and scarlet red opened up by his opposite ear. His eyes were aimed at Coco, but they were seeing something far away.

Coco was already running forward. He saw the brush moving, glimpsed a hand, then the same flash of dull steel, pointing at him now. He lunged forward and lashed out with his machete, swinging blindly into the labyrinth of green and shadow. His feet tangled in the pepperbush's roots as he swung and he went down, his ears ringing with the sound of another blast.

He lay with his cheek in the cool muck, his head still ringing from the explosion, which must have gone off at his ear. He was vaguely aware of movements through the cane, sensing only that they were moving away from him as he blinked his eyes into focus.

He was trying to push himself up when he realized what was lying on the ground before him. He hesitated, his face inches above the musty-smelling earth. He closed his eyes, thinking that perhaps he was dying and this was another vision. When he opened his eyes, it was still there.

A hand. Or a part of one, its forefinger still curled in the ring of a pistol. A thin trail of smoke rose from the barrel of the weapon. On another finger, a gold ring, twisted in some shape like vines. A thumb, still twitching. And where the rest should be—wrist, arm, elbow—there was nothing, nothing but a spray of red pepper berries and a splash of blood.

Coco pushed himself to his knees, shook his head groggily, listening to the sounds of *el jefe* crashing through the brush, of Edgar chasing after. He hauled himself up, felt his tender ear, but found no signs of blood. He found the big blade where it had fallen in the crook of a pepper root, took it up, and followed the sounds of the chase.

Coco found *el jefe*'s spoor soon enough, a fist-sized smear of blood in a sandy patch here, a swipe across a stand of cane there. He could hear harsh breathing, grunts of effort, muffled curses up ahead. He plowed through a marshy spot where the cane seemed stunted, found himself bathed in a stinging black cloud of mosquitoes.

He slogged on, fighting the urge to chop at the insects with his blade, then heard a cry up ahead, followed by the splash of something heavy falling into water.

Coco hurried on through a last canebrake, emerged on the bank of a canal. Was it the same one they'd started from or another of the endless network that crisscrossed this steaming land? Impossible to tell. Coco had lost his sense of direction long ago.

What he could be sure of was this: *El jefe* was down there in the murky water, thrashing with one good hand, one awful stump, trying to drag himself up onto the muddy bank.

"I cannot swim," *el jefe* called, but to whom it was not clear. "I cannot swim."

Edgar stood above *el jefe* on the bank, his blade poised like a housewife with a broom, daring the mouse to take one step farther. Edgar grinned as Coco emerged from the canebrake.

"I'll help him out," Edgar said as *el jefe* levered his good arm onto the shore. The old man's face was a mask of effort. He seemed strangely unaware of the spidery little man with the huge knife above him.

"I cannot swim," he gasped, dragging himself forward on the mud.

"No matter," Edgar said. He was about to strike when Coco's blade took him in the back.

Edgar stiffened, gasped, lost his grip on his knife. He staggered at the edge of the bank for a moment, clawing weakly at his back, then fell over, into the water.

Coco watched him sink, did not flinch as Edgar's sightless gaze passed over him. The last he saw of Edgar was the tiny birthmark, a doomed continent sinking with its stubbled globe.

Strange, Coco thought, how indifferent he was to Manrique's death, how he'd come to despise Edgar. How for a moment he had regarded *el jefe* almost as a comrade. It was indeed a very strange world.

He turned back to *el jefe* then, feeling weary, feeling almost sad. The world turned and turned and sometimes things were upside down. Nevertheless . . .

He was about to do what had to be done when he realized it was already over. *El jefe* lay where he had dragged himself, half in, half out of the water. His old man's eyes were closed as if in sleep, his lips parted, pressed into a shallow puddle of water.

Coco nudged him with the tip of his shoe, then again. *El jefe*, king of the sugar, Coco thought. You get what you get, but then someone else wants it, hires Coco, and see what happens.

Coco shook his head, made a sound that might have been a sigh. The world turns, he thought, and as luck would have it, he would go on turning with it. Clean this mess up now. Go back to Miami, tell this story. See what job comes next.

Strange. He pushed the old man lightly, almost gently, with his toe, and the body slid down the bank, out of sight.

"The sleep of reason produces nightmares." It was Janice's voice, lilting, echoing in the stone-floored room.

"What's that?" Deal said. They were in the largest room of a museum-cum-gallery of Latin-American art, a place he'd never heard of until a week ago. That was Miami for you. Live here a lifetime, it was still full of surprises.

He'd been studying the elaborate, other-era filigree work on the museum's ceiling molding. The whole place, which had probably been some family's mansion before taxes and upkeep drove them out, was full of touches like that. Where would you find subcontractors who could do work like that these days, he wondered. You couldn't, of course, not at any price. It was hard enough finding subs who would work, period.

"Look at this, Deal." She tugged at his arm. "Do you think it's real?"

Deal turned his attention to the piece Janice was admiring, an engraving, it looked like, a fellow in knickers collapsed at an old-fashioned desk with his head in his arms. Bats and strange-looking owls flapped in the shadowy air above him.

She had been reading the title of the piece aloud. Deal gave her a smile. "You're not imagining it. There's a painting right there on the wall."

Janice made a face. "Don't be funny, Deal. It's a Goya. I just wondered if it was *original*." There was a leather-bound book inside a glass case nearby. The book lay open at a page bearing a reproduction of the same engraving on the wall.

Deal checked the book, then turned back to the engraving. He inspected the little brass plaque nailed to the engraving's frame, then took a step back, cocking his head for a new angle. Finally he shook his head. "It's not original," he said with authority.

Janice glanced at him, curious.

He shrugged. "I feel like that every month when it's time to pay the suppliers."

"You're awful," she said. "We should have gone to the boat show."

"No," he said, making a grab for her. "This is a great building. I'm glad we came."

She swatted his hand away. A matronly woman inspecting a massive abstract across the room glanced disapprovingly at them. "Stop it, Deal," Janice whispered.

"What do you say we hide in this place?" he said, tagging close on her heels. He gestured at a massive bronze sculpture in the middle of the room, Adam and Eve with their backs to one another. "We'll pretend to be statues. When everybody's gone home, we'll reenact the Fall on that bench over there."

Janice tried to look stern, but her face was coloring. The matronly lady stiffened and turned back to her abstract.

"You're going to get us thrown out," Janice said. He could tell she was holding back her laughter.

You ever get married, make sure it's to a woman with a sense of humor, that's what his father had told him. Given him that along with a bunch of other advice, most of which had turned out to be worthless, just like the construction business he had left, Deal thought. Still, one pearl of wisdom made up for a lot.

Janice stopped in front of a Picasso. "I can't believe all these things are here," she said. They had heard about the place from a friend, David Coetzee, who collected Latin-American paintings. "A hidden gem," David had called it. "Right here on Brickell Avenue."

And he was right, Deal thought. In a city without a proper museum, it was doubly surprising to find this collection, and nearly as surprising that few people seemed to know of it. They hadn't seen a dozen others. He and Janice, along with the frigid matron, who'd fled the room, seemed to be the only visitors left, and if it hadn't been for the rain that had kept him off the job that morning, there might have been only one person in the place.

As it was, Deal had taken a rare Saturday off and fulfilled the idle promise he'd made to Janice the night David had told them about the place. He'd been cranking hard on the job, a massive home in the Grove he was rebuilding for Terrence Terrell, the computer genius who'd brought major league baseball—the Manatees—to South Florida.

Although home-building had not been Deal's major interest, the hurricane had changed all that. People had been desperate to put their lives back together, and Deal had come to find more satisfaction in that, less in throwing up storage warehouses and strip shopping centers.

Terrell had seen some of Deal's work, the renovation of a home in Gables by the Sea that had taken the brunt of the storm surge, eight feet of Biscayne Bay right through the doors and windows. Although Deal had his reservations about working for such a legendary stickler, Terrell had badgered him until he'd finally relented. And he was glad he had. He and Terrell's architects, a group Deal had worked with before, had free rein. No more project managers urging him to cut corners, find a way around the building codes. Terrell had money to burn. "Just tell me what you need to do the job right, John Deal. I plan to live here a long, long time."

It had turned out to be a sweet deal, as he'd told Janice, who laughed when he'd said it. "*You're* sweet," she'd said, laughing until he figured it out.

Deal sidled up to Janice, put his arm around her waist. He'd been grinding on the job for far too long. Forgetting his own life. She was a warm island in the supercooled room. "Let's not tell Terrell about this place," he said. "He'd just buy everything, have it put in his new entryway."

She smiled up at him, finally. "Are you going to behave?"

"Only if you want me to," he said. She was silhouetted against a pair of French doors opening onto a tropical garden. The light cast soft shadows across her features, heightened the natural pout of her lips.

"What's with you today? You never act like this."

He shrugged. "I've decided I've been working too hard. I've been too serious. But that's going to change. You're looking at a new man. The new Deal."

"Sure," she said, rolling her eyes again.

"I love this place, really," he said, pulling her closer. "I love *you*. And if you don't want to do it here, let's go get a room at the Mayfair. We'll call Mrs. Suarez and tell her we had a dead battery, they had to send a tow truck from Homestead. It'd be the truth, if we had a dead battery."

"We can't afford a room at the Mayfair," she said, twisting away from him.

"Okay, the Ramada," he said. "The Motel Six. Any place where you're not on call . . . "

"Deal . . . " she said, affecting exasperation. But she was still smiling. Their daughter, Isabel, was almost nine months old now, but she had resisted all attempts at closing down Mom's milk bar, especially at bedtime. This was their first time alone since Isabel had been born.

"I can't help it," he said. "Great art affects me this way."

"I thought maybe it was me," she said. She turned away.

"Oh, it's you all right," he said, reaching for her. She tried to duck, but he got one finger in a belt loop. He hadn't intended it, but as she spun around, he found his other hand against her breast. Her face flushed crimson. "Deal!" she said, but her voice was throaty.

"Make up your mind," he said. He hadn't moved his hand. Couldn't, somehow. He felt light-headed. Sixteen again. "The bench over there, or the Mayfair."

Her lips parted, her eyes beginning to focus on that place far, far away. Deal felt himself press closer. He could feel the heat of her stomach through his jeans. He remembered moments like this. From college? From high school? Times when it was impossible to distinguish between all the promise of life and his body's mindless urge to pop.

Then again, maybe there wasn't any difference. Didn't seem so now. He bent to brush Janice's forehead with his cheeks. Maybe the bench *was* a possibility, he was thinking, when the voice came echoing behind them.

"I must ask that you leave." It was a man in a cream-colored suit, standing in the doorway.

Deal glanced over his shoulder, deadpan. "You're not allowed to kiss in here?" He was still holding Janice.

The guy was unfazed—the elegant suit, the careful trim of his beard and hair, he must have practiced being fazeproof.

"We are closing now," the man said. His voice was neutral, slightly accented. His gaze was averted. Deal suspected he spoke Spanish in the Castilian style.

"We must prepare for an opening this evening," the man added.

"You have to close so you can open up again?" Deal said. He was wondering what it would take to get a rise out of the guy.

"You'll have to excuse my husband," Janice said. She'd extricated herself, was tugging at Deal's arm. "You have some wonderful things here," she added.

The man nodded. "The new exhibit opens Monday," he said, ushering them out. "Come again."

Deal tried to get a backward look at the guy, maybe come up with something else to say, but Janice had found the doorway, braced herself with one hand and levered him out into the bright sunshine with the other.

"This was a lot better than the boat show," he called after her.

She was shaking her head, moving quickly across the courtyard. "And I had to sign our names to the guest book," she said. She turned to glare at him, but it didn't hold. Then they both began to laugh, peals of laughter that echoed across the lush courtyard and into the Florida sky.

"Let me be certain I understand this," Marielena Marquez said to the smiling young man. "You are going to broadcast the *weather* program from our opening?"

The young man nodded confidently. "Action Weather, we call it."

Marielena shook her head, still trying to comprehend. They were standing near the fountain in the courtyard of her building, Galeria y Ediciones Catalan, while a bevy of technicians swarmed about, running cables, stationing lights and reflectors, even mounting a large blue screen that seemed suitable for projecting outdoor films near the entryway. One of the cables had snagged in the dwarf hibiscus she'd had set out last week, uprooting one of the rare plants, splitting another at the root. A large piece of carbon paper floated in the reflecting pond. There was a diet Coke can sitting in the lap of a bronze garden nymph. Someone had ground out a cigarette on the limestone paving.

She felt as if she had a summer cold coming on, but it might simply be the confusion she felt, this grinning idiot in front of her talking about ratings, a makeup woman toweling away his perspiration, patting his cheeks with powder. "This is an event of some artistic . . . some political significance," she said.

"Don't worry," he said. What was his name, anyway? Tad? Chad? He was tanned, fit, radiant with health and good cheer. He had bent down a bit so the makeup woman could reach him with an eyeliner pencil. "We do a lot of important stories. It used to be just fluff, neighborhood Christmas lights, the dog show, but now we're doing quasi-hard news in the background, stuff with a *setting*, at least, weaving that in with the weather."

He waved his hand in the direction of the building, her building, as if it were some stage set, some false front set up for his convenience. Built by Coral Gables developer George Merrick in 1927 out of solid coral rock. A mansion with barrel-tiled gables, massive overhangs, and walls two feet thick, where Paul Whiteman had once wintered, where a Du Pont cousin had kept a mistress for five years, where, it was rumored, Miami habitué Al Capone had bludgeoned a man with a leaden doorstop cast in the shape of an angel.

After World War II, a North Carolinian manufacturer of furniture had made it his second home. Facing great pressure from the import market, the furniture titan shot himself in the mansion's attic, but his widow had stayed on until her death in 1980. The place had sat in probate, untended for nearly a decade, until Marielena discovered it and made it her own.

She had walked down that overgrown pathway where a Ford van with a satellite dish atop it was now blocking the way, had stepped into the forlorn courtyard, taken one look at the fountain, the shy nymph who seemed to bow with pleasure and gratitude at Marielena's arrival . . . and had known immediately that this was the place where she would do her work.

For the past four years, she had set about making Galeria y Ediciones Catalan *the* center for the preservation and promotion of Hispanic-American art in the United States. Hers was an unusual, multifaceted approach: The building contained a modest museum where Marielena's collection, and that of her deceased father, which contained several Picassos, two pieces by Miró, and even one Goya, were on permanent display.

She had added a gallery, where the works of contemporary Spanish and Latin-American artists were featured. And there was also the publishing arm, concerned not only with the production of elaborate coffee-table books but with works of scholarship and matters bearing on the world of Hispanic-American art as well.

Marielena was herself no artist, could not draw so much as a stick figure. Yet she knew what moved her, as she knew what fire was latent in the hearts of her ancestors, her people. And while her own family had been content to live upon the earnings of a fortune so old it had lost the scent of the pressed oils it was founded upon, she had made it her mission to do something, something of importance.

She had invested every cent of the remaining Marquez wealth in her enterprise. Although she had offended some, mostly local politicians who wouldn't know the difference between a palette knife and a butter knife, she had succeeded in gaining the attention of the international art community for her efforts. This opening, for instance, was an event of great significance. And the book that she would soon publish, well, *that* would turn this community on its ear.

She sighed. On the eve of all this, she had been delivered into the hands of Chad, the Action Weatherman.

"A prophet without honor," Marielena murmured.

"Say what?" the weatherman asked.

"Nothing," she said. "Just philosophy."

"Oh." One of the weatherman's eyes seemed to be focused on Marielena, while the one being worked on by the makeup artist canted off toward the bright evening sky, where a huge seabird, perhaps an osprey, drifted overhead.

Dive, Marielena willed her thoughts toward the bird. *Carry this person away.*

"I spoke with your news director. He assured me that a reporter would come. . . ."

The weatherman pushed his makeup person aside, pulled the towel from the neck of his sports shirt. His good cheer had transformed into something more intense.

"Ms. Marquez, I *am* a reporter," he said. "I covered the ouster of Commissioner Lender, the same night a tropical wave came through. The week we broke the January rainfall record, I was live from the courthouse with the weather. Who do you think was at that big pileup on Alligator Alley, hottest February third on record?"

She stared at him, speechless. *Madness*, she was thinking, for she had spent a lifetime among artists. She was searching for some reply when he noticed something behind her.

"Shit, look at those thunderheads," Tad/Chad said abruptly. He turned to shout at the camera crew. "Let's factor those clouds in." One of the men nodded and the crew began shifting their cables.

Marielena glanced into the sky at the massive cumulus banks that were piling up over the Atlantic. Piling up so high that their tips reflected the last of the sunlight in a patchwork of pink and gold, their undersides a brawl of cobalt, gray, and purple. Sunsets that the Englishman Turner should have seen, she thought. Instead, there would be storm clouds by Chad, video replay at eleven. She sighed and bent to lift the now-gelatinous carbon sheet from the reflecting pool, then followed the director toward the *X* they'd chalked on the flagstones, the place where she and Chad would talk about art and politics.

"We're going to be back with the weekend forecast in a minute, folks," weatherman Chad said, "but first let's have a look at some of this art we came to see." He grinned and thrust his microphone in front of Marielena. "So, we've got a red one from Cuba and a blue one from Brazil, is that right?"

She forced herself to smile for the camera. The director had persuaded her to have a pair of smaller canvases brought out into the courtyard—"It's a visual medium, sweetheart"—and as the assistants holding the pieces stepped forward, she cast a nervous glance at the looming thunderheads above.

In a second-story window of her building she saw Rafael Quintana, her chief editor, smiling down upon the scene. Handsome Rafael, the picture of confidence in his cream-colored suit. There was someone else in the room, another man, but his face was lost in the shadows. Rafael gave her a thumbs-up as she began to speak.

"Yes, this acrylic, the blue one . . . "—Good Lord, was she actually descending to his level?—"is an abstract by Antonio Real. It features some striking work with the rearrangement of perspective, and though you probably can't see this on the camera, the textures are incredible—you can actually see the movement of the artist's hand."

"It's really blue, folks, that much I can tell you." Chad grinned. His thumb, apparently out of camera range, was jabbing urgently in the direction of the other canvas. "So tell us about the other one. We can almost see people here, can't we?"

The camera moved in tight on the second canvas. It was a surrealistic oil by Sucrel, a young Cuban painter with the face and demeanor of an angel. The subject was a cane field, with stooped, painfully distorted laborers in the foreground, a line of field-clearing fires in the distance, an angry sunset refracting through a haze of smoke. In the sky above the fields, the smoke and the fiery light had somehow congealed into the specter of a huge jungle cat, leaping down upon the unsuspecting workers, its claws and fangs bared.

How ironic. This young painter subtly criticizes conditions in Cuba and yet draws the wrath of exiles living in America. Perhaps if Sucrel had given the beast the face of his country's dictator . . . but she doubted anything would mollify those who were beyond reason.

"It is called *'A Tiger in Red Weather,'*" she said into the microphone, "after a poem by the American Wallace Stevens. Quite a powerful commentary on the exploitation of labor. Sucrel is perhaps the most interesting young painter in all of Cuba."

The camera was back on her now and she straightened, lifting her chin to the eye of the lens. "We are very proud to be the first to show his work in this country."

"That's created a bit of controversy in our community, I understand." Chad was still grinning, as if it was amusing.

She paused.

"Sucrel is a gifted artist who happens to come from Cuba," she said. "His subjects speak of the beauty and the anguish of everyday life. They inspire us with their strength." She tossed her hair, feeling her passion welling up inside her.

Sucrel himself stood at the gateway to the mansion, his doelike gaze upon her, the fierce-eyed, bearded Antonio Real at his side. It was they who should be before the cameras, she reminded herself, but neither artist spoke English and the museum director had scotched that idea in an instant.

"And yet," she continued, "there are those who would deny us our access to Sucrel, who would not allow him to travel here, who would see this gallery closed rather than share the beauty and the passion of his work." She glanced up to see Rafael's reaction, but he had disappeared.

"Kind of like those great cigars," Chad chimed in. "A darned shame we can't get those anymore."

Marielena felt the color draining from her face. She could only pray that the artists had not understood this moron. "I want to invite everyone to the Galeria Catalan this evening," she said, fighting for composure. "Come to see these marvelous works and judge for yourselves what . . . "

And that was when it happened. She never got to finish her sentence, would never know, in fact, just what epithet she intended to hurl at the rock-skulled, heavy-jowled men who were out there watching, if they were watching, hating her every word, hating every molecule of her. The same men who had lobbied the State Department to deny Sucrel's visa, who had pressured her bank to rescind her line of credit, who had called in the building inspectors time and again with spurious safety violation charges.

Her own countrymen, she thought, in the very moment she began to fall, but the worst of them, those so embittered by personal loss that they had become the very thing they hated most, so threatened even by art, so devoid of humanness that one of them had surely caused what was happening to her now.

In the first instant of the blast, her breath had left her. It was as if an invisible, searing hand had swept across the courtyard, hurling all of them away like so many skittles from a game board.

There were a few images of startling, slow-motion clarity: the weatherman, his grin vanished at last, soaring over her, flames trailing from the back of his shirt and trousers; the roof of the mansion exploding upward, the lovely red tiles fragmenting into shrapnel; a massive sabal palm lifting up into the heavens, then tottering, veering downward like a space missile gone awry.

Not sure any longer if she was hurtling upward or if the sky itself was rushing down to meet her, she watched as the shadow of the great tree grew and grew, enveloping her, its vast shade bringing a hint of ease to her burning body, the tree itself much closer now, finally turning the dusk to nightfall, and then there was darkness altogether.

"Why are you laughing?" Deal asked. He was behind her now, but he had caught a glimpse of her face in the mirror the Mayfair decorator had installed across from the huge bed.

"I'm not laughing," Janice said, turning her face against a pillow. Her eyes were closed, her cheeks were bright crimson, her hair, gone from blond to dark with sweat, was plastered against her forehead. She bit her lip as he moved against her, then gasped with pleasure.

"I saw you," he said, but he'd had to close his own eyes now. He clutched at her hips, as if to pull her closer, as if it would be possible to move her inside *him* somehow, but her flesh was slippery, and his hands were starting to work in some rhythm they had concocted on their own.

"I can't believe . . . " She broke off, tossing her head against the bedclothes.

He pulled back, trying to prolong this moment, then quickly gave it up, rejoined her, fell to his side. She groaned softly, keeping herself glued to him, keeping their rhythms intact. She arched upward, rocked slightly, managed somehow to work him onto his back.

He opened his eyes again as she began to rise and fall above him, her face upturned, her hair tumbling free, her lovely neck arched. "Can't believe what?" he managed. He was feeling giddy, slightly delirious, nothing in his mind but sensation. Slipperiness. A wet silk glove that clasped him, unclasped him.

"That . . . you had this planned . . . all along." She spoke in bursts, her hands digging into the flesh of his chest for punctuation.

"Mrs. Suarez . . . she was very . . . understanding," he said, surprised at this coherent voice that seemed to come from some other Deal, some version of himself he'd met on the street one day. Talking. How could conversation be an aphrodisiac?

"Oh yes," she said finally, but she wasn't talking about Mrs. Suarez anymore.

". . . yes," he answered. On his way to some other galaxy, hearing her bright cries of pleasure spiraling upward with him. Higher and higher and higher . . . until they had collapsed into the soaking bedclothes, panting, both of them gasping now with laughter.

He lay there thinking, *I am a drooling, brain-dead creature of happiness, yes indeedy*, and was already reaching out for her again . . . when the telephone began to ring.

"Calm down, Mrs. Suarez," Janice was saying. Her face was drawn into a mask of concern. "Please. I can't understand you."

Deal struggled up from the tangle of sheets, a cold apprehensiveness coming over him.

"Isabel?" he asked.

Janice shook her head, waving for him to be quiet.

"The TV?" she said, puzzled. "Wait . . . just a minute."

She jabbed her finger at the remote unit on the bedside table. Deal reached for it, punched the set on. Clint Eastwood shotgunning a cowboy off a western rooftop. He stared at Janice, puzzled.

"Channel 7," she said, the phone still tucked under her chin.

Deal skipped through the channels until he found it, where a reporter was doing a stand-up in front of a ruined building. It could have been a war zone in the tropics: a few shards of wall poking out of the smoking rubble, an overturned equipment van, still smoldering, emergency technicians combing the wreckage, all of it framed by shattered palms, scorched fronds of foliage.

". . . and those seriously injured, including our own Chad Eddings and the owner of Galeria Catalan, Marielena Marquez," the ashen-faced reporter was saying. "Meanwhile, the search goes on for other survivors. No word as to what might have caused the tremendous explosion, but fire investigators are on the scene. We'll be here to bring you details as they come to us, Reese."

The scene cut away to the studio, where the anchorperson, an overweight man with a bad hairpiece, shook his head at the news—"We'll be back with more, folks"—then on to a commercial for Craftmatic Beds. Deal pressed the mute button and turned to Janice, stunned.

"That's the place where we were today?"

She nodded slowly. He could hear the voice of Mrs. Suarez nattering away on the other end of the line. He reached out to take the phone from Janice, who stared at the TV, transfixed.

"It's me, Mrs. Suarez," he said, cutting into her rapid-fire Spanglish.

"Señor Deal, *ay Dios*. You are alive. *Madre de Dios*. How is it possible . . . "

"We're fine, Mrs. Suarez. We weren't there. Not for hours."

He held the phone away from his ear while she praised various deities for their good fortune. Then there was a lusty cry in the background and Mrs. Suarez broke off. "Is the baby," she said. "Is waking up."

"Isabel?" he said. "She's okay?"

"Is fine," Mrs. Suarez said. "Everything is fine here. Thank God for you and the *señora*."

The commercial had ended and the grim-faced anchorman was back now, a photograph of the building as it had looked before the explosion on a screen behind him. One of the grandest of the old mansions on Brickell. Deal shook his head, remembering the lush patio, the massive overhangs, the feeling of security the thick walls of the place had lent. Like being in a cave or a medieval fortress, he was thinking, then stopped himself.

There was another shot live from the scene then, the original reporter running after a fire marshal who was getting into his cruiser, pushing the reporter's microphone away.

"Look, Mrs. Suarez, we're fine, okay? But thanks for checking up on us. Go take care of Isabel. We'll see you in the morning." He was distracted, wondering what the reporter was so intent upon.

He heard something of indignation in the older woman's voice as the TV sound came up. "Sure I'm gonna take good care of her. You have a good time now." He was conscious of the disapproval in her last comment.

He heard the connection break, then focused on the TV, where the reporter was running alongside the departing fire marshal's cruiser. "Well, what *can* you tell us?" the reporter was shouting. "Do you suspect one of the exile groups?" The image was jiggling wildly as the cameraman ran after him. A uniformed cop stepped into the picture suddenly, his hand growing huge as the lens approached it . . . Then everything went black.

Janice glanced up at him, bewildered. He shrugged, reached out to put his arm around her, pulled her close as the scene cut back to the studio, the anchorperson looking into the camera, somewhat perplexed.

"We apologize for the technical difficulties," he said, gathering himself. "But you heard it for the first time here on 7. A suspicion that foul play was involved in the explosion at Galeria y . . . " The anchorman stopped to check the script in front of him, then glanced back up at the cameras, mangling the rest of the Spanish, before announcing a return to regular programming.

Deal snapped off the set as Angela Lansbury's face swam into focus. Janice glanced up at him, her eyes fearful, questioning.

"Dear God," she said. "Who could do that? *Why* would anyone do such a thing?"

He shook his head, pulled her tight against his chest. In years past there'd been other bombings in Miami—a theater that had invited a dance troupe from Havana; the set of a film rumored to present a sympathetic view of Communism; a travel agency said to be doing business with Castro's regime in Cuba.

But what answer could he possibly give that would help ease her fears? *Freedom fighters? Fanatics? True Believers?* Pick the answer that makes sense, Deal, never mind that there isn't one. The buzzer is sounding. Your time is up. There are ways to handle those like you . . .

He closed his eyes, his arms still wrapped around Janice. It had been such a good day, such a wonderful, lovely day in the tropics. And now, suddenly, all the bad memories were coming alive, snarling like wild dogs on the other side of a flimsy, rusted-out fence he'd erected somewhere in the back reaches of his mind.

Almost two years had gone by now, and though the flashes came less frequently now, they still came upon him, and when they did, they had the force of fever. He'd nearly lost her then, to a different set of madmen. True believers from the cult of get-rich-quick he'd had the misfortune to step into the path of.

And although what had happened this day had nothing to do with them, he held her now as he'd held her then: on the slanting deck of a ruined stilt home in the middle of Biscayne Bay, waiting for help to come, feeling her quiet trembling, trying to soothe her, wondering if his own hands were beginning to shake and betray him. He'd realized then who the strong one truly was.

"Deal?" she said, her voice reaching him now, as from the top of a deep, deep well. "Deal?"

He shook himself, fighting the drag of memory, forcing himself away from the snarling dogs that hurled themselves again and again against the shaking fence . . . until finally he was back, and he could see her face: the clear green eyes; the nose turned just a trace off-center; a spray of sun freckles across her cheeks in this season.

She *was* here. They were together. And Isabel was fine. They were a family, just as she had insisted they would be. He smiled down at her, feeling his breathing begin to steady.

"You went away," she said, her gaze concerned. "Like you used to . . . "

"You wore me out, that's all." He gave her a kiss on the cheek. "I'm an older guy, honey."

"You're also a big bullshitter," she said, returning his kiss. She gave him a look. "I feel it too, you know. Every time I read about a child who dies, or hear about a plane crash, anytime something awful happens." She gathered the sheets in her lap, crossed her legs, facing him earnestly.

"Part of it's because we have Isabel now, we're just more sensitive." She pushed the hair back from her forehead. "But it's also because of what happened to us. Those memories aren't going to go away anytime soon, you know."

"I'd just as soon they did," he said.

"Well, they won't," she said. "And anytime something happens like today . . . "

"That didn't have anything to do with us," he said, waving at the blank screen of the television.

"It doesn't matter," she said. "It came close. The bad thing came close again. That's all it takes to set off the feelings." She paused to stare at him. "And we're better off admitting it when it happens, Deal."

He stared back at her for a moment. Admit it when it happens. Deal with it, Deal. A bunch of guys want to take you out, your wife, anyone who's unlucky enough to be around you, all for a piece of property. How could thinking about it make it any better?

"You know," he said finally, "I saw a man who wanted to kill us die twenty feet in front of me." He took a deep breath and fell back against the pillows, staring up at the ceiling. "But it's not enough. If I had him here now, I'd want to kill him again, with my bare hands." He turned to her. "For what he did to us." He felt the look on his own face. "Does that mean there's something wrong with me, Janice?"

"Oh, Deal," she said, coming to embrace him. "Of course it doesn't. I hated him too. I always will. But you can't let it take you over."

"Yeah?" he said, smelling the shampoo in her hair, the sweat, the hint of sex. "How do you manage that, doctor?"

She pulled back, smiled up at him. "I just think of you and Isabel, all the good things we have."

She scooted up to kiss him and he twisted, feeling her sliding, still warm and damp, against his hip. He tried to keep her there, but she ducked out of his arms and hurried toward the bathroom.

"Come on," she said. "Let's take a shower and go home. All of a sudden, I'm desperate to see our daughter."

"So, Rafael, you are dead now." Vicente Luis Torreno put his heavy arm about Rafael Quintana's shoulder and laughed uproariously. The noise startled some strange bird in the darkness nearby and the thing answered with its own raucous cries, sending the surrounding shrubbery into a turmoil. Rafael could hardly distinguish the screech of the bird from Torreno's high-pitched bray. A strange sound from such a big man, such a wealthy and powerful man.

It gave Rafael an eerie feeling to be so isolated, far out from the main house, in a hut with no walls, all the strange animals he knew to be about. Torreno's estate was two hundred acres of South Dade waterfront, with an agricultural testing facility on one side, a state forest preserve on the other. Four million people within a half-hour's drive and he felt as if he were in the wilderness.

He nodded uncomfortably at Torreno. The man himself seemed zoogenic, with his thick chest and shoulders, his big head, and those eyes that fixed on you as if you were some kind of prey.

Rafael felt helpless in Torreno's grip. It seemed as if the man could crush him with a careless squeeze.

"Well, let's drink to your success, then," Torreno said, releasing Rafael. He had finally stopped laughing and was dabbing a handkerchief at the tears in his eyes. "All this walking . . . "

He trailed off, signaling to a servant in a corner of the place.

There were candles in hurricane lamps on either end of a small bar, casting ominous shadows about. The servant, a tall mulatto with an expression gaunt enough as it was, seemed cadaverous in this light. As he worked, his movements sent tiny phantasms dancing about the thatched roof above.

Rafael imagined huge bird-eating spiders nesting there, copulating with scorpions and bats. He had betrayed a lifelong friend, had caused the deaths of a dozen people a few hours before, but wild creatures were a different matter.

He felt something tickle the flesh at his neck and brushed at it nervously. Just the label on the unfamiliar clothing, he realized. He'd had to leave a lovely new suit behind, don this ill-fitting camouflage outfit.

"Here," Torreno said, handing him a tall glass beaded with moisture. "Yours has been a job well done. You have neutralized a traitor and delivered up the instrument of treason." He sipped. "To your voyage."

Rafael touched his glass to that of his host, took a swallow. He had placed a call earlier, had ascertained that the money he'd been promised had indeed been wired to his account. Where he was going, it meant a lifetime of ease. He would allow himself this moment of relaxation.

One-hundred-fifty-one-proof rum—straight, or so it seemed—chilled to near-freezing by the shaved ice, cut only with a bit of sugar, perhaps a touch of mint. The cold brought a stab of pain between his eyes and he waited for it to clear before taking another swallow. He was ready for this drink.

He hadn't seen the effects of the blast, of course, but Torreno had been graphic in his descriptions. Rafael *had* been close enough to feel the earth tremble beneath his feet and he had no reason to doubt what such force had done to those who were nearby. He tilted his head back, draining the glass.

"Coco." Torreno snapped his fingers, and the servant poured Rafael another drink.

Torreno turned to lean against a railing and stared out into the darkness. "Perhaps you are feeling a bit of remorse for what you have done, Rafael." The big man laughed mirthlessly, his gaze fixed intently upon the blackness as if he could see something out there. Rafael had read of creatures who could see in darkness, smell through walls, hear footsteps from miles away.

"It was necessary," Rafael said. It was important to remind himself of that.

Torreno turned, nodding wearily. "I have devoted a lifetime to this effort, my young friend. I can assure you that no action undertaken in the cause of liberty is too great." He stared into Rafael's eyes, as if searching for something greater than mere agreement.

"I understand," Rafael said.

"Our enemies are merciless," Torreno continued. "They have exterminated a generation of patriots, forced an entire nation into slavery. You must remember."

"It isn't that," Rafael said. The liquor was having its effect. The fire in his stomach had spread to become a warm glow in his limbs. "I was thinking of the others. The Americans . . . "

"Reporters?" Torreno's laugh was short and bitter. "The lackeys of a system that would sell its soul for the price of a television commercial?" Torreno stared at him closely, as if he had sensed some treason about to spring from his lips.

Rafael straightened his back, lifted his glass to his host. "Let me thank you, Señor Torreno," he said, "for giving me this opportunity to serve with you."

Torreno's expression softened. He touched one hand to Rafael's shoulder, squeezed, held up the bundled manuscript that Rafael had delivered in the other. Rafael felt his eyes water at the man's grip. "You have given me a valuable prize, my young friend, more valuable than you may know."

Torreno seemed to ponder something, then relented. He put the package down and raised his glass, saluting Rafael. "I am on the verge of completing a business transaction, an enormous transaction, one toward which I have endeavored my entire life," he said.

"I have committed every penny of my own wealth to ensure its success, and in turn, the success of *la revolución*," he added, fervor in his voice. "You have helped to silence those who would have brought everything to ruin." Torreno downed the rest of his drink in a gulp and gazed at him fiercely. Rafael knew he should have felt elation at Torreno's words, but what he felt, in fact, was an uneasiness deep in his stomach. The cadaverous servant had left off behind the bar to stare at him as well.

Torreno's arm was on his again, guiding him out onto an open-air terrace. Torreno pressed a switch on a railing post and a soft glow sprang up from lights tucked away in the foliage. They were on a kind of dock, Rafael realized, which cantilevered out over a pond. Torreno took a plastic bowl from a small table, opened the lid. He grabbed a handful of something, made a tossing motion out over the water. Food pellets of some kind, Rafael thought, as the murky water began to boil.

"Spoiled creatures," Torreno mumbled. He showed Rafael the contents of the container—a mass of writhing white worms as fat as finger joints. Rafael felt his stomach turn over as Torreno emptied the rest of the container into the water. The renewed surge near the dock sent a splash of water up against Rafael's leg. Rafael jerked back.

"Lungfish." Torreno seemed amused. He motioned to the servant, who came forward with a long-handled net. Torreno nodded and Coco plunged the net down into the roiling waters. He came up with something in the net, a creature that Rafael first thought was a fat snake of some kind. Coco thrust the net under Rafael's nose. It smelled of stagnant water and swamp slime; an eel-like thing with the head of a catfish lunged inside, trying to burst through the thin nylon mesh. Rafael turned away.

"Nothing attractive about them, but they have a voracious appetite"—Torreno paused—"for mosquitoes and other pests." Rafael nodded, unwilling to turn around until Coco had tossed the thing back into the water.

"They are living fossils, some three hundred million years old, the link between sea creatures and mankind," Torreno continued, following the splash.

Rafael stared at him, finding it difficult to believe there was anything to connect such creatures with himself.

Torreno gazed at the water. "They can breathe air, you see. Were this pond to dry up, the entire colony would simply gather itself and march onward until they found a new home."

"Fascinating," Rafael managed. He wondered if Torreno was mad.

Torreno nodded. "We have much to learn from nature," he said. "Some creatures teach us adaptability, while that brute over there . . . "

Torreno pointed at a spot on the muddy bank, but Rafael shook his head, seeing nothing. Torreno picked up a flashlight, snapped it on, aimed the beam across the water. There was a small island out there; it was surrounded by a fence that poked a foot or two above the surface of the water. Two spots of red appeared amid the foliage on the island's shore, as if glowing coals had been suddenly dropped there. Torreno waggled the light, and there was a huge splash in the water, a glimpse of a long ragged tail disappearing beneath the surface. Rafael had not seen the creature, but the glowing eyes had vanished.

Torreno stared wistfully at the swirling water. "The crocodile named for our country," he said. "Once it was the most aggressive creature of its kind, absolutely incorrigible near humans." He looked at Rafael. "Now they raise it in farms, to harvest its skins and its flesh."

Rafael cast a glance back toward the house. It seemed miles away, somehow. His legs were heavy, his shoulders felt slumped. He was exhausted. There was a powerboat tied off at the big dock back there somewhere. Time to board it, to be gone from this place, a fresh sea breeze in his face, on his way to South America, a new life . . .

"More than thirty years I have spent here," Torreno said, waving his arm about. "It is not my homeland, but it has become something of a home."

Something of a home, Rafael thought. The property contained a massive main house, a somewhat smaller mansion near the water that Torreno referred to as the boathouse, various gardeners' and guest cottages, and any number of gazebos, poolhouses, and chickees such as this one, all strewn amid stands of Dade County pine, mango and avocado orchards, mahogany hammocks. The most remote acreage, where they stood now, was given over to a game preserve where Torreno raised his exotic animals.

It made Rafael uneasy as he stared at one of the tall chain-linked fences dividing the far shore of the pond from the bay itself. What were the animals that could leap so high? he wondered. And if they could leap that high, who was to say they might not leáp just a bit higher.

There was another scream from the darkness on the far shore and Rafael nearly dropped his glass.

"Nothing to fear," Torreno said. "Though it sounds like a jungle cat, I agree."

After a moment, he continued. "Some think I maintain all this as a private hunting preserve." He shook his head sadly. "Nothing could be further from the truth."

He aimed his flashlight into the foliage behind Rafael and pointed. Rafael turned and opened his mouth in surprise. It was a sizable cage—not so much a cage as a clutch of screened-in trees, actually—full of nesting birds, all of them bright green, with brilliant green and red topknots. One of the birds cocked its head at the light, then fanned its wings open and gave the same lusty scream Rafael had heard earlier.

"The Cuban parrot," Torreno said. "Unique to our island and, sad to say, nearly extinct. Most of these I have obtained from smugglers." He shook his head as though the memories pained him. "Wretched men."

He glanced at Rafael. "When I return to our country, the animals will come with me. Eventually they will replenish what has been destroyed. Our enemies do not conserve nature," he said, his eyes flashing. "They consume it, and what they cannot consume, they kill."

He snapped off the flashlight, leaving Rafael blinded momentarily. He blinked, feeling Torreno's gaze upon him. "A noble sentiment," Rafael said, feeling a bit woozy. He groped about in the darkness until he found the railing they had been leaning upon, set his drink down.

"Much more than a sentiment," said Torreno, his firm grasp on Rafael's arm again. "Come, I have kept you long enough."

Torreno ushered him off the terrace and back through the chickee onto the gravel pathway that curled through the foliage. Rafael glanced about for Coco, but the servant had disappeared. Torreno was already scuttling away down the walkway and Rafael hurried to catch up. His legs felt rubbery and a glaze of sweat covered his face. He was bound for the Andes, he thought, where he would not miss this heat.

And there were so many twists and turns in the path: huge fronds swatting at his face, rough vines that clawed at him, his eyes burning as he tried to keep in sight of Torreno's heels. He heard, or imagined he heard, strange rustlings in the undergrowth on either side of him. There was another high-pitched scream somewhere up ahead—just a bird with a red topknot, he reminded himself—and he shuddered at the thought of being lost in this wilderness. Torreno was surely a madman, seeing himself riding an ark into his island's harbor, some sort of modern-day Noah. . . .

But now he had lost sight of Torreno altogether, and Rafael felt a surge of panic. He careened around a bend, his shoulder clipping something hard, and felt himself falling, his hands clawing down the fabric of a steel fence. He felt his face slap into soft mud, felt a moment of relief from the fever that had seemed to come over him . . . then he heard the clang of a gate closing behind him, the sound of metal meshing firmly into metal. He pushed himself up from the mud, groggy. There were squeals in the darkness about him, the sounds of small creatures scattering about. Then there was bright light, a supernova of a floodlamp, that had come from the forest to train itself upon him. He tried to shield himself from the beam with one hand, hooked his fingers into the fence, pulled himself erect.

He caught a glimpse of the things he had heard scampering nearby, and caught his breath: At first he'd thought they were rabbits, throngs of them, frozen in the light, but then he realized that was wrong. These creatures were more like rats, huge tailless rats, ugly things that sat up on their haunches, snouts twitching, staring at him with curiosity.

"The agouti." He heard Torreno's voice from somewhere beyond the light. "Among the largest of the rodents, but quite docile. You need not fear the agouti."

Rafael clung to the fence, his legs leaden. He'd been drugged, he realized, and he cursed himself. He'd felt safe once he was sure the money had been transferred—a terrible mistake. He shook his head slowly back and forth, trying to clear away the haziness.

"You have lost your way," Torreno was saying. "You have stumbled into a place where you should not be."

Rafael felt words forming in his throat, but his tongue seemed too thick to speak. He blinked his eyes into focus, stared out through the fabric of the fence, but instead of Torreno, saw the cadaverous Coco striding forward, a bucket in hand. The mulatto stopped, drew the bucket back, flung its contents at him. Rafael staggered back as the stuff washed over him. The stench choked him, the coppery taste of blood turning his stomach inside out.

"You are a loose thread in a tapestry that is nearly complete," Torreno said. "But take heart. If there is such a thing as karma, then you have acquitted yourself well. Farewell," he said. Then the light went out.

When the scream came again, this time much closer, Rafael knew it was no bird. He had been soaked in the blood of some hapless prey, and the predator was coming to call.

His own brain had dropped down a notch, to a more primitive level. *Puma*, he thought. Or worse, because it was so much bigger, *el jaguar*. His reason argued that it could not be, there were no such creatures in his homeland. And if there were no jungle cats there, what would Torreno be doing with them here?

Another scream as Rafael considered the question. The agouti had fled in a squealing frenzy, and Rafael followed.

He staggered away through the thick undergrowth, praying he was headed in the right direction. He had no hope of outrunning the big cat, but if he could reach the waters of the bay, he might swim out to safety.

The thought of the lungfish did not deter him in the slightest. They seemed like creatures of light compared to the thing that stalked him now. He would frolic with the lungfish, stuff them gladly down his shirt, if only he could reach that water.

He felt his feet sucking in deeper mud, then nearly sobbed with gratitude as his next step brought water inside his shoes. He tore through the last screen of mangroves, saw the broad sheet of water reflected in the starlight. He heard a howl of outrage behind him, a howl that faded as he dove forward into the brackish waters of the bay and began to swim, his movements sluggish, but carrying him out to safety.

When he was sure he was out of danger, he brought his head up, began to tread water. The big cat's screaming had stopped. Perhaps it had already slunk away in defeat. Or maybe there had been no cat at all, just another strange bird, some rat with a voice. Perhaps this was all some insane test Torreno had devised for him. In any case, he was safe. The water had also revived him a bit. He was feeling refreshed, almost exhilarated.

What he saw then made his heart stop.

It was coming toward him, impossibly, the huge yellow feline head no more than a dozen feet away. He saw the ripples where the big cat's shoulders roiled noiselessly beneath the surface.

It could not be, he thought. But there was no denying the creature that moved inexorably toward him. He could hear short powerful chuffs from the cat now, breath from the pistons of hell. He
turned, was thrashing madly in the water, trying desperately to get
away. It was like swimming inside a terrible dream—he knew what
he intended, but his movements seemed impossibly slow.

He made one clean stroke, a second, then a third. He saw a sliver
of moon slip out from behind a cloud, saw a ragged mangrove island
a few hundred yards ahead. He was a strong swimmer, after all. He
had begun to feel the slightest stirrings of hope when the first blow
struck him.

It felt like ice at first. Streaks of ice coursing down his back.
There was numbness, except for the drag of something that seemed
to hang in tatters from his back. Cloth, he told himself. Cloth. A narrow miss. He tried another stroke, but something was wrong: His
arms would not respond. He felt slippery things bumping into him
then, multitudes of them, the water so thick with the long, coiling
creatures that he thought he might rise and walk upon them to
safety.

But he could not move. He felt his face drift down into the water,
felt the rough, rasping kiss of a hundred tiny mouths about his
mouth.

Then, with the pull of the warm, salty water, came a hint of fire.
He thought of Marielena Marquez, remembered the touch of her
flesh beneath him, wondered what she had felt when the blast took
her. There was another strike from the cat, a rough jolt sending him
completely under, as the pain from the first blow finally erupted. It
would have been much quicker for her, or at least that is what he
prayed.

He felt liquid fill his throat. There was a third blow then, and a
fourth. The water boiled now with scavenging lungfish come to join
the harvest. He thought of Marielena once again, imagined the flash
of hatred she must have felt for him . . . for she must have known
how he had betrayed her. . . .

And soon enough he could not think at all.

The television was a tiny black-and-white, which made it worse somehow, the black and white. Why was that, Tommy wondered momentarily, then forgot he had wondered.

Stand at the window of the apartment—surrounded by the damp heat of a South Florida August night, palmetto bugs whispering past your ears like tiny bats to bang against the screen, tree frogs cranking it out like no tomorrow—look in, you'd think you were peeping on an ordinary guy: a Nike T-shirt, khaki shorts, and beach flops, popcorn in a supermarket bag in his lap as he stared at the tiny screen.

Slender guy, but well built, nice-looking, hair trimmed neatly, almost too short, but even that in style these days. A friendly face, unlined from a distance. You'd have to get up close to see that he was fifty, maybe fifty-five. Tanned as he was, that easy smile, short fluff of hair falling across his forehead, he might pass for thirty-five. Nice guy, Tommy. Everybody likes Tommy. Harmless old Tommy, get your finger out of your nose.

"Tommy . . . "

He hears his name called, looks up at the window in surprise, but of course there's no one there. He's used to that. Used to the phantoms who come calling, though they never hang around for long.

He turns back to the set. It happens every night, if he doesn't remember to get away in time. Right after all the programs go off.

The song . . . the . . . *star-spangled something* . . . comes on, big hairy band whomping it out, the flag flapping in some made-up breeze somewhere, and then the pictures they beam along. The nice ones at first. It always starts out nice:

Kids swimming in a creek, a panorama of some mountains, a seacoast with cliffs and waves, somebody's grandma pulling a pie out of an oven, an old man with his arm around a kid's shoulders, big sunset in the background. Tommy feels an arm around *his* shoulders, reaches up to pat the hand that's never there.

It won't stay nice like this, he knows it. But it's like being caught in a bad dream. Too late to do anything about it. He can't get up. Can't go turn off the set. He just can't.

Maybe if he had one of those kind of TVs with a button in your hand . . . he could just push it and wink it out. But no, he wouldn't be able to stop it even then.

"Tommy?" The voice all sweetness and light. "Look, Tommy."

He doesn't want to look, but he can't help it. This is the part, the part where it starts. Rockets. Red. Glare. What words are those? Where from? Nobody's singing.

On the screen are the soldiers. The jungle. They are slogging through water. That guy is tired. Tommy closes his eyes. Sees him step on something. Something sharp, up through his foot, or is it the exploding thing, the guy going up in the air like a doll some kid tore and tore, and tossed away?

He opens his eyes and the soldier is still slogging through water, of course. He just doesn't know yet. There are people on shore watching. Little people in pajamas. One man smiling, all his teeth rotting away.

If he could just get up and go to bed, Tommy thinks. But he sees the little pajama man turned upside down now, dangling from the end of a rope, the rope tied to a bent-over tree limb and someone pulling the limb down and the little man's head goes down in the water where something is thrashing and the water turns red.

Bursting. In. Air.

No little man on screen at all, of course. It's actually a black man, speaking to a crowd from a balcony. A huge crowd. Happy people shouting back, excited and crying, and in the back, police

with dogs, and other—different—people shouting and the dogs lunging for them. Then the black man on the balcony falters, throws his
hands to his throat as he staggers down.

"*Tom*-my . . . " the voice croons, but Tommy will not look.

Our. Still. Flag. Is. There.

Tommy looks again, finds he's on the screen now. Up there on
screen, at the bow of a torpedo boat that bobs in a gentle swell, just
off a beach where palm trees wave. Palm trees, just before dawn,
blue skies, and a landing craft dumping men in camouflage fatigues,
a dozen or so, onto the white sand. The men have scarcely started
toward the cover of the trees when the first explosions come. Bright
orange flowers that bloom black and toss men skyward, and then the
planes that roar as if from nowhere, out over the canopy of trees to
strafe men, crying out, flailing helpless in the surf. The sea churns
with shrapnel and blood.

Tommy waits for the planes to dive upon his boat, but they do
not, of course. One jet skims the waves nearby, dipping its wings as
if in salute, then banks away toward the beach, guns blazing again,
and Tommy feels a hand on his shoulder. He turns from the slaugh-
ter on shore to the big, dark-skinned man who smiles and embraces
him. For a job well done, Tommy knows, but he cannot feel proud.
This is bad. This is the worst. Thing. And he is to blame.

Who is this man, whom he does not trust? What has Tommy
done?

"Jesus Christ," comes the big, bad voice then, a voice from
another world.

Tommy still sitting in his chair, of course, right here in this pretty
place they call Florida, making it all up. Popcorn in his lap, but he
isn't hungry anymore. There's someone banging on his door. He can't
move. He's crying. Can't. He just can't help it.

"Jesus Christ," says the voice that's banging. "Please. Turn. That.
Fucking. Thing. Down."

And this is how it goes.

"Hell, he's got to have *that* much sense," Driscoll was saying.
The ex-cop stood on Deal's patio waving a cigarette around in the
turgid morning air. He wore a too-small T-shirt bearing the likeness
of a drooling sow along with the legend PIG—AND PROUD OF IT. The

rest of his wardrobe included a pair of plaid bermudas with boxer shorts sagging below the hems, black socks, tire-tread sandals.

Deal rubbed his face, wondering if the coffee was finished perking yet. Maybe it had been a mistake suggesting that Driscoll rent one of his units after he retired. He needed more tenants like Mrs. Suarez. Ones you'd hardly know were there.

They were talking about Tommy, or at least Driscoll was. From the moment he'd opened the front door, Deal hadn't been able to get much more than a grunt out. "You telling me you *never* hear that TV?" Driscoll asked again.

Deal shrugged. "I'm a deep sleeper, I guess."

"Well, it might as well be going off in my bedroom, every goddamn night," Driscoll said. "Maybe it's the way this place is built."

Deal gave him a look. Driscoll must have sensed he'd crossed some kind of line. He harrumphed, took a drag on his cigarette, looked out toward the side yard where Tommy was patiently weeding one of the flower beds. There was a big spot of sweat between Tommy's shoulders, turning the institutional gray of his long-sleeved shirt nearly black.

Deal guessed it was about eight o'clock on this Sunday morning. A few fleecy clouds hung motionless in the east, way out over the Atlantic. Over eighty, heading for ninety-two, the humidity already off the top of the scale. First a hurricane. In December, a freak cold snap. Now the hottest March on record. Normal Florida weather.

"Look, Driscoll, what do you want me to do, throw him out?"

Driscoll glanced back at him, his eyes hurt. But Deal could see the idea taking hold in Driscoll's mind, Tommy sitting on his duffel bag out on the sidewalk, as dazed as he'd been the afternoon he'd moved in.

Homer Tibbets had showed up a few weeks ago, Tommy in tow. Little Homer, a dwarf, maybe four-six, looking like a kid except for his adult's head and torso, holding six-foot Tommy's hand. Like a kid and his father come to collect for the United Way or something. Only Homer was the adult in this case and big Tommy was the child.

"I wundered if you still had that apartment," Homer said. No hello, no how you been, though Deal hadn't seen him in months, his voice, as always, surprising in its depth and resonance. Tommy goonying around like he'd been snatched out of some other dimension.

"You read about him," Homer said, noticing Deal's eyes on Tommy.

Deal shook his head. He had no idea what Homer was talking about.

"I found him under I-395," Homer insisted. "With those guys froze to death." Homer pronounced the word like *debt*.

It had begun to sink in. Something on TV, four homeless men, part of the growing brigade flooding downtown, left without shelter to huddle under a freeway overpass on the coldest night in a half-century. Three dead, one in Jackson Memorial, social agencies raising hell. There'd been no mention of Homer Tibbets in the stories Deal had seen.

"*You* found those guys?" Deal asked.

"I was on my way to the dealership." Homer shrugged. He was referring to the downtown location of Surf Motors. Homer was a lot boy there, had been since the days when Deal's father had traded at the place.

"They were all laid out right there by the sidewalk." Homer shook his head. "Must have froze to death up top, where they like to hang out, slid down the concrete bank in the night. They had *frost* on their faces, you know that?"

"Christ, Homer." Deal tried to imagine it. You stumbled across things like that in the Gulag, in screwed-up Third World countries, not in Miami. You didn't find people dead of exposure on your way to work in Miami.

"Then I noticed this one," Homer continued. "He looked like the Michelin Man, all puffed up. I thought maybe it's what happens when you freeze or something. Then I realize he's still alive."

Deal found his eyes locked on Tommy's. Clear blue eyes, guileless as a child's. The man smiled and Deal nodded back.

"Next thing," Homer said, "I ran out in front of a guy in a Mercedes, talking on a car phone—really pissed him off—made him call 911.

"So while we're waiting for the ambulance, I figure out why Tommy is all puffed up." Homer tugged Tommy's hand, proud. "He'd gone and stuffed a bunch of plastic bread wrappers down his pantlegs and shirt, for insulation. EMS guys said it's what saved his life. So now we call him Tommy Holsum, on account of the bread wrappers, you know. He's one smart cookie, Deal."

Tommy seemed to have drifted off somewhere, his gaze blank, his jaw slack, his head tilted as if he were tuning into a signal from a distant source.

"Did you guys want to come inside?" Deal offered.

"Funny you should ask that," Homer said. And that's how Tommy had come to stay.

Homer had gone on to explain: City officials, already under fire for their shameful treatment of the homeless, had latched on to Tommy in a big way. Got him the best treatment at Jackson, some plastic surgeon from Utah flew down to save his fingers and toes, blah, blah, blah. Then they enrolled him in one of these programs for guys who aren't exactly firing on all their cylinders, set him up with a job busing dishes, enrolled him in "life-enhancement" counseling. Now he needed a place to stay.

"He ain't all there, but he can cope in the mainstream, that's what they tell me," Homer said.

"You want him to live in my building?" Deal asked.

"Hey, I figure there's worse places than Deal House, here. And HRS will pay. American money."

The truth was, Deal had been running an ad on his last unit for nearly four months without success. The figure from HRS was only fifty dollars under what he'd been listing.

"But if you're uncomfortable," Homer said. "I mean, havin' a retard around bothers you . . . "

Homer rose, reached for Tommy, started for the door. Deal sighed and called them back.

The next day, Deal was lugging Tommy's duffel bag into the vacant apartment, showing him how this and that worked. Tommy with no name, no history, no speech, nodding, nodding, nodding. And remembering every last instruction.

In fact, he'd proved to be a faultless tenant, eager to supplement his income by doing odd jobs around the fourplex, and the check from HRS came right on time. But now here was Driscoll, making life complicated.

"You want me to do that?" Deal repeated. "Send him back to the home?"

Driscoll groaned, rubbing the back of his neck with a meaty hand. "I'm just blowing off steam, Johnny. Maybe I ain't got used to leisure or something."

Deal nodded, but Driscoll wouldn't meet his gaze.

"I'll talk to him, okay?" Deal said.

Driscoll nodded, staring off down the street where Mrs. Suarez, Deal's other tenant, was out walking her dog. "Twenty-five years on the force, maybe I worked too much crowd control."

Deal shook his head, not sure what Driscoll was getting at. "I liked it. It was a free pass. I used to do all the university games, the Fish too." Driscoll shrugged. "Now I wake up in the middle of the goddamned night, hear 'The Star-Spangled Banner,' it makes me want to jump up and salute, you know?"

Deal laughed. "I could use some help on that Terrell job," he said. "Long day of work out in the sun, you'd sleep like a baby."

"Shit," Driscoll said. "Last time I pounded a nail, I was using the butt end of a .38, trying to hang a picture. Blew a hole right between my feet. You don't want me around any construction site, Johnny."

"Well, at least you didn't shoot off your pecker," Deal said.

"Ha!" Driscoll said. Then he brightened, thinking of something. "That's what happened to that purse snatcher over in the Gables last week. You know, that moron they said on the news was running away from a holdup—stuck his gun in his belt and shot himself in the stomach?"

Deal nodded.

"Well," Driscoll said, "I was talking to Lonnie Neese, the public relations officer down at Metro. What the guy actually shot was his own dick. Blew it right off. Asshole was dead before they got him to the hospital." Driscoll laughed. "They just didn't want to say dick on television."

"I guess they wouldn't," Deal said.

"I don't see why not," Driscoll said. "Just imagine: Anne Bishop comes on saying 'Mr. Carrolton Thomas, accused purse snatcher and crack cocaine fancier, shot his own dick off in the aftermath of a crime spree earlier this evening. . . .'" He paused to stare at Deal, his face still red from laughing. "What's the matter with you, anyway? Don't you think that's funny?"

Deal nodded, though he was thinking that it would be a hell of a way to go, even for a stickup artist. Perhaps that was the result of nearly getting killed yourself, he thought. You start to sympathize with any victim, even the least likely.

"Maybe you ought to get Lonnie Neese's job," he said to Driscoll.

"Naw," Driscoll said, taking him seriously. "It's politics anywhere you look down there. Even old Lonnie has to take shit. Try and cover everybody's ass." Driscoll shook his head. "Naw, between the politics and the guys on the take, you don't know who to trust. You're on your own any way you look at it. I might as well be on my own for real."

Deal knew Driscoll was referring to the private investigation agency he'd proposed, even before the ink was dry on his retirement papers. He'd been high on the prospect at first, had even shopped various neighborhoods for office space, but he seemed to have lost interest in the project lately.

Deal glanced at him, noticed that the veins in the big man's nose were more prominent than ever, the flush high in his cheeks. Maybe it was just the laughter, but he doubted it. There was a nick on Driscoll's chin where he'd cut himself shaving, another patch of stubble where he'd missed altogether.

He heard the last sighs of the coffeemaker as it finished cycling. "You want to come in, have some coffee?" Deal asked.

"Thanks," Driscoll said, but he was shaking his head. "I took up enough of your morning as it is."

Deal nodded. He hadn't heard any sounds from Isabel's room yet. Maybe he could go back down the hallway, snuggle in with Janice, they could pick up where they'd left off last evening. The shock he'd felt yesterday had ebbed away for the most part once they'd come home, cuddled their daughter, settled in. Maybe Janice felt the same way.

"Okay, Driscoll," he said. "I'll talk to Tommy . . . " Then he broke off. "Damn, I almost forgot." He looked at Driscoll, expectant. "About Boca."

Driscoll stared at him blankly.

"You know," Deal said. "We're going to dinner tonight."

Driscoll's face fell. "Oh hell, Johnny. I don't know about that . . . "

"What, you've got other plans?"

"Naw, I just . . . "

"We've been promising Barbara for months now. Homer's coming, she's got it all set up with her boss. . . . "

There was a thud from the direction of the flower beds. They turned to see Tommy stretched out on his back in the grass, a big clump of nut grass clutched to his chest. He must have been tugging full out at the clump when it gave way, sending him flying backward.

He lay there for a moment, then rolled to his hands and knees, shaking his head like a woozy fighter. When he realized Driscoll and Deal were watching, he gave them a smile, then got up, dusted himself off, and went back to the impatiens.

"That boy's got a day job, huh?" Driscoll said.

"He's older than I am," Deal said.

"Whatever," Driscoll said.

"He buses dishes," Deal said. "At Doc's, in the Gables."

"Well, good for him," Driscoll said, heading for the stairwell.

Deal heard a noise behind him. He turned, staring in surprise. It was his daughter, Isabel, rubbing the dark curls out of her eyes, tugging at the hem of the T-shirt that couldn't cover the curve of her belly. She tottered across the kitchen floor toward him, braced herself at the doorway, and thrust an empty bottle upward. "Bah," she said.

Deal shook his head. "How did you get out of your crib?"

"Bah!" Isabel said, more firmly.

So much for his plans, Deal thought, scooping his daughter up in his arms. "Come down about six, Vernon," he called to Driscoll. "We'll drive."

Driscoll waved his hand dismissively as he disappeared around the corner. "I dunno. I don't have anything to wear."

"It's casual," Deal said.

"It'd sure as shit have to be," Driscoll said. And then he was gone.

"Whas in the bag, man?"

Coco Morales adjusted the Manatees baseball cap he wore, ignoring the rail-thin black man who slouched in the bus seat across from him. He had his attention fixed on the tiny TV he held in his palm, was fighting the glare from the sun that splayed through the filthy windows.

Two men in Mohawk haircuts and Halloween makeup were in the ring, pummeling a tall figure in black tights back and forth between them. The tall man's face wore the pallor of death beneath an artist's slouch hat. One of the big men tore the hat off and ran his fist through the top of it. If there was a referee involved, Coco could not see him.

"Yo. Whas in the bag, man?"

The bus whisked under a freeway overpass and the TV image wavered, then gathered itself. There was a small man in a tuxedo who had been trussed up in the ringside ropes; he hung there with his feet off the ground like something caught in a spider's web. One of the Mohawk men left the middle of the ring and strode over to drive a forearm into the throat of the small man, who sagged as if in death.

Coco studied all this with detachment. There was professional wrestling where he had come from, but nothing quite so ludicrous as this. He knew. He had participated himself. After his mother's death, after one tour in the regular army, another in the pay of the insurgents, he had had a chance encounter with a former *comandante.* It was a moment of relative peacetime in his revolution-weary country. A crowded bar. The former officer now an important man with a shirt pocket full of cigars and a woman on each arm. He remembered *gigante* Coco, as who would not, stood him to a drink, had one more look at his remarkable face. *El Comandante* leaned closer, ordered another round, and began to explain. The next day, Coco was working for *El Comandante* once again, in the business sport of wrestling.

In Coco's country, there were the intended victors, the heroes, as here; and there was also the lesser class, the opponents, recruited principally as victims.

The difference was that in his country, the victims were paid to absorb actual punishment. The more you were willing to undergo, the more you might earn. You would be hit, tossed, clubbed with chairs or anything else that was handy. Something extra for a bloodied nose, a split lip. And if a tooth or two happened to fly across the canvas, if you somehow broke a bone, there would be some compensation for that as well.

Coco had earned quite a good living as a victim, for pain did not greatly distress him. He *felt* pain, and did not enjoy the sensation, of course, but it did not frighten him, nor greatly inconvenience him, for he was physically quite resilient. No, the difficulty had come with his dissatisfaction at his place in the hierarchy. Coco's features were distressing enough before he began to be beaten on a regular basis. After a few months of traveling through the provinces, he was absolutely frightful to look at. Though it made him a compelling victim for the moving picture types who played the heroes, it only confirmed the fact that Coco would always be the loser.

Even that Coco could have withstood. *He* knew that he was not the pitiful representation of cowardice and powerlessness the scripts called for, but the problem was that certain of his opponents could not maintain the distinction between appearance and reality.

Eduardo Herrera, or *El Matador* as he was billed, was the worst. Herrera was the most handsome of the troupe and seemed to take personal offense at Coco's appearance. He made fun of him with the others, was always whispering to him in the clinches—*soccer head, freak, monstro*—often ridiculing him in front of fans as he stood with his foot pressing down on Coco's chest.

One night in a small fishing village not far from Coco's own home, *El Matador* had puffed out his chest for a row of local girls at ringside. *"Campesino,"* he jeered. *"Pendejo estupido!"* He leaned over Coco's prostrate form and spat a greenish glob between his eyes.

Coco had, to the amazement of the crowd, revived suddenly and miraculously, had risen up to beat *El Matador* senseless. He battered the handsome one's face with his sharp fists until blood was flying beyond the ropes, then dropped him to the canvas and ground the wounds into the grime until it was certain nothing could obliterate the scars.

Before the *comandante* and his entourage could get into the ring to stop him, he'd driven a fist into *El Matador's* throat and dragged him to the center of the ring, had left him a choking, shitting hulk under the spotlights, all this to the thunderous cheers of a crowd who took it for part of the show.

Coco lost the week's pay he would have collected that night. Lost his promising career in wrestling. But it had opened up many new vistas. He had hardly left the arena, for instance, when two of the women *El Matador* had played to at ringside threw themselves upon him.

Strange, Coco thought as the bus bounced through a series of potholes. How cruelty could transform a physical shortcoming into beauty, how the willingness to exhibit it had so improved his life.

Scarcely a week had passed before a man who called himself Torreno sent an emissary Coco's way. Now he worked in America, and had honed his craft into an art.

"Ugly fucker bringing a weirdass bag onto the bus, don't wan' to talk about it."

The skinny man had staggered up from his seat to lean across the aisle. Coco felt a scrawny hand clutch his wrist, smelled the disgusting odor of wine, of other, unknowable things on the man's breath. His own hand flashed out, covered the filthy claw on his wrist, squeezed.

The man would have cried out, but the pain was too great and too swift for that. He could only writhe about, his eyes watering, his awful teeth bared in a speechless grimace.

Coco eased him back across the aisle into his seat, careful that the bus driver should not become too curious. It was a Sunday afternoon and they were the only passengers.

"*Cabezas*," Coco hissed into the man's ear, then pointed at the sturdy woven *bolsa* that rested on the floor by his own seat. Soft and yet strong. Perfect for the things he carried. "Heads," he repeated in a whisper. "*Human* heads."

The man whimpered, his eyes growing larger as Coco increased the pressure. "A finger. A liver. Other things."

Coco gave a final squeeze, felt something snap, then released his grip. The man sagged back against his seat, his hand limp across his chest, a thing he seemed to disown. His lips were clamped together in pain, in terror. A dark stain spread down his pantlegs and the smell of urine hovered in the close air.

Coco sat back down, slipping his TV into a pocket. He glanced toward the front of the bus. The driver had his attention focused on an aging sedan in the turn lane in front of them. "Let's go, let's go," the driver shouted, leaning on his horn.

The sedan finally lunged forward through the intersection, belching a huge cloud of blue smoke behind it. The driver wrenched at the wheel, flooring the bus right after, although the light had already changed. There was a blare of horns, shouts from outside, but the driver seemed not to hear.

Coco read the sign that dangled across the thoroughfare before them. Unlike most of the storefronts around them, this one actually bore an English translation: WELCOME TO LITTLE HAVANA.

Yes, Coco thought, welcome. He lifted up his bag and stood, scanning the brightly colored storefronts for the street numbers. It looked a bit like his country, too, out there. And the driving was much the same.

He glanced at the cowering figure across from him. A few distractions to endure on these American buses, but he was just as happy that he did not drive an automobile. Think of all that he would have missed. He saw a number then, an address that meant he was drawing near.

The black man watched him warily, his eyes leaking tears. Coco reached up to pull the signal cord. The bus veered obediently to the curb. Coco gripped his bag of parts tightly and stepped out into the heat, ready to go back to work.

"She's got a crush on you, Deal."

It was Janice, glancing at him from behind the wheel. He wasn't sure if she was smiling. He was in the passenger seat, feigning sleep, didn't want to open his eyes wide enough to see. It was restful being driven for a change, even with Driscoll snoring in the backseat.

They'd spent the evening in Boca Raton, having dinner with Barbara Cooper. She'd helped them out of trouble back when, had stayed in touch even though she'd moved north, "out of harm's way," as she put it.

She was a hostess at the Sea Timbers now, a huge place on the water, massive beams and smoked glass, ship's brass everywhere you looked. Not a bad place to work for a woman who'd seen her share of hassles. Tucked into the dunes and sea grape like a little castle. The kind of place, Deal thought, you'd want to finish your meal even if nuclear war broke out.

They'd had a good time comparing notes, passing Isabel's baby pictures around, careful always to skirt the worst parts of their common history. Funny thing, Deal thought. They'd stumbled into the path of men intent on killing them all, and though they'd survived it together, they found themselves less and less willing to talk about it, even among themselves. Maybe they were as superstitious as tribes-

men, unwilling to name an evil god for fear of calling it back into existence.

Still, it had been a good evening, the oblique references and unspoken camaraderie gluing them together in spirit. Plenty of toasts, plenty of food, desserts you couldn't see over. Though Janice insisted she'd seen where Barbara's eyes had been. That's what this was about.

They were whisking down Florida's Turnpike toward home, boring through tunnels of tall slash pines, the southbound lanes divided from their northerly cousins by a hundred yards or more in this long stretch. No light save the glow from the dash, the moon breaking through the distant thunderheads from time to time . . .

It had finally relaxed him, set Deal remembering the grand road trips of his youth, long hauls through the night to the Carolinas, to New England, through the West, his mother and father in the front seat sharing a jug of coffee, Deal on a bed made up in the back, not a care in the world, so electric with anticipation he'd never go to sleep.

"We ought to take a vacation," he said, stretching luxuriously. All the glum feelings he'd had at the restaurant seemed to have drifted away. Maybe he'd just been tired.

"There's an answer for you," Janice said mildly.

Deal cocked one eye open. A smile there. Good sign. "Barbara's a good person," he said. "She's just adjusting to life in the normal, noncriminal world."

"What's that have to do with you?"

Deal wriggled around in the seat. Driscoll's snores picked up a notch. Evidently *he* found the drive restful.

"I am the very essence of normal," he said, settling deeper into the cushions. "It's like being attracted to a father figure."

"You are full of shit, that much I know."

He reached out, found her leg. "You think I'm interested in Barbara?"

"I think you're going to cause a wreck."

"We could pull over, find a place in the pine trees."

"Hmmmm-mmmmm," she said. "We've got company."

It sounded as if Driscoll was trying to snorkel a tray of flatware down a metal drainpipe. "He'll sleep right through it," Deal said. "Unless we play 'The Star-Spangled Banner.'"

She burst out laughing. "What are you talking about?" She

pushed his hand away from her thigh, but there wasn't much force in the gesture.

"Tommy," Deal said. "He plays his TV too loud right through the sign-off. Driscoll says it wakes him up every night."

"Did you talk to him?"

"How do you think I found out about it?"

She pushed his hand away again. "I mean Tommy. You need to speak with him. I'm sure if you explain it in the right way . . . "

"I promise," Deal said, shifting in his seat.

She gasped, clutching his hand in her lap. "I'm serious, Deal. I can't drive with you doing that."

"Maybe if you said 'Can't you wait until we get home,' something like that. It might give me hope."

She moved his hand down to her knee, patted it.

"Wait till we get home, then," she said. "How's that?"

"Hopeful," he said, squeezing. "Just drive fast."

"Les' go, *pobrecito.*" Gisela Suarez tugged on the leash in her hand, but the dog was unyielding. They were just beneath the window of the silent one, which made her nervous enough, but worse, the animal was rooting in one of her landlord's flower beds.

She feared that at any moment the *señor* might turn down the street, coming back home from his dinner. The bright security light that normally illuminated the building had apparently burned out, but the headlamps of his car would catch them red-handed and what then?

Señor Deal seemed like a nice man, but he was Anglo and therefore not quite knowable. He did seem to love his flowers, that much she knew. Also, he had allowed a feeble-minded man, who only watched the television and could barely speak, to live in their building. Who could tell what might happen? She could find herself out on the street again.

She had been lucky to find this place. Clean and modern, with even a *microwavio*—which, though she bragged about it at the grocery store, she used for a bread keeper. The rent, though sizable for her tiny pensioner's income, was more than reasonable. Yes, she had been lucky, she told herself.

Suppressing a shudder, she cast a glance down the block. Hidden in the shadows somewhere was the tiny bungalow that had been her home for thirty-seven years. A Nicaraguan family lived there now, parking their several cars and trucks in what had used to be a neatly tended front yard. She imagined she could hear the throbbing of the music that they played around the clock, even at this distance.

She still owned her home, but she had moved out after some-one—a madman, drug addict, who knows what kind of beast—had broken in, ransacked her home, even killed her former dog. Imagine if she had been inside at the time.

She had found herself unable to live there, yet she could not allow fear to drive her entirely from the neighborhood, either. It had been her neighborhood since she had arrived in this country, and it would be hers until she died and joined her departed husband in heaven. So she found herself in this predicament, her only compan-ion now hiking his leg to drown the *señor*'s colorful impatiens.

She laid both hands on the leash then and snatched the dog away while he was off balance. The startled beast left a curving, steaming trail across the sidewalk, but that would take care of itself. The flow-ers were saved, that was the important thing. She leaned forward, headed up the block.

And still the dog did not want to leave. He dug in his paws, scat-tering bits of grass as he fought for purchase, whimpering and strain-ing toward the corner of the building. God save her, she thought. This one was incorrigible.

Not like his predecessor, whom she had called Tuti and trained to curl up at the foot of her lonely bed after Oscar had died. Tuti danced in circles on his hind paws for a treat, barked fiercely at any-one who dared to come onto her porch uninvited, and made his busi-ness only where he ought.

And where had that gotten Tuti, she found herself thinking. *Madre de Dios.* Such a thought. Poor Tuti. Murdered by an intruder—that enormous *negro*, she thought, it had surely been him—in her own home.

She shuddered again and dragged Tuti's successor—she hadn't even named this one, how was that possible—along the sidewalk, mindless of the awful drag of his nails across the concrete, a sound that normally would have set her teeth on edge.

She was about to turn and instruct the dog to make his business there, at the edge of a scruffy vacant lot, when the dog ducked, stretched out his neck like a goose . . . and slipped backward out of his collar.

Before she could speak, the thing was gone, back toward the apartment in a flash. Mother of angels, she was thinking as she hurried back along the sidewalk. *I will kill him.* . . .

She broke off, the thought shocking her. She was immediately contrite, rebuking herself for thinking such a thing, never mind it was just a figure of speech, that she had only thought it, really. . . .

The dog, meantime, tore around the back of the apartment building. It was growling now. And barking wildly. She had never heard such antics. Perhaps it was some nocturnal animal back there, rooting in the garbage cans.

She heard snarls. A loud animal yelp. She was moving as fast as she could, cursing her aging legs.

She was nearly in front of the building when a shadow crossed her path and she caught her breath as she staggered back.

She had only a glimpse of his features beneath the bill of his cap, but that was enough. His skin was yellow, catching the reflection of the streetlamp down the block, his eyes hideous, full of loathing. It was the eyes that made him so . . . so *ugly*, even though everything about him seemed vile.

He was gone so quickly, vanished into the shadows of a pair of banyan trees that arched over the boulevard there. For a moment she thought she might have imagined him, an evil apparition from the place of nightmares and fear.

Then she remembered the dog and cast a forlorn glance toward the back of the building. There was a lump in her throat as she remembered the yelp . . . but relief flooded over her as she saw the mongrel round the corner of the building, limping gingerly her way.

Brave one, she found herself thinking as she bent down to cradle the whimpering dog in her arms, felt her own pounding heart over the rapid pulse of the animal. Perhaps this is how she would go, she thought. Like her Oscar, who looked up from his chair after supper one evening with his hand clasped to his chest, an expression of surprise on his face.

"My heart is racing," he had said to her. And then laid his head on his shoulder and died.

"*Pobrecito*," she crooned to the dog, who trembled and whined, its gaze fixed now on the forbidding shadows of the huge trees. No, it had not been her imagination.

"Poor little one." This dog had found a nocturnal beast all right.

One of the endless string of prowlers and thieves who preyed upon their neighborhood in these sad days. Yet the dog—*her* dog—had frightened him off. And though the thought shocked her, she found herself hoping he had sunk his teeth into the horrid one's flesh before he got away.

She stroked the dog's flanks until he began to calm and she herself felt strong enough to stand.

"We're not going any farther," she told him then. "Come on now, you do it here," and to her surprise, the dog obliged.

"Huh," she said, casting a last glance toward the shadows behind them. "Maybe we'll call you Tuti after all?" Though the dog made no reply, she thought she saw some recognition in its doelike eyes, and when she started back toward her apartment, he was trotting smartly at her side.

The sound of gunshots echoed across the lawn of Deal's fourplex, followed by the squeal of tires on pavement, then police sirens wailing in the distance.

"There," Driscoll said. "Tell me you don't hear that."

The three of them were on the way up the front sidewalk. Driscoll, still irritable from being awakened, clutched Deal's arm and pointed at the ground-floor window of Tommy's apartment. Blue light flickered through the uncurtained glass. There were more shots, and the sounds of a multivehicle car crash.

Deal turned from Janice's baleful gaze, nodded at Driscoll. "Okay," he said. "It's too loud. I'll talk to him." He had noticed that the security light was out. That particular type of bulb was going to cost him twenty dollars. On the other hand, he hadn't spent anything on dinner. Maybe they'd get through the month after all.

Driscoll had stopped, had folded his arms over his chest. Why wasn't he headed inside for bed? That was where Deal longed to be.

There was an Energizer commercial playing on Tommy's TV now: "Still going," the announcer's voice blared, the thuds of the rabbit's drum booming over the lawn. Driscoll seemed to be waiting for something.

"*Now?*" Deal asked incredulously. He looked at his watch. "It's

RAW DEAL

one-thirty. You want me to go banging on his door at one-thirty in the morning?"

"You want to wait 'til two? Hear the goddamned national anthem?" Driscoll fumed.

Deal was trying to think what to say when the clamor inside Tommy's apartment suddenly stopped.

There was no blue light flickering anymore, no light from the apartment at all. The three of them stared at one another in the silence. A distant glow of streetlamps. Tree frogs. A prop plane grinding somewhere in the distance.

"Sonofabitch," Driscoll said in amazement. "The set must of melted."

Maybe, Deal thought. He also thought he could make out Tommy's silhouette at the dark windows, the poor guy staring out at them, waiting for somebody's foot to fall. Deal had his arm around Janice, felt the heat of her hip beneath his hand.

"First thing in the morning," he told Driscoll. "I'll explain it to him."

Driscoll glanced around the quiet night. He cut his eyes toward Tommy's dark apartment, finally sighed and nodded wearily. "I'd appreciate it," he said. And then they said good night.

In his dream, Deal saw Janice rising and falling above him, felt her hands at his face, heard her cries of pleasure as she came, his own orgasm so intense it was almost painful. He found himself thinking, *This is a dream, but it's just as real as if it really was . . .*

. . . she was rolling off the side of the bed then, giving him a smile as she rose to go toward the bathroom, but instead, when she opened the door, it was a brightly lit terrace overlooking some Etruscan landscape, a hillside out there where workers toiled at harvesting grapes, Janice standing in the radiant light, watching. A bell was ringing somewhere. Deal flung his legs out of the bed to join her . . .

. . . and then found himself flying, a long cape fluttering back from his neck. Janice was there, too, wearing the same corny Superman costume and cape, and even little Isabel, grown up a bit, her dark curls peeled back from her forehead, her tiny hands spearing through the wash of the wind.

They were soaring over a high desert landscape, the ringing sound fading away in their wake, nothing but rocks and sand below, the heat strangely noticeable, even at altitude. It was a vacation trip, he realized. Daddy'd finally found a way to take them. And everyone was hungry, though there didn't seem to be a place to stop.

Then, suddenly, a lake came into view—Lake Powell, he thought—and he turned to Janice and Isabel, pointing Daddy-confident down below. Big beautiful fingers of blue water, tall red cliffs . . . and a marina with a wooden dock, people sitting about a waterfront cafe.

They banked downward, the three of them, the heat growing more intense as they skimmed the desert floor, abating somewhat as they planed into the water, all of them butt-first, like a family of great big ducks. They were bobbing in the water off the dock of the marina, but now there were no patrons at the tables of the cafe, no boats, no signs of life at all. And the heat was intense. He smelled the acrid odor of smoke.

This place is burning, he thought, sitting upright on the water, craning his neck for a better look . . .

. . . and found himself struggling awake on his bed.

He shook his head, groggy. He had the sensation the phone had awakened him, but there was only silence in the room. The dream had fled, but there was still the heat. *Something wrong with the air conditioner*, he was thinking, and then he began to cough.

The smoke. The goddamned smoke. He felt a surge of panic. He turned, found Janice asleep at his side. He shook her, and she mumbled something in her sleep.

"Janice!" He shook her roughly this time. She came awake, blinking.

"Too early. Back to sleep, Deal."

"Janice, something's wrong." He had her by the shoulders now, turning her to face him. His eyes were stinging from the smoke.

"Something's burning, Janice."

She stared at him, still vague with sleep. "A fire?" She shook her head, then abruptly her eyes came into focus, as though a switch had been thrown somewhere.

He glanced at their bedroom door. Closed. Christ, what did that mean? *Was* there a fire out there someplace? Or maybe it was just the AC after all. Sure, just the motor burning up. He swung his feet to the floor, trying to get his head clear.

"Isabel!" Janice cried, but Deal had risen, was already at the door.

He ran his hand across the inner surface. Pressed his cheek there. Still cool. He flung the door open, shielding his face. There was a surge of heat and a thick cloud of smoke, but no wall of flame. What had happened to the alarms? They were code. He'd installed them, picture of some TV actor on the box, one in every room.

He was coughing again, heard Janice gagging as the thick smoke enveloped her. He fell to his knees and crawled back to the bed. He found her arm, pulled her off the bed, forced her head down close to the carpet where the air was clear.

"Get outside," he said. "Stay low. I'm going for Isabel. Do you understand?"

"I'm going with you," she gasped.

He gripped her chin tightly. "*Get ... out ... side.* I'll bring Isabel. There isn't time to argue."

Finally he felt her nod. He squeezed her arms, then guided her out ahead of him. At the doorway he turned her in the direction of the kitchen, then scrambled quickly down the hallway toward Isabel's room.

The smoke was blinding now and he had to move by feel. He felt the door to the air handler closet. He'd spent an entire day enlarging that frame, making way for an upgraded unit. The door was cool. Nothing wrong with the air handler.

A few feet down the hall, then: the entrance to the hall bath, open, the marble tiles slick, almost cold beneath his touch. He'd salvaged the stone from a turn-of-the-century bank, bulldozed now, a high-rise in its place.

Next, the spare bedroom on his right, closed. This time the frame was hot. The door skin itself scorched his palm and he pulled back quickly. His computer in there, his business records, a rowing machine he'd never rowed.

He hurried on, trying to breathe, but he was taking only searing lungfuls of smoke now. He felt his head beginning to swim. The building he'd nearly killed himself to build, he thought. Getting its second chance.

Two more crablike lunges and he was at the end of the hallway, the last door on the left, Isabel's, this one closed too. He reached out, found its surface mercifully cool.

Go ahead. Burn your fucking self down, he thought. Give me five more minutes, burn yourself to hell.

He heaved himself upward for the knob and twisted.

He sensed more than heard the roar at first. It was as if a huge truck or plane were blasting down the hallway at his back. He turned as a great wave of heat and sound swept over him, and then he saw the flames: a solid wall of fire rushing toward him, the smoke disappeared somehow, leaving only the awful flames. In the second it took him to roll into Isabel's room, get the door slammed behind him, he felt his eyebrows disintegrate in a flash of heat, his lips burst into a blistering mass.

He was vaguely aware of the pain, but he didn't care about that. He dragged himself across the smoke-thick room, flailing about until he found the slats of her crib.

He gripped the wood, pulled himself up over the railing. *Why isn't she crying?* he thought, but pushed the thought away. He groped wildly about the bedclothes, his heart hammering, about to burst . . . then nearly sobbed with gratitude as his hand closed about her tiny foot.

He pulled her up to him, pressed her close, felt the reassuring throb of her heartbeat, the clutch of her sleepy hands. He hugged her once more, and then, though it seemed the hardest thing he'd ever had to do, he eased her back into the crib.

He staggered blindly across the room until his shins cracked against something hard. His hands closed on the arms of the heavy rocker, lifted. He half-slid, half-fell along the wall, then, searching, searching, until he heard glass shatter.

He stepped backward, raised the chair, spun, and threw it with his every ounce of strength. There was a crash and the air was suddenly clear, the smoke lifting as the draft rushed out through the shattered window.

Only seconds left, he was thinking. How long would that paneled door hold up? He gulped down air like a drowning man breaking the surface, then flung himself back to the crib and gathered up Isabel.

She was awake and screaming by now. He held her to his chest, soothing her automatically. Quick, careful steps across the room, eyes on the hallway door that seemed to glow, to sag inward with the force of a giant hand. *Don't run, Deal. This is the place for you. . . .*

Out through the broken window frame onto the cool grass, and never mind the glass that cracked and splintered beneath his bare feet. The flames were in her room now, snapping angrily, every stick and shred of cloth incandescent . . . *come back, Deal* . . . but they were safe outside.

Safe. *Burn yourself to hell.* He tottered toward the knot of people who had gathered on the lawn, their faces drawn, cast yellow and orange by the glare of the flaming building behind him.

There were sirens, he realized. A fire marshal's sedan bouncing crazily up over the curb, a pumper truck lumbering just behind it.

He saw Tommy on the sidewalk. Slack-jawed Tommy staring dully at the flames. Then Driscoll's face swam up out of the crowd; he saw the big man break into a run.

"Jesus God," Driscoll said. He stopped short, his expression shocked. Deal wondered what he was staring at. "Your face," Driscoll said.

"Janice?" Deal asked him. His face felt . . . his face felt strange . . . but fine.

Driscoll stared at him blankly, shook his head, glanced behind him helplessly. Mrs. Suarez was there now, a blanket slung about her shoulders. Tears were streaming down her face, but she spoke firmly, as if Deal were a child. "Give me the baby," she said. "I will take care of the baby."

Deal was feeling light-headed again. He felt Mrs. Suarez lift Isabel from his arms.

"Where's Janice?" he cried again, but Driscoll could only shake his head. He held a hand toward Deal but seemed afraid to touch him.

Deal searched the faces lined by the curb, saw the fire marshal hurrying toward him. Driscoll finally reached to take hold of him, but Deal turned away, back toward the flaming building. He began to stagger forward, oblivious to the heat.

"Janice," he screamed. Had he willed this place to burn?

He was running toward the building now. "Janice!"

He sensed someone beside him, turned to see Tommy, lumbering Tommy, joining him in a dash toward the flames. Tommy's mouth was open, his face streaked with tears. He was screaming too, crying out something unintelligible.

"Janice," Deal screamed again.

Then Tommy's anguished bellow. Tommy outrunning him, now out ahead, his arm thrown up against the heat.

"Janice," Deal cried again. His head was spinning. He prayed it was a nightmare. But the pain. The heat. Tommy and he running toward the flames. Then he felt himself going down.

"Hey, pardner."

Deal heard the voice as if from another planet. Driscoll out there somewhere, calling Deal back to life.

He tried to blink himself awake, out of the darkness, but his eyes stayed stubbornly closed. He tried to raise his hands to his face, but something held him motionless.

"Take it easy, pardner." Deal felt a hand on his shoulder. Driscoll calming him down. "They got you all tied down. They don't want you hurting yourself."

Deal saw the flames again, dancing wildly behind his sightless eyes. He thrashed against the restraints that held him, ignoring the pain that seemed to double, then double again, with every movement.

"Nurse," he heard Driscoll calling. "Get somebody in here. Now!"

Deal felt one hand come free, raised it to his face. Bandages on more bandages. It felt like he was pawing at a pumpkin with a boxing glove. Except for the pain. No blood in his veins. Just shoots of pain that surged beneath the bandages on his face and hands with every beat of his pulse.

He felt his mouth working sluggishly beneath rasping cloth, felt Driscoll's thick hand at his wrist, heard him yelling at someone—"Hurry it up, for Christ's sake!"—felt something sharp prick the skin on his arm.

He flung his head back and forth, caught bandages in his teeth, tore at them. "Janice," he said, or tried to. "Janice."

He was sliding down a cool, slippery tunnel now, a thick, soothing mist blanketing the fire on his face, his hands. He heard Janice's name echoing down the length of the long black passageway. And then he heard Driscoll's rough voice in his ear, trying to be reassuring. "She's okay, Deal. She's going to be fine."

When Deal opened his eyes again, it was dark, but this time it was darkness of a different quality. He blinked again, just to be sure he wasn't dreaming. Light filtered into the room from a hallway lamp somewhere. Driscoll was slumped in a sleeper chair at the foot of his bed, his snores rattling off the concrete walls of the hospital room. Beside him in a metal desk chair sat Homer, his head thrown back and his mouth open. He might have been snoring too, but with Driscoll's racket, it was impossible to tell. A ventriloquist and his dummy, Deal thought, as Homer began to stir.

"Hey," Homer said groggily. He reached over to shake Driscoll awake. The snores stopped abruptly. "Look who came back."

Driscoll rubbed at his eyes, struggled up out of the chair. "Deal," he said. "It's about goddamned time."

Deal ran his tongue about his lips, raised his hand to Driscoll in greeting. He counted five fingertips. Then lifted his other hand. An IV line taped to his wrist, some bandages, five more fingertips. He touched his face. Still bandaged, but there were cutouts now for his eyes, his nose, his mouth. He wondered how long he'd been in this bed.

The skin on his cheeks felt dry and tight, ready to split open. The pain, however, had subsided from agony to something that might possibly be measured. If you had the time.

"Where is she?" He swallowed. It felt like someone had run a plumber's auger down his throat.

"Down the hall, pardner," Driscoll said. Deal saw Homer's anxious glance.

"Take me," Deal managed.

"You can't go anywhere," Driscoll began, but Deal had already jerked the IV tube from his arm, was doing his best to untangle his feet from the bedsheets.

Driscoll reached for the call button dangling from the bed rail, but Deal grabbed his hand, ignoring the fresh burst of pain beneath his bandages. "Take me to Janice," he said, his gaze locked on Driscoll's. And they went.

Homer distracted the aide at the nurse's station while Driscoll helped Deal down the dimly lit hallway. Deal was light-headed, his feet seeming to barely touch the floor.

Two turns, through an automatic door, into an area where the rooms were glass-partitioned cubicles, radiating off a central command post full of beeping monitors, flashing screens, computer printouts. There were nurses and aides there, but everyone seemed too busy to notice Driscoll and Deal.

"Be ready," Driscoll said, tightening his grip across Deal's shoulders. "It looks worse than it is." The big excop turned them into one of the small cubicles, nodded at the form on the bed. "That's her," Driscoll said. "That's Janice."

Deal stared, feeling the lump in his throat grow until he wasn't sure he could breathe. She lay motionless, covered in gauze—hands, arms, head—like something from a bad horror film. A bedside monitor beeped steadily, feeding out a little paper tape that tumbled into coils on the floor.

He started toward her, then stopped, afraid. "Janice?" he said, his voice strangled. His eyes were clouding with tears.

"Who let you in here?" The voice of authority, of outrage behind him. An intensive-care nurse, doing her duty. Deal didn't budge, didn't take his eyes off Janice's quiet form.

"It's her husband," he heard Driscoll explaining.

"I don't care who he is. . . . "

Deal felt a hand on his arm. He shook it off, clutched the rail of Janice's bed.

"Just give us a minute," Driscoll pleaded.

"Mr. Deal?"

Deal glanced at her. She had a more kindly face than he expected, a broad, grandmotherly brow, wire-rimmed glasses, a flush in her cheeks. "Are you Mr. Deal?"

Deal had his gaze back on Janice's quiet form. He felt tears forming in his eyes.

"Then you'll want the best for your wife, won't you?"

The nurse's voice seemed to reach him from a distant place. Oddly, Deal found himself nodding in agreement.

"She's going to make it, don't you worry, Mr. Deal. She's out of the woods now."

Out of the woods, he thought. He wanted to touch Janice's hand, her cheek, but there was nothing but bandages and tubes and wires.

Out of the woods. What was that fairy tale? The two little kids with the mean stepmother and the wimp of a father. Took their children into the forest to die. Yet the children had survived, made it out of the woods somehow.

He felt the nurse's hand on his arm again, this time more gently. "You come out with me, Mr. Deal. We'll have us some coffee, I'm going to explain things to you."

Deal felt himself being drawn away from Janice's bed then. The nurse's big hands comforting him like the touch of some fairy godmother come to deliver him from trouble. He cast one last glance at Janice's motionless form.

How he wished it were as simple as it was in fairy tales. Didn't matter if you got your ass in a crack as long as you were pure of heart. Some genie or spirit would come along to clear things up.

But this was life. And Deal knew that he was responsible. That he *wasn't* pure of heart. That somehow he had created the circumstances that had led to this calamity. He just hadn't had time yet to figure out how.

He let the nurse guide him down the dark hallway. She knew about him, all right. He'd seen it in her eyes. He'd screwed up again. Maybe she could tell him why.

While no one was able to speak to the unutterable gnawing that Deal knew he would carry forever, he did learn a few things. From Mrs. Delaney, the nurse. From the attending physician, who arrived shortly after daybreak. And from Driscoll, who had learned what had happened during the fire.

It turned out that, despite his orders, Janice had followed him down the hallway after Isabel. She must have become disoriented, opened the wrong door, the guest room door, the very one Deal had scorched one of his hands on.

Once that door was opened, the air from the rest of the apartment fed the inferno inside and that was it, end of story. The fire turned into the freight train that had roared down the hall toward him. He knew what that heat had done to him. He could only imagine what Janice must have suffered there at the maw of hell.

The nurse and the doctor were in agreement on Janice's prognosis. Cautious, but optimistic. Burn cases were ticklish business, but as long as she escaped secondary infection, it seemed that she would make it.

"She's strong," the doctor told him. "She wants to live. That means a lot."

Deal saw the look in Mrs. Delaney's eyes. They were sitting, the four of them, on uncomfortable plastic chairs in the nurses' lounge, everyone's wretched coffee sitting untouched before them on a Formica tabletop. "What else, Doc? What is it you're not telling me?" Deal felt his lips pull and tingle with every word.

Another glance between them. The doctor and Deal's fairy god-mother.

"Nothing really," the doctor said, his gaze wavering. "There's the issue of reconstructive surgery, of course. But it's a little early to discuss all that."

Deal felt a chill run through him. He'd been so concerned that she was going to live . . .

"How bad is it?"

Mrs. Delaney coughed. The doctor looked off into that place they must teach doctors to look when the really bad shit has to be confronted. "As I said, it's a little early to assess. . . . "

Deal leaned forward, caught the doctor by his lab coat. "Tell me what we're talking about."

The doctor looked at him, his eyes helpless behind his thick glasses. "Her nose, some ear tissue, the scalp . . . " He took Deal's hand. "Please, Mr. Deal. I just don't know yet."

Deal fell back in his chair, raised his palms to his eyes, ignoring the pain. Worse than he could have ever imagined. He'd tear out his own eyes. Throw himself into the flames. If that could only make it better.

"I think you'd better get back to your bed," Mrs. Delaney was saying.

"You got to take care of yourself, partner." It was Driscoll's voice at his ear. "Lot of folks counting on you."

Deal heard the bark of laughter escape his own throat. That was rich. Counting on *him*. Sure. He could be counted on. Stick with Deal, everybody. He'll take you to hell in a handcart.

He was laughing raucously now, his hands still on his face, and then he realized he had pitched down onto the table. He felt tepid coffee soaking his arms, pouring off the table onto his legs and feet. After a moment he felt another needle prick the flesh of his arm, and heard Driscoll mouthing something else inane.

Well, fill him up with bromides, shoot him up with the pharmacy's finest, it wasn't going to do any good. Awake or in darkness, this was a pain that would never end.

Saturday night. Tommy at Doc's in the Gables, busing dishes. It's late, the place is jammed. A jazz
combo in one corner of the main room, the other
side of the big square bar. Tommy feels the bass
through his feet, the sound running up his legs and
spreading through him like something warm, feels
himself nodding to the beat as he hustles toward the
kitchen with a bin full of plates and silver.

Lots of pretty people in here tonight. Everybody
dressed up. *A party-down town*, says a voice in his head. Tommy
wonders who thought that. As if a stranger slipped in, told him
something weird.

He pauses to let some customers file by. People going out.
Always stop for the customers, Tommy. He remembers that, and who
told him. Mr. Boss. *Steve's my name, Tommy. Call me Steve. And
always let the customers go first.* Right, Mr. Boss.

There's a girl at the bar, watching him. A sparkly black dress,
milky skin, hair satiny on her bare shoulders. Tommy sees her lips
glisten in the dim light. He feels his dopey smile forming on his face,
no way to stop it. She smiles back, then there's a big guy muscling up
beside her, his arm around her, kisses her cheek. She turns to this
guy, kisses him back, moves inside his arm.

Tommy's still smiling, watching them touch and nuzzle. *That's nice*, he thinks, and knows it is himself thinking it. People liking each other. *Nice.*

"Tommy! Hey, Tommy!" a voice calls. "I need glasses over here."

Fuck you and your glasses. Tommy blinks, whirling toward Mac, the bartender. Good old Mac, every night slips him five from the tip jar, always has a joke and a wink. Who was thinking *fuck you* to good old Mac? Tommy gives him a nod and hurries on toward the kitchen.

Tommy's inside the kitchen quick. Dump the dirty stuff—wipe your hands, Tommy—over to the dishwasher that belches steam and rolls out a rubber wire tray full of shining glasses for good old Mac. Glasses on the tray, hot, hot, hot.

And he falters for a moment, his hand on the hot glasses, finds himself thinking of the flames, and Mr. Deal crying, crying so hard that it made Tommy feel like crying too, and so he had. Then all those firemen and the police that had to come and pull them away. Poor Mrs. Deal.

"Garbage!" The voice behind him bellows. "Get this garbage out." Tommy doesn't have to look. That's Dexter. The night chef. Dexter's not so nice as Mac. Tommy nods without looking at Dexter's toadlike face, puts a couple more glasses on the tray, and hurries out.

"Christ, Tommy, you stuck in slow motion tonight?" Good old Mac, smiling while he says it, gives him a wink, and Tommy hurries back into the kitchen, with hardly any time to sneak a look at that pretty girl with the long black hair.

It's later—must be the same night, but all nights are the same for Tommy. Whatever night it is, he's back to the garbage, garbage, garbage. Little cans by the food line, three of them, one, two, three into the big can—Tommy sees a whole burger tumbled faceup in the mess, he'd grab it and have a bite if it wasn't for eagle-eye Dexter over there ready for him to slip up again. *Who elected you Pope, asshole?* Tommy stops, shakes his head. What's going on, these strange voices inside his brain? He feels something hot in his head, something small and hot and glowing.

He grabs the sides of the plastic bag that lines the big can, pulls, twists, makes a knot like Mr. Boss showed him, jerks the whole thing out, hustles out the back door into the cool night.

Outside, it's suddenly peaceful. Good old peaceful alley. Quiet and dark. He glances up between the backs of the buildings and sees a slice of sky with stars, a chunk of moon floating there. *Moon over Miami.* What's that? Tommy wonders, then hurries on toward the Dumpster.

He's humming something, like a song, maybe. Trying to think of the words. But he doesn't know any songs.

Drops the bag, fishes in his pocket, key there someplace. Why's there a key for a garbage Dumpster, anyway? Who'd want to steal garbage?

Finds the key, the lock, snap, snap, the lid's up, the junk's inside, lid's down, snap-a-roo, locked up tight.

He's moving back up the alley toward the door when the man steps out of the shadows to stand in front of him.

Tommy stops. Nobody has to tell him this is bad. Worse than even Dexter's blackest moods.

Tommy looks down at the man's hand where something catches a sliver of moonlight, glinting. Looks back at the face. A face that makes Dexter's face seem kind. This is a face turned inside out. A skull that somebody tried to put flesh on. Eyes that look at Tommy and right on through him. Like he isn't anything, anything at all. A sour smell from the Dumpster drifts over them.

The man takes a quick step forward, feints with his empty hand, but somehow Tommy isn't fooled. He leans in, then steps away like a dancer or a bullfighter, and the man with the knife in his hand slips and nearly falls.

Be careful, Tommy. Be careful at night. Mr. Deal told him that. Plenty of bad people around. Tommy knows. Here's one in front of him to prove it.

But who is it who's moving Tommy's body around, he wonders as the man turns upon him with a hissing sound. He feels like a puppet, someone else directing his hands, his feet. Tommy edges away, his hands at the wall behind him, his fingers dancing along the rough bricks like nervous spider legs. He can feel the music throbbing inside the building, it's something fast and happy.

The man lunges again, and again Tommy skitters away, something just brushing the front of his busboy's coat. There's the sound of metal scraping on stone and a curse in a language that's strange to Tommy's ears.

Tommy glances at the doorway to the restaurant but knows there isn't time, no matter how fast he runs. He sees a fleeting picture of a deer on a plain somewhere, dogs tearing at its flanks and throat, pulling it to the ground.

The picture goes away and he's back in the alley staring at an old mop leaning against the wall in front of him. Old mop, Tommy thinks. And sees his hands snatch it up. And knows that he spins about in one fluid motion, one hand beneath the stick, the other on top, so it's braced. He steps toward the man who's charging after him and makes a short chopping motion.

The mop thuds into the side of the man's head so hard that the grimy sponge end flies off into the darkness. As the man staggers sideways, Tommy pivots into him, feels his right hand swinging the other end of the stick up. There's a cracking sound and a sharp cry that wings into the darkness. The man's knife falls as he throws his hands to his face. All of this so fast, Tommy hardly knows it's happened.

Wow! Tommy thinks. *Who's doing this?* He steps away, holding the stick like he's rearing backward with a shovel, then steps forward and drives the point into the man's unprotected stomach.

The man goes down with a gasp, tumbling onto his side, his toes drumming the pavement in pain. Tommy stares down in amazement. Looks at the mop stick in his hands like it's magic.

"You fucking retard." Dexter's voice booms through the night behind him, along with a blast of music. "What the fuck are you doing out here?"

Tommy turns. Dexter is standing in the doorway, shielding his eyes from the bare bulb that hangs there, blinking out into the darkness. *Ever see close-order drill, dickhead?* That voice again, that weird voice in Tommy's brain.

Tommy shakes it off, runs toward Dexter. He'll show him what he's doing out there.

But by the time he manages to pull Dexter back down the narrow alleyway, there's nothing left to show. The man is gone. There is no knife. And to Dexter the mop stick's just a mop stick, after all.

"Let me get this straight," Driscoll said. He popped another Moosehead, drained a third of it in a swallow. He closed the refrigerator door, then came back to the kitchen table where Tommy was sitting, watching him intently.

"This guy tried to stab you while you were taking the trash out?"

Tommy nodded.

"But nobody saw it." Driscoll pulled out a chair, sat down heavily.

Tommy held up the front of his busboy's coat, wiggling his fingers through a slice just above the pocket, as if he were waving to Driscoll.

Driscoll shrugged. "Clumsy as you are, you could have caught it in the meat grinder."

Tommy shook his head vehemently, his eyes flashing.

Driscoll sighed, tilted the Moosehead again, set it down empty. He had the kitchen window open for the breeze. He wrinkled his nose. "Goddamn place sure smells like smoke, don't it?"

He waved his arm around the tiny kitchen. The wing housing his and Tommy's units had survived the blaze more or less intact. A few windows shattered from the heat, some water damage, a week or so without electricity, but they'd endured all that when the hurricane passed through. Little setbacks like that were old hat by now.

At least they had a roof over their heads, had their health. They were a hell of a lot better off than Deal and his missus. Deal set to get out of the hospital in a day or two, but as for Janice, who knows how long she'd be in there. Thank heaven for Mrs. Suarez, who was taking care of Isabel.

The old lady had her little house back, reclaimed from the salsa brigade. Driscoll had gone down there, explained a few things to her scumbag renters, didn't even have to use Spanish to get through to them. A good thing, since he didn't speak any. He flashed his shield, used a little body-language Esperanto, they'd cleared out before dawn, leaving the house filthy in their wake. Mrs. S. had it sparkling again now, though.

Something he'd been able to do, at least. Didn't seem like much under the circumstances. But a little. Now here was Tommy, trying to give him something else to do.

Driscoll spread his palms open in a helpless gesture. "Let's say there *was* a guy tried to rob you. You know how many times that happens on a given Saturday night in this town? There's a zillion slimewads like that out there. You just happened to be in the wrong place at the wrong time, that's all. Think of it like the hurricane. It was bad luck that it happened, but good luck, too, because you lived through it and what are the odds it'll happen again anytime soon?"

He got up, headed for the refrigerator. He cracked a beer, came back. Tommy was staring at him, his face red, sputtering as if he were about to pop. If he hadn't looked so pathetic, Driscoll would have laughed.

"That's . . . that's . . . *not* . . . " Tommy stammered, his face glowing with frustration. Suddenly his breath flew out of him in a cry. He slammed his hands down on the table. Driscoll had to grab his beer to keep it from toppling. He was still gaping as Tommy stood and stomped out of the room.

He sat at the table, listening to the slam of Tommy's door echo from across the way. Thank God he wasn't going to have to listen to that TV now. Tommy's set had taken a blast from a fire hose and shorted out.

Still, Driscoll couldn't help feeling a little guilty. What had he said to get Tommy so worked up, anyway? He had another slug of Moosehead. The answer was clearly nothing. What did Tommy expect him to do about this robber? Nothing he could do about that either.

Deal, Tommy, Mrs. Deal, and all the rest of the goddamned world. What was *he* supposed to do about all that pain and suffering? That was one reason he'd got the hell out of the Department. Because he was sick to death of sticking his fingers into a dike that was so shot full of holes that nothing he did made any difference. Because he was sick to death of people looking at him like he was supposed to give a big shit. Because all he wanted to do was stay home and sit at his kitchen table and drink some beer and not think about a goddamned thing. Which was exactly what he intended to do. Beginning right now.

"Bad luck, nothing more," Torreno said when Coco had finished his story. They were on the veranda of the lakeside hut. Torreno was casting food pellets out across the water, making motions like a man sowing a field with grain.

"Perhaps." Coco shook his head. "Or perhaps this man is possessed."

The pellets pattered down upon the water like raindrops. Soon the sound was answered by the awful sucking noises of the fish, their mouths breaking the surface as they swarmed in for the food. Coco wished it were daylight. Better to see the things than to simply hear them. In his mind he saw a million tiny drains breaking the surface of the dark water, each one ringed with teeth like needles.

Torreno glanced at him, his face catching the faint glow of a kerosene torch. "You are going to start talking like a cane cutter, now? Bad magic? The evil eye?" He snorted. He looked like a devil himself in the flickering light.

Coco didn't waver. "You said it yourself, this is a man not right in the head." Coco's fingers traced an angry welt that lay across his cheekbone. "But he fights like a demon."

"I would not advertise it," Torreno said dryly. "The great Coco, laid waste by a man not right in the head." He turned back to his feeding. "Maybe you were drinking before you went there?"

Coco glared at him. The fish thrashed the water in a frenzy, as if ready to unfold their unnatural legs, climb onto the platform and take the food for themselves. Torreno knew he did not drink, did not use drugs. His employer was only baiting him.

Coco pondered the problem for a time. Torreno was a man of immense power and wealth. He had not achieved his position through foolishness. Surely he had not underestimated their opponent in this case. Perhaps this was a test of sorts. Perhaps Torreno was measuring Coco's worth. A possibility occurred to him.

"There is something you have not told me," Coco said finally.

Torreno lifted an eyebrow, but his face stayed in profile, his gaze intent upon the roiling waters. "You and I have been together for a long time, Coco. I would hate to see you lose your reason now."

"It is your own business," Coco persisted, "why you don't want me to know about this man, who he is. I don't care about that. But this is a question of doing what I have set out to do. If there is something I should know . . ."

Torreno flung the rest of the food into the water with an impatient snap of his wrist. He paused, stared at Coco as if assessing him. Coco felt his shoulders squaring themselves.

Finally, Torreno began to nod. "All right, Coco. You have me." A penitent's expression had transformed his normally chiseled features. "This man is not what he seems to be." He gave a wave of his hand. "Though he has adopted the guise of a fool, he is, in reality, a formidable opponent." Torreno gave a sigh, as if ridding himself of guilt. "In your terms, he is a kind of sorcerer."

Coco felt a tremor pass over him. Not fear, but the thrill of recognition, of something important about to make itself known. He had sensed this all along. "Fire does not burn him," he murmured.

"Steel will not pierce his flesh," Torreno answered solemnly.

Coco faced his employer squarely. "And you did not tell me this before."

Torreno hooded his eyes in apology. "I was not certain."

Coco drew himself up. "But still he is our enemy."

Torreno nodded.

"Then we must find another way."

"I rely upon you, Coco."

"Not upon me," Coco said. "Upon stronger magic." The fish were quiet now, gone as quickly as they had come.

"Upon stronger magic, then."

"Good," Coco said, and answered his employer's smile with a grimace of his own.

Whose hands are these? Deal found himself wondering. He was standing at a tall window on one of the hospital's top floors, waiting for the doctor, chafing in his own, unfamiliar clothes after nearly a week in hospital gowns. He could see for a mile or more, across the tops of the trees the hurricane hadn't flattened, across all the newly tiled rooftops, past the beachfront hotels, all the way to the Atlantic. It was sunny. Windy enough for whitecaps. Sailboats. Bright sails of surfboarders. People out there having fun.

He turned away. The hands were his, of course. Right there at the ends of his shirtsleeves where they belonged, gripping a red rail that divided the floor-to-ceiling windows. But for a moment there they hadn't seemed like his, not even a little.

Down below an EMS van raced toward the emergency entrance, flashers bright even in daylight. Its siren was thin, more mournful than alarming at this distance. He cut his glance away. The hair gone from his knuckles, from the back of his hands. The skin all smooth and shiny, streaks of pink here and there. He ran his hand across his face. Stubble where his eyebrows had been, nothing by way of eyelashes. He caught sight of himself in the glass. What had been a medium-cut, if untidy, mop of brown hair, bleached out by the sun, was now a colorless flattop. The best they could do under the circumstances, an orderly told him. He shouldn't feel so bad. Flattops were back in style. It was happening. It was "fly."

Fly, Deal thought. He massaged the taut skin of his cheekbones. His fingertips seemed smooth, tractionless. He drew a weary breath. Whatever "fly" was, he didn't feel it. He felt wrong, as if his body had been fitted with a new sheath, a skin that hadn't broken in yet. What was that old movie he'd seen? Some folks find this corpse that turns out not to be a corpse at all. Some creature hatched out of an egg from outer space, not quite formed when the people found it. A blank, they called it. Carolyn Jones. Kevin McCarthy. He'd get the title in a minute.

Meantime, his unfamiliar reflection stared back at him, the face still puffy, the eyes haunted. Maybe it was Kevin McCarthy, just out of the home, ready to call for help at the first false move.

"Mr. Deal?"

He turned from the window to see a tall man in a white coat approaching him.

"I'm Dr. Constantine." Deal stared at him. Stethoscope, clipboard, a couple of pens and a penlight in his shirt pocket, all that checked out. But instead of a reassuring Marcus Welby type, chiseled countenance, gray head of hair, here was this kid who had come to stand in front of him.

Fine features, rosy cheeks, a scrim of dark hair falling over his forehead. Faded silk button-down with a matching vest and stonewashed jeans under the lab coat. He looked like he'd been outfitted at Banana Republic on his way in, maybe had a razor cut and style, too.

The kid checked his clipboard. "You're a lucky man, Mr. Deal."

Deal glanced out the window. They were ten stories up, maybe more, just a thin pane of glass between them and a hundred-foot drop to a cement-lined canal at the edge of the hospital property.

"I don't feel very lucky," he said. Maybe he would kick the glass panel into pieces, hold Dr. Constantine out there in the breeze until he revised his concept of luck.

"Well, you should," Constantine said. "We're sending you home."

All that false cheer, that mindless energy. Deal felt it smack up against him like a wave. *Invasion of the Body Snatchers*, that was the title of the movie. Pods. People grow out of pods and replace the ones you know. Clearly Constantine was one of them and Deal could do the world a favor, send him hurtling out into space. He took a deep breath. "I want to know about my wife," he said finally. "Can you give me some information? Or is there someone else I can talk to?"

Constantine glanced up from his clipboard. He seemed to sense something ominous near him. Deal wondered if he'd been grinding his teeth.

"You can talk to me," Constantine said. "Or with Dr. Plattner, if you'd rather."

He pushed a lock of hair from his forehead, but it tumbled back. He looked neutrally at Deal, his smooth and rosy face a proper subject for Botticelli, if Botticelli had been a pod too.

Deal thought of Janice. Her face swathed in bandages, her brain and body numb under the drip of morphine. He looked at Constantine, a model waiting for the shutter to snap.

"Tell you what," Deal said, realizing his new hands had turned into fists. "Maybe it ought to be Dr. Plattner after all."

Plattner turned out to be a bluff man who looked like he might have exchanged a few shots in the ring in an earlier life. There were a couple of prints of hunting dogs on the walls of his office, a fisherman's vest on a coatrack, a battered copy of *From Here to Eternity* on his desk. Plattner noticed Deal looking at the book.

"He used to live here, you know that?"

Deal turned, surprised. "James Jones?" He'd seen the film. He'd grown up idolizing Burt Lancaster.

"Yeah, toward the end of his life, right after he came back from Paris." Plattner was finishing a sandwich wrapped in white paper. "I ran into him at a fish camp out in the Everglades." He made a gesture with one of his sizable hands. "I'm not much of a reader, but I read *that* book." Plattner nodded. "He signed it, too."

Deal reached for the book, opened the cover. Pages yellowing, crumbling around the edges. It gave off a smell like the libraries of his youth. On the title page was a florid scrawl in bleeding dark ink. *To Doc P, Miami's for me. Jim.*

"They had him up on an airboat, taking pictures for some tourist campaign," Plattner said. He wadded up the sandwich paper, tossed it into a waste can across the room. "One of the photographers leaned against the engine exhaust, fried a nice chunk of his shoulder, I happened to be there to fix him up."

Plattner shrugged, leaned back in his desk chair, smiled. "Anyway, Jim and I did some fishing, had a couple of drinks together. He really liked it down here."

Plattner stared off a moment, lost in thought, then turned back to Deal, apologetic. "But that's not what you wanted to talk about, was it?"

Deal put the book back on Plattner's desk. He remembered how upset he'd been with Dr. Constantine, realized how comfortable he was with this man, someone tuned into life as he knew it. "In a way, Dr. Plattner," Deal said. "In a way, it was."

Plattner stared at him a moment, then nodded. Finally he leaned forward in his chair, tented his fingers over the clutter of papers on his desk. "Your wife is in serious shape, I'm not going to kid you."

Deal felt his breath suck in, his stomach tighten. He couldn't find anything to say.

"She's going to make it," Plattner continued. "That's not what I'm talking about."

"What, then?" Deal stared at him, feeling helpless, desperate for any shard of hope or comfort.

"We're looking at a long process of healing," Plattner said. "Some intricate surgeries, a number of them, a fair amount of pain, a great deal of expense."

Deal shook his head. "The money doesn't matter."

"Most difficult may be the psychological effects," Plattner said.

Deal glanced at him. "You're talking about Janice?"

Plattner nodded.

"Janice is tough, Doctor. She's the toughest person I know."

"And she's also a woman. A wife. A person who's received serious trauma to her features."

Deal stared at him, shaking his head slowly. "You think I'd care about that? Something like that?" Anger was beginning to build in him again.

"I think *she* is going to care about that, Mr. Deal. More than you may imagine. And you're going to have to be prepared to help her."

Deal felt the anger evaporate, felt the fear rush in to take its place. He glanced at the book on Plattner's desk, found his thoughts skittering off to that movie again. Maybe the pods had the right idea after all. All these feelings, cluttering up what might otherwise be a clean and simple life. What was love but something that led inevitably to pain?

He looked up at Plattner finally, feeling numb. "Okay, Doc. I'll do my best." He was finding it hard to breathe, finding it hard to get the words out of his throat. "If you have any suggestions, I'll be glad to have them. I could use a little help."

The doctor was nodding at him then. Deal was fairly sure of that, at least. It had gotten a little hard to see through all his tears.

Coco Morales held tightly to the sides of his seat, fighting the feeling of dread that always came over him while flying. And it was worse in such a tiny craft as this. They were in a helicopter, Torreno's last-minute idea, soaring northward over a vast plain of green, its expanse dissected occasionally by razored lines of duller green and brown.

The green was sugarcane, Coco knew, thousands upon thousands of acres of it. His eyes flickered about the canopy, wondering where he had been. The brown lines were service roads where here and there a roiling of dust marked a tractor or pickup—or Jeep, he thought—on its way to some mundane task. The dull green lines were irrigation canals. He knew them well, could smell their humid muckiness even from here. Far to the south and west he could make out the verge of Lake Okeechobee, where the dull water that filled the canals below came from.

An updraft of heated air caught the craft, bucking it, and the dim line of the lake was replaced by a stomach-churning expanse of blue sky, then as suddenly by an expanse of cane tops. When the pilot finally righted them, the view of the lake was gone, obscured by a great cloud of smoke on the horizon. They were burning the fields somewhere, clearing the cane stalks of foliage in anticipation of the harvest.

Torreno turned from his seat beside the pilot to grin back at

Coco. His employer waved his arm enthusiastically out at the horizon. "From up here, you begin to comprehend," Torreno said. Coco watched his lips move, heard the words through the tinny speaker of the headset he wore. "Everything you see, Coco, every piece of it. This is what six hundred and thirteen square miles looks like." Torreno trailed off, shaking his head at the concept. Coco nodded, glancing down. Vast ripples coursed over the fields, the winds tossing the canopy of cane tops in miles-wide swaths, turning it silver-gray here, a lighter green there. "It looks like the sea," he said, almost to himself.

His mind had been wandering. He'd been thinking of the *jefe* he had killed, of the two he'd been with, of their bodies, and wondering if they were still down there in that green sea below. And then found himself thinking of all the men who had braved the waters between his country and this one, and of all those who had failed and rode beneath the waves now. Strange how one's mind traveled, skimming and skipping like the breath of the wind on the fields of sugar below.

"Yes," Torreno said with a distracted smile. "It is an ocean of money."

"There's a lot of folks hate to see this deal go through, Mr. Tor-*in*-o." The attorney was sitting across an antique conference table, an ingratiating smile on his face as he Anglicized Torreno's name. He was sitting with his back to the windows, which commanded an impressive view of Lake Worth.

Coco had attended enough such meetings, however. He knew that Torreno had not been given the seat for the pleasure of the view. The afternoon sun was slanting in, and even though the glass was heavily treated, it was intended that he would have to squint uncomfortably at the porcine man who sat across from him. Coco had been consigned to a straight-backed chair in a corner of the room, and the attorney refused even a glance in his direction.

"I've received a number of inquiries," the attorney continued. "We could make you a nice piece of change, you'd never have to turn a hand upside down."

Torreno extended his hand out over the highly polished surface of the table, turned it over and back. He smiled briefly. "I do not mind a little work."

The attorney laughed, but Coco caught sight of a flush that had worked its way up from his collar. Although the two men had treated him as if he did not exist, he had listened carefully during the meetings. He was well aware that the attorney was not eager to make this deal for his employer.

Carlos Carbonell, the *jefe* of the sugar, or so he had been until he sank beneath the waters. Carbonell had owned what Torreno was about to own. Carbonell's family, Cubans of Spanish descent, had controlled far more vast sugar holdings in Cuba before Castro's revolution. Carbonell had been wise enough to see what was coming and had transferred enough of the family fortune to the United States many years before the nationalization of his own fields.

Carbonell had come to South Florida and had begun anew, although, even with his enormous fortune, it had not been easy. While most of South Florida might be seen as a Cuban colony, the sugar lands were held firmly by Anglos—big, florid-faced men who spoke in Deep South accents, like the attorney Torreno was sitting across from now.

"They didn't take kindly to some greaser—no offense, Mr. Tor-in-o," the attorney had explained in an earlier meeting, "some His-pan-yo-le coming in and getting involved."

But Carbonell *had* become involved. He had bought a thousand acres of "sand," land on the fringes of the prime sugar-growing region, and had been among the first to make use of mechanized harvesting machinery, at a time when almost all the other growers used blacks imported from the Caribbean to cut the cane.

"It's hard work, Mr. Tor-in-o." The attorney again. "None of your American blacks will touch it."

But Carbonell had persisted. One thousand acres led to two. Then to twenty. To a hundred thousand. And on and on, until, with the purchase of a multinational conglomerate's holdings sometime in the 1970s, Carbonell became the largest of the South Florida growers.

"The thing I don't understand, Mr. Tor-in-o," the attorney was saying. "A smart man like you taking a big chance like this, when you could cash in your option and make a killing, let me lay this off for you."

"A big chance?" Torreno said.

The attorney rose, clearly summoning his energies for one last pitch. "Sugar's hard work. You're always one or two hard frosts away from the poorhouse, no matter how big you are. You got constant labor problems with these islanders you have to bring in to cut—look what happened to Carbonell."

Coco glanced at the attorney. So important, so certain of himself. What if he were to find himself in *el jefe*'s place, dragging himself up an embankment of slime, only Coco there to help?

Torreno shook his head in sorrow. "I'm sorry that we cannot continue our negotiations face-to-face."

The attorney gave him a skeptical glance. "I don't know why. He was as intent on keeping that land as you are to have it."

Torreno overlooked the comment. His eyes traveled briefly to Coco, who stared impassively out the windows.

When Torreno did not reply, the attorney remembered his pitch. "That's what you've got to look forward to. Riding herd on a bunch of crazy Jamaicans, not to mention the government hassling you about whether you paid by the piece or by the hour like you're supposed to, and did you feed them all the jerk chicken they like and so forth. You try to use machines on most of this land, then you tear up half your fields, you got to go hire the same people back to replant for you. Then you got to worry about how long Uncle Sam's going to maintain the price supports. It's a neverending source of worry, I'm telling you."

Torreno shook his head sorrowfully, as if he were commiserating with the attorney. "You make it sound a distressing prospect."

The attorney hooded his eyes in a gesture of conspiratorial agreement. He glanced briefly at Coco, then leaned down, his palms splayed on the surface of the table. "You of all people, I don't have to say this to, but Uncle Fie-del's days are numbered."

Torreno nodded. "The victory nears," he said.

"Well, that's what I'm talking about." The attorney threw up his hands. "There's not but one damn thing in the whole damn country worth fussing about and that's the blessed sugar crop. That and what's left of the tobacco is the only source of an economy. What's going to happen is, whether Fie-del croaks or somebody croaks him, next thing some senator will stand up and give a speech: 'My fellow Amercuns, we got a choice between giving our newly freed neighbors to the south about a gozillion dollars in foreign aid to get them off their backs, and ours, or we can shitcan the import tariff on Cuban sugar and let them *earn* their way into a capitalist society while the consumer enjoys a lower price on his Coca-Cola and Hershey bar.'"

The attorney broke off, his face flushed as he played his trump card. "Which way do you think the boys in Washington are going to lean?"

"Yes," Torreno replied evenly. "I see your point."

"Then you'll be sitting up there in Okeechobee, no tariff protection, with everything you've got sunk in one big albatross around your neck. You're going to pay twenty-seven million dollars for a property that'll net you less than five percent of that, in a good year. I don't know how deep you're into the banks for this purchase, but you'll have a hell of a time just servicing your debt." The attorney nodded and Torreno nodded solemnly in return.

"As your adviser in this matter then . . . "

Torreno held up his hand to cut him off. "Are we agreed that the option price is a good one?"

The attorney nodded. "Sure. Carbonell's kids don't want anything to do with sugar. They think the old man was a throwback. Now that he's gone, they're happy to be rid of it. You've got a fair price, I'll give you that much, Mr. Tor-in-o."

Torreno tapped his fingers on a sheaf of papers before him. "And the income projections for the current year are sound?"

The attorney shrugged. "As long as the frost keeps coming when it ought to."

"Then schedule the closing, Mr. Taft," Torreno said. "Let me worry about the money." He stood up and gestured to Coco.

"But these offers I was telling you about. I can turn you a quick two million, you'll never see the first problem . . . "

Torreno raised his chin and sighted in on the man as Coco joined him.

"Tell your friends to consider it a disease, if it helps you, Mr. Taft. Call it the throwback disease of the Cubans. Say that sugar runs in my people's blood."

He gestured to Coco again, and then the two were gone.

They were outside now, on the roof of the building that housed the attorney's offices, moving through a stiff breeze toward a pad where the helicopter idled. The pilot stood down by the open door of the machine, his face impassive behind mirrored sunglasses, his hands folded before him in an undertaker's pose. An irresistible curiosity had gripped Coco. Though he seldom questioned his employer, he couldn't help doing so now. He placed a hand on Torreno's arm, interrupting his stride. Torreno turned, his tie fluttering loose in the wind like a banner, his close-cropped hair going askew.

"Something is wrong?" Torreno asked, his eyes scanning the rooftop.

Coco shook his head. "I just wanted to know. What you told the man inside." Coco gestured out over the buildings and the houses below, toward the west, where sixty miles inland the unseen cane fields sprawled beneath a towering bank of thunderheads. "That's what we will do now, raise the sugar in this place?"

Torreno laughed, a short, barking sound. He put his hand on Coco's shoulder. "I told that man only what I wanted him to hear, Coco. This business today is only a necessary step. It may have taken every cent I can put my hands on, but it is nothing compared to what's to come." He smiled and squeezed the hard flesh of Coco's shoulder. "All that land you saw today, Coco, conceive of it as a seed, a mere seed, from which a massive tree will grow."

"And all this will serve *la revolución*?" Coco asked.

Torreno seemed surprised. "You would doubt me, Coco?"

Coco dropped his gaze, shook his head slowly.

Torreno laughed and circled his arm about Coco's shoulders. "We must let nothing stop us now, Coco." He had to raise his voice as he guided them toward the waiting helicopter. "We are far too close for that."

"Janice?" Deal spoke her name softly. He was sitting at the side of her hospital bed, had her unbandaged hand clasped in his. She'd been asleep since he'd come into the room. Now he felt a stirring in his grasp. He squeezed her hand again, gently.

"Deal?" Her voice was faint, raspy with sleep. She ran her tongue along her lips. Her face was still covered with bandages, but they'd made new openings, tiny slits for her eyes.

"You want some water?" he said.

She nodded, took her hand away to fumble groggily for the control that raised her bed. He stood up, reached for the water pitcher, stopped. It was filled with flowers. Flowers he'd bought from a vendor on the corner outside. He drew the water from the bathroom sink and brought it to her. He didn't mention the flowers.

"How about some ice?"

Janice shook her head weakly. He helped guide the water to her mouth. She drank, then settled back on the pillows.

"Something new," he said, pointing at the bandages on her face. "Can you see now?"

She nodded. "I can see *you*."

He reached for her hand, felt her squeeze back, hard. He blinked at the tears that were forming in his eyes. She was still speaking, her voice a little more than a murmur.

"I couldn't hear," he said, leaning closer.

She cleared her throat, her voice just above a whisper. "I said, you look terrible."

Natural enough, given how he felt. Still, here was Janice, worrying about *him*.

"I'm fine," he said. "Isabel and me, we're both fine. She's having fun with Mrs. Suarez. She wants to come see Mommy." He glanced around the room, feeling helpless. "I didn't want to bring her until . . . " He trailed off. "I wanted you to be able to talk to her, so she wouldn't be scared. . . . "

"Her mommy's . . . a mummy," Janice said.

Deal forced a laugh, but it left a silence in the room. A candy striper passed down the hallway by the open door, pushing a cart full of magazines and books.

He raised Janice's hand to his lips. A faint medicinal tang at her fingertips, but still, the familiar smell of her flesh, that good, wonderful Janice smell. "Jesus," he said. His chest felt as if it would burst. "I was afraid we lost you." He had to stop, afraid his voice would break. He kept his smile, though.

"I had to go after her, Deal." Janice was squeezing his hand again. "You know I had to, don't you?"

He nodded. He pressed his cheek against the back of her hand.

"Isn't this a *mess*," she said finally. She broke off, coughing.

"We're going to be fine," he said when she was resting quietly again. "*You're* going to be fine." He sat up, his eyes glittering, keeping that smile. Cut off his arm right now, he would smile all the way through it. "I talked to the doc. He says you're going to do great . . . "

"Don't," she said, squeezing his hand vehemently. Her voice was unexpectedly firm. He stared at her. "We've done without the bullshit for a lot of years, Deal. We don't have to start with it now."

He cleared his throat. "Janice . . . " he began.

"It's going to take *years*," she said, and he sensed that she was losing control, "and we may as well get used to it." She was choking back the sobs now.

"Janice, whatever it takes, we'll do it." His own eyes were wet now. "I *love* you, Janice."

She pulled her hand from his grip. Her head was rocking side to side on the pillow: No, no, no.

"Janice . . . "

"I have to go to sleep now, Deal." Her voice was faint, barely audible in the quiet room. "I have to go to sleep."

 "How could I buy something so expensive without knowing that it works?" Coco said to the man behind the counter.

The man didn't bother to look up at him. He was sitting in a lawn chair, staring off at nothing, running a string of worry beads in one hand, sipping from a cup of tea in the other. You'd never be able to see him from the doorway. When Coco walked in, he'd thought the shop was untended. Strange shop, strange town.

"Works," the man said, his gaze still fixed in front of him. "Turn on. Look."

Coco stared at him. He had finally registered that the man was blind. Arab guy in his sixties, bald, tufts of hair sprouting from his ears, his nose. How did a blind Arab end up in a place like this, selling television sets?

Coco glanced at the tiny portable television the man had taken out of the display case for him. Except for the three-dot color logo painted on the front, the thing seemed identical to its black-and-white cousin still on the shelf. Coco was thinking, *Imagine being blind, all the little things you would have to learn.*

"I have turned it on," Coco said finally. He held the snow-filled screen out toward the Arab. He'd been about to say, "See for yourself," but that wouldn't help. Instead, he flicked the volume control wide open.

A fine static hissed above the hum of a rotating table fan the Arab had placed on the floor behind him. It must have been ninety degrees in the closed-up shop. Coco found himself yearning for Miami, as if it were a place where things were sane.

The Arab shrugged. "Too far," he said. "Work in city. Or up high." He jabbed his thumb toward the pressed tin of the ancient ceiling. "As good as Sony." He sat back in his chair, apparently worn out by his sales pitch. He began to cough, great racking, growling hacks that sent the aluminum lawn chair into a squeaking dance.

Coco thought he saw a shadow flit past the curtain that shrouded a passageway behind the counter. Pungent smells, lamb and spices possibly, drifted in from behind the curtain. A tiny apartment, maybe the Arab's wife back there tending to life's affairs.

Coco considered things. It would be far more enjoyable to have a color image when he watched, even if it was the size of a postage stamp. And the price seemed more than reasonable. But he'd never heard of this brand. What if the set did not work?

He glanced about the sparsely furnished shop again. Many of the shelves were empty, with squares and circle of dustless glass that showed where goods once had been. It looked like a place going out of business, but there were no signs to say so. In fact, he'd had to squint in the darkened windows, try the door, to be sure the place was open at all.

Had this been Miami, one of the electronics shops near the downtown port, there would have been flashing lights, banners, music throbbing onto the sidewalks, a swarthy young man with many rings and necklaces to pull him inside. Here in Belle Vista, "The Sweetest Town in the World," life seemed very odd.

The Arab had stopped coughing and was wiping his mouth with a handkerchief. "You want Sony, maybe? Come back at night, my son has. At the camps right now."

Coco pondered the Arab's meaning. It was a Saturday afternoon, payday. They'd passed a cane workers' barracks on the way into this forlorn town. There were a number of vendors with their wares set out in a dusty roadside clearing. Brightly colored rugs, bins full of vegetables, racks of shining watches. Maybe that's where all the goods from this place were. In the back of some battered station wagon, being haggled over by men risking a season's wages.

Had there even been a proprietor's sign outside this shop? Coco had the sudden feeling that he had stumbled into a bedouin's tent beside some watering hole in the desert. Were he to return here a week or a month from now, wanting to exchange the set—forget the warranty, Coco's here and he wants it fixed—what would he find? No sparsely laden shelves, no blind man, no building at all. The black ashes of a campfire and piles of camel dung.

"One hundred twenty-five," Coco said, turning down the volume on the hissing set. He spun the channel dial, saw a wavering image— a soldier in a parachute?—coalesce briefly, then disappear.

"One seventy-five," the Arab said evenly. "Dollars," he added, as if it were necessary. He had repeated the figure named on the tag inside the case.

"One hundred and fifty," Coco said. He glanced at his watch. "I am having to leave now," he added in a warning tone.

"Leave," said the Arab, unperturbed. "Without TV."

Coco glanced at the door. It was a thought. Just take the thing and walk out. He had an image of men in scarf-wrapped faces bursting from behind the curtain in the back, big curved blades in hand.

"One hundred fifty-five," Coco said. He was trying to find the image of the soldier in the parachute again.

"One seventy-five," the Arab said. "Layaway. Pay end of harvest."

"I don't work here," Coco said, hearing his voice rise. "One seventy."

The image he'd spotted was nowhere to be found. The dial spun freely beneath his thumb. What was wrong with him?

He was sure this was a mistake, the TV a worthless phony in a made-up case. Crazy. Let the blind man turn him down. Torreno back there waiting while Coco haggled over a TV set. He was out of here. Hurry back to his employer, buy Sony in Miami.

"Good," the blind man said. "One seventy." He was on his feet, deftly producing a box for the tiny set, some earphones and a power cord in there. The blind man held his hand out for the money. All in the blinking of Coco's eyes.

Coco hesitated. He wanted to tell the man the deal was off. Turn and walk out the door. Forget it. But he had offered. And the image had returned to the tiny set: hundreds of men in parachutes now, raining down from big planes overhead. Look out below . . .

Coco found himself counting three bills into the man's hand, gathering the box and earphones up, backing toward the doorway as the man fingered the bills.

"Good TV," said the man. "Good color."

Coco nodded, wondering how the guy could be sure he wasn't clutching three one-dollar bills in his callused hand, but then he was out into the street and realizing he was truly, truly late.

He hurried down the cracked concrete sidewalk toward the restaurant where he had left his employer, checking his watch again. He stuffed the small television into an outside pocket of his coat, along with the plug and earphones. He crumpled the box and the instruction sheet and stuffed that into an overflowing trash can bearing the legend KEEP OUR SWEET CITY CLEAN.

It was nearing sundown and there were a number of workers on the streets now, mostly dark-skinned men, with the high cheekbones and narrow-eyed haughty good looks of the West Indians, and Coco had to weave his way along past them.

Men out of the sticky, smothering fields, on the loose for a few hours. Some drinks, some real food, and, with luck, a woman. A saloon door swung open, loosing a gust of fermenting beer and reggae music across the sidewalk. For a moment Coco felt disoriented.

First that business with the shopkeeper, now this gust of beer and music. His head was light. In that instant he was transported: There had been an earlier life, when he too could amble down a sidewalk with no destination in mind, with nothing to concern him save the need to wake up for a day's inconsequential work, and that a distant care, to be sure.

"Yes, and in those days it would take three months' pay to put that toy in your pocket." It was a voice from now that reminded him of how things were. "A better life. A better life," he found himself agreeing. No matter what he had to do to maintain it. He plunged ahead, ignoring the curious stares of the cane cutters in Belle Vista who stepped aside, seeing a light-skinned man talking to himself as he hurried down the crowded sidewalks.

As luck would have it, Torreno was *not* pacing the sidewalk beside the limousine, nor was he inside the big car, impatiently drumming his fingers for the arrival of his tardy driver. In fact, Coco saw as he pushed through the heavy door of the restaurant, Torreno was still where he had left him, in a wide red booth in the rear corner of the place, the same two men in nondescript dark suits still on either side of him, listening.

Now, however, the atmosphere seemed considerably loosened. The other tables had emptied of the luncheon customers, leaving the place nearly deserted. A waitress idled near the server's counter, casting an occasional glance toward the group in back.

The coffee cups on Torreno's table had been cleared away and replaced by cocktail glasses, even though this place resembled a diner more than any place where drinks might be sold. Torreno held a bottle of brandy in one hand and was replenishing the glasses of his two companions when he saw Coco enter.

Coco hesitated inside the door and was about to make for the counter, where a man in coveralls and a baseball cap sat eating soup. When he saw Torreno's gesture, he shifted his gait and made his way down the shining linoleum aisle. Had there been signs in Spanish on the walls, this place could have come from his home city.

"This is my associate, *Señor* Morales," Torreno said as Coco approached the table. Coco nodded to the two men. So far as he could remember, Torreno had never introduced him to anyone, certainly not as a gentleman. The two men, cautious types with hair trimmed high above their ears and steely eyes, showed little interest. They returned Coco's nod with curt ones of their own.

"Sit down, Coco," Torreno said expansively. He found a clean glass and poured another drink. Coco sat, casting a surreptitious glance at the bottle. How much of the liquor had his employer consumed?

"These gentlemen have been explaining to me some very interesting statistics, Coco." Torreno lifted his glass, waiting for Coco to raise his. Coco sipped. It tasted like fire, but went down smoothly.

"Nearly half of all the sugar in America is produced within fifty miles of where we are sitting. Did you know that?"

Coco shook his head.

"And of that amount, the American Sugar Corporation, which we now count among our holdings, controls more than twice as much as any other grower, am I correct?"

"Two point three," one of the men said. He nodded with Torreno, but he did not seem enthused.

"Which makes me among the largest growers in this country." Torreno smiled at Coco.

"You better pray the price supports hold up," the second man said. His face was flushed, as if he'd had plenty of the brandy himself.

"That's hardly his concern, Claude," the first man said. He picked up a sheaf of papers from the table, handed them to his partner. "Tuck these away."

"We'll review the sale, but I'm sure there will be no problems." He turned back to Torreno as Claude worked a combination on his briefcase. "Congratulations, Mr. Torreno," the man said. "You're not only the largest sugar grower in Florida, you're also the only one who will never have to worry about bringing in a crop."

"If he lives that long," Claude said.

Torreno saw Coco tense, laid a hand on his knotted forearm. "It's all right," Torreno said. "He means, if we live to see our enemies fall."

"And as for living long enough," he said, turning to Claude, "I can assure you that our time is near."

The man eyed him. "Nothing's for certain. Not where sugar's concerned."

Torreno's smile broadened. "Then we must work hard to *make* it certain. Yes, gentlemen?" He raised his glass again and downed it. Coco watched as the two took polite sips and rose to leave.

He gazed through the window as the two men strode across the street in the fading light, got into a dark sedan, and drove away. He took a sip of his drink and turned to his employer, who sprawled expansively against the red cushions of the booth, his smile positively radiant now.

"Those two," Coco said. "They are other growers? Men who are unhappy to have you as a competitor?"

Torreno glanced up at him as if he were awaking from a dream. "Growers?" His smile broadened. "No, Coco. Those men are from the government."

Coco felt his eyebrows go up in surprise. He glanced around the ill-lit restaurant. The farmer in the ball cap seemed oblivious to them, had tilted his bowl to his lips to drink the last of his soup. The waitress reached to slide a tray of glasses onto a high shelf, exposing the substantial flesh of her thighs. *This* was where a government sent its emissaries?

"The United States government . . ." Torreno continued, shaking his head as if even he found it difficult to believe, "because of Castro, they allow very little sugar to come into this country." He gave Coco a satisfied smile. "It makes the growing of sugar, *big* sugar, a most profitable business."

Coco shook his head, puzzled. "You spend a lifetime to topple Castro, and you say the time is almost upon us when that will happen," he said. "Then you buy the sugar, which is profitable only because of this same man. I do not understand. What will happen to your sugar if Castro falls?"

Torreno shook his finger reprovingly. "*When* Castro falls, Coco." He poured another drink and toasted the departing sedan. "Those men will carry proof of our acquisition back to Washington now." He smiled almost dreamily. "And when Castro falls, *those* fools will make me the richest man on earth."

"The water meter, Emilio!" Deal was on the side-walk, shouting over the roar of the backhoe.

Emilio was in the seat of the big machine, grind-ing gears, revving up for another pass at the ruined north wing of Deal's fourplex. He finally glanced up, saw Deal jabbing at the ground by the pile of charred beams he'd just deposited, dropped the backhoe into neutral. The roar subsided by half and Emilio leaned forward, cupping his ear.

"You covered up the water meter!" Deal shouted. "You have to move this shit."

Emilio widened his eyes, acknowledging his mistake. "I forgot about that thing," he said. The meter lay under a concrete door that sat flush with the ground between the sidewalk and the curb. It was easy enough to overlook, especially when the grass hadn't been cut for a while. Now it was piled over with wreckage. Deal turned away from the sight of one of Isabel's teddy bears amid the tangle. It was headless, its body charred, a splinter of two-by-four spearing its one good arm.

"Yeah, well, this stuff's got to be cleared. And try not to tear any-thing up while you're at it," Deal said, moving on toward the build-ing.

He ignored Emilio's hurt expression. He'd had Emilio out on a number of DealCo jobs in the old days, carrying on as Deal's father and Emilio's father had before them. In fact, Emilio had been the cabinetmaker when Deal put the fourplex up, but that was before the hurricane. A week after Andrew hit, Emilio's cousin had showed up, down from Tampa in a battered Chevy pickup, a backhoe he used to dig septic tanks lashed to a flatbed trailer behind it.

Before long, Emilio's Fine Cabinetworking had died, replaced by Emilio and Rodriguez, Backhoe Service. The two had nailed signs on light poles all around Dade County and at last count had worked two hundred days straight, digging stumps and clearing debris, $65 an hour plus travel time. The battered Chevy had, along with a step-van Emilio had inherited from his father, become a pair of Eddie Bauer Explorers, and the backhoe had a twin now too. Deal assumed Rodriguez was across town, still stacking hurricane deadfall, or maybe digging a pool for someone with leftover insurance money.

Deal supposed he should feel fortunate getting Emilio over right away, but he didn't. He didn't feel much of anything. He had decided to put the fourplex right again, but he was hardly enthused at the prospect. Once he had it in shape, it was going up for sale. He never wanted to see the place again.

He'd put in a call to Terrence Terrell and they'd agreed to let Deal take some time off the rebuild of Terrell's house in the Grove, bring in a third party to get the place dried in. By the time the roof was watertight and the doors and windows were on, Deal would have the fourplex back together and would come back on board for the finish of Terrell's place. That was the plan, anyway.

In the meantime, Deal would have the old gardener's cottage on the back of Terrell's property to stay in. It was a Coconut Grove arti-fact, one big room with a foldout bed, a shower bath, and a nook for a kitchen, and Deal was grateful for Terrell's insistence that he stay there. Decent housing was still tough to come by in Dade County, even more than a year after the storm. The place wasn't really big enough for him and Isabel together, but Mrs. Suarez was going to help out in that regard for the time being.

One thing at a time, Deal reminded himself. Focus on one prob-lem at a time. Were he to dare to let it all crowd into his mind at once, he worried he would crash under the weight. For the next few hours, he was going to work at clearing a damaged fourplex. Then he'd come up for air and go on to the next thing.

He put away his troublesome thoughts then, and stood surveying the building in front of him. He'd built the place in a shallow V shape, two wings with two units in each, separated by a shaded breezeway, upstairs and down. That design, along with a southerly breeze the night of the fire, had spared the half of the building where Tommy and Vernon Driscoll were still able to live. The stuccoed exterior of the south wing was dusky with smoke, the gray paint baked darker on one end than the other, but it was still livable. No one there now, though. Tommy at work at Doc's, Driscoll off somewhere, driven away by the grinding of the backhoe, Deal supposed.

Emilio had pretty much cleared away the fallen material from the north wing. One back wall on the second floor would have to come down, though, along with what was left of the roof and joists. They'd need to gut all the interior walls, top and bottom, for what the fire hadn't reached had been ruined by the smoke and water. It would cost a hundred thousand, easily, and that was with him doing a good chunk of the labor and contracting out the rest.

He shook his head. Another insurance claim to file. First the hurricane, slight though the damage had been, now this. So much for his homeowner's policy. Next anniversary date, he'd be out there shopping along with the thousands of others whose carriers had gone belly-up, or quit issuing policies in Florida, or simply walked away from their old clients. Sure, he could understand that, Deal thought. What good was selling insurance if you actually had to pay claims?

He put his hand on the front doorknob, its brass finish cooked to the color of oil scum on backwater, and pushed. The door gave inward at his touch. Didn't swing. *Caved* inward. Fell. A crash, a puff of ash as it glanced off a wall and landed facedown in the hallway like a joke in a slapstick movie.

Deal stared dumbly down at his hand, then at the door, its back side charred black from top to bottom, the hinges flapping where they'd torn loose from the ruined jamb. He glanced down the hallway. Wallboard bulging as if there were tumors growing in the framing behind, the ceiling sagging, tatters of yellow insulation dangling down. The smell rushed down the hallway to greet him: wet carpet already gone rancid, old smoke, sweet rot of food growing its haloes of mold among the ruins.

He'd been in a hundred houses like this since the storm, seen all this and worse, but it had never struck him as now. Walking into someone else's ruin, homeowner griping over his shoulder about his penny-pinching insurance adjustor, the rock-bottom estimate he needed, Deal had seen each and every house as a project, as a job, as a prospect for renewal.

Two feet of scum carried in on a storm surge, changed your sunken living room into a mangrove swamp? No problem. Your roof's sailed into the Everglades, all the walls along with it? Got it covered. Have to jack your whole foundation up six feet in the air, above the floodplain, before the city'll let you rebuild? Can do. Sailboat in your family room, brick chimney up its ass? Piece of cake.

And he had reveled in the transformation of those wrecks back into homes, always felt a pang at the expressions of the families who'd come back, wide-eyed and weeping themselves to see what Deal had done. Watch a kid run inside his house, find his room put back together, hear him yelling up and down the halls, that made him feel good. Better than good. Like a minor god, or Superman, at least. Superman Deal.

A far cry from what Deal's father had done with the company, of course. DealCo had been a giant. Syndicate hotels on Miami Beach. Funny-money condo palaces on Brickell. A massive bank tower downtown that no one seemed to have paid for. His old man, legendary high-roller, a smile, a buck, a clap on the back for everybody. He'd taught Deal everything there was to know about building, but by the time he died, dead drunk at the time, he wouldn't have known which end of a hammer worked, and he died without a cent, the company books a joke.

It had been a long climb back for Deal, first the fourplex, then a warehouse here and there, a strip mall, a small office building . . . and then, suddenly, the hurricane and he had become a *re*builder. A fixer. And, in truth, the feeling it gave him was what made all the hassles worth it. Scrounging for materials all the way from Hialeah to West Palm Beach. Keeping his crews on the hustle and out of the clutches of rival contractors desperate for help, fighting to keep the subcontracting crews honest. Putting up with the endless delays from inspectors who had a million places to check and an endless succession of code changes to apply. Recalls to replace a cracked tile here, a loose doorknob there. Listening to outraged homeowners sure they were being screwed, by their adjustors, by the inspectors, by Deal himself.

Seven A.M., outside a tract house down on Old Cutler, a guy in his sixties, Bermuda shorts, I SURVIVED ANDREW T-shirt, cordovan shoes, white socks pulled high up his shins. Squinting behind thick glasses and waving a copy of his contract as Deal gets out of his pickup.

"You quoted my roof at ten thousand dollars."

"Yes sir."

"The roofer told me it was going to cost twelve thousand dollars."

"I'm not surprised."

"Well, I'm not paying a penny more than what it says right here."

"No sir, you don't have to."

Guy looking at him funny, like he's got the wrong man, the air starting to leak out of his sails.

"You're darned right I don't have to."

"We've got you a good roofer, that's the important thing."

Relief, suspicion, confusion rolling over the guy's face, one after the other.

Leaving Deal to fight it out with the roofer, or with the insurance company where it was possible, or to simply take it in the shorts and absorb the loss. Some jobs went smoothly, some didn't. It tended to even out.

The guy on Old Cutler had turned up at Deal's office, in fact, a month after the job was wrapped, a check for $2,000 in his hand.

"I made the bastards pay," he said, thrusting the check at Deal.

"What bastards?" Deal asked.

"My neighbors. It was their palm tree busted up my roof in the first place."

Hundreds of estimates. Dozens of homes repaired, some small jobs, some total redos. And he'd been can-do, even-keeled, unruffled, all the way through. No job too big for Superman. No Kryptonite around here.

Now he stared down the ruined hallway of his own gutted house and felt his resolve vanish. He felt shaky, disoriented, as though he was going to throw up. He saw Janice—stubborn, fearless Janice—dragging herself down the smoke-filled passage, as iron-willed as Deal himself, intent upon finding Isabel, her hand reaching up for the door, the wrong door, and all those flames blasting out upon her . . .

. . . and he had to lean against the spongy, crumbling wall at his side to keep from going down. This was how helpless felt, he thought, and just as suddenly felt a rush of anger at himself for being so smug, walking into all those ruined homes, those battered lives, full of pep and vim, don't worry, folks, we'll have these boulders out of your bedroom before you know it. . . .

Christ, that wasn't all those people wanted. They wanted somebody to sympathize before the heavy equipment came in, they wanted someone to *mourn* a little. . . .

"You look a little peaked, son."

Deal was startled by the voice. He turned to find Driscoll picking his way through the rubble toward him, a sack of what looked like donuts in his hand.

"It's a mess, iddn't it?" He shook his head in commiseration. "I was over here yesterday, poking around." He glanced back down the hallway at the fallen door. "I set the door up to discourage somebody just walking in, you know. Looks like it fell down again."

Deal nodded. He didn't see the point of getting into it. "It's a mess, Vernon." He felt infinitely weary.

"Well," Driscoll said, "if anybody can fix it up, you can."

Deal stared at him. Another conversation he was going to pass up.

Driscoll gave him a look. "So what's going on out there with the water?"

Deal shook his head, puzzled. "The water?"

"That kid out there on the backhoe. Looks like he busted the water main or something." Driscoll was pawing around in the donut bag. "You like chocolate?"

"Jesus Christ," Deal said, pushing past him. He could see it now, a spray of water glittering in the morning sunlight, a million diamonds tumbling down onto the place where once a lawn had been. "Jesus H. Christ!"

They were sitting on the tiny patio off Driscoll's apartment now, watching the guy from Metro Dade finish up the patch on the water line Emilio had ripped up.

It was nearing five and Emilio was long gone, off to pull some construction permits down at City-County. The backhoe sat quietly near the pile of soggy debris, its clamshell poised half-open. It looked like a mechanical dinosaur, about to plunge in for a bite.

"You want that?" Driscoll said, pointing at a sugared donut he'd set out for Deal earlier.

Deal had another sip of the brackish coffee Driscoll had brought and shook his head. The coffee tasted like paper pulp. He imagined the donut would taste the same. Driscoll picked it up, polished it off in a couple of bites.

The guy from Water and Sewer was walking toward them. "You got water *now*," the guy said. He handed Deal a form on a clipboard to sign.

"Thanks." Deal nodded. He stood up, inspected the form. "Do I get a bill for this?"

"Naw," the guy said. "We'll call it hurricane-related, write it off."

Deal gave him a look. "After all this time?"

The guy shrugged, jerked his head toward the silent backhoe. "Emilio," he said, "his cousin married my sister-in-law's niece."

Deal nodded, handing the clipboard back. The guy tore off the top copy, handed it to Deal. "This is a receipt for the new meter. If somebody steals it, you'll lose your original deposit."

Deal thought about it, somebody hard up for a water meter, ripping his off in the middle of the night. Pipe wrench, geyser of water . . . sure, anything was possible.

The Water and Sewer guy was on his way back to the truck now. "Emilio was one good cabinetmaker," the guy said over his shoulder.

"Yeah," Deal said, nodding. "That he was." His voice was nearly lost in the roar of the guy's departing pickup.

When he turned, Driscoll was shaking his head. "That's why our taxes are so high," he said. "All this high-level fraud."

"Maybe you ought to run for public office," Deal said. His mind was occupied, trying to figure the odds of all these things happening to him alone.

"It's a thought," Driscoll said. "Or maybe I could get one of those TV shows like that Al Whatsisname. You know, he finds out the restaurants where they serve crab salad only it's really processed sea legs or something?"

"*Shame on You*," Deal said absently.

"That's it," Driscoll said. "This Al found out laundries'll charge you a buck for a guy's shirt, but two seventy-five for a girl's, just because the buttons are on the wrong side." Driscoll made a gesture with his mouth. "Guy with my experience, I ought to be able to come up with better stuff than that."

"Big-time contractor rips off meter reader," Deal said. "Is that what you mean?"

"You're big-time now?" Driscoll arched an eyebrow. He was turning something over in his thick fingers, shaking his head. "Naw, I was thinking bigger than that even. What do you figure a guy like Al Shame on You makes?"

Deal shook his head. His stomach had settled again, or at least was back into its familiar knot, same as it had been since he'd awakened in the hospital a week ago. He tried to remember what hunger felt like, or that big, full feeling after a wonderful meal, couple of drinks, a bite or two of some artery-clogging dessert. Dreams from another world. What he had now was a stomach that had pulled itself into the size of a walnut. It would accept some bad coffee, or a couple of drinks, but not much more.

"I've got work to do," he said, turning to Driscoll. He felt very, very tired.

"Sure," Driscoll said. He was studying the thing in his hands again, seeming to debate something. He glanced up as Deal was about to leave. "I had a look at the fire marshal's report."

Deal stopped. He hesitated before he spoke. "Tell me, Driscoll."

"It was the same thing I told you in the hospital. Electrical short."

Deal nodded. Electrical short, he thought. One of those catchall phrases you hear after a disaster. Like pilot error, wind shear, act of God. They sound authoritative, but explain nothing. What could explain Janice lying in that hospital bed, every movement bringing her a wave of pain, cutting right through the Demerol, the morphine, everything they gave her?

Why not call it God's error? God tosses some shit down, maybe it's intended for a guy on the next block, but it happens to land on you, on your wife. Sure, that makes sense. The only problem was, Deal had miscalculated. He'd been thinking they'd taken all the shit there was to take, for a good long while, at least.

"It was the air conditioner, they think," Driscoll continued.

Deal stared at him. "The air conditioner?"

"The circuit-breaker box, it shorted out."

Deal nodded, was about to walk away. Then he felt his legs go weak. He pulled a chair out from the table, sat down again. Forget pilot error, wind shear, act of God. The nausea had returned full-bore now. His head was reeling. No mouse in the attic, chewing insulation. No power surge, no random spark. This *could* be explained, after all. He fell back in his chair, held on to the edge of Driscoll's patio table with both hands.

Driscoll gave him a puzzled look. "You okay?"

Deal nodded. He was not okay. Way beyond not okay. But how could Driscoll know that? The ex-cop was going on, something about the report and him poking around the apartment . . . Deal's head was throbbing too powerfully for him to concentrate.

". . . so *you* take a look," Driscoll was saying. He tossed the object he'd been worrying in his thick fingers across the table. The thing spun around, fell silent on the white resin top.

It was made of tin, a charred tin cap off something, a can, or a large bottle, maybe. Deal picked it up. "Yeah, so?" He was more attuned to the way his body was shifting beneath him, rearranging itself into various alien configurations, one after the other. At this instant he was feeling weightless, hollow, in fact. A mirage. A hologram with a voice.

"Look inside the top."

Deal looked at the ex-cop. Sure. Why not. Listen to the nice man. Do anything but think about what has just made itself plain to you, Deal.

He turned the charred cap over. There was a crusted ring inside the rim, where the threads met the top. Most of the crust was undifferentiated ash, but here and there were flecks of what looked like cork. He wanted to *be* undifferentiated ash.

"You smell anything?"

Smell the cap? Sure. Deal brought it to his nose. The scent of smoke, wet ash, the same as everything else in the vicinity of the ruined apartments. He shook his head.

"Me neither," Driscoll said, still intent on wherever he was taking the conversation. "I can take it to the lab boys, but it's been lying out in the rain and all, all this time."

Deal stared at him. It was time to end this conversation. Get away from Driscoll before he came completely apart. Go someplace to wallow in some heavy-duty self-loathing. "What's this about, Driscoll?"

"It looks like the top off a gasoline can to me," Driscoll said. "That seem like a good guess to you?"

Deal had placed the charred cap on the table between them. He stared at it, the thing seeming to register in his mind for the first time. "You found it in the apartment?"

"Outside the apartment," Driscoll corrected him. "Between the air-conditioning compressor and the wall where the circuit breaker was," he nodded, "where they think the fire started."

Deal stared at him for a moment. "It was an electrical short, Vernon. You just said that."

"Nobody's saying otherwise, not right now," Driscoll said. "Of course, it seemed like it spread so quick, nobody heard the smoke alarms, all that's been bothering me . . . " He broke off, noticing the expression on Deal's face. "You sure you're okay? You want some water . . . "

"Goddammit, Driscoll, what is it with you? You can't get a case on your own, you want a job with the fire marshal? Leave it alone."

Driscoll stared at him, then down at the charred piece of metal between them. "Does this conversation upset you?"

Deal looked up at him. "Does it upset me? You playing detective, suggesting somebody's torched my apartment? On the basis of what?" He flipped the charred cap away, into Driscoll's lap. "That thing could have been out there since the time this was a vacant lot."

"Of course it could have, but wouldn't it be all rusty?"

Deal stared at him. "Who the hell would want to burn down my apartment building, try to kill me and my family? Have another drink, Driscoll."

Driscoll raised his hands in surrender. "I think you're acting a little strange about this. . . . "

Deal felt it all break loose, finally. He leaned across the table suddenly, grabbed Driscoll by the front of his shirt.

"There's no mystery here, Vernon. *I* fucked up. *ME!*" He stared hard at Driscoll. "I installed that AC unit. I did it because the guy brought the wrong breaker panel and had to knock off at five on Friday and I was in a hurry to move in, okay?" Driscoll stared at him, astonished.

"I went over to Home Depot to pick up the breaker switches and put them in myself. I figured I'd get the electrician back out, go over my job." He threw up his hands.

"Only the first thing Monday came and I had some other things to do, and every time I thought about it after that, I had a few *more* things to do, and a few more after that, and finally I forgot about the goddamned things altogether, because if it isn't the fuck broke then why in the fuck worry about fixing it, and that was over a year ago, okay!"

Deal was nearly screaming by the time he finished. He looked at his hand, noticed he'd crumpled Driscoll's sport shirt into a wad, and let go, falling back into his seat. "I'm sorry," he said, his voice a whisper.

Driscoll smoothed his shirt front, ignoring the apology. "That's quite a guilt thing you got going," he said.

Deal glanced up at him. "Don't fucking joke with me, Vernon. Not about this."

"I'm not joking," Driscoll said. "You don't want to listen to me, then don't."

Deal lifted his gaze. "Do you have the slightest proof that this was arson?"

"Forget it," Driscoll said. "I don't want to spoil your day. Why don't you go roll around in broken glass?"

Driscoll stood up, stomped through the open doorway into his apartment. Deal sat there for a moment watching the vertical blinds clack together in the wake of the big man's passing. He heard the sounds of the refrigerator opening and closing, the pop of a can tab.

Driscoll reappeared in the doorway, a beer in his hand. He glanced at Deal as if he'd just appeared on the patio. "You still here?" Driscoll said. "I thought you'd be off whipping yourself by now."

"Vernon . . . " Deal began.

"'Course if you want to get into a pissing contest about who's the most pitiful around here, I guess I got a few marks in my favor."

"I didn't mean anything . . . "

Driscoll waved him off. "You meant exactly what you said. I'm an old boozehound, scared to death without his job to go to. Well, old buddy, I'm sorry I bothered you with my thoughts."

He raised the can to finish it, but Deal rose up, swinging. He slapped the beer out of Driscoll's hand and the two of them stood frozen for a moment, watching the thing soar out over the yard, spewing foam like a tiny rocket gone awry.

As Driscoll turned, Deal held his hands up. "I'm sorry, goddammit. I didn't mean that stuff about you."

The beer was on the grass now, oozing a few last suds. Driscoll glanced at it, then at Deal, a mournful expression on his face. "That was my last goddamn beer," he said.

"I'll buy you a beer," Deal said.

"You damn bet you will," Driscoll said.

"I'm sorry about the beer, too," Deal said.

Driscoll eyed him. "That's okay," he said. "You were upset. I seen it happen before. I didn't handle it very well. I was thinking about this notion of mine and I got a little excited. Maybe you're right, maybe it was the AC. Maybe it was even something you did. But hell, it's worth looking into, isn't it?"

Deal nodded. He could feel his heart racing, but it seemed a distant sensation. Settle into self-pity, it's hard to find comfort in anything else. "Your notion," he said to Driscoll finally. "What about it?"

Driscoll made the shrugging expression with his bloodhound's face. "We got to go to college first. I'll tell you a few things on the way."

"I won't promise anything," Driscoll was saying from behind the wheel of his Ford, "but if the boys heard about this down at Metro, then it's worth a try. It's the kind of thing that draws these people out."

"You're the cop, Vernon," Deal said.

They were headed out Coral Way, bound for the state university. A former colleague of Driscoll's had tipped him to the program on for this evening, a contingent of "Student Youth for Cuba," talking about the good life under Communism.

"It ought to be good for a Molotov cocktail or two," Driscoll called over from the driver's seat. "You never know when you'll get lucky. At the very least, you'll see what gets these assholes all worked up."

Deal nodded, staring aimlessly out the window. What was the alternative? Sit in his gardener's cottage and brood like Heathcliff?

He sighed. A lot of traffic lights out this way now, it seemed. And a lot of traffic. Much more development than Deal remembered.

This had been a neighborhood once. Six homes to the acre, two bedrooms, one bath, and a carport in each, good value for twelve thousand dollars. His father had built a block of the houses some-where just north of where they were.

He gazed out at all the little bungalows that had once been people's homes, now turned into doctor's offices, insurance agencies, even a palm reader over there with a brick driveway and a picket fence. Maybe they should pull in, see what Madame Rosalinda had to say about the future.

"You want the air on?" Deal glanced up at the sound of Driscoll's voice. They were stopped at a light and Driscoll was motioning at the passenger's window. "It's a nice evening. You ought to roll your window down."

Deal nodded. He knew how to get along. He cranked the window handle as they pulled away from the light. It *was* a nice evening. The humidity had backed off, and it seemed the temperature had as well. A balmy late-summer evening, more like California weather than Florida's. A couple more weeks, they could start thinking about days in the eighties, nights in the sixties. They would have fall in the tropics.

In another lifetime, he and Janice would be getting the bicycles out of the garage, getting ready for little forays into the Grove. They'd been talking about the seventeen-mile swing into Shark Valley, out in the Glades, wondering if Isabel was old enough for it this year. Once the temperature dropped enough to put the mosquitoes down for the season, you could truck out to the northernmost visitor's center, park, unlimber your bikes, and pedal down these asphalt lanes through the sawgrass, past the foraging herons, the raccoons, the turtle families, dodge old alligators asleep on the paths . . . but he broke off, reminding himself that it wouldn't be happening, not anytime soon.

Driscoll had been talking while Deal drifted. His pal, Driscoll. Driscoll, who wanted him to believe the fire wasn't his fault, wanted him to believe it so bad, he was going to find an arsonist to blame. Good old Driscoll. Maybe he could turn up the Easter Bunny while he was at it.

Now Driscoll was hammering on the horn at an old man stopped dead in the left lane of traffic. He was still talking as he glanced behind them and swung the car into the middle lane to pass. ". . . so when the salesman asks me if I want power windows, I told him, 'Look, I been drivin' nothing but what the county gives me for thirty years. What do I need with power windows?'" Driscoll laughed, glanced over to see if Deal was paying any attention. "The guy gets so frustrated trying to sell me power this and automatic that—I don't want any of it—he finally takes me in to the fleet manager, who asks me what is it I really want. 'Nothing,' I told this other guy: 'Four wheels, a motor, and an AC unit, paint it if you have to.' So he cuts one of the units out of this year's allocation for Metro Dade." Driscoll pounded the dashboard happily. "Now I got a plain vanilla Ford sedan and everybody's happy."

Deal pointed at the spot in the dashboard where most cars would have had a radio. "Don't you ever miss the ball games?"

"Hey, I asked for an AM radio, they told me nobody *makes* an AM radio anymore. You know what it costs for the cheapest thing they got?"

"I don't care," Deal said.

"Yeah." Driscoll nodded, but he was wounded. "Anyway, I'm going over to Pep Boys. I'll have them put in some kind of radio, come out way ahead."

"Sounds good to me, Vernon," Deal said. It was true. Everyone ought to come out ahead, if they could.

It was nearly dark by the time Driscoll found the entrance to the campus and located the parking lot for visitors. The University of Florida at Miami sat on a big chunk of land way west of the city that had once been a county airport. The old control tower was still there, looming over the weedy asphalt lot that had probably once been a runway. CAMPUS POLICE, read a sign on the side of the tower.

"When the Pope came to Miami, he did his thing right over there," Driscoll said. They were walking toward a cluster of tall concrete buildings in the distance. Driscoll pointed off toward another section of abandoned runway. "They had me on security for that little number. The hot rumor was that the *comunistas* were going to pull something during the Mass."

"Was there anything to it?"

Driscoll shook his head. "Not unless they were the ones who cooked up the thunderstorm." Driscoll laughed. "The Pope got up there on the platform, saw a wall of lightning rolling in, that was the end of it. He said a couple of Hail Mary's, two hundred thousand people went home. I guess he figured his connections weren't *that* strong."

Deal glanced around the open field. The sky was crystal blue, holding a thin slice of moon, one star in its cusp, a narrow band of orange in the west. Crickets and tree frogs had set up a racket, but he could hear the background roar of traffic on the Turnpike extension. The wide road was out there, a few hundred yards beyond the trees marking the ragged edge of the horizon.

A few miles beyond that lay the Everglades. Hundreds of square miles of sawgrass and water, the Gulf on the west, the Atlantic on the south, Lake Okeechobee and the cane fields on the north. Nothing in between but grass and water and the things that liked it just that way. He felt a powerful urge to be out there, to be part of it, barely sentient, a creature with his snout just out of the water, his belly sunk in the warm muck below.

"You sure you know where we're going?" he said to Driscoll.

Driscoll took his arm, guiding him onto a sidewalk that took shape amid the weeds. "Just stick with me, pardner."

". . . so what we say, it is not in Cuba the way what you hear, and we say thank you again for this visit to tell you the conditions the way they really are in our country,"

Or words to that effect, Deal thought. He'd been drifting again. The young man who'd been speaking pressed a button on the slide-machine controller he held and the image of a smiling cadre of field workers vanished, replaced by a blinding square of light.

It was stuffy in the crowded auditorium and Deal had been nodding off during a mind-numbing recitation of facts and figures about the delights of life in Castro's paradise. No hint of any trouble, except death by boredom. He held up a hand, shielding his eyes from the glare of the blank screen, then blinked fully awake as the fluorescent lights flickered back to life.

There was a polite round of applause from the audience, a mixed bag of tweedy professor types and yuppified students, as the three representatives of the Cuban Youth Brigade stood and bowed. Two young men, one woman, all with steel-rimmed glasses and bad haircuts. They seemed a joyless-looking trio to Deal, hardly the crew he'd hire to travel about U.S. college campuses to boost a country's image.

"So what'd you think?" Driscoll said, turning in the seat next to Deal.

"Really, truly fascinating, Vernon. They live on an island, they can't buy fish to eat, but everybody's happy anyway," Deal said as Driscoll nodded agreement. "Can we go home now?"

Driscoll held up his hand. "Hold your horses."

Deal scanned the audience again. The professors were gathering their briefcases, heading for the aisles, the students were yawning, chatting, the girls comparing clothing styles, the boys comparing notes on the girls. Down in front of the stage, there were a half-dozen scruffier types wearing armbands that read USHER directing traffic in a desultory way. If this was college politics, things seemed to have lost their edge since Deal had been in school.

Deal sat back, impatient, as the three Cubans started down off the stage. The ushers joined ranks and blocked off the aisle there. Someone had opened an exit door and Deal felt a cooling draft from outside.

One of the professor types was hurrying the Cubans outside, with the ushers closing ranks behind them. Deal had just turned to ask Driscoll what he was expecting anyhow, but the big man was already shoving himself out of his seat.

"I knew it," Driscoll said. He was on his feet, trying to wedge past a trio of bookbag-lugging coeds. He called over his shoulder to Deal, "That's him, the little prick in the back."

Deal followed his gesture to the rear of the auditorium. There was a tiny Hispanic man near a set of doors, dressed incongruously for this crowd in lime-green slacks, a yellow guayabera, and a porkpie hat. He was carrying a canvas duffel bag and was rooting around inside it, until he looked up and saw Driscoll, lurching out into the aisle, trying to kick his foot free of a huge knapsack.

The little man dropped his duffel bag, had bolted for an exit before the thing hit the ground. As Deal stood, the rear doors of the auditorium flew inward with a crash, and a mob of chanting students streamed inside, blocking Driscoll's pursuit of the little man.

"*Cuba sí! Castro no!*" the intruders were chanting as they streamed down the aisles. "*Cu-ba yes! Cas-tro no!*" All of them Cuban, apparently. Mostly males, in their twenties, some women. Razor cuts and perms. Shirts by Polo, crisp chinos, lizard boots and alligator shoes. No shortage of jewelry or manicured nails. Deal remembered his own student days from the sixties, the ragtag crew that had taken over the student newspaper, camped out in the administration building. By contrast, this looked like a noisy contingent of business majors.

Shouts and screams erupted at the exit door where the Cuban

brigade was on its way out. Deal turned to see the Cubans and their escorts dodging missiles flying through the open doorway. Rocks, Deal thought. Big white rocks. Then realized what they really were. One egg splattered against the Cuban guy who'd been speaking, another broke over the face of an usher.

The little man had long since disappeared and Driscoll was being carried with the tide of protestors toward the disturbance at the exit doors. Deal saw him elbow one of the protestors aside, trying to get to the unoccupied stage. He jostled past a short Latina carrying a sign with a NO CASTRO emblem on it. She yelled something in Spanish, then raised her sign and rammed the wooden standard into the back of Driscoll's head.

Driscoll lost his balance, went down sprawling into a group of screaming coeds. One of the ushers, egg yolk still dripping from his chin, turned to see what had happened. A guy in a pinstriped shirt stepped forward, bringing his fist up from deep right field.

It was the perfect sucker punch, catching the usher, a black man with close-cropped hair, flush on the cheek. The usher's glasses flew straight up. He went over backward, his arms windmilling into the group still dodging eggs at the door.

The place was pandemonium now. Everyone screaming, throwing punches. A professor, Coke-bottle glasses askew, had made it up onto the stage. He clutched the lectern, pounding the mike, shouting, "Order! Order!" until somebody jerked the power cord and the mike flew out of his hands.

Deal vaulted the aisle in front of him, clearing an elderly couple quaking in their seats. He landed across an empty row, felt a chair arm gouge his ribs, take his wind away. He came up gasping for air, staggered toward the place where Driscoll had gone down. A kid with slicked-back hair was dancing into the midst of the screaming coeds, shooting some kind of karate kick at someone, darting back, then lunging forward again.

Deal had a glimpse of Driscoll—a smear of blood across his mournful face—trying to lift himself off the carpet. His big head snapped back as the kid danced forward, skittered back. Deal lurched out into the aisle and drove his shoulder into the karate dancer's chest. The blow took the kid by surprise, sent both of them crashing into the opposite bank of seats.

Deal felt a fresh jolt of pain in his side as they went down. He flailed for the kid, had him for a moment, then lost his grip. He felt a sharp blow on his face, then another. The same karate kicks nailing him now. He felt another bloom of pain as his nose flattened under the kid's heel.

He rolled backward, lashed out with his own feet, caught the kid in a leg whip that would have cost him fifteen yards in his playing days. The kid went down, losing his breath as he slammed against the floor. That was the thing about institutional carpeting, Deal thought. Thin stuff, thin padding underneath. Not much between you and the concrete slab.

He caught the kid by the foot as he tried to scramble away, twisted till he heard something pop. The kid screamed and twisted, and Deal found himself holding an empty shoe. There was another kick, a stockinged foot bouncing off his forehead now.

"You little asshole," Deal said, and grabbed the kid by his pant-leg. He got a good grip, twisting the fabric in his fist, dragged the kid close, and sank his teeth into a set of stockinged toes. His head was throbbing. He wanted to lock into a toe joint, grind down until he felt digits separate, maybe work on up: ankle, knee, an arm or two—*weaselly little bastard*—but eased off despite himself, was going to be content to climb up onto the kid's chest and slap him silly . . .

. . . when a bright star exploded in his head and he felt himself tumbling backward, his arms, his legs, everything gone suddenly numb.

He found himself lying across Driscoll's lap at the bottom of the aisle, the two of them wedged up against the apron of the stage. The place was swarming with campus cops now. Most of them seemed no older than the students, but they were laying about with their batons in what Deal thought was a satisfactory way.

Deal got a glimpse of a kid in camel-colored slacks limping out a doorway at the back of the auditorium, glanced down to find himself still holding a shoe.

A brand-spanking-new loafer, the leather buttery-soft in his hands, a gold logo glittering brightly at the instep: a guy on a pony with his mallet raised.

"Ain't that just the way." It was Driscoll's voice, the ex-cop grabbing the loafer, tossing it away in disgust. He found a handhold on the stage, helped Deal up too. "It used to be the hippies beating the shit out of the rich folks," Driscoll said, helping Deal upright. "Now look what's happened."

Deal glanced around. The melee was over. The Cuban Youth Brigade members were gone, most of the protestors had disappeared, even the elderly couple had made it out one of the rear exits. A couple of the protestors were in handcuffs, hollering that they wanted "counsel." A campus cop was headed toward Deal and Driscoll, a wary look on his face.

Deal coughed, felt fire in his chest. He turned to Driscoll. "There was a reason why we came here, wasn't there?"

Driscoll was breathing heavily, swiping at the blood on his upper lip. He pointed aimlessly toward the back of the room. "There was a reason, all right. Only thing is, the little bastard got away."

They were in a room on the ground floor of the control tower now. A kid in a yellow windbreaker had driven them over in a golf cart, had called an EMS team on a portable phone as they jounced along.

One of the medics, a slender Hispanic woman with long sleek hair, ran a penlight across Deal's eyes, probed his rib cage, stood up with a smile. "Nothing for me to do," she said cheerily. "Take some Advil when you get home."

Deal nodded, drew a breath as deep as he dared, the pain still dancing there. He'd need a crane to get out of bed in the morning. Across the room, the medic's partner was fixing a broad strip of adhesive across the bridge of Driscoll's nose.

"Don't worry about it, pardner. It's been broke plenty of times before," Driscoll said. He fingered the tape as the medics packed up. "Might have straightened it out a bit, in fact."

A young cop came out of an office, closed the door behind him on more angry shouts for "counsel." The cop consulted a clipboard under his arm, shook his head, walked over to where Deal and Driscoll sat. "One of the guys in there punched an usher, hurt him pretty bad. The guy claims he was defending his girlfriend from an attack by the usher. Either one of you see anything?"

"If it was the same little shit that hit me with her sign, she didn't need any protecting," Driscoll said. He rubbed the back of his neck stiffly.

Deal shook his head. "It was a sucker punch, all the way. If it's the same kid, anyway. I didn't see his face."

The cop shrugged. "There's a tooth still embedded between this kid's knuckles. Besides, he admits it. He says it was self-defense."

"Bullshit," Driscoll said.

The cop gave him a look. "We called downtown. They corroborated *your* story, Lieutenant."

"I'm not on the force anymore. You don't have to call me Lieutenant."

"What they told me about you, you're still Lieutenant in my book," the young cop said.

Driscoll looked uncomfortable with the compliment. He gestured across the room where the duffel bag the little man had been carrying sat on a tabletop, a couple of strange-looking jars beside it. "What was in the bag?"

The cop glanced at the things. "A carbide and water setup," he said. "Stink bombs." He turned back to Driscoll. "You saw the guy who was carrying it?"

"Not really," Driscoll said.

Deal stared at him in surprise. Driscoll avoided his gaze, looked back at the cop. "It was kind of crazy in there, you know?"

The cop didn't seem convinced, but after a moment he turned to Deal. "We've got the statements of two of our officers, a couple of professors, some of the students. That should be enough. But if we need you again . . . ?" He left his question unspoken.

"Sure," Deal said. "Whatever."

"Don't forget to put out an APB on that other guy: a kid with one shoe and a set of teeth marks on his big toe," Driscoll said.

The young cop laughed and started away. Then he seemed to think of something. He turned back, his face solemn. "The sad fact is, that one'll probably be sitting in class over there tomorrow, taking notes on hospitality management." The cop jerked his thumb in the direction of the classroom buildings. "Feeling justified about what he and his buddies pulled here tonight."

Deal rubbed his forehead where a lump had formed. You could get a lump from a stockinged foot, apparently. Something he'd have to remember. He took another look at the cop. At his nametag. Corporal Oller. Jet-black hair, olive complexion, dark eyes. "You're Cuban?" Deal asked.

"Sure," he said. "But I'm not crazy." He shook his head. "You can't really blame these kids, though. They hear it at home, they hear it on all the Cuban radio shows, they even hear it from some of their professors—they're bound to start to believe it."

"What's *it*?" Deal said.

"The whole back-to-Cuba myth," he said. "That someday soon Castro will fall, we're all gonna get on our boats and go sailing home, make everything just like it used to be." He shook his head. "Meantime, we all have to stand united against the commies and the pinkos here in the U.S. to make sure this all happens as soon as possible. And man, you better believe you're with the program or you're against it. That's how you get stuff like what happened here tonight."

Oller checked over his shoulder at a glassed-in office where a graying, heavily jowled man with captain's bars sat engrossed in paperwork. He lowered his voice and leaned closer to Deal. "One of the 'Free Cuba' groups hears that Jose Feliciano wants to do a concert in Havana, that's it. He doesn't even have to go there. It's enough he was *thinking* about it. Poof! No Cuban store sells Jose's records any longer. No Cuban is supposed to buy his stuff. As far as the Cuban community in the United States is concerned, Jose Feliciano doesn't even exist. He might as well be dead."

"It can't be that bad," Deal said.

Oller didn't seem to hear. "I don't even *like* Jose Feliciano," he said. "But this stuff pisses me off so bad, I buy everything of his I can get my hands on." He grinned. "Of course, I'm not going to drive down Calle Ocho playing it real loud."

He might have gone on, but the captain had left off with his paperwork and was coming through the door of his office now.

"We are nearly finished here?" The captain said, giving Oller a sharp glance.

Deal stared at the captain's nametag: J. Acevedo. He wondered what Acevedo's feelings on Jose Feliciano might be.

Acevedo turned his gaze on Driscoll. "I heard you retired, *viejo*. You come out here to go to school or something?" He wasn't smiling.

Driscoll stood up. "Just showing my friend here the sights," he said. He pointed at the bulge over Acevedo's belt. "*Viejo* means old fart in Spanish, don't it? How is it you say lardass?"

Oller turned away, hiding a smile. Acevedo's face went crimson. Deal wondered if he might have to try to break up another fight.

"We about ready, Vernon?" he said. He stood up, getting himself between the two men.

Driscoll looked down over Deal's shoulder at Acevedo, who glared back at him. "Sure," Driscoll said. "Let's leave the captain to his crayons and paperwork."

20

"So why did you lie to that cop?" Deal asked.

They were sitting at a battered picnic table in a back corner of Edgar's, a bar on 57th Avenue north of Bird, where Driscoll had insisted they stop.

The ex-cop turned from the TV, where a ball game was in progress. "Leverage," he said.

Deal shook his head. "What's that supposed to mean?"

Driscoll shrugged. "Maybe nothing," he said. "Let's see what happens." He went back to the game.

Deal stared around. It didn't seem like the place for another gathering of communists. Sawdust and peanut shells on the floor, making grimy little drifts in the corners, the smell of grill grease in the air, the blare of a couple of ten-year-old TVs over the bar competing with an electronic pinball game in the corner. Nobody was playing pinball, but still the machine cycled through whoops and kazoo-like noises, as if some ghost were squandering invisible quarters there. A half-dozen old geezers, the only other customers, sat at the bar, as intent on the game as Driscoll seemed to be. The Manatees and the Rockies in from Denver by cable, players with pink faces, playing on blue grass. A fly ball had just bounced off the forehead of a Rockies outfielder. Replay after replay now, the fielder's cap and glasses flying one way, the ball another, the announcers in hysterics.

"Expansion baseball," Driscoll said finally, shaking his head.

Deal had a sip of his beer. "Why are we here, Driscoll?"

Driscoll waved him off. "This is how you do it, Deal. Just sit tight."

Deal took a deep breath, favoring his sore ribs, took another inch or so out of his beer. No wonder Driscoll had left the department—all that hassle having to talk to other people, explain what he was up to. On the other hand, the ache at his side had begun to subside. Maybe he'd have several beers, get into the game, see if the old codgers at the bar would make a space for him. He glanced at Driscoll, his expression bland. "You been using your Manatees tickets?" The Manatees were the hometown version of the Rockies. Some of the other detectives down at Metro had given Driscoll a season's pass to the young team as a retirement gift.

Driscoll paused, as if he had to think about the question. He polished off his beer, made a wave toward the bar for a refill. The bartender was fiddling with the controls of one of the sets. "Naw," Driscoll said, finally. "I keep meaning to, but . . ." He shrugged, shook his head. "Funny thing is, if I was still working, you couldn't keep me away from the stadium, know what I mean? Now that I got all the time in the world, I don't do shit." He had his eyes on the bar. "Yo! *Garçon!*"

The bartender gave them a look, then got grudgingly down from the stool he'd been using to reach the set, drew Driscoll a beer. A Rockie in a green-haloed uniform drilled a homer into a fuchsia sky. Driscoll drummed his fingers absently on the tabletop, abruptly turned to Deal. "It's like the agency I keep saying I'm gonna set up. Easiest thing in the world, right? All the businesspeople I know, scared shitless the cops can't keep 'em safe? And they're right. There's a fortune to be made in executive security in this town."

"Sounds good to me," Deal said. "Do it."

"Yeah," Driscoll said. The bartender arrived with his beer and Driscoll took it straight from his hand. "Thanks, pal."

Driscoll downed half the mug in a swallow. The bartender stood waiting for his money. Driscoll put down his mug, fished around in his pockets, gave the guy a bill. "What's wrong with your TV?"

The bartender followed Driscoll's gesture. Another green-haloed player was circling the bases, kicking up clumps of bright red earth.

"This Manatees, they are too good," the bartender said.

Driscoll stared at him. "Right," he said finally.

When the guy left, Driscoll threw up his hands. "I gotta get out of this town. I mean, you can't even come into a bar, run a tab, talk a little baseball anymore."

"Learn Spanish," Deal said.

Driscoll seemed to consider it. "Yeah. I got plenty of time on my hands, right?"

"Is this what we came down here for?" Deal said. "If it's all the same to you, I'm ready to go home."

Driscoll was about to answer when the front door to the place opened. A smile came over Driscoll's face.

"*That* is why we came here," he said, pointing at the door. "The guy is so predictable it's scary."

Deal glanced up, did a double take. It was the same little man who'd carried the duffel bag into the auditorium hours before, still wearing his lime-green slacks and yellow shirt, the hat perched jauntily back on his head.

The little guy was inside now, had one hand on the bar rail, was about to pull himself up onto a stool when he caught sight of who was sitting at the picnic table. In one unbroken motion, he pushed off the rail, made a smooth pirouette, and headed back out the door. Driscoll was up and after him faster than Deal would have supposed the detective could move.

Though none of the other patrons seemed to take notice, Deal watched the drama through the window of the place: the little guy scurrying through a pool of light toward an aging silver Cadillac, the plastic near its tail fins eaten away, Driscoll on his heels. The little guy got his door open, his hand in his pocket, his keys out. He'd actually made it into his seat, cranked the Caddy over, sent a blue puff of smoke from the exhaust before Driscoll caught up with him.

Driscoll reached through the open window, wadded the guy's shirt in his big hand and pulled. The little guy came out through the open window, kicking like a minnow in Driscoll's grasp. Driscoll held him aside with one hand, reached inside the Caddy with the other. He pulled the keys out of the ignition, turned, and jammed them into a pocket of the little guy's guayabera.

He shook the little guy a couple of times, pointed in the direction of the bar, and when the little guy shook his head, rattled him again. Finally the little guy nodded. Driscoll set him down then, mashed his hat back into place, and pushed him toward the door.

"Say hi to Chuy-Chuy," Driscoll said, guiding the little guy into a seat against the wall. "He's kept his office in this place for years, right up there at the bar."

Deal stared. "You knew he was coming? Why didn't you say so?"

Driscoll shrugged. "After that trouble out on the campus, I couldn't be *sure*."

Deal shook his head, turned back to Chuy-Chuy, who listened silently, looking fearful for his life.

Driscoll slapped his hand on Chuy-Chuy's back hard enough to dislodge his hat. "My old buddy Chuy-Chuy," Driscoll said. "One name used to be good enough for him, but after he became a multiple offender, we gave him two, just like the golfer. Right, Chuy-Chuy?"

Chuy-Chuy shrugged. He seemed ready to bolt under the table, go for the door again. "Don't get any ideas," Driscoll added, nodding at Deal. "This man here will break your spine."

"I done nothing," Chuy-Chuy said, surly.

"Uh-huh," Driscoll said. "What about that little number out at the university?"

Chuy-Chuy shrugged. "I didn't do shit, man. Besides, all they wanted was to stink the place up."

Driscoll shook his head. "It doesn't matter, my friend. We got an explosive device, we got intent to assault, a dozen other things. A guy like you takes another fall, you can kiss your ass goodbye."

Driscoll turned to Deal, his arm still resting on the little man's shoulder. "I explained to Chuy-Chuy we just wanted some of his expert advice, but he's a nervous kind of a guy. He'll calm down in a minute." Driscoll slid what was left of his beer to Chuy-Chuy. "Drink up."

Chuy-Chuy hesitated, saw the expression on Driscoll's face, drank. When he was finished, Driscoll prodded him with an elbow. "Now tell the man."

Chuy-Chuy looked about, considered his chances. The old geezers were still intent on the game. The bartender glanced over, but turned away when Driscoll waved him off.

"Liquid paraffin," Chuy-Chuy mumbled.

"Speak up," Driscoll said, jabbing him again.

"I said it coulda been liquid paraffin." Chuy-Chuy was rubbing his ribs.

"Who is this guy?" Deal said to Driscoll.

"An arsonist."

"Bullshit," Chuy-Chuy said.

"Shut the fuck up," Driscoll said. He leaned across the table, his arm circling around Chuy-Chuy's shoulders. "Chuy-Chuy is known about town as the man with the torch, the dude who loves to play with matches." Driscoll's thick fingers massaged the flesh near Chuy-Chuy's collarbone. From a distance, it might have looked like they were pals. Deal could see tears welling in the little man's eyes.

"Remember the Winchester Chemicals fire up in Lauderdale?" Driscoll said. "Chuy-Chuy lit that one."

"The fuck I did," Chuy-Chuy managed.

"Couple of firefighters I know sucked in some real choice fumes trying to put it out," Driscoll said, ignoring him. "What they got now makes emphysema seem pretty."

"Man . . . " Chuy-Chuy was writhing in Driscoll's grip.

"He is also the firestarter of choice for the right-wing yahoos who burned up those travel agencies last year, the places selling tickets to Cuba." Driscoll paused. "You may recall there was one where the pretty lady manager dropped by the office unexpectedly one night, had her little boy with her? They got there just in time for the fireworks, all there was left for her husband to bury was a handful of teeth."

"That wasn't me." Chuy-Chuy's face was white now. He could hardly get the words out.

"What *is* true," Driscoll said mildly, "is that we couldn't prove a thing. Cuz Chuy-Chuy has gotten very good at what he does. He hasn't seen the inside of a prison cell for a long time now."

Driscoll gave a last disgusted squeeze and released his grip. It took Chuy-Chuy a moment to get his breath back. "Because I didn't do anything," he said, gingerly rubbing his shoulder.

Driscoll turned to him, his face bland. "That may be, pal. But I'm going to suggest something to you. A guy who plays with matches is bound to get burned. In fact, somebody might find you inside that silver bomb out there one night, fried to a crisp because you forgot what you had under your seat. And I know for a fact nobody would question how it happened, you get my drift?"

"Fuck you," Chuy-Chuy said, but he seemed a shade paler.

"So do me a favor," Driscoll said. "Talk to my friend here. Maybe it'll help convince me you've gone straight, you got the public interest in mind these days."

"Could I get a beer," Chuy-Chuy said.

"Sure," Driscoll said. He snapped his fingers and the bartender hopped to.

". . . in which case you'd want to use something doesn't leave that gasoliny smell," Chuy-Chuy was saying. He paused to wipe beer foam off his lip. "That's why liquid paraffin's good. But it's slow. You want a fire that's gonna accelerate quick, you might use carbon tetrachloride, the stuff dry cleaners used to use."

Deal frowned, remembering his own trips to the cleaners. "Can't you smell that stuff?"

Chuy-Chuy shook his head. "Not after it burns. A sniffer can usually pick it up, though."

Deal turned to Driscoll, who explained. "It's a detector the fire marshal uses where they suspect arson. It's a little battery-operated thing with a wand on the end, looks like a walkie-talkie. It'll pick up traces of carbon-based accelerators that a person can't smell."

"Even paraffin," Chuy-Chuy volunteered. He'd become more voluble the deeper he'd gotten into his subject. "It can pick that up too."

Driscoll reached into his pocket, produced the metal cap he'd found in the wreckage. "Liquid paraffin, carbon tetrachloride, they come in a can with a lid like this one?"

Chuy-Chuy glanced at it and shrugged. "They could."

Deal stared at him a moment. "What about that detector? Is this something they used after . . . " He broke off. "After my fire?"

Driscoll nodded. "Any time there's an injury."

"Then they would have known . . . "

"Not always," Chuy-Chuy said. "I seen them miss plenty of times."

Deal wondered if he heard a touch of pride there.

"He's right," Driscoll said. "The things aren't foolproof. Maybe the batteries are low, or the guy doin' the checking doesn't really have any reason to suspect anything, he's not as careful as he might be."

"The classic thing is," Chuy-Chuy broke in, "an inspector can walk into a room that is burned to shit, he can still tell where the fire started, because fire burns up and it burns hottest from where it starts. So they take a look at your place, they figure it started at that junction box, went up and out from there because there ain't shit left in that spot and everywhere else is just charred."

"So the case is closed," Deal said. "It was an electrical fire."

Chuy-Chuy shrugged. "Not necessarily. Somebody could know the same things what I just told you. He soaks a rag in paraffin, stuffs it in the junction box for a starter, uses the carbon tetrachloride to spread things quick. Inspector could have missed it."

"Could we go back over it now?"

"After all this time, the place been open to the weather and all? You had a firebug in there, you'd have a hell of a time proving it now."

Chuy-Chuy waved his hand in a dismissive gesture. The perfect crime. A piece of cake for the accomplished arsonist. Deal had felt sorry for him a few minutes ago, writhing in Driscoll's grasp. Now he felt his own hands twitching, ready for a turn at the little man.

"Guy knows his stuff, don't he?" Driscoll said it dryly.

"Isn't it kind of dangerous when you light it, being around those chemicals?" Deal asked.

Chuy-Chuy shrugged. "Guy who did your place, *if* that's what happened, he could have been miles away when it went up."

Deal stared at him, uncomprehending.

"There's a couple dozen ways. He could have used a timer. Or say the phone lines come in through the same service box. All he has to do is bare a couple phone wires, then call you up in the middle of the night, spark jumps the lines, there she goes."

Deal felt a sickness deep inside. Had he heard the ringing of the phone? Him fighting up out of the bedclothes. Someone calling at that time of night? And the smell of smoke, the fear, Janice coming awake, groggy at his side.

"... one call and there she goes ... " Chuy-Chuy raised his hands, outlining a blossom of flame as if it were something beautiful. Deal felt himself rising, ready to go across the table.

Driscoll reached out, held him back. "You know anything about this job, Chuy-Chuy?"

"Not shit, man."

"It sure sounds like you do," Driscoll insisted.

"You ask me 'How could it have happened,'" Chuy-Chuy said. His eyes were still on Deal. "I told you how it *could* have happened. I'm outta that shit, man."

"I drag your ass out to the cops at the university, you're gonna be right back in it."

"That was *nothing*," Chuy-Chuy whined.

"Let's go see what they think," Driscoll said. He wadded Chuy-Chuy's shirt in his fist, started up from the bench.

"Okay, man," Chuy-Chuy said, batting at Driscoll's hand.

"Okay *what*?" Driscoll said, hesitating.

"Somebody might have called me about this kind of job."

Driscoll sat back down, gave Deal a look. "Tell me, Chuy-Chuy," he said.

The little man glanced at Deal, hesitated. Driscoll elbowed him sharply in the ribs. "This man's wife is lying in the hospital right now, you little prick. You either start talking or I'm going to lock you in a room with him, *then* I'll take what's left to the cops."

Chuy-Chuy saw the look in Deal's eyes, turned away. "I got a call couple weeks ago. Somebody interested in a couple of hits. One of them might have been what you're talking about, I dunno. We never got around to it."

"What was the one you talked about?" Driscoll asked.

Chuy-Chuy shrugged. "A big job."

"Like that museum over on Brickell?"

"Hey, it never got that far. I told you."

"Yeah," Driscoll said. "You're out of that shit now. Who were you talking to, Chuy-Chuy?"

Chuy-Chuy laughed. "You gotta be kidding."

Driscoll wiped a meaty hand over his face. "Trust me, Chuy-Chuy. I am not kidding."

"Well, you might as well be," Chuy-Chuy said. "I'd as soon be back in jail."

"It was Torreno, wasn't it?" Driscoll said.

Chuy-Chuy turned away.

"Torreno or one of his slimewads," Driscoll said. "And you didn't just say 'Sorry, I'm busy.' I seen enough of your work around this town. You gave them a goddamned by-the-numbers kit, didn't you? That's the least you did."

Chuy-Chuy whirled back on him then, his face full of venom. "Fuck you, Driscoll. Fuck you and this asshole and this asshole's old lady, cuz the worst thing you can think of isn't worth what you want from me . . . "

And that was when Deal went after him. A beer spilled, and there was cold wetness across his legs, and a roaring white noise had come to fill his head. He didn't care about any of that, though. He was lost in the satisfaction of his hands closing around Chuy-Chuy's throat and the gurgling sounds he made until Driscoll had pulled him off.

He could barely hear Driscoll's rough voice barking at Chuy-Chuy—"Get out of here. Get the hell out of here"—was only vaguely conscious of a bad TV picture of a baseball game and a vague blur of the little man fleeing through the door, but it was all dim and unreal compared to the picture of the night when his world collapsed, the picture that was never going to let him go.

"I'm sorry about that," Driscoll said, breaking the silence. "I had to grind the little prick, though. It's the only way I'd know whether he actually did it." They were twisting down Ingraham Highway in Coconut Grove, the moon flittering through the tangle of branches overhead.

Deal glanced over. He'd been listening to the thudding of his own pulse as it gradually slowed, watching the big man drive, thinking that he could have killed a man earlier, very well might have, had Driscoll not pulled him off. And on what grounds? Because Chuy-Chuy had pissed him off? Because Driscoll had bullied Chuy-Chuy until he was willing to say anything? Time to get a grip, Deal.

They were very nearly home now, the place Deal was calling home, anyway. Before the hurricane, the trees had interlocked over the roadway, creating a solid canopy, leaving a broad tunnel beneath them, through the green. Now the branches were just starting to touch again. Like old friends, Deal thought . . . or lovers. And felt the ache that came with every thought approximating emotion.

He forced the image of Janice in her hospital bed from his mind, tried to find something mindless to focus on, but it didn't seem possible. Before he knew it he was reliving the satisfaction he had felt trying to bite a kid's toe off earlier in the evening.

He took a deep breath, glanced over at Driscoll. "What's your interest in this Torreno character, anyway?"

Driscoll snorted. "Vicente Luis Torreno? You don't know who he is?"

"He's a businessman." Deal shrugged.

"Maybe that's why you went bust as a builder," Driscoll said dryly. "Your old man sure as hell knew what Torreno could do. His crowd, anyway. The Unacknowledged. They control half the City Council seats, the Chamber of Commerce, the builder's association . . . "

Deal decided to ignore the issue of who ruined DealCo. "So there's a Cuban business association, Driscoll. The city's half Hispanic now. It's natural they're going to exert some influence . . . "

"Some influence?" Driscoll rolled his eyes, turned back to the road, too disgusted to reply.

No point in debating the ex-cop on the inevitability of change, Deal thought. Nor in pointing out that it had been just as much a good-old-boy network for the Anglos thirty years ago, when Deal's father had built DealCo into a leviathan. Good timing for Deal's money-from-anybody father, bad timing for straight-arrow Deal. Complaining about it was like complaining about the weather. What you did, Deal thought, was go out and do your work. Do the thing you were good at. Do your work and hope for the best.

"I read about some of these guys, Driscoll," Deal said. "Jorge Vas, some of his pals . . . "

"Forget Vas," Driscoll said. "Those are the politicians, the guys who go to Washington, get their pictures taken with the president. They're out there where you can keep an eye on them. It's a guy like Torreno who's the real problem."

Driscoll spotted the gap in a tall hedge that bordered the narrow lane they were on and hit his brakes. He had to back up to make his turn down the entryway to the Terrell estate.

"Torreno's a behind-the-scenes player," Driscoll continued. "A money man. A bad actor. And he controls the war chest."

"What are you talking about?" Deal asked, his gaze following the path of the car. They were crunching down a graveled alleyway now. In the distance were the unfinished turrets of Terrell's one-day-to-be mansion. Just ahead was the cottage where Deal was staying. A possum scuttled across the road through the lights. Go to bed. Get up. Go to work. Kick it down the road, he thought.

"Every Cuban who's doing major business in South Florida—in the U.S., for that matter—kicks in. That's where the money for the Bay of Pigs came from, for Chrissakes. It's been coming in ever since, in a flood. Nobody knows how much, but it's way, way up in the millions. They run a major lobby in Washington, a paramilitary camp out in the Everglades, a firing range. They got association houses, after-school programs for kids, a whole operation."

Driscoll pulled up in front of the cottage, killed the engine, the lights. A trash can toppled over behind the house, probably the possum foraging. Deal was ready to get out. "So they're getting organized. I'm happy for them. It's the American way."

Driscoll had turned toward him now. "According to Department intelligence, they got enough weapons and ordnance stored away in Dade County alone, they could take over most small countries if they had the army to use the stuff." Driscoll shook his head. "Meantime, they bankroll these half-baked incursions you hear about in the papers, five or six kamikazes hit the beaches in Cuba, take a hosing from Fidel, anything for *viva la revolución*."

Deal turned. "You're telling me this megabucks Torreno also sends out college kids to break up a pissant program like tonight's?"

Driscoll shook his head. "*He* doesn't have to. You heard that campus cop. Torreno and his buddies got so many people brainwashed, they make Barry Goldwater seem like a liberal. It's worse than Scientology. The guys at the top work on the important stuff, the flunkies take every opportunity to raise hell."

Deal looked at him wearily. "I've lived here all my life, Vernon. A lot of things have changed. But I still don't see what any of this has to do with me. Why would Torreno or any of these people want to burn down my building?"

Driscoll stared, a little of the wind going out of his sails. "I dunno, exactly. But you heard Chuy-Chuy. I think *some*body torched it. And another thing I know is, it don't take much to set these people off." He paused, gave Deal a look. "Now you were at that art museum a couple weeks ago, right? They invite a Cuban guy to show his paintings, BOOM! Bunch of people dead, a big chunk of Coral Gables goes sky-high."

Deal nodded.

"Earlier that same day, right?" Driscoll said.

Deal nodded again. "So what?"

"So maybe nothing. But think back. Did anything happen while you were there? Anything unusual?"

Deal stared at him, but he wasn't seeing Driscoll. He remembered Janice, the feel of her in his arms, the cool, cavernous room.

He finally shook his head. "They asked us to leave. They were getting ready for the opening that night . . . " Deal trailed off. He could still hear her laughter ringing into the crystal Miami sky.

Driscoll took him by the arm. "You sign anything? A guest book, a ledger?"

"Driscoll, you must be crazy. Just because I went into a museum . . . "

"I'm not saying anything's for sure, Deal. But Chuy-Chuy as much as told us . . . "

Deal put his arm on Driscoll's shoulder. "I heard him, Vernon. And I was ready to kill him, but that doesn't mean anything, except he was ready to say anything just to get away from you and he happened to push the wrong button. Don't you understand? I was ready to kill that guy, and over what? Some vague suspicion?" Deal broke off, shaking his head. "I appreciate the help, Vernon. I really do. But tomorrow's going to come early. I'm going to bed."

Driscoll started to say something, then thought better of it. He clapped his big paw over Deal's. "Okay, pardner. I'll see you around the fourplex."

He was about to drive away when he stopped and leaned over, shouting through the open passenger window. "Hey, Deal. Maybe it'd be easier on you, I took this place, you moved into my unit for the time being."

"Thanks, Vernon, but it's okay. I need your rent."

"Hell, I'd still pay the rent. I'd be living here, wouldn't I?"

Deal tried to imagine how Terrence Terrell would find Driscoll as a tenant. "That's all right. It's your apartment, Vernon. I'll feel better if you stay in it, as long as you're happy, of course."

"Whatever you think," Driscoll said. He lifted his big hand in a wave, and then he was gone.

Deal watched the car go, heard the sound of the motor die away, heard the rustlings of the possum around back, tearing through a Hefty bag for a midnight snack. The air, ripe with the scent of the bay and with a hint of coolness in it, held him there, thinking about Driscoll's suspicions.

It was tempting to fall in with Driscoll, of course, fix all his sadness and outrage over a changing world on someone else. But it was loony. What interest would someone like Torreno have in Deal's affairs? And as for the museum connection . . .

Deal closed his eyes, willed himself to reconstruct their visit. A chance trip, something they'd decided on that morning, no one else even knew they were going. Nothing strange on the way in, nothing but interesting art to look at while they were there, save for a few other nondescript visitors—an elderly matron, a Japanese guy with a camera bag, a knot of high school girls in uniform—nothing memorable at all, except for the picture of Janice gathered into his arms, and he wasn't going to think about that. Still, he could see her moving away from him, out of the gloomy building into the sunlight, laughing at his adolescent behavior. "And I had to sign our names to the guest register, Deal. . . . "

He stopped then, her words echoing in his mind suddenly. He was already turning toward the sound of Driscoll's departing car, ready to call out, "Wait . . . you were right, there was something. . . . " And then, just as suddenly, his excitement vanished, and he was left feeling more foolish than before. Sure, their names were on a guest register, all right, a register that would have gone up in smithereens in the blast, along with the guy who'd thrown them out. And even if there'd been time for someone to study the guest list, what did that mean? There hadn't been any wave of fire-bombings on old folks, Japanese tourists, and high school girls, had there?

The garbage can rattled again, and he saw the shape of the possum waddling away into the shadows, making snorting noises as if it were disgusted at the slim pickings there. No, Deal thought, they had seen nothing, done nothing, there was no hidden connection. That was the stuff of mysteries, of films that gave you the double and triple twist, and this was simply life. What seemed most logical was that Driscoll had quit the department too soon, before he had gotten to nail the bad guys he wanted worst, that was the only connection there was. Deal shook his head and turned back toward the cottage.

He was tired to the point of wooziness, nearly asleep on his feet, the quiet of the forested Grove hissing into his ears until, for a few blessed moments, he had almost forgotten who he was, very nearly *that* he was. His eyes had adjusted to the darkness by now. He saw the pale white bloom of the possum waddling away into tall grass. He saw the glow of the city lights arc up into the sky, lap up toward the stars, and give out. He saw a shadow whisper past his ear, flutter to a halt in a live oak a few feet away.

An owl, he realized. A tiny owl, the size of his fists clenched together. It sat on a branch a dozen feet from Deal's nose and cocked its head at him. Its eyes were in shadow, but Deal felt himself being measured. Being measured for prey, he thought. And for a moment, although it was just a moment, he felt willing. Yes. Come on down, owl. He'd let himself be carried away.

Driscoll parked the Ford on the street in front of the fourplex, rolled up the windows, but left the thing unlocked. He'd rather a thief just opened the door to see there was no radio, no CB, no nothing inside. Better that than having a window broken out first.

He fished under the seat, found the gizmo that clamped on the steering wheel—something the dealer had tossed in—locked that into place. He shouldn't have to worry about a car such as this being stolen—you'd think the thieves would have better taste—but Miami offenders seemed to be indiscriminate. His last car, a Ford Taurus, had been carrying 180,000 miles and practically no paint when somebody stole it for the third and final time.

He stood back from the car and glanced through the windshield: The gizmo had a fluorescent plastic covering around its steel frame—it looked like someone had welded a neon axle to the wheel. Of course, a determined thief might simply hacksaw through the wheel on either side of the clamps, toss his unbeatable, cop-approved gizmo away and drive off, but Driscoll would just have to take that chance.

He had seen a movie once where an engineer rigged his car up so that when the bad guy got inside, the doors locked themselves, the inside handles wouldn't work, next thing a bomb went off and blew the asshole all to snot. Driscoll would love to have such a setup, minus the bomb, of course. Come out early in the morning, stretch, have a smoke, saunter down to the old sedan, see what you'd snared in your car trap. Be a glorious way to start the day. He glanced around the quiet neighborhood, saw nothing, heard nothing—especially no damnable TV blaring away—and was about to move on toward the house when he thought he saw a flicker of movement near the ruined side of the building. He checked his back again, thought about going inside for his piece, then decided against it. No more movement. Maybe it was just cop paranoia.

Still, he thought, it wouldn't hurt to check. He was across the dewy lawn quickly, up against the smoke-smudged walls and out of the glow of moonlight. He edged on toward the entryway, saw the door ajar, remembered he and Deal had left it propped that way the last time they were there.

He waited a few moments, listening intently. He breathed in the still-pungent odor of scorched wood and smoke, heard the sigh of a breeze through the open timbers. But there was nothing else. Whatever he had seen had been his imagination playing tricks on him. Maybe Deal was right. Too many years looking for trouble, assuming the worst. Maybe the fire *had* started in an electrical box. Maybe he *was* turning into a sorry old bigot. Maybe . . .

He had taken a couple of steps back across the lawn toward his apartment when something hit him hard from behind. He staggered forward, trying to keep his balance, then felt an arm lock across his throat. He tried to lurch back from the pressure, but whoever it was had his head clamped firmly in his other hand.

Driscoll felt a pinging in his ears. Whatever there was to see in front of him—broken sidewalk, torn-up lawn, plainest new car in Miami—had been replaced by a red sheet of pain. He felt his fingers beginning to tingle already, his legs going numb. A few more seconds, he'd be out. A few seconds after that, he'd be dead. He had a flash: all the guys down at Metro waving goodbye, *So long, Vern . . . Can we use those Marlins tickets . . .*

He flailed about with his arms reflexively, but it was useless: All he could grab was air. So this was it. No chance to get his papers tidied up, no putting in one last call to his brother in California, and who would take back the videotapes in his apartment, already two days late and he hadn't stayed awake through either one of the goddamned things.

They were staggering backward now, he and his assailant, guy wanting to get him back in the shadows, finish the job, leave his body in the burned-out shell. Pinwheels and skyrockets exploding before Driscoll's eyes now. *Wheeeeee!!! Whoooaaa!!!* Real Fourth of July stuff, Driscoll thought, feeling his legs still mince-stepping beneath him, but something else crowding into his brain too, a feeling that he had grown heavy, off balance, *Sure, dumbshit, that's why they call it "dead" weight,* but maybe that meant he was a little heavy for whoever was holding him, surely having to support most of his weight now.

Why had he been so careless? Why hadn't he gone inside for his piece? Why had he gone over to the burn site in the first place? He could have missed this party altogether . . .

. . . thirty years on the force and no gunshot wounds, no knife zippers, just a couple bottles over the head and his nose punched sideways a few times, he retires and look what happens, some piss-wad takes him out in a breeze.

Driscoll felt a little of the pain go away in a sudden surge of anger, anger directed as much at himself as the guy who was killing him . . . and he willed—no other way to put it, without question *willed*—his feet to keep on moving backward, urging them both backward, picking up the pace, in fact: one step, another, a bigger one, a bigger one yet . . .

He felt himself gaining leverage now, the two of them hurtling along, and all he could hope was that they were going where he hoped they were, hoping that at least that something—*anything*—would get in their way. He felt the walk under his feet then, one solid foothold, then his heel hooking over the edge, and he shoved with all he had left, was either going to accomplish something or kick himself free, right off the planet . . .

And felt a satisfying crunch as they hurtled into the side of the apartment building. They made a sandwich momentarily: Driscoll, the guy on his back, the scorched stuccoed side of the building. Driscoll heard a gasp as the breath went out of his attacker and took a momentary satisfaction in being way, way overweight—*that's what two-fifty feels like, friend.* In the same instant, the grip at his throat was gone, and he could breathe again.

He reached over his shoulder automatically, caught a fistful of shirt and hair, leaned forward, and threw. The same jujitsu moves he'd learned in Korea. Forty years later, and still going. There'd been a karate craze down at the Department a few years ago, and they'd tried to force Driscoll into the class. He'd had to throw half a dozen Japanese guys through the walls before they'd left him alone.

The guy who'd been trying to kill him was writhing on the ground in front of him now, his face covered by some kind of ski mask. He didn't seem like he was going anywhere, but Driscoll wasn't taking chances. He dropped down, pinned the guy's chest with his knee, and snatched off the mask.

"Jesus H. Christ," Driscoll said when he was finally able to talk. This was some kind of night, all right.

It was Tommy's face staring pathetically up at him in the moonlight. His guileless eyes were wide, his mouth popping soundlessly open and shut as he tried to get his own breath back.

"What in the *hell* are you doing?" Driscoll said, and then remembered to ease the pressure on the poor guy's chest.

"You thought I was that same one, the guy tried to do you in the alley at work? Is that it?" He popped a beer, put it on the kitchen table, slid it across to Tommy.

Tommy fumbled for the can, nearly missed it, ended up sloshing suds into his lap. He sniffed the can, shook his head, pushed it back across the table at Driscoll.

"Drink the goddamned thing," Driscoll said. "Maybe it'll do you some good."

Tommy gave him a look, picked up the beer, sipped cautiously at it. "Wow pend?" he said. He was pointing outside, puzzled.

"Wow pend?" Driscoll repeated. He turned to follow Tommy's gesture.

"Wow pend," he said again.

It was like hearing Deal's little girl jabber, trying to interpret what she wanted. Suddenly a light went on. He turned back to Tommy. "What happened? Is that what you said?"

Tommy nodded vigorously.

"When you tried to kill me, you mean?"

Tommy stared at him. His mouth twisted up and he put his hands awkwardly against his chest, a pained expression in his eyes. Driscoll had never gone in for charades, but as a cop he'd seen this one about a hundred million times: "Who, me?"

138

Driscoll wiped his hand across his face. He tried to imagine how they dealt with this guy down at the restaurant where he worked: "Here's how we grill a burger, Tommy. No, no. Don't put your hand on the grill. It's the meat patty. That's right. . . . "

He rearranged his features, started over again. "Tommy, I'm coming home a minute ago. I park my car. I get out. I think I see something moving around in the other apartment, the one that's burned. I walk up to see." Driscoll paused. "You with me so far?"

Tommy nodded, a guy eager to please.

"Then you goddamn jump out of the shadows, put a move on me. You remember that?"

Tommy shook his head vehemently.

"You were choking me, you jerkwad. You were trying to fucking kill me and you don't remember??" Driscoll slammed his hand down on the table between them. Tommy's beer went over on its side. He tried to catch it, but only sent it into a worse spin. A band of foam shot across Driscoll's chest, more into his lap, before he could kick his chair back and stand.

"Jesus Christ," he growled, trying to brush himself clean. "What the hell is the matter with you . . . "

He glanced up at Tommy, feeling his own face glowing with anger. Then he stopped. Tommy had the empty can in his hands now, clutching it against his chest hard enough to mangle it. His face was beet red, twisted in anguish. "Sowry," he gasped, as big sobs racked his body. He looked like a kid who'd been scolded to the point of abject shame. "I'm *sowry.*"

Driscoll sighed, put his hand out to soothe him. "Tommy," he crooned. What was going on here? Tommy the killer? Tommy the baby? A two-hundred-pound, fifty-five-year-old baby? Driscoll felt the shudders beneath his heavy hand, and his weary heart gave.

"It's okay, Tommy," he murmured, trying to stanch Tommy's tears. "Come on. Cut it out. It's okay."

22

"I think he needs some help," Driscoll said.

Deal was busy at the ruined doorway, trying to get the hinges set in the battered frame without straining his aching ribs. He paused, looked up at Driscoll, who'd already removed the tape from his nose. It was true, Deal thought, Driscoll's nose did seem straighter. He set down his drill, took away the screws he'd been holding in his mouth.

Tommy was heading down the sidewalk, away from the building, spiffed up in T-shirt and jeans for work. He stopped to lean into the playpen Deal had set up under a ficus near the sidewalk. Isabel was in there playing with a crew of stuffed animals. Tommy poked her in the ribs and Isabel squealed happily. She jabbered at Tommy, who smiled and made gestures back at her. Isabel screamed with laughter. Tommy turned to Deal and Driscoll.

"Bipe," he called, waving.

"Bye, Tommy," Deal said.

Driscoll gave him a wave in return.

"You ought to keep your voice down," Deal said as Tommy moved out of earshot.

"As if he knows what I'm talking about," Driscoll said.

"Driscoll," Deal began, feeling pained. "If he's smart enough to do what you said he did, he's smart enough to understand."

"Wait a minute," Driscoll said, "you don't believe me? You think

140

this is my imagination, too? The numbskull tried to kill me. He put a first-class move on me and damn near pulled it off. You don't hear my voice? I sound like a frog."

Deal stared at him. "Driscoll, you've been on his case since he moved in. Maybe he finally snapped, decided to give you some of your shit back, I don't know."

"I'm telling you, the guy is goddamn dangerous. First he's telling me somebody tried to kill him at work . . . "

"At *work?*"

"Out in the alley." Driscoll waved at his disbelief. "Then he comes after me." Driscoll stopped. "You ever talk to his keepers? The ones who sent him over? Maybe he's a psycho."

"Come on . . . "

"Bullshit, come on. Do you know anything about this guy, really? For all you know, he's our firebug."

Driscoll stopped abruptly, as if the thought had just occurred to him in its speaking. Deal too felt stunned. He turned and stared off after Tommy, good old Tommy, whistling a cockeyed tune and waving hello and goodbye to things you couldn't see.

"You don't believe that, do you, Driscoll?" Deal's gaze was on Isabel now, Isabel playing nonchalantly in her crib. "Bah," she was saying. She bopped one animal over the head with another. "Bah bunny."

"Call HRS, that's all I'm telling you. They got shrinks on the payroll, they must have. Take the guy in, let 'em check his valves. Then you'll know. Know who you got living in your house, anyway."

Deal went over to the playpen, hefted Isabel up into his arms. He hugged her, breathing in the scent of her baby's tender skin, then turned to face Driscoll. He realized a faint sickness was gathering in the pit of his stomach, and he held Isabel even tighter.

"I can't believe Tommy is dangerous," he said, sensing how hollow his own words rang.

"Uh-huh," Driscoll snorted. "Jeffrey Dahmer's mama said the same damn thing."

They stood upwind at the edge of a broad canal that cut through the endless cane, Torreno and Coco Morales, along with Dagoberto Real and his men, all of them save for Coco dressed up like bankers, waiting for the signal from the state forestry offices for their private ceremony to begin.

Real was, in name, a partner of Coco's employer, a man whose name was often linked in print with Torreno's: For the record they were fellow businessmen and leaders of the expatriate community, united in their desire to lead their countrymen back home again. At least that was the public front. In private, Coco thought, matters were not so clear-cut.

Coco studied the two with Real carefully. Although they wore coats and ties and were intended to appear as businessmen, he knew they performed the same function for their master as he did for his. He knew also that they had measured him as he was now measuring them. After all, anything might happen. At any time.

There was a shrill ring, and Torreno removed a folding telephone from his breast pocket. He listened a moment, nodded, then turned to the group of dark-skinned men standing a hundred feet downwind, at the edge of the rustling cane field. Torreno, who might have allowed a momentary smile, motioned with his arm, and one of the workers picked up a strange-looking can. The worker struck a match and the snout of the can blossomed into flame.

The others stood back as the man tilted the can and began to stride quickly along the edge of the canebrake, dispensing bright burning gobs of fuel oil as he went. One of the field workers followed along, a machete beating time idly at his side. The Jamaicans called the big knives "collins," or "bills," and while they were the principal tools of the harvest, this man would not be cutting cane tonight. He had his eye out for the things that might come bolting out of the brush, especially the snakes. Coco was glad to be where he was, with but two creatures to keep his eyes on, and those two of small threat, he had already decided.

Real's men were nudging each other excitedly as the flames grew, their eyes sparkling in the reflection. Fools, Coco thought. The sort who amused themselves with matches as children.

"If the wind turns, we'll have to jump in the canal," Torreno said, his own grin reflecting the glow of the flames.

Dagoberto Real, dapper in a double-breasted suit that lay like a silk glove about his shoulders, glanced at the water as if it was the last possibility in his mind. They had scarcely stepped down from the Jeep that had brought them to witness the burn when he had stopped to wipe the muck dust from his shoes with a handkerchief. Coco was surprised the man had not ordered one of his bodyguards to do it.

The flames were climbing high into the twenty-foot stalks now, crackling and snapping with heat's own voice. The sky was suddenly alive with birds swirling in the updrafts, drawn to the clouds of insects fleeing the fire. Coco saw a gull wheel and dive straight into the flames, rise again with something struggling in its beak. He heard a shrill scream and turned to see a flurry of movement near the group of workers with the firepot.

A flock of rabbits had burst out of the flaming underbrush and darted about in a panic, caught between the men before them and the flames at their back. One of the creatures sprouted fire from its fur. It fell to its side and made a frantic, scrabbling circle in the dust, its screams louder now. Coco saw the worker raise his long blade, bring it down, and the screaming stopped.

Closer by, a creature that might have been a dog emerged from a screen of tall grass, trotted forward a few paces, then stopped. A gray fox, not a dozen yards away.

Coco looked to see if the others had noticed, but the two bodyguards still had their eyes fixed on the fire, and Torreno and Real were engaged in intense conversation, leaning close together over the roar of the flames.

The fox, who must have grown fat on a diet of rabbits, his coat sleek in the glow of the fire, gave Coco a last, disinterested look, then padded quickly down the bank of the canal. It paused, tested the water with a paw, cast a backward glance at the fire, and dove. The fox paddled rapidly across the canal, head held high at the front of a spreading V. It emerged on the far bank, shook itself once, and disappeared into the gloom.

Although the fire had advanced a good hundred yards into the cane, the heat had grown intense. Coco felt sweat trickling down his armpits, saw Real pull out his handkerchief again, this time to pat down his face.

Torreno's face glowed like a foundry master's. He swept his arm at the wall of flames. Sparks and embers were shooting up from the twisting cane stalks, dancing past the egrets and gulls like fireworks. Black smoke had spread like a giant thunderhead high into an otherwise crystal evening sky. The group with the firepot was nearly lost in the distance now, their silhouettes seeming to drag the sheet of flames along into the night.

"Magnificent," Torreno called. "Is it not magnificent?"

Coco, rarely given to enthusiasm, found himself nodding in agreement.

"Hot," said Dagoberto Real, mopping at his face and heading back toward the waiting Jeep. "Damned hot, is what I'd call it."

Torreno and Coco shared a look. Then Torreno shrugged and motioned everyone along.

"The fire burns away the leaves," Torreno was saying. "The men cut the stalks that are left." Miles away from the burn now, the group followed him through the door of the building that looked incongruous in the rural landscape, an ironworks, possibly, plucked out of an urban setting and dropped down in the middle of nowhere.

Coco flipped on a light switch, illuminating the cavernous interior. Looming boilers in a far corner, huge turbines crouched closer by. They walked on inside until they came to a railing. Below them lay a series of glowing pools connected by conveyor belts and heavy steel rollers placed here and there along an apparent processing route.

"The cane is piled and gathered, brought here by truck," Torreno continued, his voice echoing up to the vast corrugated ceiling. He nodded at Coco, who moved across the dusty concrete floor to a control panel nearby. Coco found the proper breaker switch, pulled sharply. A heavy rumble began, as much vibration as sound.

Torreno had to speak louder now. "The stalks are fed in through the hoppers over there," he pointed into one gloomy corner, "then go down the conveyors through the rollers."

Real stared without interest at the heavy manglers. Steel rollers like silos laid side to side, they whirled noisily, whining for something to crush.

"A few passes through those gears, and every atom of liquid has been driven out of the stalks, into the catch-basins you see," Torreno said, indicating the glowing pools. "After it is done, we burn the fiber that's left to help fire the boilers. Those power everything to begin with."

"A neat circle," Real said grudgingly. He had the look of a schoolboy being dragged through a field trip.

"Precisely," Torreno said. If he noticed Real's distaste, he was ignoring it. "The waste fiber was originally used to make a kind of wallboard, until they found that mice had an inordinate appetite for it. Now it is burned, the excess power sold off to the local electrical cooperative." He smiled at the efficiency of it.

"By the end of the week, this plant will be in full operation, twenty-four hours a day. It will not stop until the last stalk of cane is processed."

He motioned Real to a table near the switchbox, a place where workers might take lunch when the plant was operating. Real swiped a disapproving finger across a dusty chair bottom, brought his handkerchief out again before he sat.

"So," Torreno said, spreading his hands out on the wooden tabletop between them. "To our proposal. What are your thoughts?"

Real shrugged his shoulders. "Vicente," he began, as if it was painful, a pain he had endured many times. "We have had our differences . . . "

Torreno started to protest, but Real held him silent with his upraised palm. "And yet we have always managed to accommodate one another in the pursuit of a common goal."

Torreno held himself in check as Real continued. "But now,"

here Real's eyes flicked away, toward his two men, who loitered in the shadows, "this *sugar* business." He spat out the word, threw his hands up helplessly.

"We have here the opportunity of a lifetime," Torreno said.

"I have had my people look into this 'opportunity.'" Real withdrew a sheaf of papers from a breast pocket, donned a stylish pair of bifocals, and began to read. "You rely on a price of twenty-one cents per pound for a product that sells on the world market for roughly half of that. The present quotas restrict imports to something less than twelve percent of United States consumption.

"However," Real said, pausing for a glance at Torreno, "there is considerable political opposition to the maintenance of such protections. The Hemispherical Free Trade Agreement could allow the importation of sugar from Mexico, perhaps even from Cuba, into this country. The proposed General Agreement on Tariffs and Trade would end all agricultural price supports worldwide."

"This is all political talk," Torreno said dismissively.

"Also," Real continued, "as one of the largest holdings in this area, Florida Sugar is liable for a significant part of the proposed Everglades Restoration Project, estimated cost: four hundred million dollars, not to mention what might come in the future."

"We are already working on alternatives to that plan. . . . "

"It is an environmental nightmare that will only get worse," Real said. "And you are also a signatory to a negotiated settlement on behalf of the sugarcane workers of Florida in the amount of fifty-one million dollars. . . . "

"The attorneys have filed for an exception to that ruling . . . "

Real sighed, waved away Torreno's protest. He was about to read on but something seemed to stop him. He folded up his papers and leaned earnestly forward. "My question is this, Vicente: Have you lost your mind?"

For a moment, the only sound in the enormous room was the low-pitched rumble of the big rollers. The two men stared at one another across the dusty tabletop. It occurred to Coco that were he to pass his hand through the space that held their gaze, he would feel heat.

"There is risk in all things," Torreno said, breaking the silence at last.

"Vicente . . . " Real began, shaking his well-coiffed head. The aggrieved tone had returned to his voice.

"Hear me out," Torreno said, growing exasperated. Real glanced up, startled.

"You will forgive me for feeling strongly on the matter," Torreno continued, "but we are speaking here of something more than money, or of the petty politics of the Americans."

He reached across the table to grasp Real's shoulder. "My father grew the sugar, Dagoberto. The lifeblood of our island. He tended to those fields as if they were his children. He cared for his men, he saw to the welfare of their families."

He broke off, his eyes glittering, and pointed at Coco, who stood nearby, listening impassively. "That man there, for instance. He owes his life to my father."

The look that Real gave Coco did not suggest it was a matter of great concern to him. Torreno continued on, forcing his voice to calm. "He built schools, he built roads. He was a magnificent citizen. He was an *institution*.

"And for all this," Torreno said, "his reward was to be gutted like a pig, murdered by *comunista* shit while his own wife and child watched." Torreno slammed his hands on the table. The noise rang off the tin walls of the building.

"It is regrettable," Real said. He had found a thread to worry at a buttonhole of his fabulous suit, snapped it clean. He glanced up. "But this is no political rally, Vicente. I admire all your father did. And he was first and foremost a businessman. He would be the first to tell you: Do not base your investments upon emotion . . ."

"Nothing could be further from my intentions," Torreno interrupted. "I know this sugar. I am offering you an opportunity of unrivaled possibility."

Real shook his head. "And he would also say, 'Never throw good money after bad.'" He stared around the vast interior of the processing plant. "I understand your desire to become a sugar baron, Vicente. Though I wish you well, I think you are doomed."

Torreno shook his head. "You misread me. It is an opportunity for yourself and those who depend on us . . ."

Real held up his hand. He would hear no more. "Not a penny from me, not a penny from the funds we control. I could not in good conscience allow such a risk."

"The risk is already taken," Torreno said flatly.

Real stared at him, not certain he'd heard correctly.

"Others were interested. I was forced to act quickly," Torreno said.

"You have committed our funds?" Real was shaking his head in disbelief. He stared at Torreno, making sure he understood. "To what extent?"

Torreno shrugged. "Some twenty million."

Real shook his head, dazed. "That is everything. Every cent in the foundation treasury."

"And it will earn itself a hundred times over," Torreno said, his gaze hard now.

Real's face had turned scarlet. "This is outrageous. Unbelievable. You had no right, no authority . . . "

"What's done is done, Dagoberto. I am asking for your support. There is no need to publicize this matter. And one day, with your assurances, the others will not question my actions." He gave Real a significant look. "You must trust me. There are aspects of this arrangement which I cannot discuss. But, rest assured, there will be benefits for everyone involved. Unbelievable benefits." He paused. "I am prepared to share these with you, Dagoberto."

Real stared at him. "You would offer to bribe me?"

Torreno raised his hands in a gesture of acquiescence.

The two stared at one another, the quiet palpable once again. This time, Real broke the silence. "I am sorry, Vicente. You have placed yourself in a position of great financial strain, but it cannot excuse what you have done."

"It *is* done," Torreno repeated.

"It will be undone," Real said. "As you say, there are other suitors, American corporations seeking a tax loss. Let them preside over this doom." He rose, ready to go.

Torreno nodded. "You intend to inform the others then."

Real stared at him. "How can I help it?"

Torreno raised his hands in surrender. "And your desire to lead alone . . . that has nothing to do with your decision?"

Real seemed not to have heard the question. His face was expressionless. "I am sorry, Vicente."

"I am sorry too, Dagoberto." Torreno made a hopeless gesture with his hands.

Real turned to leave.

Then Torreno lunged, his heavy hands finding Real's throat.

The two bodyguards started forward. Coco stepped in, his hand flashing upward in an arc. One of the bodyguards stumbled backward, one hand still caught inside his coat where it fumbled for a pistol. His other hand clawed at a band of scarlet that had magically appeared above his collar. He tottered a moment, then fell, spraying blood, making the hacking noises of a dog with a bone caught in its throat.

In the same moment, Coco brought his hand down again, and the second man, who had glanced aside at his fallen partner, looked up in surprise. With Coco's motion, his face had been suddenly divided. It was like a drama mask: surprise on the half that could still respond, a sag toward the earth where the nerves no longer held.

His one good eye traced a scarlet line down his chest, on down to his belt, which now flapped open, neatly sliced in half. When he finally understood, his hands jerked up, clutching, as if he might join his stomach back together. His mouth opened, but instead of a question, there was only a bubble of blood. Coco stepped aside as he tumbled to the floor.

A few feet away, Torreno still struggled with Real. The two fell across the wooden table and disappeared for a moment. As Coco started forward, he heard the sound of a blow landing, a heavy grunt, and then saw Real rise up from behind the fallen table.

Real's eyes were bright with fear. He stared at Coco, at the blade in Coco's hand. He shoved the table forward and the heavy wood cracked into Coco's shins. Coco meant to dance away but felt his feet slipping in something. Then he was falling. He felt his hand strike the railing sharply, felt his knife fly from his hands.

Coco heard the rustling of feet near his head, threw his arms up in reflex. There was a stinging sensation at his arms suddenly, bright lines of pain crossing and recrossing his flesh. Something splashed on his face, into his eyes, blinding him. *The knife*, he thought. Real slashing at him with his own knife. The panicked strokes of an amateur. In a moment, Real would come to his senses and finish the job.

Coco drew his legs to his chest, rolled to his side, and kicked. He felt his heels dig into Real's chest, and thrust on with all his strength. There was a cry as Real fell backward.

Coco came up, wiping his own blood from his face. Real tottered for a moment, balanced upon the railing that separated the floor of the plant from the processing line. His arms windmilled once, twice, then flatted outward like angel's wings. He cried again and fell hard, half a dozen feet onto the clattering metal belt below.

Torreno pulled himself up from the toppled table, dragged himself to the railing beside Coco. Beneath them was Real, who had fallen onto the conveyor that fed the massive rollers' jaws. Real struggled to raise himself on one elbow, staring stupidly at the knife blade that seemed to sprout from his own ribs. He was twisting about, clawing at his back, trying to find the handle of the knife he'd fallen on, when the conveyor chattered, dipped, and abruptly tossed him down the chute.

Real might have felt something, at his foot, up his leg, down the whole length of him. But it happened in a motion so rapid, it was hard to comprehend what was happening. Was there pain, Coco wondered, or was such a thing beyond all sensation?

Real might have meant to call out. But if he did, the sound was swallowed in the growl of the machinery. The last Coco saw of him was his face—an instant's expression of utter surprise—then a glimpse of an outflung hand, wrist and palm bared, fingers extended as if in an aristocrat's wave—"Ah well, so be it . . . " Then the massive rollers growled again and gathered him in altogether.

The machinery still howled, though he was accustomed to it now. Coco righted the table and turned to inspect the floor once more. A smooth concrete surface, soon to be covered with dust, the ooze of sugar settling from the air, the clomping of a thousand filthy boots. He had wrapped bandages about the shallow cuts on his forearms, donned a fresh uniform shirt. There was pain, of course, but nothing of significance, nothing to what others had felt.

Below him, the conveyor carried stacks of cane toward the implacable rollers. Beyond, the catch-basins glimmered, pristine in the reflection of the few lights that remained. A furnace in the far corner roared, consuming the evening's waste. *The snake eats its tail*, Coco thought, *and the circle is closed.*

Torreno emerged from a workman's latrine, smoothing his suit, pressing his hair into place. *He will never see the inside of such a place again*, Coco thought.

Torreno glanced about and nodded approval of Coco's work. He actually seemed at ease.

"Those men in the fields," Coco offered. "They saw things."

Torreno shook his head. "Those men kill one another to come to this country, to work here. You could feed them to the rollers inch by inch. They would never talk."

"Others must know Real came here."

"Yes," Torreno said, giving him a look. "And come he did. And leave." He put his hand in his coat pocket and withdrew some documents. "He signed these papers. He congratulated us on our mission here. And left."

Torreno shook his head and gazed off into the distance, as if gathering strength after a great disappointment. "Our movement has many enemies, Coco. Perhaps Señor Real has gone into hiding, as is often required." He shrugged. "Or perhaps he *has* fallen prey to a misfortune. If that is so, we must all of us find the will to draw together and press on."

Torreno turned to Coco, his face as open as if they had not shared this evening together. Coco nodded. His employer had concluded the matter then. "In the name of the *revolución*," Coco said at last.

"In the name of the *revolución*," Torreno echoed. And led them toward the doors.

Deal sat in the waiting room, trying not to look at
the guy in the chair across the room from him. Short
guy, pockmarked face, good suit, leather clutch
briefcase. Deal had caught all that, as well as the
haunted look in the guy's eyes when he pushed the
call button to let one of the therapists know he'd
arrived.

Deal knew without looking that the guy was still
tearing at the ragged flesh around his fingernails—
he had been since he'd come in. He could hear the little nips of the
guy's teeth, the little grunts of satisfaction when a good-sized chunk
came free. He also knew the guy had his eyes on him, maybe trying
to figure out what Deal's problem was.

*Hmmmm, a fellow in checked shirt and jeans, tooled-leather
boots, retro cowboy with something of a tan, needing a haircut and
certainly a manicure—those nicked-up hands a disgrace—yes . . .*

Deal found himself sliding his hands out of sight beneath his
thighs, then stopped himself. Christ, sit in a shrink's office long
enough, you'd develop problems whether you had any or not. Guy
probably thought he was wearing lacy underwear beneath his work
clothes.

An inner door popped open then and they both looked up. It was
Dr. Goodwin there, beckoning to Deal. Deal got up. He couldn't help
but glance at the guy across the room. The guy was working hard on

152

one of his thumbs. When he saw Deal looking at him, he blushed furiously and turned his head away. Deal shook his head and followed Dr. Goodwin.

"I appreciate you doing this," Deal said as the door closed behind them. He was following the doctor down a long carpeted hallway. Plush fabric, thick padding, muted light from deco sconces along the walls.

Quite a contrast to the paint-peeling HRS clinic where he and Tommy had started off their day. There a young Pakistani doctor had listened impatiently to Deal's vague concerns, shined a light in Tommy's eyes, whacked him on the knee with a rubber hammer a couple of times, and sent them packing with a suggestion that they come back in a month to check that blood pressure again. Deal couldn't blame the overworked HRS doctor. The place was full of society's forlorn: pregnant mothers herding their squalling children, zombied-out street people with tubercular coughs and festering sores—it was a scene out of Delhi. Whatever might be troubling pleasantly addled Tommy, he was clean and disease-free, knocking back three squares a day, next patient, please.

Still, Deal had set aside his day, and on a hunch had called Dr. Plattner, the bluff physician in charge of Janice's case. Someone had been in to "see" Janice, Deal knew, but he didn't have the name, hoped Plattner could direct him. Plattner listened to Deal's story about Tommy for a few minutes, then made a call of his own and sent them along to Dr. Goodwin's clinic.

Dr. Goodwin stopped at one of the doorways and turned to wait for him. She was forty, maybe, maybe forty-five, a tall, handsome woman with a thick mane of sandy hair. He'd expected someone severe, someone in a lab coat and steel glasses who'd shunt his concerns about Tommy aside, get down to business about what he was contributing to his wife's mental welfare.

But there hadn't been a word about Janice. Dr. Goodwin had taken Tommy along and invited Deal to park himself in the waiting room, where he had read through two issues of *Elle* and one of *US* without encountering a single thought. Only the entrance of the nail-biter had interrupted the tedium.

Now Dr. Goodwin turned from the doorway and gave Deal a smile. "Thank Steve Plattner," she said in her nasal accent. At first he'd thought she was British. Now he suspected Australian. "He piqued my interest."

Deal glanced at Dr. Goodwin's ringless left hand. He could imagine this woman holding her own with Plattner, long weekends in the Keys: skeet shooting to start, fly-fishing for bonefish later, martinis at sunset. Doctors in love. He found himself wishing she *had* brought Janice up.

"Mind the chairs," she said. Had she noticed him staring at her? If so, she didn't let on. "It's a bit dark in here."

Deal stepped inside carefully. He blinked, his eyes adjusting to the dim light. It was an observation room, the only light coming from a window at the far end. The window allowed a view into another office, a comfortably furnished room where Tommy was sitting in an upholstered recliner chair, his eyes closed, his head resting on a cushion.

There was another woman in the room with Tommy, a younger woman with dark curling hair, wearing jeans and a polo shirt. She sat in a chair nearby and was in earnest conversation with Tommy, stopping every now and then to jot a note on a pad.

Deal had learned to read lips when he was a kid, something he'd undertaken on a whim. If he worked at it, he could still catch a phrase, especially if the context was clear, the speaker precise. He could catch some of the weather on a muted TV, read a coach reaming out an official. Once, at a fancy restaurant in the Gables, he had glanced across the room, watched the wife of the mayor smile sweetly, elegantly, and call her husband a pencil dick.

Now, even straining, he couldn't pick up anything through the glass. The light was dim, the woman spoke quickly, and as for Tommy, it was hard enough to decipher what he was saying if you could hear him. Deal thought he saw him form the word "mother," but it could just as well have been "mashed potatoes."

"Quite an interesting lad, your Tommy," Dr. Goodwin said. She'd come to join Deal. They stood before the window together.

"He feels quite terrible about what happened to your wife," she continued. "Guilty, in fact."

Deal turned to look at her.

"They can't see or hear us, you know. One-way glass. Soundproofed." Dr. Goodwin gestured through the window. She regarded Deal for a few moments. "I'm not certain it's appropriate for me to discuss Tommy with you," she said. "But under the circumstances . . . you *are* his personal representative . . . "

She trailed off, as if waiting for Deal's confirmation. Deal nodded slowly. Plattner must have done that, given him official status.

"Guilty?" Deal said. "Why would he feel guilty?"

Goodwin shrugged. "We were just talking with him, trying to ease him up a bit, chitchat, really, about his job, about you and what you've done for him—he's *very* grateful, you know—and then he burst out crying."

Deal glanced at Tommy, then back at Goodwin. He shook his head. "I'm not sure I'm following you, Doctor. Tommy ..." He broke off, searching for the right way to say it. "I mean, we communicate, but it's not exactly like conversation."

Goodwin nodded. "Yes, well, that's what I meant about *interesting*." She pointed through the glass. "We had the same problem at first, but then there was something about the look of frustration on his face, as if he had things to say that he just couldn't get out ..." She broke off and gave him her quiet smile. "We put him under, you see, and he's been chattering away like a house afire. . . . " She broke off again, clapping a hand to her mouth. "Good Lord. I didn't say that."

Deal stared at her. It took him a minute to figure out what she was talking about. "It doesn't matter," he said finally. Here was a therapist embarrassed by something she'd said? "What do you mean, 'put him under'? You drugged him?"

Goodwin was still coloring from her gaffe. She shook her head. "Hypnosis," she said, and pointed at the young woman in the other room with Tommy. "Dr. Craig, my associate, specializes in hypnotherapy. It can be an effective aid in working around certain dissociative disorders."

"Dissociative disorders? What are you talking about?"

"A defense mechanism," Dr. Goodwin said. "Doesn't matter what you call it. It's common enough. A patient may *want* to express something on one level, but then there's another part of the psyche that just won't cooperate." She stared at Deal as if she was wondering how intelligent he was. "Blocking," she said.

Deal had begun to revise his opinion of Dr. Goodwin. "Tommy's brain-damaged," he said. "He's been that way since birth."

"Whoever told you that?" Goodwin was staring at him in mild surprise.

"The people who sent him to me," he said. "At HRS." He felt a wash of doubt sweep over him suddenly, remembering the morning's visit to the clinic.

Goodwin raised her eyes skeptically. "I'd want to see his files, of course, but the perceptions of that man in there, skewed as they may be, are those of a thoroughly functioning adult."

Deal turned to stare at Tommy, who in fact did seem to be babbling along. In all the time he'd been living in the fourplex he hadn't strung more than a few words together at a time. Isabel had begun to outstrip him, in fact.

"I wouldn't rule out tissue trauma entirely, of course," Goodwin continued.

"Tommy?" Deal shook his head, trying to get Goodwin's drift. "You're saying Tommy's . . . " Deal broke off, picturing Driscoll there in the shadows, whirling his finger around his ear, rolling his eyes and making cuckoo noises.

Goodwin frowned. "Tommy is sick, yes indeed. Do I think his problems are psychological, yes again." She glanced in through the windows. Tommy's face had twisted up once more. He clutched the arms of his chair and began to toss his head back and forth.

"He's worked out a fairly vivid persecution scenario, Mr. Deal. He feels a great need to be punished. It's a bit early to say, but it's all in the paranoiac vein." She glanced at him. "Apparently, he has conflated your tragedy with his own need for punishment, which only exacerbates his feelings."

Deal shook his head.

"He's taken credit for any number of tragedies," Goodwin continued. "The assassinations of the Kennedys, Martin Luther King, the bombing at Lockerbie." She raised her eyebrows, her gaze on Tommy now. "He was describing the invasion of a Caribbean country when I left to bring you in." She turned to Deal with the hint of a smile on her face. "You seem to find this hard to digest, Mr. Deal."

"I can't," Deal said, stunned. Bad enough to think of Tommy barely able to cope, withstanding all the "look at the dufus" shit he'd have to take from the world, but to think that he had all these demons raging inside him as well? Deal felt a twinge of anguish, another of shame. Good old Tommy. Whistle a tune, Tommy. Deal had been as bad as anyone else, attributing happiness to this fractured man just because he had a job and a roof over his head.

"I can't digest it," he repeated. He turned to the doctor, choosing his words carefully. "About my house . . . " He broke off, tried again. "You said he felt guilty about what happened . . ." He paused again. "To Janice and all."

Goodwin nodded, waiting. She showed no reaction.

I'm just a bug, Deal thought. *A bug with a voice whose wife got scorched.* He bit back his anger and continued. "Did Tommy say he'd done something . . . "

"Start the fire, you mean?" Goodwin shook her head. "No, Mr. Deal. It's not that he claims to have *done* all these things, you see. He simply believes them to be his fault somehow."

"I don't follow you, Doctor."

"That's why it's so interesting," Goodwin repeated. "Most people limit the scope of the sins they take on to personal matters, 'I've ruined the lives of my wife, my father, my family,' that sort of thing. Tommy seems to have taken on the sins of an entire nation."

She leaned forward, flipped a switch on a console beneath the one-way window. "Let's just have a listen, shall we?"

Tommy's voice drifted eerily into the room then, the same child-like tones Deal was familiar with, but the words clearly formed now, the sentences halting but coherent, and cohesive, and somehow impossible:

". . . good guy, Charley. He was coming up out of the water onto the beach. I'm thinking, hurry, Charley. Hurry into the jungle. And the other guys, a dozen guys, they're still in there, in the ALC, picking up their gear." Tommy's face twisted.

"Go on, Tommy" came the soothing voice of the therapist.

After a moment, he found his voice. "He just flew apart," Tommy said. "Charley. Like blew up. Never saw that. A tank round, I don't know. Hit him and he blew up. A ball of fire where he was a second before. I saw his arms, both of them flying through the air, that's all. The noise. The noise was awful. Because the planes were coming then. Shooting. They all blew up. All of them. They said captured, but it didn't happen. Every one of them, blown up. In pieces. In the water." He clutched the rails of the chair and gave a wail that seemed to shake the glass between them.

The therapist in the room dropped her pad and jumped up to soothe Tommy, who was thrashing in his chair. He was trying to get up, but Deal saw them now, for the first time, thin rubber straps across his chest, others at his knees. The restraints held him down, but his arm snapped out, catching the therapist, sending her flying over a coffee table.

Dr. Goodwin shoved past Deal, found a key at a ring on her belt, unlocked a door into the observation room. She jerked it open, slammed the door shut behind her before Deal could move. Tommy was still thrashing in his chair, threatening to send it toppling. Dr. Goodwin urged her colleague up, urged her toward Tommy's flailing arm. They were all struggling like people caught in an awful windstorm.

Goodwin reached into the pocket of her lab coat, pulled out a hypodermic syringe, uncapped it with her teeth, and jammed it into Tommy's flesh. She injected the contents and pulled the needle out, tossed it aside. The two women held on grimly as Tommy's movements became gradually less violent, then calmed altogether. Deal watched it all, stunned. Tommy spouting *Back to Bataan* fantasies, suave and sophisticated Dr. Goodwin charging in there to sedate him, as practiced as a keeper out of *The Snake Pit*. He felt as if he were watching some impossible movie on a giant-screen TV.

He sagged into a chair behind him, watching dumbly as Dr. Goodwin checked Tommy's pulse and respiration, said something to her colleague, then turned and came back through the passage door to where he sat.

"I'm sorry," she said. She glanced back through the window. Her colleague was hooking up a blood pressure monitor to Tommy's arm. "He'll be all right." She straightened her coat. "I might have seen that coming. *Should've* seen it." She gave Deal a severe look, as if it had been his fault she'd been in there gabbing.

Deal took a deep breath, glanced at Tommy, who seemed to be sleeping blissfully now. He looked like a guy who'd come home from the factory, crashed in the middle of *Cheers*.

Deal found himself shaking his head again. "Where does he *get* all that stuff," he wondered aloud.

Goodwin sat down heavily in a chair beside him. He'd been talking to himself, but she seemed to take him seriously. She sat quietly for a moment, then turned to him. "It's our culture, Mr. Deal. It's all around us. You don't like your president, you shoot him. A man offends you because of his skin color, you beat him to death." She gave him a wan smile. "'Turning and turning in the widening gyre/The falcon cannot hear the falconer . . .'" She broke off, sat back in her chair. "It's a wonder more of us don't buckle under the weight."

She'd been quoting Yeats. One of the few poems he'd understood, back in the days of literature class. College. Another life, of course. Another dimension. The one where life made sense and poems didn't. Deal felt himself revising his opinion of the doctor yet again.

"What can you do for him?" Deal said.

Dr. Goodwin gave him a look. "Help him," she said firmly. "It will take time. But we will help him."

Deal nodded. He would have to ask the question again now. He hated himself for it, but he thought of Janice, and of Driscoll and his cold eye, and so he asked again. "Could he be dangerous? Could he do something?"

"To himself?" Goodwin said. She paused. "It's quite possible." She gave Deal a thoughtful look. "To others? It's very doubtful. He blames *himself* for things, Mr. Deal. Not other people."

Deal glanced back through the heavy glass. Tommy stirred in his sleep, licked his lips, formed a childish smile on his face. Dreaming, Deal thought. Back to being good old Tommy, having a little lie-down, and a happy dream.

Deal found himself wondering what Dr. Goodwin had shot him up with, and, momentarily, if she might be willing to share a little of her stash. He could use a couple weeks of sugarplums and toy soldiers himself. Then he sighed, shook himself, and got up to go.

Driscoll piloted the white Ford down US 1, past the University of Miami, where the elevated Metrorail train whisked past him going the other way. Something he'd have to take a ride on, one of these days. Something a retired old fart should be doing.

He drove on through South Miami, then swung west, out Kendall Drive, past the Dadeland Shopping Mall, its lots bursting at 2:00 P.M., a Thursday, middle of a recession, or so they said.

Apparently no one had told the throngs piling into the mall. He shook his head, pulling around a long line waiting to turn into the parking lots. Driscoll had never been to Dadeland, not to shop, that is. He'd had a few calls there, once had to chase a purse snatcher through an indoor fountain, ruin a good pair of shoes, but he couldn't imagine shopping there. The immensity of the place overloaded his circuits, made him sleepy. Besides, all those things to buy, how could you ever choose?

Some people liked that, lots of glitter, lots of action. Driscoll preferred quiet and grubby. When he needed something, he went to Gabby's, an outlet store in West Miami, a place that sold stock overruns and discontinued items of every stripe: clothes, small appliances, even canned goods. You had to be careful the pants you bought had the pockets sewn in, check the expiration date on the canned hams, but it was quiet and dimly lit, and the shoppers pawed silently through the bins like numbed survivors of disaster.

On top of that, the prices were right. He'd been going to Gabby's for years, had even outfitted the new apartment with things from there, including the first piece of art he'd ever bought: a big painting of a zebra running across a plain, which he had hung over his sofa, first thing you saw when you walked in, $49.95, frame included.

He liked the zebra painting a lot, even if the animal seemed a bit too big, too sleek, too graceful-looking when you really studied it. That was one thing about living alone. If Marie were still around, he'd have had to settle for a seascape or still life or something. At the very least, he'd have had to hear about how his zebra looked like a horse with stripes, bunch of shit like that.

Now, with her in California, living with her sister, he could do exactly as he pleased, she could too. He'd given her all the furniture—good riddance to a lot of floral-printed rubbish—and he had let her sell the house and keep the equity. She'd also taken the good car, a three-year-old Chevy wagon. Never mind it was Marie leaving *him*. He'd kept the Taurus—long since stolen—his books, his collection of 78s, and his less than glorious pension fund: Sayonara, Marie, it was a great twenty-eight years and write if you get work.

He hung a left in front of a wall of oncoming traffic—more people headed for Dadeland, he supposed—ignoring the blasts of horns behind him as he bounced across the low storm curb and entered the long curving driveway of Presbyterian Hospital. Thirty years on the force, catch you later, guys. Twenty-eight years with Marie, ciao baybee. A lot of change when you thought about it. And, none of it having been his idea in the first place, he did his best not to think about it.

He took it easy up the drive, a half-mile or more, enjoying the look of the place, more like a Venetian palace than a hospital, big rust-colored towers and clay-tiled roofs poking up into the blue sky, a sizable pond off to the right surrounded by rangy malaeluca trees and an exercise path that was full of people doing just that: young women jogging in spandex, old codgers walking determinedly, a stroke victim struggling along in a walker.

It made Driscoll tired just looking at it. He tried to imagine jogging, getting himself up in a pair of bike pants (as if they made them that big), trailing along after one of those skinny butts. He imagined the engine of his body, all the chambers getting the news. Organs: "Jesus Christ, what's going on?" Brain: "Batten down the hatches, men, lardass is *jogging*!"

He could see it, every blood vessel in his body, rigid as old PVC tubing, suddenly sloughing off God knows what kind of crud in the surge created by actual exercise. All that stuff would slosh up to his heart, if he was lucky he'd get in half a lap around the pond before he keeled over, be dead before they could gurney him the hundred yards to the emergency entrance.

Still, he needed to make some kind of effort at regrouping, didn't he? He'd made exactly zilch progress on his big postretirement plan of opening his own investigative agency. He'd reneged on his promise to himself to move out to a place near the beach. He'd seen exactly one Marlins game with the season pass the guys had given him at his going-away party. Pitiful.

He'd seen it in plenty of ex-cops before him, the life-implodes-upon-you syndrome: All those big talkers, full of plans, "just wait 'til I'm out of this place, I'm going fishing, hunting, golfing every fucking day . . . " and three years later they're sitting at home alone, wife long gone, sick of being around a guy so batshit crazy he can't get out of his pajamas before it's time to go back to bed, sitting there alone at the kitchen table with a bottle of store-brand booze, and forget the ice—shit, forget the glass—spinning the old .38 around in circles on the Formica, waiting to see if it comes up pointing at you . . .

Driscoll wiped at a sheen of sweat on his face, guided the Ford up to the curb near the entrance, killed the motor, and got out. So maybe that was why he was running around, poking his nose into Deal's business, trying to make something where there really wasn't anything, because he could look down the barrel of the future and see his mouth closing around the opposite end. Elementary, my dear Driscoll, elementary.

"'Scuse me?"

The voice brought Driscoll out of his reverie. He realized he was already at the entryway of the building. The rent-a-cop who patrolled the front was staring at him as if he'd said something. Driscoll wondered if he'd been muttering to himself as he walked.

"Nothing," Driscoll said. He flashed a shield, a joke badge that said HONORARY MIAMI VICE COP—SONNY CROCKETT, CHIEF if you were given the time to read it, another going-away present from the gang. "The car okay there?"

"Sure," the rent-a-cop said. Even if he had any doubts about the badge, one look at the white Ford, another at Driscoll himself, the rent-a-cop put them aside.

It was the same at the reception desk, again with the records clerk. "Marielena Marquez," the clerk repeated after a glance at the badge, already punching the name into her computer. She was in her twenties, a perky young woman with dark, frizzed-up hair and an ingenuous smile, like maybe she hadn't been fried one bit poking around in computer records from nine to five, five days a week. Watching her pound the keys, the color high in her cheeks, her tongue poking out of her frosty lips, Driscoll found himself wishing he were twenty years younger.

"Lots of Marquezes," she said. "Would you believe it?" She glanced at him, smiling. Driscoll found himself with an irrational urge to weep. It was just a young woman being nice to him. Lord, he would have to get a grip.

She was back to her screen before he had thought of anything to say. "Here it is," she said cheerily. "Marquez, Marielena."

She smiled and swung the monitor around so he could see. She pointed. "Checked out ten days ago, Blue Cross/Blue Shield, copayment by check, missed an appointment with therapy last week."

Driscoll nodded his thanks. "I don't see an address there," he said.

She nodded, spun the monitor back, tapped some keys, squinted at the screen, hit another key. A printer sprang to life, whined a couple lines of type, chinked out a sheet of paper that the clerk handed to him with her open smile. "What else?" she said, ready to please.

Driscoll had to smile. He stood, folded the address away, patted her on the shoulder. "Sweetie, if you only knew," he said.

She stared at him. For a moment he thought he'd offended her.

"And thanks," he added, going out. He felt her gaze on him all the way to the door.

He had the computer printout in one hand, the wheel of the Ford in the other, was poking along halfway down the block checking house numbers before it hit him. "Jesus Christ," he said, gliding the Ford to a stop.

He got out, walked around the front of the car, went across the sidewalk, stopped at a little strip of raggedy grass. He stared out over the faded police ribbon at the place where a house had once been. A fairly substantial house, to judge by the size of the property, and by what was left of the foundations. A fairly impressive house, to judge by its neighbors. But why hadn't he thought to check the address that clerk had given him, anyway? Some cop. He'd driven all the way back across the city, mooning about some girl thirty years his junior, thinking he was going to Ms. Marquez's house, to find himself staring at the ruins of the bombed-out museum.

He ducked under the plastic ribbon, walked closer. A broad stone entryway led up five steps into nothingness. A few feet away, another set of steps led down into what had once been a basement. A basement. That was a rarity in Miami, he thought.

He glanced around. This side of the street seemed to be elevated. Most likely he was standing on a coral ridge, an ancient deposit of shells and sea life, one of many that criss-crossed this city where everything had once been under water. The ridges, seldom more than a few feet high, gave the landscape what little variation there was.

The rear of the property was a tangle of ficus and underbrush that hid the waters of Biscayne Bay not more than a hundred yards away. Once the water had covered the spot where he stood, had covered most of Florida, for that matter. He was tempted to think of that as a better time, nothing but sun and tide—but even then there had been little fish and big fish, he thought.

He walked around the basement and found some shade under a big poinciana tree. Or what was left of one. The side of the tree away from the building still had most of its limbs. The other half had been sheared away by the force of the blast. He caught a glimpse of something shining in the dirt at his feet, bent down to check.

It was a shard of wood, half-buried. He caught the edge, pulled, brought up a foot-long chunk of gilt picture frame. He dusted it clean on his pantleg, had another look. One edge smooth, elegantly curved, glinting in the sunlight, the other a series of jagged splinters. He stood, hefting the wood, trying to comprehend. What had it been like, anyway, when it happened? One moment you're walking along with a bunch of nice people, drink in hand, looking at all the pretty paintings, the next instant a bomb goes off, you're flying through the middle of Hell. And all because somebody doesn't like your politics? Not even *your* politics. The politics of the guy who runs the country where the guy lived who painted one of the pretty paintings.

He tossed the fragment into the quagmire of shattered boards and brick and muck where a wonderful house had once been and turned to go. Then stopped short. There was a face staring at him, over a hedge that separated one side of the museum property from one of the neighboring estates. An Hispanic guy in a battered straw hat, his leathery face a map of wrinkles stubbled with a grizzled beard, watery blue eyes that stared at him for a moment more and then disappeared.

"*Momento*," Driscoll called. "*Momentito!*" A bit louder. He found himself ready to run after the guy, but where would he run *to?* The thick hedge stretched unbroken for a city block in either direction. By the time he got around, the guy could have gone anywhere.

Then the old guy appeared, coming around the other side of the poinciana tree. "You are wanting something?"

Driscoll craned his neck, trying to see around the tree. "How'd you get over here?"

The old man followed his gaze and shrugged. "Walking," he said.

Driscoll still hadn't spotted any gap in the hedge. He gave up, flashed his phony badge. The old guy barely glanced at it. Apparently Sonny Crockett was as good as any other cop. The old guy waved a gnarled hand over the ruined lot. "Bad business, eh?"

Driscoll looked at him. "Bad all right," he said. The guy might have been seventy, might have been eighty, his skin a relief map in bronze. "You here when it happened?"

The old guy stared out at the rubble. "I was in my country. On one vacation."

Driscoll gave the guy another look. "Not Cuba?"

The old guy shook his head. "I am from Zacatecas," he said solemnly. "In Mexico," he added.

Driscoll tried to imagine the guy flying on a plane, but the image didn't work somehow. How long would it take to go to Mexico by bus, about a month and a half? "You're a long way from home, pardner."

The old guy nodded. Driscoll pocketed his shield, was ready to pack it in. He'd go down to City-County, see if he could pick up another address for Ms. Marquez, maybe something on the tax records.

The old guy was rooted to his spot, however. Apparently he'd come to talk. "You don't see this kind of things in Mexico," the old guy said.

Driscoll followed his gaze at the rubble. "Yeah?" he said. "Why not?"

The old guy gave him a grin. "Too tired," he said. "Everybody too tired."

Driscoll smiled back, gave him a clap on the shoulder. It felt like he'd struck a gnarly fence post covered by a work shirt. "Well, you take it easy, Pop."

The old guy gave him a look, the same one he'd used on Driscoll's phony badge. "The lady," he said. "She is better?"

Driscoll hesitated. "Ms. Marquez?"

The old guy nodded.

Driscoll shrugged. "I guess so. She's out of the hospital. She must be."

The old guy considered it. "At home?" he asked.

Driscoll had taken a step toward the car, but stopped. He turned back to the old guy. "Yeah," he said. "She went home. You wouldn't happen to know where she lives, would you?"

The old guy nodded.

"You *do* know where she lives?"

He nodded again. Driscoll took out a pad. "Well, that's good, because I need to talk to her." He found a pencil stub in his jacket pocket. "You want to tell me where it is?"

"Maybe she does not want to talk to you."

Driscoll looked up at the guy in surprise. "I'm trying to help her. Find out who did this."

The old guy shrugged. "Maybe she does not want to talk to you anyway."

Driscoll took a breath. What was he going to do? Lean on an eighty-year-old guy? Offer him a sawbuck? Somehow he didn't think it would work. He certainly couldn't threaten to take him downtown for questioning. He glanced back at the neatly trimmed hedge, at the jungly estate on the other side of it.

"You do yard work over there?"

"I am a gardener."

"You work other places?"

The guy pursed his lips. It meant it would be considered.

"How about Ms. Marquez here? You ever cut her grass? At her house, I mean."

The guy shrugged. Driscoll took it to mean that he had.

"Well, how'd you like to take a look at my place? I could use somebody every couple of weeks."

The same shrug.

"Of course, I'd have to have a reference, talk to somebody you worked for, right?"

Lips pursed *and* the shrug this time.

In the end, Driscoll got the address, but not before he'd written out careful directions for the guy to Deal's fourplex, made an appointment for Saturday morning. What the hell, he thought as he got back into the Ford. Tommy could always use a little help with the groundskeeping.

The house was a mile or so away, a modest Mediterranean bungalow a block or two from the Venetian Pool in Coral Gables, its lawn and flowerbeds immaculate. Don Pedro, as he had made himself known, was obviously an able gardener, no matter how old he was.

Driscoll drove past slowly, noted the empty carport, parked under a big ficus tree in front of a neighbor's house. As he was moving up the front walk, he saw a lamp snap off inside.

There was a brass knocker in the shape of a lion's head on the wood door and the thing echoed mightily when he clapped it, then clapped it again. He noticed a sweet fragrance, glanced down at a flowering bush by the steps: little white flowers. He made a note to ask Don Pedro about it. They could use something to cover up the smell of charred wood up at Deal's place.

He heard the sound of a door closing somewhere and waited, but there were no footsteps. He backed down from the entry and hurried around to the drive that led under the carport, just in time to collide with a nervous-looking woman in a white housekeeper's dress.

"*Jesucristo,*" the woman said, backpedaling. She had a string bag hooked at her elbow. Driscoll saw a pair of slippers inside, some folded clothes.

"Sorry," he said. "I'm looking for Señorita Marquez."

The woman glanced over her shoulder as if she were considering a dash for the backyard. There was a high chain-link fence there blocking access to the neighbors' yard. A pair of Dobermans had appeared on the other side and had begun to bark furiously.

"Is she inside?" Driscoll said, producing his shield.

The woman turned a shade paler and shook her head. "Es no home!"

"Where is she? When's she coming back?"

"Es gone, *no se.*"

"Uh-huh," Driscoll said, thinking about it. *"Habla inglés?"* he asked.

"No," the woman said, shaking her head vehemently. "No *inglés.*"

"Geez, that's too bad," he said finally. "Cuz now we'll have to go down to the immigration office, find somebody to translate." He smiled affably at the woman. *"Tu sabes? Immigración?"*

The woman's terrorized expression fell away and was replaced instantly by a sullen glare. She hiked her bag up in front of her body like a shield. "What do you want with me?" she asked, her English impeccable.

Driscoll nodded at the bag she was clutching. "I'd like to talk to Señorita Marquez," he said.

"She already talked to the police," the woman said.

"I'm not a policeman," Driscoll said.

The woman glanced out at the white Ford, then back at him.

"What are you then?"

"A friend," he said.

She studied him, still suspicious. "Don Pedro sent me," he added. And with that, she followed him to the car.

Her directions took them north, into a shabby neighborhood a couple of blocks from the intersection of 79th and Biscayne. "Here," she said, pointing to a two-story block building on a corner.

There was a sign painted there, advertising a botanic shop, an herbal medicine store, along with a big mural of what Driscoll supposed was a lady saint: She was depicted wearing a kind of habit with a white cloak, carrying a torch, a Bible, and an urn of some sort. There was a placid-looking dragon that looked more like an alligator curled at her feet. Saint Alligatrix, he decided.

He followed the housekeeper out of the car and past the windows of the shop, where herbs of unknowable types hung upside down in great fan-shaped clumps. Two guys in ball caps had been standing down the curb near the hood of a decrepit Chevy discussing something in earnest Spanish; they took one look at Driscoll, glanced back at the Ford, and clammed up instantaneously. They couldn't have looked more guilty if they'd have been wearing ARREST ME signs around their necks.

The woman shooed a couple of kids away from a paint-peeling entranceway and started up a flight of steps. She hadn't bothered to check to see if he was following, but when they reached the landing at the top, she turned and held her hand up.

"Wait," she said. She turned the lock on an iron gate, then two more deadbolts on an inner door, slammed both shut after her.

Driscoll stood in the hallway, trying to calculate what the heat might be in the dark, airless space. A hundred? Hundred and ten?

Sweat was trickling down his armpits. He could be home drinking beer. Furthermore, *home* could have been an apartment in Hallandale, close enough to get an ocean breeze, with an easy drive over to Joe Robbie Stadium, where he could be making use of those Marlins tickets. Instead, he'd moved into Little Havana, had nearly gotten himself fried to a crisp, and now was dragging ass over the whole of Dade County, chasing phantoms, and for what?

"*¿Por qué?*" he heard one of the kids at the bottom of the stairs whisper. He glanced down at them, a boy and a girl, maybe five, giggling, pointing up at the big gringo standing on the steps. *¿Por qué?* What *was* he doing here?

He could tell himself that it was just the luck of the draw, that this was just the way things had worked out, of course. But a part of him knew that wasn't true. The truth was, he'd probably worked it out this way on purpose.

He'd felt pushed out of the department, not only because he'd reached retirement, but because he'd felt like he hadn't belonged anymore. Most of his contemporaries had long since retired, or gone off to softer jobs in small towns upstate. And he detested the new hold-the-fort attitude that had come in with all the new faces over the years: He'd been a cop long enough to know that the streets were never going to be swept clean, of course, but he and his contemporaries had rarely been so brazen about the matter.

In Driscoll's book, you at least aspired to make a difference. The way it was now, what most of the guys aspired to was not to look bad, put in the time until something better came along. You could blame it all on the overwhelming rise of crime, on the amount of drugs on the street, on the flood of immigrants into their part of the country, on the failure of the economy and the decline of social services in general, you could blame it on a million things, but what it all came down to was accommodation. Driscoll suspected you could plop yourself down in almost any big city at any given moment of history, look around the streets, listen to the pundits, you could convince yourself, "Hey, the world's going to hell in a handcart."

Then you could make your choice: try to do something about the situation or find a convenient excuse and accommodate yourself to it. The only thing was, these days most everybody down at City-County seemed to be an accommodator, and that left Driscoll, still behaving as if he could make a difference, feeling pretty much like a dinosaur.

The city manager buys his suits for pennies on the dollar from a well-known fence? Hey, Vern, chill out. Everybody loves a bargain. A commissioner gets picked up smoking crack with a hustler in a South Beach flophouse? Yo, Dris, we all gotta kick back once in a while. Somebody's blowing up museums and travel agencies that do business with Cuba? Well, Detective Driscoll, we have to understand the passions of the dispossessed, don't we? If there were a thousand crimes being committed at that very moment, there were a thousand pleas to cop. Driscoll could feel his blood pressure building, forced himself to calm.

Face facts, Driscoll. You may have left the department, but you're still a dinosaur. Maybe there's a comet coming, got a bead drawn on Dade County, on your fat ass, going to blow you to kingdom come with all the other dinosaurs, but never mind, you're not going anywhere. You're going to hang around your turf, because it's your turf, and retirement or not, you're going to keep on doing what you've always done, and now that you've got a sniff of something, your tiny brain is fixed on finding it. . . .

His thoughts broke off as footsteps sounded inside the apartment. In a moment the locks on the inner door clacked open and the woman in white reappeared, opening the gate, ushering him in dourly. The air inside was still close, stirred only a bit by an ancient window-unit air conditioner at the far end of the living room, but it felt icy in comparison to the heat on the landing. Driscoll opened his mouth to say something, but the woman had already turned, with a brusque motion for him to follow her.

She took him down a narrow hallway, the uneven floorboards creaking as they went. The building suddenly felt lopsided to Driscoll, as if the whole second story had been added as an afterthought by a weekend carpenter and was now teetering, about to collapse and dump them down into the *botanica* below. Just the heat, he supposed, but he had to put out a hand to steady himself as he trailed along after his guide. A chunk of flaking wallpaper came off in his fingers.

She stopped abruptly and flung open a door. Driscoll went past her, crumpling the wallpaper out of sight, suppressing an absurd nudge of guilt.

The door slammed behind him and he glanced about, fighting the sensation that he'd been lured into a trap. The room was cool and dimly lit, the only window obscured by a yellow blind that had been pulled down and that was now rustling in the breeze from another wall-unit air conditioner.

There was a single bed pushed into a corner, a nightstand with a pitcher of water, a vase with some drooping flowers beside it. A figure was propped up against some pillows there, a woman, her dark hair spilling down over her nightgown. Driscoll couldn't really see if she was awake, but he sensed eyes upon him.

"Miss Marquez?" he said. His voice sounded loud in the tiny space.

He thought he saw a nod. He walked closer, his eyes adjusting to the light.

Her face was puffy and taut, her eyebrows and lashes gone, the skin ruddy and scaling. Her eyes followed him eerily, like the lidless gaze of a snake.

"I'm Vernon Driscoll," he said. He didn't bother to produce the phony shield.

"You're with the police."

It was a statement, not a question. Though her voice was faint, he heard the caution there. He shook his head. "I'm retired," he said. "I'm a private detective now."

He surprised himself, saying it. All these months telling himself he had to get busy, file the forms, rent an office, get his act together, and suddenly he'd just cut through the crap, appointed himself.

He put his hand on the back of a wooden chair by the nightstand. "You mind if I sit down?"

She nodded at the chair, closed her eyes briefly. As he sat, he scanned her face again. There had been real beauty there once. Would be again, in time.

"Margaria says you have threatened her, Mr. Driscoll." The voice was still soft, but Driscoll found himself offering an apologetic shrug.

"I wanted to ask you some questions," he said.

She shook her head gently against her pillows. "I've already spoken to the police. I saw nothing, I know nothing, I cannot be of help."

Driscoll nodded, letting the silence take them for a moment. He glanced about the room. Other than a crucifix above the bed, the walls were bare. He got a glimpse of a couple of nightgowns on hangers inside a tiny closet, saw a suitcase and the bag that Maria had been carrying as she left the Gables house on the floor inside. Despite the wheezing of the air conditioner, the air carried a scent of mustiness, a decay that seemed to emanate from the walls themselves.

"You're afraid, Miss Marquez," Driscoll said. "That's why you're hiding out here. I'd be afraid, too, after what happened."

She was silent. He tried another tack. "The thing is, somebody's got to find out who did it, see they're brought to justice . . ."

She laughed then, a short, barking sound. The victim's laugh, the one that comes when you find out who the joke's really on. Driscoll had heard it plenty of times before.

He leaned forward in his chair, working his hands together. His fingers felt stiff and awkward. "You see, why I'm here, some friends of mine were hurt pretty bad. In an accident . . ." He broke off, correcting himself. ". . . in an *incident* that had some similarities to what took place at the museum . . ."

"An accident," she said, almost dreamily. Her gaze was on the ceiling now. "That's what I have been telling myself it was." She turned and smiled bitterly at him. "A terrible accident. But one which I will survive."

She held up her hand between them, palm toward her face. Driscoll saw a thumb, a forefinger, the skin swollen and flaking like that of her face. Gauze covered the stumps where the rest of her fingers had been. "I am going to go away from here, Mr. Driscoll. And put this behind me and pray that I never have an accident again."

Her eyes found his, burning. After a moment she rolled back on her pillows, her gaze on the ceiling again.

"Does the name John Deal mean anything to you?" he asked after a moment. There was no response. "Or Janice Deal?"

172

She lay quietly, staring at the ceiling as if he weren't there. "They'd been to your place the day of the explosion," he persisted.

Her eyes flickered at that.

"Maybe you ran into them . . . "

"Mr. Driscoll, I do not know these people. I have never met them. If they were guests of the museum, I can only be happy they were not there when the others were killed. Now leave me alone, please." Her gaze had not left the ceiling.

"Maybe they saw something while they were there, who knows. Something that could have put them in danger . . . "

She turned on him then, her eyes flashing. "Then ask *them*, Mr. Driscoll. Ask *them* what they saw!"

He shrugged. "The missus," he said. "She's still in the hospital. Burned over most of her body."

Her gaze faltered and he nodded at her. "But her face got it the worst. They're not quite sure how that's going to come out. . . . "

She fell back on her pillows, uttering a cry. Anger, frustration, pain, all of it mixed together in a peal that brought Margaria to the door in alarm.

"*Señorita?*" Margaria called.

Miss Marquez lifted her hand, waved at Margaria in dismissal. "Nothing. I turned in the wrong way."

Margaria gave Driscoll a suspicious glance and edged back down the hall. Driscoll listened to the boards signaling her departure, then continued.

"My friends," he said. "They're not mixed up in international politics. They're just average people. He builds houses. She's interested in art. They've got a little girl. . . . "

"It wasn't the paintings," she said, her voice flat and listless.

Driscoll glanced at her. Her gaze was back on the crumbling ceiling, but it wasn't defiant this time. She looked defeated, as if she were staring at something in the pattern of water stains that made her infinitely sad.

"Excuse me?" Driscoll said.

"The bombing," she said. "Everyone assumes it happened because of the paintings. Because of Sucrel, the young artist I had invited to this country." She paused then, biting her lower lip.

"You think it wasn't," he said cautiously.

"That is correct," she said. "At first I thought it was all about the paintings, too." She paused then, still staring deeply into the pale brown swirls above her. For a moment he thought he had lost her, but then she turned to him. He thought he saw tears forming in her eyes.

"I try to understand them," she said, her voice fervent. "I *try*. My own parents were driven from their homeland. I understand the outrage. I understand the dream of return." She fell back on her pillows, the tears flowing freely now. "But these things that some of these people *do*."

Her voice had risen dangerously and Driscoll nodded in what he hoped was a reassuring way. He'd done some checking on Ms. Marquez. Her father had been an international trader, a man smart enough to see Fidel coming. He had maintained foreign accounts for years, had cashed in his Cuban holdings and sent the money out months before Castro and his forces descended like apocalyptic weather from the mountains. It occurred to him that Ms. Marquez's views were tempered by the fact that she was sitting on a $100 million nest egg, but he kept the thought to himself.

"When a group of people is so violently wronged," she said, her voice intense, "you would think they would understand. That they would never do such things themselves. Would you not?" She turned to him, her eyes beseeching.

"You'd like to think so," he said. "But then you go out on a thousand domestic abuse calls, some guy beating the crap out of his wife and kids, you come to find out he's just doing what his daddy taught him to do, when he beat the crap out of *him*."

He shrugged, turned away. He should be encouraging her, not making her feel stupid, but he couldn't help it. Maybe he was getting tired.

People were stupid, that's what he'd found himself thinking. Creatures about a minute and a half removed from the jungle, cosmically speaking. You can't count on reason, logic, or judgment. The best you could do was to find somebody to love, hang on tight, hope you could find cover when the shitstorm hit. He found his thoughts wandering back to the fresh-faced clerk at Presbyterian Hospital. Say she was twenty-eight. Sure, Driscoll, what's thirty years' difference? Time she gets to be your age, you'll be crowding ninety. Jesus.

He shook his head, came out of his reverie to find Ms. Marquez staring at him.

"You were saying you didn't think the bombing had anything to do with the painter you brought in," he said. His brain felt fuzzy. The words were coming automatically, out of the part of him that had coaxed victims and witnesses to talk since before he could remember.

"I think it was because of the book," she said.

He glanced at her. "The book?"

He'd had a reasonably thorough chat with various of his contacts in the department. A detective here, bomb-squad technician there, asking just enough of each to keep the collective guard down, getting just enough to piece things together: Sure, we know what type of device was used; yes, we suspect the group or groups responsible; no, we have no firm suspects, no arrests on the horizon; sure, the investigation continues, along with about six thousand other things we're looking into, Vern. Nobody had said anything about a book.

"What book are you referring to, Ms. Marquez?"

He was careful to keep his voice quiet and casual. Finally, as he had hoped, the dam broke. And as she began to talk, he reached into his pocket for his pad and pencil like the good detective he was. And then he began to write.

Deal circled the crowded visitors' parking lot of Coral Gables General Hospital twice before he gave up and parked on a grassy berm near the street. There was just enough room between two NO PARK-ING signs to angle the pickup in and still open his door wide enough to get out.

He stopped a moment to lock the toolbox that sat out in the bed, up against the cab, then hesitated when he noticed a shovel and pickax lying there. Both had picked up a patina of rust, rattling around exposed the past couple of weeks. Someone had managed to get roofing tar all over the handle of the pick and the thing looked welded to the bed liner. You'd probably need a pry bar to lift it up. If a person wanted the things that badly, they were welcome, he decided. For that matter, why not just leave the keys, let them take the tools, the whole damned truck?

A strange attitude, he had to admit. The truck was nearly new, a spanking candy-apple-colored machine that Janice had christened "Big Red" the day he brought it home, all excited about the bells and whistles he was hardly accustomed to in a work vehicle. They'd buckled Isabel's car seat inside, cranked up the air conditioning, the powerful stereo, and driven around for a couple of hours, just being together to celebrate getting the truck and Deal's landing the big Ter-rell renovation in the Grove, alternating the three cassette tapes he'd picked up on the way: Delbert McClinton and his raspy blues for Deal, Natalie Cole's ballads for Janice, Raffi for Isabel.

They'd ended up far out Tamiami Trail at The Pit, a down-home barbecue shack with a screened-in porch and a bunch of picnic tables scattered around outside. He and Janice had sat at one of the tables under a chickee hut, braving the mosquitoes, watching a stray rooster scratch in the dust, while Isabel dozed in the air-conditioned truck, the engine purring under its brush-barred nose a few feet away.

"It's not a good idea to leave her alone like that," Janice had said. She licked barbecue sauce from her fingers, stared thoughtfully through the windshield. The sun was no more than an orange band out over the Everglades, but Deal had switched the dome light on inside the truck. The interior glowed like some kind of jeweler's showcase. Isabel lay in her car seat, her eyes closed, her head lolled back, her hair dark against the white quilting. It *was* a jeweler's showcase, he remembered thinking.

"Jesus, Janice. She's six months old. She's buckled in. You could reach out and touch her." He smiled, swiped at a dot of sauce on her cheek. He'd had two beers, what seemed like five pounds of ribs and thin sliced pork, was working on his second round of key lime pie.

He had a new truck, a half-dozen good jobs lined up, a wife he loved, a baby girl. They were sitting on the edge of the Everglades on a night still too cool for the bugs to be out in force, listening to the tree frogs' chorus, watching the sun paint the sky in fiery streaks of orange and red. An occasional car or eighteen-wheeler hauled past out on the Trail, headed across the glades for Naples, or boring in toward the glow of Miami. He felt so good he ached.

"I know," Janice said. She gave him a wistful smile, took his hand, licked away the sauce he'd taken from her cheek. "But things happen, Deal."

Things happen. Sure. He was standing now in the afternoon sun, not six months later, alone, watching the heat ripple off the bright red hood of the truck. Things happen. They sure as shit did. Were a Scud missile to come piling into the parking lot at that very instant, blast Big Red and those tar-laden tools to kingdom come, Deal would not express surprise when he reached the pearly gates. "Things happen" is what he'd say.

"Hey, buddy," a voice called.

Deal turned. There was a city cop who had stepped out of a traffic scooter a dozen yards away, out on the street. The guy had been writing a ticket on a car nosed up to an expired meter by the curb.

"You can't park there," the cop said, gesturing with his ticket book. He wore aviator's sunglasses, his hair cropped short. His sleeves were so tight around his biceps, it looked like they'd been taken in after he got dressed. A weight lifter on traffic patrol.

Deal still hadn't spoken.

"You can't park on the grass in Coral Gables," the guy said. He was walking toward Deal now, working up his badass glare.

"There's no place else to park," Deal said.

"Well, you can't park there."

They both turned to look at the truck. The cop was beside him now and Deal put his hand on the cop's shoulder. The cop started, but Deal kept his hand there a moment, not really grasping, just making contact.

"I'm going to see my wife," he said. He patted the cop on the shoulder then and walked away, toward the looming hospital.

"I'll have to write you up," the cop called after him. His voice was somewhere between a warning and a whine.

"Things happen," Deal said, nodding. But he was only talking to himself.

For a moment Deal thought he had wandered into the wrong room. He stopped in the doorway, glanced over his shoulder, then stared back at the person in the bed.

"It's me, Deal." It was Janice's voice, faint but unmistakable. "Don't look so surprised," she said.

He looked up and down the empty hallway again, then walked on inside. Some of the bandages that had wrapped her head and neck had been removed. Her face was still covered, and her ears, but they had left decent-sized openings for her eyes and nose and mouth. He could see her lips now, smooth-skinned and tender-looking, little stubble where her eyelashes were coming back, a shiny pink hint of skin at the bottom of her nose.

He came to the bed, took her outstretched hand. He ached to hold her in his arms, squeeze her with all his might. They had pulled the gauze away from the top of her head, revealing a sizable portion of scalp and a peach fuzz of hair growing in.

"You've got a crew cut," he said, nuzzling her fingertips. He thought he saw her lips curl into a smile.

"Sinead O'Connor has nothing on me," she said, her voice faint, straining to sound upbeat.

He felt her squeeze his hand. "When did all this happen?"

"This morning," she said. "Dr. Plattner changed the dressings himself. He cleaned me up, snipped away some of the underbrush. He said the danger of infection has passed. We're ready to begin the renovation work." Another squeeze as she continued, "I told him you had plenty of experience in that line of work, maybe he'd want to talk to you."

"That's great," he said. And it *did* seem great. Still, he felt a hesitation. Kicking out the walls of a house, tossing up a few partitions, that was one thing. This was another.

"We're going to take some skin off my bum," she said, her voice determined to sound cheerful. "and a little fatty tissue, see if we can fix my ears up. I told him he could take all the fatty tissue he wanted from down there. . . . "

Deal felt the tears rolling down his cheeks before he realized what was happening.

"Deal? What's wrong? I thought you'd be happy. . . . "

He was shaking his head. "I am happy," he said. "Jesus Christ, Janice. I *am*. It's just that . . . it just seems . . . I don't know . . . *unfair*, you having to go through all this, that's all." He had her hand at his cheek, felt the coolness of her skin. "I guess it just took me by surprise, seeing you."

"Well," she said, settling back on her pillows, "I'm the one who's supposed to be emotional. Buck up, buckaroo."

He laughed, gave her hand an answering squeeze. "You look great," he said.

"Let's not get carried away," she said. "Straightforward encouragement will do fine." She took a deep breath and let it out. When she spoke again, her voice sounded faint, as if she'd used up her store of energy. "How is Isabel?"

"Great," he said. "Mrs. Suarez buys her a toy every hour on the hour. She's starting to babble in Spanish."

"How do you tell what language someone's babbling in, Deal?"

He ignored her. "She wants to come see her mommy."

Janice nodded. "Mommy wants her to come."

"I'll talk to Plattner," Deal said. "I'll smuggle her in if I have to."

"That would be nice." He saw the smile come back again, briefly. "And you, Deal. How are *you* doing?"

"Great," he said, hating the forced sound of his voice. "I took some time off the Terrell job."

"That's probably good," she said. "You've had a lot to take care of."

He shrugged. "I want to get the fourplex fixed up." He paused, looked off toward the windows. Outside a crane was at work, swinging a heavy beam atop the skeleton of a new wing for the hospital. "I want to put it on the market. I don't want us moving back in there."

She made a sound in her throat, something like a laugh. "I remember a time when I couldn't get you to consider such a thing."

"Yeah," he said. "I know. But it's served its purpose. DealCo's back on track. We can afford something else. Besides, I want to get rid of the place. It's a jinx."

She held the sleeve of his shirt between her fingers. "I don't believe in jinxes, Deal."

"You were right in the first place, Janice. If I'd have sold the place like you wanted, none of this would have happened . . . "

"Stop it, Deal." Her voice was soft, but surprisingly authoritative. "You stop blaming yourself right this instant." She struggled to sit up straighter against her pillows. "You were right to finish the fourplex. If you had listened to me, there wouldn't be a DealCo anymore. You'd be working for someone else right now. I was just being selfish. I was big and fat and pregnant and worried about feathering the nest."

"All this apologizing is pretty disgusting" came a voice from behind them.

Deal turned to see Driscoll standing in the doorway. "I didn't mean to eavesdrop," the big man said. He jerked his thumb in the direction of the nurses' station. "I said I was Uncle Frank come all the way from Kansas. I don't know if they believed me but they told me I could come on back."

"Come in, Vernon," Janice said. "We were just voting on what my new nose should look like. Do you prefer aquiline or Roman?"

Driscoll shambled in, shrugging. "Just make sure they don't do Karl Malden," he said. He glanced at Deal, held something out in his hand.

Deal took it, puzzled.

"Caught one of the Gables uniforms puttin' it on your truck, son."

Deal shook his head, started to wad the ticket up.

"Better take a look," Driscoll said, pointing.

Deal glanced down at the envelope in his hand: It was a traffic ticket all right, but someone had written across the face of it, big block capitals in what looked like Magic Marker. "WARNING— YOU HAVE PARKED ILLEGALLY—FURTHER INFRACTIONS MAY RESULT IN PENALTY."

He stared at Driscoll. "A *warning* traffic ticket? I never heard of that."

Driscoll shrugged again. "That's Coral Gables for you." He turned to Janice, took in the new bandages, her stubbly scalp. "How you doing, little lady?"

She nodded. "Much better," she said. "Just weak . . . and awfully achy."

Driscoll nodded. "Well, I won't stay. I just wanted to say hi at you, tell you to come on home soon as you can."

"I will, Vernon," she said.

Driscoll looked as if he wanted to do something—hug her, pat her hand—but finally he backed off. He turned and gave Deal a nod. "I ran across something," he said. "I'll just wait for you outside if it's okay."

Deal nodded, surprised, then turned back to Janice as the big man walked out.

"What's that about?" she asked.

"Nothing," he said. "I don't know. He's got this idea it wasn't an accident . . . " He trailed off.

"What are you talking about, Deal?"

"The fire." He threw up his hands. "He thinks maybe somebody set it. He's been poking around."

"Deal?" Her voice had risen in alarm.

He took her hand again.

"Do you believe him? Is there some reason to?"

He shrugged again. "No. I don't know. It's just . . . " He knelt down by her. ". . . I think he feels just like I do, Janice. We'd like to be able to *do* something, you know. Set the world right, find a scape-goat . . . " As he spoke he felt the force of it inside him. If he *were* to find a focus for his outrage . . . he knew it was a fantasy, the concept of revenge, but still, the possibility tantalized him, teased him with its prospect.

She shook her head. "What good would that do?" she said softly.

He nodded glumly. "It wouldn't do any good," he said, and laid his cheek against her hand. "It'd just make some of us feel better."

"Oh, Deal," she said then, and began to stroke his head. "We just have to go on now, don't you see? We have to accept what's happened and go forward."

"Sure," he said. And let her stroke him until her hand went quiet and her breathing fell away into sleep.

Torreno flipped through the document quickly, then held it up, testing its weight in his hand. It *felt* substantial, promising everything that its language professed. He scanned the title page, noticed the official seal embossed in the lower corner: an eagle, a clutch of arrows in one talon, the familiar Latin inscribed across the ribbon in its hooked beak. That's what it was, he decided, rubbing the cover sheet between his thumb and forefinger: *money*. The document felt like money in his hands.

"Articles Pursuant to the Orderly Transition of Power," he said, reading some of the typescript aloud. Besides Coco, who sat in a distant corner, apparently intent upon a tiny television wired into his ear, there were two men in the office with him. One was one of the agricultural officials who had met with him at the restaurant in Belle Vista. The other was a heavyset man whose status had not been clearly defined.

Torreno noticed, however, that the man he knew was clearly deferential to the stranger. "Show him the paperwork, Claude," the big man had said, with scarcely a pleasantry beforehand, and Claude had practically torn the snaps off his briefcase to get the document out.

"A lot of what you'll see in there is boilerplate," the big man said now. "We've had to set up contingency plans in a number of areas:

casinos, banking, utilities. We can't trust that any of the existing infrastructure will be operational once we get that bearded asshole out of the palace, excuse my French." He gave Torreno a wisp of a smile.

"Because of the tariff and treaty implications, yours is a bit more complex, of course, but . . . " There was a dull thump from outside and he broke off then, glancing out the window that gave on to a view over the rear of Torreno's South Dade estate.

"What the fuck is that?" the big man said. Claude too stared over Torreno's shoulder, his face reflecting shock.

Torreno turned, saw what they were staring at. The creature had escaped from the fenced compound and made its way up to the house. It had leapt up onto the outer window ledge and now stood there on its haunches, pawing at the glass, its whiskered snout twitching inquisitively.

"Agouti," Torreno said, smiling as he swung his chair back to face them. "They are quite harmless."

"That's the biggest goddamned rat I ever saw," the big man said. Claude remained silent, but his face seemed pale.

Torreno shoved his chair backward, rapped sharply on the glass with his knuckles. The agouti sprang off the window ledge and scuttled away.

Torreno waved his hand toward the lake and the surrounding expanse of land in the distance. "It is a passion of mine, to collect certain species—many of them hunted and trapped to extinction in my country," he said. "I intend to reintroduce them to our island."

The big man lifted an eyebrow. "I was your island, I'd be happy to leave well enough alone on that score."

Torreno shrugged, reappraising this man. He was almost certainly an attorney, wore an expensive suit, had his hair expertly cut, his hands carefully manicured, and yet he spoke like a longshoreman. An unusual representative from the halls of power, to be sure.

"There are many more striking creatures on the grounds," Torreno said, nodding. He waved a hand at Coco, who stood up from his television watching, instantly alert. "I would be glad to show you about."

Claude's face showed alarm. The big man waved his hand. "Some other time, Mr. Torreno. We've got to get on back up north."

Torreno nodded. He made a gesture and Coco sank back into his chair. The sun was going down now, and the light in the room was dim. Coco's gaunt face reflected the flickering of the screen.

"So," the big man said, turning his attention back to the document, "what you'll find in there is more or less what you and Claude hammered out."

"More or less?" Torreno said.

The big man smiled again. "Don't worry, Mr. Torreno. You've got what amounts to a five-year monopoly on sugar production in Cuba and a guaranteed favored-nation status for your dealings with the U.S. and the European markets we control. As it makes clear in the document, this is to ensure an orderly transition to a free economy. We don't want any goddamned free-for-all down there once Castro's gone. We want to make sure we have a nice, well-managed, capitalistic country. After the five years is up, you'll be faced with a free-market system, of course."

"Of course," Torreno said.

"Though you'll certainly have a decided competitive advantage," Claude added.

The big man turned and stared at Claude. "I think the man can understand that for himself, Claude."

Claude ducked his head behind the lid of his briefcase and began fumbling with some papers. The big man turned back to Torreno. "I'm sure I don't have to tell you how sensitive these arrangements are, Mr. Torreno. It's not that much different from conducting biological weapons research. We all know it's necessary, but it's not the kind of thing we like to put in the public eye.

"Besides," he added with his phantom smile, "there are quite a few people in the sugar industry in this country would love to be in your shoes. If word on this issue were to get out, we'd have a mess on our hands. We don't need a lot of haggling. We're just trying to provide for a smooth process."

Torreno returned his smile, placing the document on his desk. The phrase did have a solid, reassuring ring to it. He would return to his country in a position he could scarcely have dreamed of only months before, before a certain friendly senator had explained these matters to him in exchange for an astronomical campaign contribution—the largest in the history of congressional politics, if his sources were to be believed. "We'd dearly love to involve a Spaniard in all this," the senator had drawled. "'Course they'd have to have an oar in the sugar industry in *this* country already," he'd added with a wink.

And now Torreno had his oars in, all right. He laid his palm flat across the papers and leaned toward the big man in a display of sincerity. "I am not only the holder of the largest block of sugar-producing land in this country, but I am also one of the few Hispanics involved in the industry. I find our agreement a testament to the political sensitivity of our leaders. You can trust my discretion."

The big man nodded. "I'll pass your sentiments along," he said. "Now you go ahead and give us your John Hancock, we'll get the papers back to Washington."

Torreno stared at him, uncertain, then glanced down at the document before him. "You'll provide me with a copy?" he asked.

The big man made a snorting sound at that. "Not just yet," he said, his affability wearing thin. "Once you indicate your agreement, everything is reviewed and countersigned at the top. You'll hear from us by and by."

Torreno shook his head, held up the document. "But I thought that was the purpose of this meeting, to confirm the arrangement."

The big man gave Claude his bemused look, glanced out the window again. When he turned back to Torreno, his smile had grown into something approaching true amusement. "It's confirmed, all right. It's just going to stay off the record. What did you think, Mr. Torreno? That the President was going to come down here and play with your agouti?"

Torreno felt himself flush. His gaze flickered away to Coco, whose face glittered and shifted in the light from his tiny set. If the man before him was not crucial to the fortune of a lifetime, they would go play with the agouti, all right. . . .

He flipped the document open, found the signature page, and withdrew his pen. When he had finished, he stared at the page for a moment, fixing the reality of it in his mind: his own name in bold script beside a blank line that would soon bear that of the President. One simple signature that would eventually catapult him to the very top.

He looked up at the big man then, closed the document, and slid it across the burnished surface of his desk, smiling. He would allow nothing to disturb him, to alter this course of events. Absolutely nothing.

The big man barely seemed to touch the document before Claude was tucking it into his briefcase. "There now," the big man said, nodding at the briefcase. "This'll all be taken care of inside a couple of weeks. Then all you'll have to do is wait for Uncle Fee-dell to come to his senses and step down."

Torreno lifted his eyebrows. "As you say, everything is just a matter of time."

The big man chuckled at that. He rose and motioned to Claude. "Let's get that chopper revved up."

As Claude made for the door, followed by Coco, the big man leaned forward and extended his hand. Torreno rose and took it.

The big man spoke quickly, in a voice too low for anyone else to hear. "You've got yourself a sweet, sweet deal, my friend." Torreno felt the pressure of the man's grip increase and he looked up into the intensity of his gaze. "Now don't you go and fuck it up."

Torreno stood with Coco at the fringe of the helicopter pad, watching the machine lift off into the darkening sky. The air was crystalline, the evening star already bright. He waited until the roar of the props had faded, until the warning lights of the craft were tiny dots beneath the star, then turned to take Coco's arm. "We have arrived at a most sensitive time, Coco."

Coco looked down at him, his eyes inquisitive, his gaunt face otherwise impassive. "We have unfinished business," Torreno continued. "Matters that, left untended, might disturb these most delicate negotiations."

He waved his hand in the direction of the departing helicopter. Coco nodded, following his gesture.

"That man," Coco said thoughtfully. "He is an important one, no?"

Torreno nodded.

"Still," Coco said. "I would like to have him."

Torreno patted him on the shoulder. "Forget that man," he said. "We have other things to deal with."

Coco nodded. The tiny earphones that connected him to his set bobbed at his neck like strange jewelry. Though his expression had not changed, Torreno saw the readiness in his pose. He would be happy to go back to work. Television and murder. It was surely a simpler life, having only two passions, Torreno thought.

The sound of the helicopter was gone now, replaced by the sounds of the nocturnal menagerie that surrounded them. The two of them stood that way for a while, listening as the howling grew.

Deal let Driscoll guide him across the hospital parking lot to the white Ford, which was parked, ticketless, on the grass beside the pickup. "Are you going to tell me what this is about?" he said.

"It's a long story," Driscoll said, motioning for him to get inside the car. He wiped at his brow with a handkerchief. Although the sun had fallen below the trees, the heat seemed to have only intensified. "Let's get in the air conditioning."

Deal got in and managed to get his seat belt fastened as Driscoll took them straight across the grass and over the curb onto the street.

"Is this an emergency?" Deal said, holding on to the door handle as they swerved onto Le Jeune Road.

Driscoll shrugged. "You go out the right way, you have to pay your parking tab."

Deal stared at him.

"Hey, I'm living on a pension now," Driscoll said. "I got to watch my cash flow."

"Maybe you need a wealthier client," Deal said.

"Hah. This is pro bono work, son. All for the public interest." He'd turned his attention to his driving.

Deal studied him for a moment. "You really must be desperate."

Driscoll didn't look at him. He blew his horn at an old woman about to shove a shopping cart across the intersection in front of them. "Old bat," Driscoll said as they sped past her. "Jaywalking, stealing a Publix cart." He glanced over finally, gave Deal a smile. "Crime rampant on the streets. How do you figure I'm desperate?"

"Where are we going, Vernon?"

"Answer a question with a question. This is a classic evasive technique. You trying to confuse me or something?"

"I'm trying to make a point. Tell me where we're going."

Driscoll sighed. "I talked to that Marquez woman. The one who ran the museum that got blown up."

Deal nodded. "I figured it would be something like that."

Driscoll shook his head, puzzled. "She checked out of the hospital against her doctor's advice, got herself a half-assed hideaway up in Little Haiti. She's so scared she's taking voodoo treatments rather than take care of herself properly."

"What's the bottom line here, Vernon?"

"She had an interesting theory about why they bombed her place."

"Let me guess," Deal said. "Castro did it himself, to discredit his enemies. Either him or little green men."

Driscoll pulled at the wheel suddenly, swerved over to the curb. He turned to Deal, ignoring the chorus of horns behind them. "Why don't you just tell me what's eating your butt?"

Deal stared back at him. "I appreciate your trying to help, Vernon. I really do. But I'm just not a conspiracy-theory type of guy. We had a bad accident, that's all. You've got me involved in Cuban politics somehow. What I know about Castro is this: that's the name on the daybed in your apartment—Castro Convertibles. Now if that ties me into your theory, I'd be glad to hear about it. Otherwise, I think it's time for me to stop brooding on what's past and get on with my life. That's the way it's supposed to work, Vernon. You spend a certain amount of time brooding and grieving, and then you have to go on with your life."

Driscoll took it all in, nodded calmly. They were still idling, blocking the right one-third of the busiest thoroughfare in Coral Gables. Someone in a Cadillac was behind them, leaning on a horn that played a four-note tune.

Driscoll motioned for the guy to pull around with his thumb, then turned back to Deal. "Interesting you should mention conspiracy theory, because the one I got for you is a lulu. Now I could either

190

try to explain it to you myself or I could take you right to the source."

"The source," Deal repeated. He felt weary, as if no matter how much time he spent explaining things to Driscoll, it would come to the same end.

"Well, the next thing to the source," Driscoll continued. "It seems that Ms. Marquez had a publishing venture tied into her other operations. She'd put out fancy catalogues for her shows, commission some academic to write a book on Latin American art, that kind of thing. She never expected to make any money off of it, but then that whole shebang was nothing but a money pit. She did it all out of the love of art." He waved his hand again, and the Cadillac finally pulled around them with a squeal of tires. Its windows were heavily smoked, its license plate and undercarriage outlined in glowing neon light.

Driscoll shook his head, watching the car speed away. "I remember a time you couldn't drive through the Gables in a car like that."

"I'm sure it was a better era," Deal said.

Driscoll turned back to him, his face bland. "You're upset, so I'm going to forgive you a lot of things," he said, continuing before Deal could respond. "Anyways, as things got busier down there at the gallery, she hired a guy to handle the publishing matters, which were mostly matters of course, so she could travel around, recruit new artists and all that."

Deal glanced out, trying to read the name of the cross street on the tombstonelike street marker nearby. Maybe he could just walk home from here. How long could it take? Forty-five minutes?

"Then one day she comes back from Brazil or wherever to find her new editor in her office hopping straight up and down, a big thick manuscript in his hands."

"I know this is going to come to something, Vernon."

"You're damn straight it is," he said. "It turns out this book is not the kind of thing they're used to publishing at all. But it's so hot, it's so tied into the very thing that motivates her to do the things she does, she feels like she's got to take the opportunity."

There was a screeching of brakes then, and Deal glanced back to see a step-van sliding to a halt behind them. "Jesus, Vernon. Can't we move?"

"In a second." He had pulled a little pad from his shirt pocket, was flipping through the pages. He held it up to the glaring lights of the step-van to see something, then went on, excited.

"This book, see, in addition to being a general diatribe against the politics of the expatriate Cuban community, has got some extremely incriminating stuff in it about the activities of the Patriots' Freedom Foundation and one of its honchos, Vicente Luis Torreno. According to the stuff in the book, Torreno is tied directly to most of the terrorist activity down here the past few years—which comes under the heading of things we always suspected. But what's new is, he's been skimming from the foundation coffers for years, trading on the fervor of his compadres to make himself a rich man. If that came out, we wouldn't have to prove he was guilty of murder; his own people would tear him to shreds."

"Who wrote this book?" Deal asked. He was watching out the windows over Driscoll's shoulder as a guy in a khaki uniform got down out of the step-van and approached the driver's side of the car.

"A guy name of Valles," Driscoll said. "He used to be a professor out at the state university until he got a bit too noisy about his ideas. They bumped him from the faculty a couple years ago, and he turned to writing his book."

The guy in the uniform was rapping on Driscoll's window with his knuckles. "What's wrong with you jerks?" the guy's voice drifted faintly through the glass. "You can't park here."

Driscoll gave a wry laugh. "How many times we heard that today?"

Deal shook his head. "Valles?" Why did the name sound familiar?

Driscoll nodded, satisfied that Deal was finally getting with the program. "He was one of the guys blown to smithereens at the museum that day . . . along with the editor, supposedly."

"Supposedly?"

"They found pieces of Valles. All they found of the editor was articles of clothing, some jewelry. The bomb squad figures that's because the publishing office was ground zero. The two of them— this Valles and the editor—were supposedly up there having a pow-wow when the thing went off."

Deal considered it. "Even so, all you have is the word of some dead crackpot who lost his job because of his theories, Vernon."

The guy from the step-van rammed the window with the palm of his hand hard enough to rock the car. Driscoll turned, cranked the window open a couple inches. "Go around me, asswipe. I have to come out there, I'll tear your arms off."

The guy stood staring openmouthed as Driscoll closed the window and turned back to Deal. "Ms. Marquez was worried about the same thing, but he showed her solid evidence."

"Such as?"

"Such as Valles's brother used to work as the accountant for the Patriots' Foundation."

"The crackpot's brother," Deal said.

"I'm supposed to be the hard-nosed cop," Driscoll said, waving him off. "The brother had plenty of records in his possession, according to Ms. Marquez. She had a chance to look at them before she gave her editor the go-ahead."

The guy in the khaki uniform was still standing in the street, his fists clenched, trying to decide what to do. A Coral Gables police cruiser passed by, heading the other way up Le Jeune. Deal saw its brake lights flare up, its flashers go on.

"And there was one other independent source of confirmation," Driscoll continued. "Valles had found some kind of spook—a guy from some version of the CIA—who'd been assigned to assist Torreno with his train-the-troops, let's-invade-Cuba projects. The government knew these incursions weren't going to amount to anything, but they'd thrown the Patriots' Foundation this spook as a kind of a sop—go help them shoot their guns in the Everglades, that sort of thing.

"But according to Valles, the guy was a burnout case. He figured out what Torreno was up to and realized he was in danger. He came to Valles with the story: Torreno's whole operation the last several years has turned into a sham, designed to keep the pot simmering between the U.S. and Cuba so Torreno can stay in place and profit off the proceeds to the cause of liberty.

"The last thing Torreno wants is normalization of relations between the U.S. and Cuba. But it doesn't have anything to do with politics, because he doesn't want Castro to fall either. That's the beauty of it, you see." Driscoll's face was glowing in the reflection of the dash lights.

The cruiser had found a break in the median and pulled up behind the step-van, its flashers whirling. A uniformed officer was getting out, heavy flashlight tucked under his arm like a baton. The guy in the khaki uniform looked relieved now that justice was about to prevail.

"Don't you see?" Driscoll went on, oblivious to the scene outside. "Torreno's like all the guys at the Pentagon were when they found out the Soviet Union was really in disarray. Once the rest of the world figures out the Cold War threat is empty, then they're out of a job, so they were busting their butts trying to convince us that we should still be scared to death. That's Torreno's scam. He comes on like Castro's worst nightmare, sends these boatloads of amateurs off to 'invade,' then tips the Cuban government off so nothing can get out of hand."

"That's crazy," Deal said.

"That's not what the CIA guy says."

"Who is he?" Deal said. "*Where* is he?"

Driscoll shrugged. "That I *don't* know." He threw up his hands.

The uniformed officer was approaching their car now. The guy in the khaki uniform was jabbering excitedly in his ear, but the cop was holding up his hand, waving him off. "Just hold on a second," Driscoll said. He turned and got out of the car, closing the door behind him. He flipped open his wallet, showed the cop something, then pointed at the guy in the khaki uniform and back at the Ford.

The cop nodded, unhinged his flashlight, and used it as a pointer for the guy in the khaki uniform, directing him back to his step-van. The guy made some protest, but the cop's jaw hardened, and the guy went along.

Driscoll turned and got back in the Ford, stopping to wave his thanks to the officer.

"I could call a tow truck if you want, Detective," the cop said.

"Thanks anyway," Driscoll said. "Just a vapor lock. She's all right now." He got in, slammed the door.

"The thing is, Valles is dead, the government spook is who knows where . . . "—Driscoll paused, grinning at him—". . . but I *do* know where Valles's brother is. And that's where I'm headed. You interested in coming, or not?"

Deal sighed. "I still don't see what all of this has to do with me, Driscoll."

Driscoll paused. "That's the part we're working on, Johnny." He put his meaty hand on Deal's arm. "It was the same people did your place and that art gallery. I get my hands on them, we'll find out the *why* of it."

Deal hesitated. He remembered Janice's hand on his cheek, her tired voice. She was right, wasn't she? What good would all this do, what purpose would be served, other than to cater to the whims of a retired cop who never got the bad guy he had traced for the last half of his career? So let Driscoll go off on his wild-goose chase. If something really came of it, Deal would find out. Meantime, he had to get up in the morning, he had jobs to resume. And still, something held him. That faint possibility, that slimmest of chances, if Driscoll was right, if he was on to something, if someone, never mind who, had done what had been done to Janice, to his family, to him, intentionally . . .

He turned to Driscoll then, nodding his head, as he had somehow known he would all along. "Let's go see this brother," he said, and felt his head rock back as Driscoll grinned and floored his Ford.

Driscoll took them through a maze of cross streets to a section of the Gables close to US 1. They cut down a narrow lane between two shuttered warehouses, pulled up before a row of shabby apartments done up in a false Tudor style. Some of the facing boards had warped, exposing crumbling plaster underneath, and most of the east-facing units featured aluminum foil in the windows to block out the morning sun. There was an old Chevrolet Vega parked in some knee-high grass just over the curb. A Gables address, all right, but a far cry from the likes of Ms. Marquez's digs.

Driscoll checked something on his little notepad and nodded at Deal. "This is it," he said, motioning Deal out.

Except for the hum of traffic drifting over from the highway, the area was quiet. Deal glanced at a sign hanging from one of the warehouse fences: PATROLLED BY ATTACK DOGS, it read, but there were no dogs in sight.

He looked at the apartment building again: six units, maybe more. But no cars at the curb, no TV or radio noise seeping out, no kids in the street or in the tiny, treeless yard at the side of the place. It didn't seem as if anyone had lived there for years. And who would want to, he mused. A gauntlet of warehouses to run on your way home, invisible attack dogs in your front yard, what looked like a lumber-storage compound in the back.

"Doesn't look too promising," Deal said.

Driscoll nodded. He checked the address again. "We *could* be getting the runaround," he said. "Let's find Unit Two."

They discovered an entryway in the middle of the building, a short gloomy hallway that gave on to an airless courtyard: There was a battered set of mailboxes recessed in the wall, all nameless, four paint-peeling doors downstairs, each odd-numbered, an iron staircase leading up. Ancient advertising circulars littered the corners of the courtyard.

Driscoll glanced at him. The air was stifling, the quiet intense. Deal thought he could hear the far-off sounds of locusts buzzing, but it hardly seemed likely in this barren neighborhood. "Nobody lives here, Vernon." Deal glanced back down the dark hallway. He felt a sudden wave of claustrophobia, a yearning to make a dash toward the dim square of light that marked the street.

Driscoll shrugged. "We've come this far." He turned and started up, his footsteps thudding on the metal treads.

Deal took one more look around the courtyard, feeling the hair rise on the back of his neck, then hurried after him. He found Driscoll at the top of the stairs, poised before a door that listed ajar. A brass "2" dangled sideways on the frame, hanging by a single tack. A doorknocker's ghost was outlined in old paint on the door front.

Driscoll held up a cautioning hand as Deal joined him. The ex-cop rapped on the door frame sharply with his knuckles, the sound jarring in the silence. There was no response.

Up there, the buzzing sound was louder. "You hear that?" Deal asked.

"What?"

"It sounds like locusts," Deal said, trying to home in on the source. "Or maybe radio static."

Driscoll shook his head. "My wife was always doing that," he said.

Deal stared at him blankly. "Doing what?"

"Hearing things I couldn't." Driscoll shrugged and lumbered on.

Deal searched the catwalk that connected the four top units. The others seemed similarly neglected. The skeleton of a potted ficus leaned by the doorway opposite. Deal was sure now that the place had been evacuated after the hurricane. There'd been probably been some major roof leakage and the tenants had taken the opportunity to find greener pastures. He and Driscoll were just wasting their time there.

And that noise. Whatever it was, the sound was giving Deal the creeps. He glanced over the railing, but the courtyard below was empty.

"Look here," Driscoll said, behind him.

Deal turned. Driscoll had nudged the door to Unit Two open with his toe. The door swung back, giving them a view into a darkened apartment. The buzzing sound was distinctly louder.

Deal peered in over Driscoll's shoulder, squinting. There was a clear zapping sound and a sudden flash of light.

Driscoll looked back at him, then reached inside, flipped a wall switch, but nothing happened. He flipped it again, and the same flash of light came again, accompanied by the angry snapping sound.

Driscoll reached into a pocket of his rumpled coat and withdrew a tiny flashlight that gave off a surprising amount of light. They stared down its beam at a hallway that was lined with books. Or had been.

The shelves were empty now, except for a volume tossed askew here and there. Most of the books had been swept to the floor where they lay in mounds, spines cracked, pages adrift. *The storm*, Deal found himself thinking. Just like the messes he'd seen in half a hundred homes ripped apart by the hurricane. But something was wrong there. There was no overwhelming smell of decay and mustiness, no stench of ruined carpet, spongy plasterboard, soggy furniture.

He bent down, picked up one of the books, ran his fingers across the dry pages. He heard the angry crackling noise again, glimpsed another pop of light.

"Lookit," Driscoll said, directing his attention with the little pocket flash.

Deal followed the beam down the hallway. There was an old floor lamp there, its bulb sputtering on and off. He got a glimpse of the rest of a living room as if in strobe flashes: upended furniture, shattered lamps, a wild swirl of papers tossed everywhere.

Driscoll moved past him, picking his way down the hall over the mounds of books. "Stay back," he whispered to Deal.

Deal waited a moment, then followed after the big man. They were in the tiny living room now, Driscoll's light sweeping the wreckage. Deal got a glimpse of the windows. Heavy red curtains tied back, yellowed blinds pulled down to the sills. No hurricane had torn this room apart. The sound he'd been hearing was distinct now, an angry buzz that waxed and waned with the sputtering light that the floor lamp threw.

Driscoll led them to a doorway off one side of the room, threw his light into a small bedroom. The wreckage there was similar. Clothes tossed from a closet, dresser drawers dumped, the mattress shredded.

"This is one lousy housekeeper," Driscoll said. He swung his light into a bathroom, where the medicine chest door dangled by one hinge, its shelves swept empty except for a blue box of Polident. Deal felt an unaccountable wave of sadness. Someone's common, everyday life, torn open before his eyes.

They picked their way back across the littered floor, and for a moment Deal thought they were on their way out. Then Driscoll veered off past the sputtering floor lamp and through another doorway.

"Mother of God!" the ex-cop called. He was backpedaling as Deal hurried after him, his big head cracking into Deal's chin. Deal staggered back, catching the door frame to steady himself.

"Holy mother of God!" Driscoll called again.

Deal stared over Driscoll's shoulder, holding his throbbing chin. The crackling noise was intense now. He blinked away the tears Driscoll's blow had put in his eyes . . . then stopped, stunned.

Driscoll's flashlight beam was fixed on a man tied to a kitchen chair. His head was thrown back, his tongue lolling out, his mouth twisted open in a gesture of agony. Someone had slashed the power cord from the air-conditioning unit above the Formica table, stripped away the insulation, twisted a foot of bare copper wire about each of the man's hands, then turned the electricity back on. Instead of flowing to the air conditioner, however, the power had surged into him. Thin skeins of smoke were still rising from his fingertips. His whole body seemed to tremble in time with the crackling and snapping sounds that filled the room.

"The box," Deal said numbly. "The goddamned fusebox."

Driscoll turned to him, uncomprehending. Deal snatched the flashlight from the big man's hands, swept the beam over the kitchen walls. He found it between a plaster crucifix and a cheap reproduction of the Adoration, its little gray door still waving open.

He ran across the room, glanced at the exposed electrical panel. An ancient one, full of fuses that glinted back at him like blind eyes. He reached out, hooked his finger into the bright ring of one main, yanked it free, then tore out the other.

The angry buzzing stopped. The man in the chair seemed to relax, his head lolling forward on his chest. For the first time, Deal became aware of the terrible smells in the room: the cloying sweetness of feces, the choking odor of burned flesh. He felt his stomach heave.

"Fucking A," Driscoll said, staring at the dead man.

Deal bit his lip, fighting the nausea, stumbled past Driscoll out of the tiny kitchen. He made his way down the narrow hallway, his feet plowing through drifts of books. It was like a bad dream. He was a kid again, fighting his way through snowdrifts, his feet leaden, while something terrible rushed up from the darkness at his back.

He made it to the railing outside the door of the apartment before he lost control and vomited into the courtyard below. He stayed bent over for a moment, rolling his forehead against the cool iron of the railing until Driscoll stepped out to join him. He straightened then, wiping his mouth on his sleeve. "Is that the guy we came to see?"

Driscoll nodded, held up a battered wallet. "Alberto Valles. Forty-two dollars, an Amoco card, a Discover card. I don't suppose that's what they were after." He turned back toward the apartment, let out a long breath. "The poor sonofabitch."

Deal stared after him for a moment. "I'm sorry, Vernon," he said.

Driscoll gave him a look. "What are *you* sorry about?"

"About not believing you," he said, gesturing at the open door of the apartment.

Driscoll shrugged. "You could've been right. I wasn't sure myself." He pointed inside with his thumb. "Until now."

Deal shook his head in disbelief. "He must have had *some* kind of proof."

Driscoll nodded. He bent down, picked up a copy of the *Aeneid* that had tumbled out onto the catwalk, riffled through the pages. "At least they thought he did." He tossed the book back into the clutter of the hallway. "Files, a copy of his brother's book, who knows?"

"Does anybody have a copy of this book?"

Driscoll shook his head. "Everything went up in the blast," he said. "That's what Ms. Marquez says."

There was a pause. Their eyes met.

"Where is she?" Deal said.

"In deep shit." Driscoll nodded.

And then they were pounding down the stairs.

**30** "Slow down, Driscoll. You're not a cop anymore," Deal said. He had to raise his voice over the roar of the Ford's engine. They were barreling down an I-95 exit ramp, then fishtailing eastbound onto 79th. An old black man, waiting to cross the street on a three-wheeled bike, stood staring as the Ford slid through the intersection. Deal's gaze locked on to the old man's for an instant. "Poor fools," the man's expression said, and there wasn't a chance to disagree.

"Yeah, there are certain benefits you miss," Driscoll said. He wrested the wheel to the left suddenly, roared past a half a block of stalled traffic, using the opposite lanes. He made it back onto their side, swerving away from an oncoming bread truck at the last moment.

"We're going to get pulled over." Deal was clutching the armrest, trying to keep himself upright. Driscoll slowed as they approached a red light, glanced to the left and right, then floored the accelerator.

Deal closed his eyes, steeling himself for impact—beer truck, eighteen-wheeler, speeding low-rider—but there was only a teeth-cracking jolt as they bottomed out in the crosswalk, on the far side of the intersection. He thought he heard a wail of sirens somewhere behind them but realized it was only the receding blare of horns.

There were a few more blurred blocks—a collage of liquor

stores, shuttered businesses, a peep show, a long stretch peppered by the gaping faces of men holding themselves up on parking meters—then a power-slide turn off the boulevard down a side street for several dark blocks, and a screeching double-parked stop in front of a *botanica,* deep in the heart of Little Haiti.

Something was going on inside the store, Deal saw as he piled out after Driscoll. Shelving had been pushed back to clear a space for folding chairs, all of which were full: matronly black women in checked dresses, fanning themselves; skinny old men in white shirts and dress pants, their eyes rheumy and glittering; children in T-shirts and shorts, some standing on their seats, others milling about. What room was left for standing was jammed as well, with people clapping, sweating, chanting in a frenzy. They were all staring at an extremely tall man at the front of the room shaking what looked like a feather duster over his head.

As he hurried after the lumbering Driscoll, who passed the brightly lit windows without a glance, Deal saw that the feather duster was in fact a rooster in the tall man's grasp. The tall man raised his other hand to the rooster's neck, made a slashing motion. The head of the thing fell away and a spray of blood splattered down on the shoulders of the tall man's white shirt. He began to swing the now headless bird back and forth, anointing the faithful at the front of the crowded room. Some kind of *santería* rite? Deal turned away, saw Driscoll disappearing into a stairwell up ahead.

By the time Deal reached the entryway, Driscoll was already at the top of the stairs, swinging an iron gate aside, hammering at a locked door there. Deal took the steps two at a time.

Driscoll pounded again, the blows echoing in the airless landing. The chanting from the *botanica* downstairs reached a sudden crescendo, and Deal wondered what they might be sacrificing now.

"Watch yourself," Driscoll said, bracing himself against the wall behind him.

Deal stepped aside as Driscoll strode forward, pistoning his big foot into the door. No contest there. The cheap frame splintered and the door flew inward, banging off the foyer wall. The sound was lost in the din of the faithful from below.

"Jesus, Vernon," Deal said, but Driscoll waved him quiet.

He had a gun in his hand now, was holding it by his ear as he went through the shattered doorway. He brought the pistol into firing position, as if he was ready to blaze away, then relaxed.

"Well, kiss my ass," Driscoll said, his face a mask of disgust.

Deal hesitated, then poked his head inside. The unshaded bulb on the landing threw a bright slice of light across the barren floor of the living room. No rug, no lamps, no furniture of any kind. Dust clumps drifted in the corners. You could see all the way into the alcove of a tiny kitchenette where a broken stool leaned in a corner.

Driscoll moved across the room, down a hallway. He had his flashlight out now. Deal followed cautiously after him. Driscoll checked an open door on his right, shook his head, moved on to a closed door on the left. He gave Deal a cautioning glance, then turned and eased the door open. He glanced quickly inside, drew back, battered the door all the way open with his foot.

The chanting from downstairs had stopped, leaving an eerie silence in the hallway. Driscoll holstered his pistol inside his coat and stepped into the bedroom doorway. Deal peered in after him, following the beam of the flashlight as it played over the deserted room. A streetlight outside threw angular shadows about the walls.

Driscoll shook his head in disgust. "She was right in here . . ." he began, then broke off. His eyes widened, and his hand scrabbled at his coat for his pistol. *Someone's there,* Deal heard his brain clamor, but it was too late to do anything about it.

He felt an arm clamp about his throat, felt his feet lift off the floor. He heard a muffled thud and a grunt from Driscoll, sensed others rushing past him in the darkness. He flailed his arms about, trying to reach his attacker, but it was useless. He struck out with his heel, felt a satisfying crack when he struck bone.

He was readying himself for another kick when there was an explosion of pain in his head, a brief, glorious burst of light behind his eyes, and, as he might have expected, a darkness that rushed up and swallowed everything.

"What you be messing around up here for, mahn?"

Deal heard the voice, but he couldn't be sure if the speaker was talking to him. He'd been lost in a swirling dream where giant roosters chased him about a series of barren rooms. They pecked at him, slamming their beaks into the walls and floors with the force of pile drivers, drawing great gouts of blood from the wood itself.

His head was splitting, as if one of the creatures had caught him flush behind the ear. He blinked his eyes open carefully, saw the tall *santería* priest looming above him. The rooster's blood had dried to a rusty brown on the man's shoulders.

"Why you be busting into a person's home?" The man spoke with a British islander's accent. His voice was soft, inquisitive, as if the question was rhetorical, more a complaint than a request for information. Deal felt hands on his arms, realized he was being held by two others. When he tried to turn, the tall man reached out, held his chin fast in a hand that was slender but surprisingly strong.

"You wanting to hurt the sistah, was you?" Again that melodic inflection, more wonder than accusation.

Deal shook his head, groggy. An unshaded bulb dangled behind the priest's head, burning like an angry sun. His throat felt swollen from the choke hold they'd laid on him earlier. "What sister?" he said, his voice strangled.

He had to cast his gaze down, his eyes tearing. He saw cartons with strange trademarks stamped on their sides, glimpsed a pile of flour bags bunkered against a wall. They must have dragged him into a storeroom of the *botanica.* He wondered if the congregation was still out there, waiting. Maybe he and Driscoll would be the final act.

He heard the sounds of a struggle somewhere behind him, heard a sharp cry. He twisted in the grip of the men who were holding him, saw Driscoll being hauled in through a doorway, trying to shake loose from two burly black men even bigger than the ex-cop. A third man tumbled against a stack of rice bags, clutching a foot Driscoll must have stomped on.

The priest gave Driscoll a glance as the big men subdued him, then turned back to Deal. "This mahn saying you a friend of the sistah, that so?" He shared a grin with the others. "Say you wanting to *help* her."

Deal swallowed, not sure his aching throat would cooperate. "A man was killed tonight," he managed. "We were worried about a woman who was staying here. We came to warn her."

"*Warn* her?" the priest said, as if the idea were miraculous. "Well, now. Come to *warn* the sistah."

"She was hiding a woman named Marquez," Deal said, insistent. "She could be in danger."

The tall man nodded thoughtfully. "The sistah say so. Say bad men maybe coming here. Maybe you do. Maybe that's why we got you now."

"We didn't come here to hurt anyone," Deal said, his anger rising. He struggled in the grasp of the men who held him, to no avail. He nodded at Driscoll. "This man used to be a police officer. . . . "

The priest's eyes lit up at that. He reached into the pocket of his shirt, produced a gold shield. He held it in front of Deal's nose. As Deal read the ridiculous inscription, the tall man withdrew Driscoll's pistol from his waistband with his other hand, tapped the phony badge with the stubby barrel. "Is looking like a policemahn, sure. But I don't think this is the real thing, sir, I do not."

"Jesus, Driscoll," Deal muttered.

"It's just a joke," Driscoll said.

"No," the priest said thoughtfully, still tapping the shield with the pistol. "I think it is not so funny."

"Where is she?" Driscoll demanded. "Where's Ms. Marquez?"

The priest lifted his delicate eyebrows. "Wherever that is, mahn, she is being safe now."

Deal saw the look in the priest's eyes. If Ms. Marquez had been hidden away by these people, he did not doubt that she was safe. And they could forget ever finding her. He had an image of himself and Driscoll traipsing house to house through nighttime Little Haiti. They wouldn't last an hour.

"We need to talk to her," Driscoll insisted. "My friend here was nearly killed by the same people who blew up Ms. Marquez's place. His wife was badly burned. She's still in the hospital. They have a baby." The priest gave him a thoughtful look. "They're in danger," Driscoll added. His voice had taken on an uncharacteristically pleading note. "Ms. Marquez is in danger too, and she has information that could help us."

The priest considered it. He turned to Deal. "That true, what he say?"

Deal nodded.

The priest glanced at one of the burly men holding Driscoll. "He the one come to the sistah before?" The burly man made a gesture with his eyes.

The priest nodded, thoughtful. Deal saw his own wallet materialize in his hand. The priest was staring at him now. "You John Deal, yeah? That your real name?"

"That's my real name," Deal said.

The priest turned to the man whose foot Driscoll had stomped on, said something in soft, guttural Creole. The man took Deal's wallet and another that must have been Driscoll's, then limped out of the room, giving Driscoll a surly look as he passed.

Deal turned to Driscoll, who did his best to shrug. "Shut up, you," said one of the burly men holding Driscoll. The other man stepped in, blocking Deal's view. The priest had sat down on a mound of flour sacks, his long arms crossed across his chest, his gaze drawn inward, waiting.

Deal chafed in the grip that held him, trying to understand. Perhaps it was true, all the things Driscoll had claimed about this supposed book, about Torreno and his Patriots' Foundation. If you were in such a position, it might motivate you to kill a few people. But Deal still couldn't figure out where *he* came in. Did walking through a museum constitute him as an enemy, a fellow traveler? Even granting Driscoll's most paranoiac view, he didn't see how that was possible.

Then something occurred to him. He was about to call out to Driscoll when the storeroom door opened and the man who'd taken the wallets limped back in. The priest conferred with the man in hushed Creole again. Finally he nodded and turned back to them, his face impassive.

"Okay, now," the priest announced. "We going for a little ride."

From the outside, the vehicle had resembled any other tradesman's van. There were crudely stenciled signs on the tailgate and sliding side door, advertising X-pert lawn service. A tiny flag—from some Caribbean island, Deal supposed—fluttered from the radio antenna.

Inside, however, things were hardly what he'd expected. Instead of holding a welter of rakes and lawn tools, the rear cabin had been converted to a limousine's layout, with a pair of broad, comfortably upholstered seats facing each other, a small table and a serving bar bolted to the floor in between. One wall held a bank of electronics gear, including a tiny television. The rear windows had been carpeted over and a glass barrier between the rear area and the driver's compartment had been treated with a reflective surface.

There were three men up there, Deal knew, including one carrying an automatic weapon who had supervised their loading. He imagined that the man was watching them now through the one-way glass, his Uzi at the ready.

Deal stared back at his own reflection, which looked pale and wavering in the soft chaser lights that flittered around the outline of the ceiling. He was sitting between the priest and one of the men who'd been holding him, a man with a weight lifter's body and the face of a divinity student. That man wore a suit and a tieless white shirt buttoned to the neck and kept his right hand hidden inside the vest of his coat.

Driscoll sat opposite, wedged between the two burly men who had held him captive inside the storeroom. He stared back at Deal expressionless, rocking with the steady motion of the van. "Did you ever think," Deal said, returning to the thought that had occurred to him inside the storeroom, "that it wasn't me at all? That maybe somebody could have been trying to take *you* out when they burned the apartment."

"Shut up, you," the man next to Driscoll said. Deal wondered if it was the only English he had learned.

The priest held up his hand. "Let them talk," he said.

Driscoll gave his customary shrug. "I considered it. But I didn't think much of the possibility," he said.

"Why not?" Deal persisted. "Maybe it was one of your old enemies, figured you were vulnerable, off the force and everything."

Driscoll shook his head. "Naw, the way things are in the department these days, they'd have had too many better opportunities when I was still around. Something happens when I go out on a call, it would've been an unfortunate accident in the line of duty. Sayonara, Vern." He glanced up at Deal. "I don't think it was me."

Deal nodded. It made sense, but still left him unsatisfied. Maybe that was the problem, trying to apply logic when the whole thing made no sense. Look where he was now, riding through the streets of Miami, the prisoner of some voodoo warlord. How did that stack up on the rationality index?

The van took a sudden turn, then slowed, jouncing over a set of speed bumps. Deal heard what sounded like a boat horn as the van pulled to a stop. They sat there in silence for a moment, listening to the muffler creak beneath them, then the sliding door flew open.

The priest nodded to the big men across from him, who urged Driscoll out. The priest withdrew a tiny handheld phone from a recessed compartment, punched in a number. The man beside Deal motioned impatiently for him to follow Driscoll. Deal stepped out of the van, blinking, sensing the soft warmth of water nearby, smelling it even before his eyes adjusted to the darkness.

Everyone stood quietly outside, waiting as the priest held a muffled conversation inside the van. They had parked inside a storage compound a few blocks up the Miami River. A half-mile away, the glittering bank and hotel buildings towered, their floodlights chewing up wattage Las Vegas–style.

The reflected glow of the big buildings outlined the ship that was docked alongside them, a rusty hulk of a freighter that looked incapable of navigating this barge canal, much less the high seas. The deck was jammed with bicycles, hundreds upon hundreds of them, stacked haphazardly under tarpaulins. The ship was a typical Caribbean shuttle: It'd be off before dawn, bound for the islands, there to drop off the bikes, the electronics gear sure to be swelling the hold, for pennies on the dollar. Ten days from now it would be back, offloading fruit, rum, a few woven goods and craft items, and the most lucrative cargo: a sizable number of fare-paying stowaways desperate to reach the streets of gold.

Deal glanced back at the glittering towers. Their lights would be visible for miles out to sea, he knew, well past the surging Gulf Stream, a kind of tropical stand-in for the Statue of Liberty, and every bit as enticing to a load of rafters from Haiti or Cuba. He found his mind drifting to the things Driscoll had told him. How could anyone be so cynical as to trade upon the hopes of such people for the sake of money? How could people who'd lost everything to tyrants turn murderous and tyrannical themselves? Naive, perhaps, but it still confounded him, infuriated him.

"That boat's got so much hot shit in it, it glows," Driscoll said, breaking the silence.

The priest was unfolding himself down from the van as Driscoll spoke. "Property is a relative concept," he said.

"Only when what you're talking about doesn't belong to you," Driscoll said.

The priest stopped, considering Driscoll's logic for a moment. "They are ready for us," he said by way of answer, and led them toward the ship.

The gangway shuddered under their weight, as if it might pitch them into the oil-slicked waters between the ship and the docks at any second. A man who dwarfed the two guarding Driscoll stood at the rail, watching them climb. He held what looked like an AK-47 in one hand as if it were a pistol. When the priest joined them on deck, the huge man nodded and directed them amidships with a wave of his weapon.

Deal was considering the possibilities as he followed Driscoll's heavy footsteps down the peeling decks. He reasoned that if the men had intended to kill them, they wouldn't have gone to the trouble of bringing them there. On the other hand, maybe they would be taking a short cruise out to open waters, he and Driscoll would be converted to chum where it was more convenient.

They came to an open bulkhead then, and one of the big men stayed back to guide them through the passage. Driscoll moved on inside. When Deal hesitated, the guy behind gave him a shove.

Deal stumbled into the passageway, saw light flooding from an open cabin a few feet away. Two women were in there, staring impassively at Driscoll, who had already stepped inside the room. Deal heard the bulkhead door slam shut behind him. He hesitated for a moment, then went to join Driscoll.

It was a modest cabin, with two fold-down bunks and a doorless recess you might call a closet. A narrow bulkhead gave on to a john the size of a phone booth, with a shower that would soak everything when you used it. Ms. Marquez was wearing street clothes, the bandages on her hands disappearing up under a loose-fitting long-sleeved blouse, a turban-styled scarf about her head. She was lying back against some pillows on one of the bunks. Margaria sat by her side.

Driscoll surveyed the room, gave a backward glance at the big man who remained at the doorway. "You should have told me you wanted to take a cruise," he said "I know better ships." Margaria turned her gaze to Deal, contemptuous.

"This is John Deal," Driscoll continued. "The man I was telling you about."

Deal saw Ms. Marquez's eyes flicker, as if she'd felt a jolt of pain. Margaria took her hand, soothed her cheek softly with her hand. "You have no business here," Margaria said. She didn't bother to look at them this time.

Ms. Marquez put her fingertips on Margaria's lips to silence her. "I am sorry, Mr. Deal," she said weakly. "For what has happened to you and your family."

Deal nodded. "I'm sorry for you, too," he said, meeting her gaze.

She was a beautiful woman. Or had been, at least. He found his thoughts drifting back to Janice, her bandages, her blistered skin . . . had to will himself to stop.

"You had a lovely place. Some wonderful paintings," he said sadly. "My wife and I enjoyed it very much."

She nodded, sinking back into her pillows as if the memory of it exhausted her.

"I guess they told you someone killed Alberto Valles, Ms. Marquez," Driscoll cut in. "They wrapped him up in copper wiring, plugged him into a two-twenty socket. He was still smoking when we found him."

Ms. Marquez's face had turned a shade paler. She shook her head weakly against her pillow. "Animals," she said, her voice faint. Even Margaria seemed shaken by Driscoll's words. In the silence, Deal heard the distant sound of a powerboat on the river, the muffled sounds of men talking out on deck.

"Whoever it was had torn Valles's place apart, ransacked his files," Driscoll continued. "The police'll go through everything, but it looked like a pretty thorough job to me. I expect they got everything they were after."

"They always do," she said.

"Pardon me?" Driscoll said.

Ms. Marquez was staring at the ceiling, forlorn. "They are ruthless, Mr. Driscoll. They take what they want. They take and they take and they take. And they let no one stop them."

She struggled up on one elbow. "Now what do you want from me?" She stared at them wild-eyed from her bed, ignoring Margaria's comforting hands at her shoulders. In a moment, Deal thought, the voodoo brigade would come through the door, put an end to this.

Driscoll gave his imperturbable shrug. "I thought maybe you'd have something stashed away. A copy of the manuscript, some of the files. Anything that might substantiate the charges . . . "

Ms. Marquez's eyes were on Deal now. Her face was haunted, as if Deal and Driscoll were demons come to rob her of her last shred of repose. "I have told you. Efrain Valles was very protective. He left nothing with me. He was to deliver the completed manuscript the day that he was killed. So far as I know, there was only one copy."

"I checked with the boys downtown," Driscoll said. "They never found a trace of any manuscript after the blast."

"It was written on paper," she said. "Not stone tablets. The explosion took place in the editorial offices. You told me that yourself."

Driscoll nodded as if she was reminding him of the obvious. "What do you know about this Rafael Quintana, your editor?"

She stared back at him, spots of color coming into her cheeks. "What about him?"

"How long did he work for you?"

"Not long," she said finally. "A few months."

"Where did you find him?"

She turned away from Driscoll's gaze. "A friend in New York recommended him. She knew I was looking for someone to help expand my publishing activities and she knew Rafael. He was a junior editor in a small firm in New York City. He was quite anxious to come back to Miami, quite enthused about our goals." She glanced up at Driscoll, her face pained. "I wanted to provide a forum for other voices in the exile community, Mr. Driscoll. Rafael understood that. He was excited at the possibility. He actually went out searching for authors who had important things to say, manuscripts of value. . . . " As she spoke, her gaze clouded, until, as if she'd heard the suggestion in her own words, she finally trailed off.

"Were you involved with Quintana, Ms. Marquez?" Driscoll asked the question softly, but she seemed to expect it.

"What relevance would that have?" she said. She seemed very tired.

"Maybe none," Driscoll said. "Except if you were, you might not have noticed certain things."

"What sorts of things?" she asked. She was staring off somewhere far away, her voice faint.

"Did this person who recommended him tell you what kinds of books Rafael Quintana used to publish in New York, Ms. Marquez?"

She shook her head, numb. Driscoll reached into his pocket. Deal saw the guard at the door tense, then relax as Driscoll withdrew his little pad and began to flip through the pages. He found what he was looking for, glanced up at Deal, then began to read.

"*El Problema de las Razas de Cuba,*" he managed. He screwed up his face. "*Cuidado la . . .* " He broke off. "The hell with it," he said. "Bottom line is it's all racist, fascist stuff, things that would make the Ku Klux Klan Press seem liberal. In New York, Rafael

Quintana worked for an outfit committed to the spread of right-wing propaganda. Its whole operation was funded by the Patriots' Freedom Foundation."

"How do you know these things?" Ms. Marquez asked dully.

"I'm a suspicious person by nature," Driscoll said. "I look at a situation, I try to imagine the worst about everybody." He shrugged. "After that, it's simple. You just get on the phone, ask a bunch of questions."

"What are you getting at, Vernon?" Deal asked.

"Rafael Quintana was a plant in Ms. Marquez's operation, that much seems certain . . . "

"You think he would sacrifice his life for those madmen, just to stop the publication of a book?" Ms. Marquez broke in.

"Maybe he didn't." Driscoll shrugged. "They still haven't found his body."

She stared at him for a moment, absorbing the implication. Finally she gathered herself.

"In any case," she said, "it is over. The manuscript is destroyed, Alberto's records are gone. . . . " She shook her head, weary.

"If we could prove a link between Quintana and the bombing," Driscoll offered, "link Quintana to Torreno . . . " He shrugged. "You'd make a pretty credible witness. . . . "

Ms. Marquez gave a dry laugh that sounded more like a cry of pain. "My word against that of Vicente Torreno? And that is assuming I would live long enough to testify. Spare me, Mr. Driscoll."

"Sure," Driscoll said. "I can understand. You're ready to go off on vacation, who wants to get tangled up in some messy trial." He glanced around the stark cabin. "You got yourself a first-class stateroom, a nonstop ticket to Haiti—jeez, you're the first people to willingly go to Haiti in years. They'll probably give you the key to the island . . . "

"Leave her alone, Driscoll," Deal broke in. "She's right. They'd eat her alive."

"Stay out of this," Driscoll said.

"Find some other way to do it, Vernon. You want the guy that bad, find another way."

Margaria had gotten Ms. Marquez back on her pillows, was smoothing her hair from her sweat-dampened brow. The guard was watching the confrontation between Driscoll and Deal with something resembling a smile. He could watch them fight, then finish off whoever was left.

Driscoll turned back to Ms. Marquez. "How about the man who was mentioned in Valles's manuscript?" Driscoll said. "The man from our government who knew what Torreno was up to. Do you know his name, where we might look for him?"

Ms. Marquez gave him a forlorn look. "He is dead," she said, giving them a bitter smile. "I too wanted to speak to this man, to hear it from his mouth. I insisted to Efrain Valles that I speak to him, but he told me he was dead, shot on a Cuban beach during one of the 'raids' Torreno manufactured."

"Why didn't you tell me all this before?"

She shook her head, helpless. "I thought it would sound too convenient. That it might make you doubt me."

Driscoll shook his head. "What was this man's name?" he asked.

She shook her head. "Efrain would not tell me," she said, falling back on her pillows. "He wanted to protect him." She gave her bitter laugh, and turned her face to the wall.

"Now, please," she said. "I am very tired. You must leave me alone."

The big guy turned and motioned them out. Deal heard footsteps on the decks. Driscoll was making a note on his little pad as the big guy shoved him on through the bulkhead. Something they'd be able to check out in the afterlife, Deal supposed. He gave Ms. Marquez a last glance, then felt a thick hand on his arm propelling him out into the humid darkness.

He stumbled back down the decks, something hard and unyielding prodding him in the back all the way to the gangway, where the same enormous man stood with his AK-47 in his paw.

"Down," one of the big men behind him said, pointing toward the docks below. Deal followed Driscoll down the swaying gangway, steadying himself along the rope handhold. When they reached the parking area, Deal saw that the priest's van had disappeared. In its place was Driscoll's white Ford, the paint glowing softly in the reflection of the Miami skyline.

"Go," said the big man behind them. And Deal and Driscoll went.

"You never thought they were going to hurt us, did you?"

It was Driscoll's voice, filtering back to him through the underbrush. It was still dark, and Deal struggled to keep Driscoll's jiggling flashlight beam in view. They were on a wild stretch of property behind the ruins of the bombed-out museum, although Driscoll had refused to tell him what they were doing there.

"I suppose you didn't?" Deal called to him.

"I'm suspicious," Driscoll called. "Not paranoid."

He had stopped, and Deal fought his way through the clutch of a Brazilian pepper bush into a clearing where Driscoll stood.

Deal stopped short, surprised by the unexpected view. They were on a rare elevated stretch of ground that overlooked Biscayne Bay. To the north, the same brightly lit buildings they had viewed from the banks of the Miami River were visible, now jutting up over the fringe of mangrove and banyans to mirror themselves on the placid backwaters of the Atlantic.

To the south he saw the graceful arch of the causeway looping out from the mainland to Key Biscayne. One car made its way up the span as he watched, silent at this distance. Its lights coned steadily through the darkness and then disappeared abruptly at the crest of the bridge, as if it had driven off the edge of the world. A million-dollar view, he thought, forgetting himself for a moment.

From where they stood, it was a dozen paces down an embankment to the water, which lapped gently at the shoreline. Driscoll guided his flashlight beam in that direction. There was a foot-thick band of seaweed at the verge, studded with chunks of Styrofoam and plastic jugs, a few pilings, and what was left of a dock that listed half-in, half-out of the water.

"Lookit that," Driscoll said, guiding the beam over a tumbledown boathouse that ran back from the dock onto the shore. The rear of the building was bunkered into the embankment where they stood, its roofline ending just about level with the ground beneath their feet. "Come on," Driscoll said. "I'll show you something."

He took Deal's arm, guiding him down the incline to the boathouse entrance. The outer door to the place was long gone. Inside, a pair of rusty davits listed like skeletal arms waiting for a phantom ship. A dank mustiness emanated from the open doorway. The walls were streaked with mildew, prodigious sheets of it, fed by the constant heat and humidity. Every board of the place, Deal thought, doing its best to succumb to the call of the tropics, transform quickly back to mulch.

Driscoll directed his light against the rear wall inside. There was some kind of doorway there, covered by a rusty steel grating. Driscoll started forward and Deal took his arm.

"You're not going in there, are you?" he said to Driscoll. "You're not going to walk across that floor?"

Driscoll ran the light over the boards. The planks of the rotted dock where they stood continued on inside, becoming the floor deck of the boathouse. The whole structure looked ready to fold into the water.

"Why not?" Driscoll said to him. "I bet Rafael Quintana did."

Deal stared at him.

"I ran into an old guy that does the groundskeeping for some of these places around here," Driscoll continued. "He had some pretty interesting stories. You'd be surprised what's come ashore right where we're standing."

Deal shook his head. "I'm tired, Driscoll. Show me what you wanted to show me and let's go home."

Driscoll nodded. "That's what I was getting to. Come on."

He stepped through the open doorway of the boathouse. As he took a second step, there was a mushy, snapping sound, like someone slapping a wet towel against concrete. Driscoll's right leg plunged through one of the rotted floorboards, sending him down to one knee, his hands splayed, the flashlight skittering across the deck like something alive.

"Jesus Christ," Driscoll muttered, struggling to get his leg free.

Deal stared at him, caught in the beam of the flashlight that had come to rest in a corner. In another context, it might have been funny. Now he found himself wishing the rest of the floor would give way, teach Driscoll a lesson.

"You gonna give me a hand?" Driscoll stared up at him, helpless.

"Only if you promise we can go home," Deal said.

Driscoll glared up at him. Finally he nodded. Deal picked his way carefully along a row of nails that marked where a stringer would be running underneath the decking boards. He edged on across the musty room, bent to pick up the flashlight, then came back to Driscoll, ran the beam over his beet-red face.

"I wish I had a camera," Deal said, hesitating.

"Kiss my ass," Driscoll said.

Deal found himself laughing then. It started off as a child's giggle, but when he tried to stifle it, it turned into gulps, then full-throated, bellyaching whoops that seemed to go on forever. Finally the laughter subsided to sighs, and he was able to breathe normally again. He wiped at the tears that leaked from his eyes. He couldn't remember the last time he'd laughed. His stomach ached and he felt drained, but he also felt better, as if some of the tension that had been eating him up these past weeks had finally found a vent.

"Sorry," he said to Driscoll, who had endured it all in silence. "I couldn't stop."

"Just help me up," Driscoll said impatiently.

Deal swung his other foot over to a parallel course of nails, braced himself, and bent down to take Driscoll's meaty hand. He caught hold, felt the man's bulk up the length of his arm.

"Go," he called, giving it everything.

Driscoll heaved back. There was another great slapping sound and Deal felt the floor give way beneath his feet.

In the next instant, he was weightless. Then he was plunging into bath-warm water, his head going under, his nose and mouth filling, his feet shooting down into bottomless muck.

He was still holding on to Driscoll, he realized. He shook his hands loose and kicked wildly at the muck until he felt himself begin to lift free. They broke the surface together, sputtering, Driscoll thrashing about like a rhino trying to tread water.

Deal noticed the flashlight bobbing in front of him, still sending out its light into the silty water. He reached out and snatched it, aimed it up at the gaping hole in the decking above their heads. Driscoll was already moving toward the shore in an awkward breast-stroke. After a moment Deal turned and followed after him.

They struggled up onto an outcrop of coral boulders that marked the edge of the breakwater and sat together, still sheltered by the list-ing dock, dripping water back into the bay. "Honest to Christ," Driscoll said finally.

He stared at Deal, his hair plastered over his forehead, the pic-ture of exasperation. Deal slung a reeking piece of seaweed from around his neck back into the water.

And then they both began to laugh, great honking, gasping bursts that echoed off the sides of the rotting building and out across the water, where the moon cut a long path of glittering light.

"Oh, shit," Driscoll managed finally, getting himself under con-trol. "What a night."

He glanced at Deal, who nodded his agreement in return.

"Take me home, Vernon," he said.

"If you insist," Driscoll said. He put his hand down and was about to push himself up when he saw something and stopped. "What's this?"

He reached his hand into a cleft between the boulders and with-drew a wrinkled sheet of paper. "Let me see that light," he said.

Deal handed him the flashlight, watched as Driscoll scanned the paper. The ex-cop nodded, handed the sheet back to him, holding the light so that Deal could see.

The paper had turned a pale yellow, but the type was sharp and unmistakable. "*Master of Deceit*, by Efrain Enrique Valles," Deal read aloud.

Deal turned to say something to Driscoll, but the ex-cop was already on his hands and knees, the flashlight in his teeth, pawing at the boulders beneath them like a man who'd just caught the glimmer of a vein of gold.

"Well, at least it proves what I figured was right," Driscoll said. He'd spread the single sheet of manuscript on the seat of the Ford between them, nodded at it as they swung off Brickell and onto the northbound approach to I-95.

They had spent another hour or so combing the shoreline and mangrove outcroppings near the boathouse, to no avail. Driscoll had even persuaded Deal to tiptoe back across the floor of the boathouse and venture into the passageway that, as Driscoll had learned, had been hacked through the coral back toward the house. Deal had felt the ghosts of countless pirates, rumrunners, and dope smugglers crowding in on him as he inched up the airless passage. He was not disappointed to find the whole thing blocked by a slide the blast had likely caused a dozen feet inside.

He was leaning back in the seat of the Ford, groggy with exhaustion, listening to Driscoll's continuing monologue: "So I figure this Rafael Quintana had to have been hotfooting it down the passageway toward the boat he's got docked there, he isn't going to miss one little page when the bomb goes off and lights a rocket in his ass."

Deal glanced over at him. "So you have a title page to some book. Congratulations."

"You get a map of that coastline," Driscoll said, unfazed. "Draw yourself a line from that piece-of-shit boathouse straight south, you'll come to Vicente Torreno's waterfront estate. That's where the rest of that book is."

"So we'll just go knock on the door, see if we can borrow it, right?"

Driscoll gave him a dark look but said nothing.

Deal fell back in his seat, weary, his thoughts a jumble. What if Torreno *had* blown up the Marquez estate to destroy the manuscript or cover its disappearance? They still couldn't prove it. And nothing they had heard or seen suggested any link to the fire at his fourplex. Driscoll was mistaken about that, at least. He had to be.

Deal glanced out the window, felt a start. In his daze, he hadn't paid much attention to Driscoll's driving. Now, he realized, they were heading away from the Grove, away from the little gardener's shack and the swaybacked bed he so desperately craved.

"Where are you going, Vernon? I've had enough for one night."

Driscoll shook his head. "I figure you can come on back, spend what's left of the night with me, pardner." He looked over as they dropped back down off the expressway onto Flagler Street, heading west toward the fourplex. He'd pushed his graying hair straight back from his forehead where it had dried in an irregular pompadour. There was a big scratch on one cheek and a smear of mud on the other. Deal wondered momentarily what *he* must look like.

"I don't think it's such a good idea, you sleeping all by your lonesome out in the middle of that jungle."

Deal struggled up in his seat. "Goddammit, Driscoll. I have to be at the hospital early tomorrow. They're taking Janice in for a skin graft. I want to go home and get some sleep. . . . "

"We're *going* to your home," Driscoll insisted. "You built the goddamned place. And you put a nice foldout couch—Castro's Convertible, wasn't it—right there in my living room."

"You don't seem to get it, Vernon. This doesn't have anything to *do* with me."

But Driscoll was resolute, using his jaw to point them down the broad street through a series of traffic lights that were reduced to clicking yellow at this time of night. "Maybe you're right," he said as he turned down the side street toward the fourplex. "But why don't you just humor me a little while longer. I'd feel a whole lot better if you just bunked with me the next couple of days. Is that a whole lot to ask?"

Deal felt a headache mounting over his right eye. He wasn't going to argue anymore. He was going to stay calm, wait until Driscoll stopped. He would simply call himself a taxi and . . .

"Well, kiss my ass," Driscoll blurted, his eyes widening at something in front of them.

Deal turned, following his gaze. Impossible, yes, but there it was. A bulky Metro-Dade fire rescue van pulled up at the curb in front of the fourplex, its red and white flashers spinning wildly. He shook his head, sure he'd been sucked into a dream now, into some horrendous time loop.

It was all alive for him, instantaneously—running from the burning fourplex toward the rescue team at the curbside, Isabel clutched tightly in his arms, his eyes scanning the crowd desperately for any sign of Janice—the whole terrible night rushing before him in a series of images . . .

. . . and then they were sliding to a halt at the curb, Driscoll flinging the door open while the car was still moving, making a dash for his half of the fourplex. A technician was backing out of the hallway, guiding one end of a steel gurney toward the waiting van. There was another medic on the other end of the gurney and a third by their side, that one holding a bottle of fluid attached to the person on the stretcher.

"Isabel?" he cried as he ran toward them, the sound rising involuntarily from his throat. But it couldn't be. It couldn't. His limbs had gone heavy with dread. He felt as if he were trying to run through molten lead.

"Señor Deal! Señor Deal!" He heard Mrs. Suarez's voice and spun about. He paused and stared, feeling relief sweep over him. Mrs. Suarez, her face drawn, tears streaking her cheeks, stood there at the curbside, Isabel gathered up in her arms.

"Dah," Isabel called, her face radiant. "Dah!" She had her arms outstretched.

Deal ran toward them, pulled his daughter into his arms, smothering his face with the reality of her. "Oh, sweetie, oh, honey," his voice thick with emotion. Finally he turned back to the old woman.

"What is it, Mrs. Suarez? What's happened?" In her halting English, she explained how a neighbor had heard the shot and summoned her.

"Is terrible," Mrs. Suarez said, sobbing freely now. She pointed at the approaching gurney, a handkerchief clutched in one of her gnarled hands. "Terrible. He shoot him*self*!" Her face twisted in anguish.

Deal turned, caught a glimpse of the form as the medics folded down the gurney wheels, slid it into the back of the van.

He caught his breath. The face swollen, slathered in blood, disfigured in the angled lights. But unmistakable.

"Poor Tommy," Mrs. Suarez wailed behind him, as the ambulance doors slammed shut. "*Pobrecito* Tommy!"

Tommy. Now it was Tommy.

Who else, Deal found himself thinking as the vehicle gained speed down the narrow avenue. And *what* else? What else could happen in this awful, forlorn place?

33

"Sometimes I am sitting out here, Coco," Torreno said, feeding another page to the fire, "and I can imagine that it is our homeland."

They sat in low-slung canvas chairs in a clearing near the lake. Coco turned from the considerable blaze, one he had built from deadfall and scraps of lumber, and stared out across the lake at the pines marking the farthest reaches of Torreno's estate, silhouetted against the waning moon.

To him, the vast, flat landscape, dotted here and there with hammocks of taller trees, looked more like Africa, or at least like the pictures he had seen of that place. He would not have been startled to see a herd of giraffes come thundering across the plain toward them. A howl from one of the creatures that Torreno kept behind the tall fences only confirmed his impression. Much more like Africa.

"You have done good work," Torreno said, brandishing a sheaf of papers in his hand. Coco turned back and nodded impassively. Torreno tossed the rest of the papers into the blaze, watched them curl into nothingness.

"Our enemies are many, Coco. We must be vigilant." How many times had Coco heard the refrain repeated? His employer was staring into the fire as if the ghosts of those he feared danced among the flames. Finally he turned back, thoughtful.

"I have spent all my life as an exile, Coco. My entire life, when you think about it, has been determined by the whim of a madman."

Coco stared at him, waiting. While Torreno pretended to philosophize, he did not require discussion. From Coco nothing would be required save an attentive ear. And Coco did not mind. Coco had ceased searching to justify his own actions a long time ago. "Perhaps you do not feel as I do, Coco," Torreno continued. "You are a vagabond, a mercenary. As the Americans like to say, 'Home is where you hang your hat.'"

Coco lifted an eyebrow in response. The fire was making him sleepy. He had worked hard this day. The fact was, he *was* comfortable here, in this chair, before this fire, which, though hot, had the advantage of keeping the insects away.

He shifted irritably in his seat, wondering why Torreno could not be content with all that he possessed. He had left Cuba with nothing and become a titan in this country. Now he would not be content until he was an even bigger titan, returned to the country he had left. The concept of such ambition tired Coco even further. And brought another annoyance to his mind.

"The woman," he said. "She is still alive somewhere. . . . "

"She means nothing now," Torreno said, emptying the box of papers onto the fire. They watched one sheet swirl up in the draft above the flames. For an instant it seemed that the paper might escape unscathed, flutter aloft, rise out into the world. It wavered in the updraft, then abruptly burst into flame. Torreno smiled. "You see," he said as if the little drama were proof of something, "it is done." His eyes glittered in the reflection of the fire, and he settled back, returning to his theme.

"I could have allowed myself to accept a terrible injustice, Coco. Most men would have compromised. Made accommodation. I have seen it in those who have worked alongside me. Over the years, as their comfort has grown, their zeal has faded. Every year it has become more difficult for me to convince them of the need to support the struggle. Men like Dagoberto Real." He waved his hand dismissively. "But now it is different. I will no longer need to beg, Coco."

He turned to Coco, his face half-shadowed. "I have dedicated every particle of my being to the redress of that injustice, Coco. I have not relied upon the courts, or armies, or quavering politicians." He paused. "I have done it myself," he added fervently. "And I will have my reward."

He took Coco's shoulder and shook it. "Soon all this will come to an end. We will return in magnificent victory, will we not?"

Coco nodded again, feeling the heat of the nearby flames, of his employer's intense gaze. He was nodding, but he felt resistance deep within. That nagging voice that he had heard before, and had ignored, and would ignore again, despite its incessant refrain. "Never," the voice crooned. "Never. It will never be."

"Rise and shine, pardner." Driscoll's voice drifted to him as if down a well. "They're coming out of surgery."

Deal blinked awake, pulling himself up by the arms of the waiting room chair. He was on a surgical floor somewhere in the bowels of Jackson Memorial, the sprawling public hospital complex just west of the city. There was a television playing in front of him, its sound turned down low. It looked like a group of bikers on a talk show. One guy was pointing out a tattoo on his shoulder to the female host.

Driscoll stood in front of him, glancing down a nearby corridor impatiently. He looked fresh, as though he'd showered and changed, though he wore the same kind of white shirt and shapeless gray pants as the day before. Maybe he had a dozen outfits like that.

Deal shook his head groggily. His vision was foggy and his head felt as though it had been filled with cement. He stared at Driscoll, still trying to connect.

He'd been dreaming. Isabel was in the hospital, needing an operation. A doctor explained patiently that he was overdrawn at the bank, that there could be no operation. Deal had pulled out his wallet, wanting to prove to the man that he could pay, but there was nothing inside. No money. No driver's license. No credit cards. No pictures of his family. Nothing.

226

His hand went automatically to his hip pocket. He felt the familiar shape of his wallet there and repressed the urge to take it out, inspect the contents. He massaged his face, his fingertips tingling with exhaustion.

Relief at the dream's dissipation was fading quickly into the dread of his actual life. He had a brief image of Janice, could feel her weak fingers in his grip . . . then just as quickly remembered Tommy. Poor, miserable Tommy, who'd put a gun to his temple last night and tried to blow his addled, paranoid brains out. Deal should have insisted that Dr. Goodwin institutionalize him the very day they'd been in the psychologist's office: get him in a hospital, run tests, find some medicine that might even him out . . .

Deal broke off, just awakened and already exhausted, thinking of yet another thing that he should have done, like the little Dutch boy, except he didn't have enough fingers for all the holes in this world's dike.

On the television screen, another biker had stood to drop his pants, point out a tattoo on one of his buttocks.

Deal glanced up at Driscoll. "What time is it?"

"Almost noon," Driscoll said. His gaze stayed fixed on the hallway. "I just got back, brought you some clothes." He waved his hand and Deal saw a paper sack in the chair next to him. "When I came past the station, the nurses told me they were about done with Tommy. . . . "

He broke off as a group of doctors in scrub greens and soft-soled shoes emerged from a set of swinging doors. Deal pushed himself up and hurried down the hallway after Driscoll.

One of the doctors saw them coming. He left the group and turned to Deal, who had forged ahead.

"I'm John Deal," he said. "I'm . . . " He broke off, searching for the right explanation.

"Tommy lives with him," Driscoll said.

"I know," the doctor said. "I read the story in the paper." The doctor gave Deal a nod. "I do some work with the homeless with Joey Greer, over at the Camillus House. That was a kind thing you did, Mr. Deal, taking Tommy in."

Deal nodded. He knew it was supposed to make him feel good, but it only seemed like the doctor was stalling, holding off more disastrous news.

"How's he doing?" Driscoll said.

The doctor gave Driscoll a look, then turned back to Deal, his face grim. "It's a miracle he's still alive," the doctor said. "We were able to relieve some of the fluid pressure, get him breathing on his own, which is a good sign . . . " He trailed off. "It's anybody's guess, Mr. Deal. I wouldn't get my hopes up."

Deal shook his head, putting his hand against the wall for support. "Poor Tommy," he said, hearing himself echoing Mrs. Suarez. "The poor sonofabitch."

"We had to leave the bullet in his brain," the doctor continued. He hesitated, as if he was trying to find the right words.

"But when we were prepping him, we found something . . . " The doctor paused, shaking his head. "It's the strangest thing," he said. He reached for something in a pocket of his greens. "Incredible, in fact. I've certainly never heard of anything like it."

"What are you talking about?" Driscoll said.

The doctor held up what looked like an oddly shaped pebble. "We picked it up on the initial x-rays," he said.

Deal shook his head, puzzled. His head was still fuzzy, his eyes burning from fatigue.

"It's another bullet," the doctor said. "Lodged in the tissue between the skull and the brain itself." He gave them a look. "It was in the way," he shrugged, "so we took it out."

"Wait a minute," Deal said, bewildered. "You're saying he shot himself *twice*?"

"Of course not," the doctor said. "This thing was encased in a good deal of old scar tissue. It had to have been in the man's head for some time. Months, at the very least."

Deal shared a look with Driscoll.

"That's what I meant," the doctor continued. "For a man to suffer two serious gunshot wounds to the head at different times, well . . . " He glanced at them. "What would *you* calculate the odds to be?"

Deal shook his head. He was remembering his visit to the psychologist, could see Dr. Goodwin's expression: "I wouldn't rule out tissue trauma entirely, of course. . . . "

He took the doctor's sleeve. "Could this earlier gunshot . . . " He broke off, trying to phrase it the way he wanted. "Could that injury have accounted for Tommy's mental state?"

The doctor thought about it a moment. "It's hard to tell," he said finally. "I never actually observed his behavior, of course. And now, under the circumstances . . . " He gave Deal a helpless look. "Tommy never talked about this injury to you? Never mentioned it?"

Deal glanced at Driscoll, who shook his head.

The doctor shrugged. "It's possible, of course. He might have been a normally functioning adult before he was shot the first time . . . " He turned and gestured toward the operating room. "It would be difficult to determine, but if he ever regains consciousness . . . " He trailed off, letting the implication hang.

"You mind if I take that old bullet, Doc?" Driscoll said finally.

Deal turned, saw with disbelief that Driscoll was holding out his phony shield. He opened his mouth to say something, then closed it at Driscoll's warning glance.

"I don't see why not," the doctor said. "It's certainly not connected to this incident."

"I'll get it back to you," Driscoll said.

The doctor nodded and dropped the slug in Driscoll's palm. He checked his watch, seemed to remember something. "If there's nothing else then?"

"No," Driscoll said. "Thanks for your time."

"Thanks," Deal added. He gestured toward the nurses' station. "You'll tell them to keep me posted on Tommy's condition?"

"Sure," the doctor said. "We'll see how he does. Maybe we can let you see him a little later on." He paused. "If you want."

"I'd like that." Deal nodded.

The doctor clapped him on the shoulder then and started off down the hall.

When he had disappeared, Deal turned to Driscoll. "Christ, Vernon. Suppose he tells someone."

Driscoll shrugged. "What do you think the boys at Metro would do with this slug? As far as they're concerned, old Tommy tried to kill himself last night and botched the job. You tell them he had an old bullet in his noggin, they'd just figure he was king of the screwups, screwed up twice in a row."

Deal shook his head, trying to understand where Driscoll was headed. "They found a gun beside his head, his prints all over it."

"I know they did," Driscoll said.

Deal stared at him. "But you think someone tried to kill him?"

"You tell me," Driscoll said. "I'm supposed to believe a guy like Tommy goes down to the pawnshop, buys himself a Colt and some high-velocity loads? I can't see it happening."

Deal considered it. "Maybe he had it all along."

Driscoll gave him a look, refusing to grace the remark with a reply.

Deal turned, looked off down the hallway. The doctor had disappeared. A maintenance man worked his way slowly down the corridor with a mop, sending a peppermint odor their way. Deal could feel the pieces trying to mesh together in his own foggy brain.

"And you're guessing that maybe the night of the fire, somebody was actually trying to kill Tommy?"

"You gonna get pissed off at me if I say yes?" Driscoll asked.

"But *why*, Driscoll? Why would anyone want to kill Tommy so badly that they'd be willing to kill us all in the bargain?"

"Somebody who didn't want to call attention to the matter," Driscoll said. "Somebody who wanted it to look like an accident. Some retard and an ex-cop die in a fire, ain't it a shame."

"And me," Deal said. "And Mrs. Suarez. And my wife and child." He glanced up at Driscoll. "Who would do that? Who could do a thing like that?"

Driscoll looked at him as if he was a slow student. "There's basically two reasons why people kill other people," he said wearily. "One has to do with love, which I think we can eliminate here. The other's money. Put enough money on the line, a person's liable to do just about anything."

Deal thought about it for a moment. About Driscoll's dogged pursuit of the case he never cracked. "Torreno," he said finally. "You think he did this too, don't you?"

Driscoll gave him his who-would-think-otherwise look. "I think that he had *somebody*—even if it wasn't Chuy-Chuy—set the fire, and I think he sent somebody back to finish the job."

"But there isn't any proof!" Deal said, exasperated. "What connection could a guy like Tommy have with Vicente Torreno?"

Driscoll gave his philosophical shrug. "I dunno, Deal. But there *is* one. We keep digging, we'll find it. That's the way it works."

He broke off then, and Deal knew that for Driscoll speculation time was over.

"I got an old buddy lives up in Broward, still does some work for the ME," the ex-cop said. "I'm going to let him have a look at this slug, see what he can tell us. That is, if you don't turn me in for impersonating an officer first." He gave Deal a neutral stare.

Deal was about to say something, tell him what he could do with his bloodhound's "instinct" and his phony badge, when he noticed the clock on the wall above Driscoll's head. "Oh my God," he said.

"What?" Driscoll said, turning in alarm. But Deal was already at a dead run toward the elevators.

"Janice," he said. "Her operation . . . it was at ten o'clock." He reached the elevators and stabbed the buttons until he thought his thumb would break. He was pounding on the panel with his fist when the doors finally slid open and he rushed inside, heedless of the crowd of orderlies and visitors who had to squeeze aside, then shift again as Driscoll lumbered into the car.

"I should've woke you," Driscoll said. "I forgot all about it."

Others stared at them, curious. Deal held his hands up to cut him off as the car inched maddeningly down through the floors. He massaged his face again, feeling ready to explode with anger, with frustration. The entire blessed world, he thought. The entire world was coming apart. If the cables on this elevator car were to part and send them hurtling toward the center of the earth, he would not be surprised.

Never mind that there was no logical reason for him to be frightened. If a man could do what Driscoll claimed had been done, then what was a mere elevator car? Or an explosion here or there. Or, he thought, his blood chilling inside him, arranging that a knife should slip during routine surgery.

 For once, Deal had no quibble with Driscoll's driv-
ing. The ex-cop covered the few miles from Jackson
Memorial to Coral Gables General in what seemed
half the normal time. Even a brief morning thunder-
shower didn't slow him. They took the last several
blocks down a low-lying residential street leaving a
high rooster tail of water behind the Ford.

"All these hospitals, I feel like an ambulance
driver," Driscoll muttered as he sped up the circular
entryway.

Deal didn't bother to reply. He flung open his door, was out of
the Ford before it had stopped, sprinting through a curtain of water
that cascaded off the side of the canopy, then down the covered
walkway and inside the crowded lobby. He took one look at the
crowd in front of the elevators and headed for the stairs, taking them
two at a time up to the third floor.

He hesitated when he came out of the stairwell onto the ward,
then got his bearings and hurried down the broad corridor, doing his
best not to break into a run. He passed the nurses' station without a
glance, ignoring the call of someone behind a typewriter. He ticked
off the doorways as he passed—one, two, three—and then reached
Janice's room, catching the door frame by one hand, swinging himself in.

He stopped, thinking for a moment that he might have miscalculated. There was a heavyset black woman in a pink uniform stripping the sheets from Janice's bed. The monitors, the glucose bottles, the charts had disappeared. The closet door stood open. Where the robes and duffel bag had been, placed there by Deal himself, a few empty hangers dangled.

The black woman stared at him warily. Deal heard a sound behind him and turned. The nurse who'd called after him from the nurses' station stood in the doorway behind him.

"Can I help you?" she said. He did not recognize her face. Weeks of coming to this hospital, and he did not recognize this woman's face. He could feel his heart thudding in his chest.

"My wife," he managed. "She was in this room. She was having an operation this morning. . . . "

"They told me that lady isn't coming back." The aide said it defensively, as if someone were criticizing her work.

"Are you Mr. Deal?" the nurse asked.

Deal ignored her question. He was ready to leap upon these women, pummel them, strangle them.

"Where is my *wife*?" He heard his own voice rising dangerously.

The nurse shook her head. "They didn't tell you?"

"Tell me what?"

"She's graduated," the nurse said. Deal realized she was smiling. "She's been moved to a regular ward."

Deal stared. His heart was still pounding, and his knees felt as if they might give way. But he could breathe again.

Deal shook his head. He still could not speak. He felt incapable of movement, as if the molecules of his body were busy, reorienting themselves to this new state. The two women stared at him, uncertain.

Finally, the nurse broke the silence. "Well, I'll bet you'd like to know what room she's in, wouldn't you?" she said. And still all Deal could do was nod.

"She's asleep," another nurse told him, intercepting Deal on her way out of the room. "Don't worry. Everything went just fine."

Deal nodded his thanks, resisting the urge to sling the nurse out into the hall. He even managed a smile, edging on past her, inside the room. The blinds had been pulled shut, but enough light spilled in for him to see Janice's quiet form, her chest rising and falling in rhythmic sleep.

She lay with one cheek upturned. He stared at that one taut, shining patch of skin that had been bared, ready to burst into tears of gratitude. Just a few square inches of unmarred skin, and yet it seemed he was witnessing a miracle. How long had it been? All the bandages had been removed from the top of her head now. He could swear that the stubble of her hair had thickened measurably in the recent days.

He sank down on his knees beside the bed, brought his lips to her hand. After a moment, he felt her fingertips flutter. He glanced up, saw her eyes open momentarily. Her lips worked beneath the bandages that still covered the other cheek, the lower part of her face.

"What do you think, sailor?" she said after a moment, her voice faint, raspy.

"You look great," he said. He laid his head against the back of her hand.

"I told the doctor to make me look like Sean Young," she said.

He smiled. "Janice is just fine," he said.

"I've seen the way you look at her," she said.

He squeezed her hand. "That cheek is one hundred percent Janice Deal," he said.

"Well, too bad," she said. "I tried."

He gave her another smile, kissed the inside of her palm, her wrist. He was vaguely aware of some antiseptic scent beneath the bandages on her arm, but it seemed as fragrant as perfume. He was quiet then, listening to the beat of his own heart as it slowed to something near normal.

"I missed you," she said after a bit.

"I know," he said. He looked up, meeting her gaze. "I was with Driscoll," he began, trying to gauge how much to tell her.

"And?" she said, giving his hand a gentle squeeze.

He took a breath. "It's Tommy," he said finally. "Something terrible happened to him."

"What?" She was trying to push herself up on her elbows. "What's happened, Deal?"

He hesitated, but knew there was no holding back now. "He shot himself last night," he blurted. Janice sank back on her pillows with a groan.

"Mrs. Suarez found him. He's still alive. They took him to Jackson for surgery. I was waiting to see how it turned out, and fell asleep. That's why I wasn't here for you. . . . " He realized he was beginning to ramble.

"Shhh . . . ," she said, cupping his face in her hand. "It's all right, Deal. You're here now. I'm so glad you're here."

She stared at him for a moment, her eyes glittering, and then she lay back, already drifting off.

"Poor Tommy," she murmured. "Very sad Tommy . . . " Her words had begun to slur.

He knew he might have let it go at that, let her drift back into sleep, let her dream some hopefully untroubled dream, but he couldn't. It would have been like trying to keep some awful secret from a part of himself.

"He didn't do it, Janice," he said. He squeezed her hand, waiting until her eyes flickered open again. "He didn't shoot himself."

"We think someone tried to kill him, Janice," he continued. "I think that's who they were after when they burned our place."

Her eyes were wide now. She shook her head in confusion. "Tommy? Someone wanted to kill Tommy?"

"I know," he told her. "It sounds crazy. But . . . " He thought of Alberto Valles, his hands still quivering as the current jolted through his lifeless body. He turned back to Janice.

"Driscoll's turned up some things. Nothing you could take to court, but enough to make me believe it's possible." He gripped both her hands in his now. "I'm still not certain, but if it's true, if they'd do what they did trying to kill Tommy . . . " He stopped short. There was, after all, no reason to frighten her, no real reason to believe they were in danger. Even if Driscoll was right, he and Janice had been mere bystanders, hadn't they?

"We've got to find out, Janice," he went on. "If someone did these things, they're going to pay, goddammit. They're going to pay . . . " He broke off when he realized she was asleep, her hand gone limp in his.

He waited a moment, watching her breathing deepen. Her lips twitched as if she *was* dreaming. If she was, let it be a pleasant one, he prayed. Set in a place where the world was bright and vengeance was a word that no one knew.

The phone call came as they were stepping down from the new truck that Torreno had had delivered that morning. It was a boxy all-terrain vehicle that he had decided was perfect for forays into the farther reaches of his estate. They had spent an hour splattering through the bogs at the far end of the lake, and Torreno had been so pleased at his inability to mire the thing, no matter how deep the mud, that he had asked the salesman to deliver a second to the offices of American Sugar in Belle Vista.

"It is British," Torreno said proudly to Coco, waving at the mud-covered vehicle. "They know how to build these things."

Coco nodded. The salesman who'd delivered the vehicle waved happily to them as he drove off with his partner in a similar truck. Coco had seen the price on the contract the salesman carried. His employer had spent nearly a hundred thousand dollars on two massive toys.

The mechanical chirping sounded again, and a look of annoyance crossed Torreno's features. He reached into the pocket of a bush jacket he had donned despite the heat, and withdrew a tiny wallet-sized phone. His employer often used it to place calls, but almost never had Coco heard it ring.

Torreno unfolded the phone, held it to his ear. "I am here," he said tersely. He listened to someone on the other end, his face showing gathering concern. "Repeat," he said at one point, his face coloring.

His accusing gaze had come to rest on Coco. "You are certain?" Torreno said into the phone. Coco could hear the gnatlike whine of a voice on the other end. The sound broke off abruptly as Torreno snapped the phone shut and slammed the side of the muddy vehicle with his fist. He stared down at the ground in the gathering heat, ignoring the dent he'd put in the side of the door, his gaze focused somewhere far away. Finally he glanced back up at Coco.

"Something is wrong?" Coco said.

"He is alive," Torreno said after a moment. He glanced up sharply at Coco. "You tell me you have killed him, and yet he is alive."

It was impossible, Coco thought. Some mistake on the part of one of his employer's minions. If either of the men he had dealt with the night before were to be living, it would be no less a miracle than the Resurrection itself. Still, there was no mistaking the expression on Torreno's face. He stared back impassively, waiting for the rest of it.

"You shot him. You told me there was no doubt. . . . "

Coco felt a momentary start, though the furious expression on his employer's face had nothing to do with it. "This man, he has been marked," he heard himself saying.

Torreno stared at him, his face turning even darker. "Don't give me idiotic superstitions. You have failed, Coco. It is as simple as that."

Coco stared back at his employer mildly. Coco could not have put it into words, yet what he sensed was undeniable. But his employer, despite the years of fervent rhetoric, despite his elaborate vision of a glorious return, had left that place behind in a way that he would never fully appreciate.

"Perhaps this man cannot be killed. Not by me, at any rate," Coco insisted.

Torreno pounded the side of the vehicle again, turned away from Coco to stand poised in thought.

Coco stood, readying himself, though he was uncertain just what he might do. The picture of the *jefe* from the sugar fields had come into his mind. The picture of panic, of utter desperation on a face that had never known such an emotion. "I cannot swim," the *jefe* had called, and then had died with his face in the mud and the slime.

Coco had seen a glimpse of that same expression on his employer's face, though it had been supplanted with rage, and now with calculation.

"It is true," Torreno said, as if he had given thought to Coco's words. "The spirit of this man is very strong."

Coco stared silently at his employer.

"But your spirit is stronger yet, Coco." Torreno took him by the shoulder. "We must see it as a test," he continued.

"A test," Coco repeated.

"This one last thing," Torreno said, almost whispering now, "that is all I am asking of you, Coco. You will finish this and then we are done."

Coco hesitated. He had never heard a note of supplication in his employer's voice before. Perhaps Torreno understood more than it seemed.

"You must protect me," Torreno said, his voice as fervent as that of the *jefe* who had died in the sugar fields.

And finally Coco nodded.

"You could have provided me with a better specimen, you know." There was real annoyance in the little man's voice. He had stopped his work on the computer keyboard in front of him to stare up at Driscoll and Deal, his eyes growing momentarily large and luminous behind a pair of Coke-bottle glasses. He was balding, and wore a short-sleeved dress shirt and bow tie, even here, in the garage of his own home.

"I'm sorry as shit, Osvaldo," Driscoll said. "Imagine the nerve of the guy we took it out of, busting it up with his head the way he did."

Osvaldo gave him a disdainful look but said nothing. He turned, tapped some keys on the computer. They had followed him down a ramp that led from the kitchen of a nondescript suburban home into his "office," a corner of the garage set off by a partition that still lacked a door. Door or no door, the place was freezing, chilled by the blast of a massive wall unit AC that must have been there for the sake of all the electronic equipment arrayed on a series of doortop desks laid end to end.

Osvaldo had lifted an image of the slug Driscoll had given him, using a photomicroscope, then loaded a copy into a flatbed scanner. Now he had called up what looked like a phone directory onto the screen of his computer, was paging down through the listings. He seemed to find what he was after and punched another series of keys. Deal heard the muted sounds of an autodialer, then a series of electronic squeaks and howls.

"That's how computers fuck," Driscoll observed.

Osvaldo didn't look up from his screen. "*If* computers were to fornicate, they would find a far more creative way to do it," he said. His voice was comically high-pitched, as if he had been inhaling helium.

"Osvaldo's wound a little tight," Driscoll said. "I have to drop by a little more often, get him to lighten up."

"Be still, my heart," Osvaldo said. He consulted a notebook full of pencil scratchings, typed in more commands.

"Who we fornicating with, anyhow?" Driscoll asked, pointing at the screen.

"A certain high-level governmental agency that shall remain nameless," Osvaldo said.

"Got a way with words, doesn't he?" Driscoll said to Deal. He turned back to Osvaldo. "I'm surprised they still let you hook up."

"Who said anything about *let*?" Osvaldo was tapping keys intently as he spoke. "I'm a taxpayer. I'm just exercising my rights."

"Osvaldo used to work for the Broward sheriff's office," Driscoll said. "Until somebody ratted him out, reported his own fornicative habits. Now he stays at home and dreams up ways to use computers illegally."

"Fornicative habits." Osvaldo sniffed. "I like that, Driscoll. All these years there's been an intellectual hiding behind that *lumpen* facade."

Deal stared at the tiny man, trying hard not to imagine what the "fornicative habits" were that had gotten him tossed from his job.

"All that shit over there, he uses to make phony ID for teenagers," Driscoll continued. He pointed at another bank of equipment in a corner: There was a camera on a tripod, a color copier, a laminating machine, bins of different-colored paper.

"I'm an industrial surveillance consultant," Osvaldo said to Deal. "Your friend is just upset because I'm doing well."

"He does do well," Driscoll said agreeably. "A seventeen-year-old kid'll pay a couple hundred bucks for a phony driver's license."

"I should have left the public sector years ago," Osvaldo said. "I had no idea what was waiting for me out here."

The computer had started to beep. "Aha!" Osvaldo said, smiling behind his thick glasses. "That didn't take so long."

Deal craned his neck, trying to see the computer screen, but the little man held his hand up to block his view. "You can't tell anything from this. We'll get better resolution on the scanner. I'll just download . . ."

He broke off to type more commands, then flipped another switch. Another sizable piece of equipment hummed into electronic life. He waited until the thing began to feed out a sheet of paper, then consulted his little book, tapped his keyboard again.

He smiled up at Driscoll. "Won't they go crazy," he said, "trying to figure out why the Smithsonian Institution was running a ballistics test?"

"You're a genius, Osvaldo," Driscoll said dryly, pointing at the sheet that had dropped into a tray near the man's tiny hand. "What'd we match up *with*?"

Osvaldo flipped the paper over, exposing a facsimile of the battered slug they'd taken from Tommy's head. Beneath it was a regularly shaped bullet, its riflings clearly defined. Deal shook his head. He didn't see how it was possible to tell anything from the few discernible markings on their slug. Osvaldo glanced up as if he'd read his mind.

"The computer does it," he said. "Extrapolates from what we've fed in. Either it can figure it out or it can't. There's no maybe. If it gives us a match, then it's a match."

"Well, what the hell does it say?" Driscoll demanded.

Osvaldo turned calmly back to the text beneath the images. He made a sound that Deal guessed signified satisfaction. "Ivan and Ivan special," he said to Driscoll.

Driscoll shook his head.

"You know," Osvaldo insisted. "The same kind of handgun they did Neon Leon with."

"Yeah?" Driscoll said, surprised. He turned to Deal. "It's a Kalashnikov. A rare one, a pistol they used to issue to Russian army officers. We had a hell of a time getting a make on it."

Deal shook his head.

"The Russians mothballed them years ago," Osvaldo said. "Later a few of them turned up in Angola and then Cuba, part of the military aid package. Only time I saw it used around here was the case I mentioned."

"Guy ran a restaurant down in South Miami," Driscoll said by way of explanation. "A place he used to launder his drug money. Everybody figured it was just another drug deal gone bad until they found out what kind of gun was used. The Feds've been harping on it ever since. They're using it as part of the drug thing they're trying to pin on Castro."

Deal stared at them. "Are you saying the bullet that came out of Tommy was fired by this same gun?"

Osvaldo shook his head. "There's no way to know, not with what you brought me. We can be certain what *kind* of gun was used, but you'd need to be able to identify some anomaly within the pattern to prove it was the same weapon. There's just not enough to work with here." He gestured at the computer, helpless.

Deal stood in the frigid blast of AC, trying to make sense of it all. Tommy shot by a Russian pistol, the same kind used by drug-dealing Cuban nationals. Tommy with another bullet in his head, one he'd fired himself, or hadn't. How would they ever know which universe was operating here? Who was Tommy? Where had he come from? How long had he been living on the streets before Homer found him, nearly frozen to death beneath an underpass?

Then Deal stopped. He turned to Driscoll, who'd been studying the printout Osvaldo had handed him. "Tommy would've been in a hospital for that first gunshot wound, wouldn't he?"

Driscoll nodded. "I'd say it was a safe bet."

"And any hospital would have to make a police report, wouldn't they, on any gunshot wound?"

"Sure," Driscoll said. "But it could have happened anywhere in the country. We don't even know *when* he was shot the first time. It'd take forever to run down."

"Okay," Deal said, his excitement growing. "But let's try the most obvious possibility first, just for the hell of it."

"What are you talking about?" Driscoll asked.

"Tommy was found last December, right? We could work backward from there, check the local hospitals. How hard would it be?"

"There's only one trauma center down your way," Osvaldo offered.

Deal and Driscoll looked at each other. "The same damned place where he is right now," Driscoll said.

They started for the door together. Abruptly, Driscoll turned back to Osvaldo.

"How about cranking your machine up for one more favor?" he asked.

Osvaldo gave him a suspicious glance. "As long as I don't have to go back into the same data bank anytime soon. Those particular guys are smart—I don't want to press my luck."

"No problem," Driscoll said. "This is easy stuff."

He bent down and scribbled something on a pad by Osvaldo's keyboard. "Check him and the assumed names register for anything this guy's connected with. Cross-check the probate listings, from West Palm on down through Dade County. Any holdings he's got his fingers in, I want to know about it."

Osvaldo glanced at the pad and nodded. "It'll take a while," he said. "Where can I reach you?"

"That's okay," Driscoll said. "I'll call *you*." And then they were gone.

"You ever think of computerizing all this?" Driscoll said as the clerk dropped another set of patient files on the table of the tiny room where they were working, combing last winter's admissions logs hour by hour, day by day.

The clerk, a thin, pale man in his thirties with a tattoo of footprints on the web of his thumb, gave Driscoll a look, waved a hand at the paint-peeling walls around them. The musty records had given the room a hopeless, claustrophobic character. Deal wondered what it would be like, coming to work there most of the days of your life.

"Sure, we've thought of it," the clerk said. "But the hospital's still a little short on bed space and bedpans. The records room is going to have to wait awhile."

Driscoll nodded, turned to a new ledger dourly. They'd already checked a dozen gunshot-to-the-head victims, discounted each one. Half had died or were of the wrong race, a few were in jail, the rest were citizens who could be accounted for.

"I can't believe so many people get shot," Driscoll said. "And I'm a cop!"

Deal resisted the urge to correct Driscoll. He still had not been able to shake the notion that real policemen were about to burst into the room, drag them off to a cell somewhere.

"It's a rare day we don't get at least a couple," the clerk said. "Gives you a new perspective on life, doesn't it?"

"Take a look at this one," Driscoll said, handing a patient folder across the table to Deal.

"Anthony Everett," Deal read, flipping the file open. "White male, five eleven, one sixty-five. Admitted November 11, possible gunshot wound."

Driscoll took the file back, flipped on through, looking for something. Finally, he glanced up at the clerk. "How come there's no compliance report on this guy?"

The clerk took the file from Driscoll, scanned through it. "The incident was never confirmed." He shrugged.

"What do you mean, never confirmed?" Deal said.

"You have to have an attending physician perform an examination," the clerk said. "Apparently the examination on this guy was never completed. He walked."

Driscoll stared at the clerk in disbelief. "He came in here with a gunshot wound to the head and walks out under his own steam before a doctor ever sees him? Is that what you're telling me?"

The clerk glanced at the file again, then shrugged. "Dr. Hassan *saw* him, he just didn't finish up with him before he disappeared." The clerk looked over at Deal. "People wander out of here all the time, right in the middle of treatment. They calm down, realize they're not going to die, maybe they start to worry they're going to get in trouble."

The clerk turned to Driscoll. "November 11 was a Saturday. You ever been down to the emergency ward on a Saturday night? That'd be the least surprising thing could happen, if you ask me."

Driscoll sighed, covering his face with his massive hands. "This Dr. Hassan," he said finally, giving the clerk a patient look. "How might we get in touch with him?"

Deal and Driscoll were waiting in the interns' quarters, a battered place with a worn carpet and a musty smell that reminded Deal of his high school locker room, when Dr. Hassan arrived for his shift. This time when Driscoll displayed his phony shield, Deal didn't even flinch.

Hospital records had already told them that Hassan was an Iranian immigrant who'd studied in London, gone to med school in

Madrid, was completing an internship in the States. He turned out to be a slightly built man in his mid-thirties, his face framed by owlish horn-rimmed glasses.

He removed the glasses a couple of times as he studied the Xeroxed file Driscoll had handed him. Another intern lingered near the locker area until Driscoll fixed his glare on him and the man eased on out of the room. Hassan looked up from the file as the door closed behind his colleague.

"Yes, I remember this man," he said finally. "He is the one who vanished." His doleful eyes reflected wonder as he thought back. "Those men from the raft brought him in and left and then he disappeared as well."

"Men from the raft?" Deal asked.

"Yes," Hassan said, unruffled. "Unusual men. Quite an outlandish story, really."

"Try us," Driscoll said.

Hassan glanced at him. "I'm still not sure it was true, of course. And my Spanish was a bit rusty—"

"Doc . . . " Driscoll interrupted. "We're kind of in a hurry."

"Of course," Hassan said, giving him an agreeable nod. "The two men who brought this one in told me that they had floated here on a raft from Cuba. They said to me they'd plucked this man out of the water the night they left. They'd heard shooting, and at first assumed it was meant for them. But then they realized it was something else altogether. They said the sky was filled with planes, the beach behind them full of explosions . . . " He broke off, shrugging.

"And then sometime after the firing had stopped, they came upon him, floating in the water, with his arm clutched to a piece of wreckage. They'd argued about what to do, the two of them, but they finally came to the conclusion that since he was an American and they were on their way to America, it was an omen of sorts. They were sure he'd never make it, but he had, in fact. He was still alive when they washed up on shore. By that time they were certain their fate was entwined with his and so they brought the man here."

Deal shook his head. "Why didn't you report all this?"

The intern gave him a puzzled glance. "To what end? The story was quite incredible. The patient had vanished, as had the men who brought him here."

"But still . . . "

"You must understand, I might treat fifty persons on a weekend shift." His eyes grew large behind his glasses. "And in this hospital, one encounters many strange stories."

Deal turned to Driscoll, shaking his head in amazement. "It couldn't be Tommy, Vernon. It just couldn't be . . . "

"There's one easy way to find out," Driscoll said. He stood and placed a hand on the intern's shoulder. "One hell of an easy way."

"Again?" Hassan's voice was a whisper. He glanced back at them as he bent over Tommy's inert form. "He has been shot again? How could it be?"

"That's him, Doc?" Driscoll gestured for him to take a closer look. "You're sure?"

Hassan's hands moved carefully to Tommy's head, pushed a shock of his hair aside, inspected something. He stood back, held his hands out like a film director framing Tommy's face. Finally he turned, shaking his head in disbelief.

"It has been some time," he said, pointing back at Tommy. "But you see the scar there, just above the ear. That was the location of the wound I saw . . . "

Driscoll nodded.

"Are you certain?" Deal said, impatient.

Hassan shrugged again. "Yes. In my best estimation. I would have to say yes."

"Well, thanks a million, Doc," Driscoll said, propelling him toward the door.

Hassan held back, as if he'd be glad to put off his rounds to stay and chat. "It is quite some story, no?"

"You bet your boots," Driscoll said. "We appreciate all your trouble."

"There is something else I can do?"

"Just tell the ladies down at the nurses' station to give us a couple more minutes. We won't bother him," Driscoll said, guiding Hassan on out into the hallway. He gave the intern a reassuring nod, then closed the door and hurried to the phone without a word to Deal.

"Yes," he said, dialing an operator. "This is Dr. Hassan. Can you get me a Broward County number, please?"

Driscoll waved away Deal's inquiring look as he waited for a connection. After a minute his face lit up. "Yeah, Osvaldo, it's me, Driscoll." He paused, waiting for a moment, then took out his little pad and made a couple of notes.

"That's great, Osvaldo. But there's just one more thing . . . "

He held the phone away from his ear, letting Deal hear a stream of high-pitched curses. When Osvaldo's voice had calmed, Driscoll took up again.

"I appreciate it, Osvaldo. All you have to do is check out a guy named Anthony Everett. I've got a Social Security number and a Maryland driver's license with an address." Driscoll repeated the information they'd taken from the hospital's admissions form, listened while Osvaldo repeated it. "Yeah, just verify that stuff, run him for outstanding warrants, call up a credit report, anything that's easy." He held the phone away from his ear again at Osvaldo's reply, then thanked him and hung up.

Driscoll studied the notes he'd made for a moment, then looked up at Deal. "Seems our buddy Torreno's been busy," he said.

"Doing what?" Deal asked.

Driscoll tapped his little pad in his hand. "Osvaldo says he's dumped about thirty-five million dollars into real estate over the past six months, and that's just what the computer was able to pick up on the quick."

"So?"

"So, all of these transactions are recorded in Torreno's name, or companies controlled by him. Five'll get you ten most of the money for those deals came out of the Patriots' Foundation coffers."

"What did he buy with it?"

"Some of it's parcels of land over in Collier County. That's where they busted a couple of paramilitary training camps tied to the foundation last year."

"Maybe he's just buying the land in his name to keep things quiet."

"Maybe," Driscoll said, tapping his notebook. "But that only accounts for a small portion of it. What do you think the Patriots' Foundation cares about American Amalgamated Industries," he said, pausing for emphasis, "for which Torreno forked over twenty-seven point one million dollars."

Deal stared. "Twenty-seven million? What *is* American Amalgamated Industries?"

"American Sugar," Driscoll said. "*Big* sugar, up by Lake Okeechobee. It's the biggest single processor in the U.S. It used to be controlled by a family named Carbonell. The old man died recently, his kids finally got to sell."

"Osvaldo told you all this?" Deal's eyes were on Tommy, his waxy skin, his slack mouth, the tubes and lines that held him to the world.

Driscoll shook his head. "Naw. I met Carbonell a couple years back. He was a real independent old cuss, a guy who came over here long before Castro. His family had been in the business down there for a hundred years. He read the handwriting on the wall, came to the U.S., built his sugar empire, never looked back. He hated Torreno and his activities. Somebody put me on to him, thought he might be able to give me some leads on some of the things we were looking into."

Deal glanced up from Tommy with a sigh. "And did he?"

Driscoll shook his head again. "He didn't know shit, really. Torreno had come to him for money to support the foundation early on, Carbonell threw him out on his ass. Old guy talked my ear off about making your own way, America the land of opportunity, all that. What he knew about was growing sugarcane."

"How did he die?" Deal said. He was tired. Funny how that worked. Get beaten down to the bone, things made more sense than when you were rested, your mind firing on all cylinders.

"He drowned," Driscoll said, giving him a look. "Slipped into one of the canals on his farm. Couple of his sons found him, that's the story, anyway."

"A guy that only cared about one thing dies in an accident, now Torreno owns his pride and joy," Deal said.

Driscoll nodded. "I thought I was the conspiracy theorist around here."

"Maybe it's rubbing off," Deal said. He was trying to comprehend it, all the things a man might be willing to do if enough money was involved. Or maybe he was looking at it from the wrong end, picking all the nits. To Torreno, a killing here, a firebombing there, those were tiny details in an operation that was so big it dwarfed old-fashioned notions like morality.

"Still," Driscoll said. "I don't know why he'd do it. I mean, you hear all those stories," he continued, "a guy gets bad service, he buys the restaurant and fires everybody. But twenty-seven million dollars. That's a lot of revenge."

"Maybe that's what Torreno wants to do next, become a sugar baron."

Driscoll shook his head. "He's got to be smarter than that. Carbonell himself told me he was losing money. The land's eroding, they got all kinds of labor problems, the price of domestic sugar is propped up by price controls that everybody in Congress is pissed off about . . . " He trailed off. "The entire industry's on the edge. It'd be like buying a steel mill in Pittsburgh because you liked the football team."

They stood quietly for a time then, Deal running it all over in his mind, fighting the feeling that threatened to overwhelm him altogether. If it was true, if Tommy was the target of Torreno, then he was simply an afterthought; he and his family were mere nuisances caught up in the backwash of a high roller's rush to the money trough. Driscoll, Tommy, Janice, Isabel, all of them like fleas to a man who, apparently, could do anything without fear of reprisal.

He stared down at the inert form before him. Tubes ran from both nostrils, both arms, a battery of equipment stacked near the bed. What had he done? What threat could *this* man have posed to Torreno?

"Anthony Everett," he said, shaking his head. "Whoever the hell *he* is."

He was about to turn to Driscoll when he felt the brush of something at his pantleg. He glanced down, surprised to see Tommy's fingers clutching feebly at the bedclothes. Tommy's lips moved then and a sound came. At first he thought it was a moan or Tommy babbling nonsense in his sleep . . . then Tommy's eyes flickered open and his hand reached toward Deal.

"Suh . . . " Tommy said, "suh . . . suh . . . ," his mouth twisting as if each syllable racked him with pain. One of the monitors at his bedside had begun to beep urgently.

"A nurse," Deal said to Driscoll. "Get a nurse."

He grasped Tommy's hand as the ex-cop bolted for the door.

"Easy now," Deal said. He felt a spasm run through Tommy's body. "Take it easy."

"Suh-gah," Tommy said, his voice almost a wail. Deal leaned close, hearing shouted orders, footsteps approaching in the hall.

Tommy's gaze was locked desperately on Deal, his mouth still twist-ing painfully. "Gave . . . him . . . suh-gah. *We* did . . . "

He squeezed Deal's hand once more. His eyes began to roll, and he fell back on his pillows. ". . . gave him the *suh-gar!*" He fought to stay awake, reaching out to Deal with a panicked expression, like a man about to go backward off a cliff. "We . . . gave . . . him . . . the . . . sugar . . . " he said, his voice halting but clear. And then, as if the effort to articulate the words had taken everything, he collapsed. The machine was beeping furiously now.

Deal looked up as the door to the room flew open and a cadre of nurses and technicians rushed inside.

"You, out of here!" one of the nurses barked.

An orderly stepped in front of Deal, taking Tommy's hand away. Deal allowed himself to be guided into the hall, where Driscoll waited.

He still felt the charge that had transferred itself from Tommy's urgent grasp, could still hear his words echoing in his mind.

He turned back to Tommy's room, where the beeping of the bed-side monitor had mercifully slowed. An aide hurried out, heading back toward the nurses' station.

"He okay?" Driscoll demanded.

"He's still alive," the aide said. He didn't look at them, didn't break stride.

Driscoll gestured through the open doorway where the crew still worked. Tommy lay quiet again, unprotesting as they probed him, reattached lines and tubes. "That guy is one tough sonofabitch," Driscoll said, marveling. He glanced at Deal. "He say something to you?"

"Something." Deal nodded. Deal felt the heat inside him gather-ing, focusing into the tip of a blue-white flame.

"Well?" Driscoll asked, waiting.

"Let's go see Osvaldo," Deal said. He glanced up, seeing that for once the puzzled expression was on Driscoll's face. "Let's find out who Anthony Everett really is."

"Well, whoever Tommy Holsum really is," Osvaldo said, "he ain't any Anthony Everett." He'd gathered a sheaf of papers from the tray of his printer, tossed them on the desk in the direction of Deal and Driscoll.

Deal reached for the papers, scanned them as Osvaldo continued.

"I ran the license first—stuff on that comes back fast, so if you got a guy stopped at the side of the road, you can get a make on him before he decides to pull out his MAC-10, give you early retirement."

He glanced at Driscoll, who motioned for him to get to the point. "Anyway, there's no such license issued by the Maryland Department of Motor Vehicles. Never has been."

"How about the Social Security number?" Deal said, flipping through the papers.

"There was an Anthony Everett who had that number once," Osvaldo said. He was trying to sound authoritative, but his absurd voice didn't help. "That Anthony Everett died in Fargo, North Dakota, in 1972, at the age of eighty."

Deal stared at him. There was silence for a moment, broken only by the steady rush of the air conditioning. The room seemed colder suddenly.

"He's a spook," Driscoll said. "Somebody made him up, gave him a cover."

"Torreno?" Deal asked.

Driscoll shook his head. "I doubt it. The bad guys usually don't bother with that kind of stuff."

Deal nodded. Letting it sink in.

"Who wants to go first?" Driscoll said. "Guess who it was, which famous Uncle created Anthony Tommy Everett Whoever?"

Deal nodded. "The government. Our own government."

"They gotta cover themselves, just like anybody else," Driscoll said. "The foundation has a well-funded lobby in Washington. You lend Torreno and his cronies a guy like Tommy, some spook from an agency you never knew existed, let him train true believers how to play guns in the jungle. Makes it seem like you're doing the crazies a favor, also gives you a way to keep track of what they're up to."

Driscoll gave Deal a look. "You told me Tommy had a pretty vivid fantasy about a bunch of guys invading a beach in the tropics somewhere, right? Everybody got the shit shot out of them?" He waved his hands like he was building something in the air.

"He was there," Deal said, the realization flooding over him. "He had to be. He was part of it."

Driscoll nodded. "So Torreno put a bullet in his head, tossed him into the ocean. Told whoever that Tommy got blown away in the operation and figures that's the end of Anthony Everett."

Deal had a vision of Tommy Holsum on the deck of a boat, good old Tommy, Tommy the spook, seeing it all go bad. Turning, throwing up his hands, just that much too late, tumbling into the water, where he'd surely die. And might as well have died, given what had happened to him. Two rafters bound for freedom in the U.S. pick up the guy who's helping to run the last great Cold War scam of the century, give him a new life. All the irony. It would make quite a story, except the ending had gone to shit.

Deal shook his head finally. "It just might have worked, until Tommy showed up in the newspaper on his way to my house. Torreno or one of his people sees he's still alive, they come after him."

Driscoll nodded. "Makes sense to me."

"But why go to the trouble?" Osvaldo said. "What's this Tommy or Everett gonna say? Everybody's gotta know we're helping train these Cuban commando guys. Who cares if they're dumb enough to get their brains blown out?"

"According to this book," Driscoll said, "this book that doesn't seem to *exist* anymore, Torreno set his own guys up. Sent them in there knowing they'd get blown away."

Osvaldo shook his head. "For what?"

"It's a long story," Driscoll said, "but the bottom line reads money." He threw up his hands. "Only thing is, there's no way to prove it."

"We gave him the sugar," Deal said abruptly. He'd been listening to the two of them going back and forth, the words Tommy had uttered twisting through the thoughts in his mind like some musical counterpoint.

"What's that?" Driscoll said.

"It's what Tommy said in the hospital when you went for the nurses," he said. "'We gave him the sugar.'"

"So what's *that* supposed to mean?" Osvaldo said.

"Means the guy's been shot twice in the head," Driscoll said, disgusted.

"Think about it, Driscoll," Deal said. "You're the one who compared Torreno to the guys in the Pentagon, profiting all those years of the Cold War. If that's so, then he'd have to know the foundation's days are numbered, right?"

Driscoll nodded.

"So if he's the kind of businessman you think he is, he's got to think ahead."

"We already went over that," Driscoll said, impatient. "He bought a sugar farm that's likely to bankrupt him or the foundation, whoever it belongs to. It'll happen even quicker if Castro goes."

"That's right," Deal said. "It doesn't make sense." He glanced at Osvaldo, who was listening thoughtfully, then turned back to Driscoll. "*Unless* there was another reason he made that purchase."

Driscoll shook his head. "Such as?"

"'We gave him the sugar,'" Deal repeated. "Think about it for a second. What if we *did*? What if the government really did?"

"I don't know what the hell you're talking about," Driscoll said.

Osvaldo was nodding. "You're thinking we franchised him, right? Found the bull goose Cuban with ties to sugar and gave him the franchise."

Driscoll was still shaking his head, bewildered.

"There was economic disaster in Eastern Europe, there has been ever since the Wall came down," Deal said. "But Cuba's on our doorstep. We can't afford chaos once Castro's out of power. Somebody else could step in, screw up things even worse. There has to be a game plan to prop up the infrastructure so we don't end up spending a ton to keep Cuba friendly.

"Once Castro's out," Deal continued, "what's Torreno going to have left, a pension from the Patriots' Foundation? Somebody's got to run big sugar in Cuba. Somebody from the States. Just like every other concession that'll be worth a dime down there: hotels, casinos, banking. We're sure as hell not going to let Castro's ministers stay on. That's what Torreno's doing with American Sugar: He'll be the natural choice. Twenty-seven million's a drop in the bucket compared to what he'll have one day."

Osvaldo chimed in. "Somebody gets telephones, somebody gets airports . . ."

". . . and somebody gets sugar," Deal said. "Just like a big game of Monopoly."

"Except that the money's real," Osvaldo said. "Sugar's the only thing in Cuba that's worth a damn these days. Everything else— tourism, the casinos—that's going to take years to bring back. You're talking a billion-dollar industry, conservatively, ready to throw open the door."

"That's what Tommy knew about?" Driscoll said. "It's a stretch . . ."

"Sure it is," Deal said. "But give me another scenario that makes sense."

"It would explain why they've been trying to kill him," Osvaldo said, leaning back in his chair. "Possibility of him screwing up a deal that big . . ."

"Well, he isn't dead yet," Driscoll said.

Deal turned to him then, as did Osvaldo. They shared a gaze, three people on a street corner who've just caught sight of an old woman in a crosswalk, an out-of-control bus headed her way.

"Call the hospital," Deal managed finally.

But Driscoll's hands were already on the phone.

"I let them die," Tommy heard himself saying. Heard his own voice, sure and strong, even though he knew it was a dream. Such a long time since he had heard the sound of his own true voice. "I let good men die," he repeated.

He was standing in a vast room, a courtroom, he realized, before a black-robed tribunal, his confession echoing off the unseen walls like a mantra: "I let good men die. . . . "

The judges wore faces from the history books, all the leaders and would-be leaders who'd died the wrong way themselves, even the one from another century with the beard and the birthday, the back of his head blown away, nodding and chatting with the others, who no longer seemed to be taking notice of Tommy. Then a stoop-shouldered man with a massive head and a bloodhound's face, no bullet wounds on his body, stood up to say, "My fellow Americans, it is a tough life." He smiled, and pulled a lever that yanked a square of marble floor from under Tommy's feet and sent him hurtling, breathless, down a chute for what seemed like miles that ended when he plunged into icy water.

Tommy came up out of the water gasping, clawing for life . . . and then his eyes flickered open, and, with relief, he found himself in a hospital bed. *This is real*, he understood. *This is my life now*. There were lines and tubes that ran up from his arms to places he could not see. He heard the muted beeping of some machine that he sensed was counting out the pulses of his body, saw someone in hospital greens working at a table near the door.

Although his tongue was thick, and his throat felt the size of a needle's eye, his mind raced with a clarity that had eluded him since . . . since when, really? That awful day on the boat?

So many things had happened, he knew. And yet he had been graced. He had been brought back. Given a chance to atone for mistake upon mistake compounded into tragedy. And still there was time to do something. At the very least he could confess his sins and bring justice to the man who had betrayed him, betrayed them all.

He swallowed, willing his voice to return to him, and called out then. The man in the green gown turned. He was tall and wore a white mask that covered his nose and mouth. He held a syringe aloft. His long, glove-clad fingers clenched, and a spray of liquid shot into the air. Tommy felt something spatter his cheek. A bitter smell overwhelmed him.

The eyes, Tommy was thinking. The same awful eyes. Then the man pulled down the mask and he saw who it was. For a moment he thought he was back in his dream. Impossible that *he* should be standing above him in a doctor's clothing, an expression that looked strangely like fear on that ruined face.

Tommy tried to call out. What words were they, he wondered, as Coco bent over him? What final words?

"Sow-wry," he heard himself moan then, in Tommy's pitiful voice, as the needle struck home. "I'm *sow-wry!*" And then everything was starry light.

It seemed to take an eternity, waiting for Driscoll to get through. From what Deal could tell by listening to half of several conversations, there was no information available from the operator. When he finally got a number for the nurses' station on Tommy's floor, a nurse transferred him to the administrator's office. After another five minutes on hold, Driscoll was ready to hang up. Then a voice sounded on the other line.

Driscoll started to explain, then broke off. Deal couldn't make out the words on the other end, but the look on Driscoll's face was enough. He knew before the big man had replaced the receiver on the hook.

"Tommy's dead," Driscoll said. "His heart just stopped." He looked around the room, shaking his head like a boxer who'd taken a stop-the-bout shot. "That's what they said."

"Bullshit," Deal said.

The room was quiet again. The same three bystanders on the corner, who've just seen the old lady get flattened while the bus goes hurtling on, somebody scrapes the body off the pavement, and the world turns merrily on.

"He'd do anything," Deal said. "Anything at all."

Driscoll glanced at him as if he'd just remembered there were other people around.

"He'd kill me, you, my wife, my daughter," Deal continued, "if he thought we were in the way." So much seemed so clear now, Torreno's motives apparent, Deal's rage equally clear in its focus. But still, the greater mystery nagged at him: Why had Deal been so loath to accept it? What was there inside himelf that made him so ready to blame himself for what had befallen him and his family?

"Hey," Driscoll said. "He doesn't care about you. It's over. Even if it's the way you say it is, Tommy's the last one who could hurt him."

"Is that right, Vernon? What if he's sitting around right now wondering whether Tommy came to his senses for a moment while he was living with us, said something to me, or Janice, or Isabel, for that matter? Where does a guy like that draw the line?"

"We'll get him," Driscoll said. "We'll get an autopsy on Tommy . . . "

"They won't find a thing, Vernon. And even if they do, how would you implicate Torreno?"

Driscoll started to say something, then stopped. He threw his hands up helplessly.

"So that's it, huh?" Osvaldo said. "This slimewad just goes on his way, you guys sit around and wonder whether you're gonna get whacked someday?"

"If we had *any*thing," Driscoll said. "Valles, or Tommy, even that cockamamie book . . . " He drifted off, still wondering.

The book, Deal thought. It *had* existed. They had the title page to prove it. But now . . . He stared about Osvaldo's office, at all the equipment, the computers, the printers. It seemed as if Osvaldo had the capability to put his hands on almost any information that had ever been stored. Too bad they couldn't access the ether, pull Valles's records or that manuscript out of thin air somehow . . .

. . . and then, even as the thought of giving up, gathering his family for a flight somewhere far away had occurred to him, he felt the vague stirrings of a plan. It was a long shot, but under the circumstances . . .

"Osvaldo," he said abruptly, and the little man looked up from behind his thick glasses. "How about the State Department? You think you could get into their files?"

"It depends on what you want," he said. "We won't find any memos on the stuff you're talking about, trust me."

"No," Deal said. "That's not what I had in mind. Compared to that, what I want ought to be easy."

They swung down off Old Cutler, heading east toward the water. The sun had been reduced to a tired thumbnail of reddish orange, sinking beneath the horizon behind them. This far south, the houses were scattered, separated by vast stretches of pines and mango farms. A lonely place to live, Deal found himself thinking.

On the right ran a tall chain-link fence, the wire clad in black vinyl and topped with coils of razor wire. Deal had always assumed it was part of the neighboring agricultural station. Now he knew it marked the boundary of Torreno's estate.

Osvaldo had called up an aerial map on one of his computer screens—*You want maps? Piece of cake!*—and Deal had seen the whole elaborate place—main house, guest cottages, lake, private marina. They'd also spent enough time manufacturing phone calls in the little man's office to confirm Torreno's movements. If their luck held, Torreno would arrive in Miami from the offices of American Sugar within the hour. And if he didn't, they could always try Plan B.

He wanted to laugh. Plan A was flimsy enough—he couldn't imagine what might come next. He glanced down at the thick sheaf of paper in his lap, still warm from the bowels of Osvaldo's speedy printer.

He caught sight of his own feet then, momentarily startling himself. It took him a moment to believe that the wingtip shoes there were on his own feet. He was more accustomed to Top-Siders and tennis shoes. At the same moment, his hand went involuntarily to the tie that formed a strangling knot at his throat. How many years since he'd worn a tie? He'd had to get the salesman at the clothing store to knot it for him. It had taken three stops before they found a place with suits that seemed suitably "Washington" by Driscoll's standards.

"So let me get this straight," Driscoll said, his eyes on the road. He reached into a pocket of his coat, withdrew a tiny tape recorder from Osvaldo's endless cache, and held it up. "We're going to walk in and tell the guy, 'We think you stole about thirty mill from your foundation's treasury, plus killed a few dozen people so you could take over the sugar business in Cuba one day. Could we have your confession now?"

He replaced the recorder and glanced over at Deal.

"You spent the last ten years of your life trying to nail this guy, Driscoll. He's still walking around, doing all the things he likes to do. Does that suggest anything to you?"

"Yeah," Driscoll said. "It suggests he's been awful lucky."

"Well, it suggests to me we try something different."

Driscoll glanced at him again. "You don't have a gun in that suit, do you? That's one way we're not going to do it."

Deal shook his head. Driscoll reached over, opened Deal's coat. "Good," the ex-cop said.

"I'm surprised, Driscoll," Deal said.

"What surprises you?" Driscoll drove past a break in the tall wire fence where a massive wooden gate had been set between two coral-rock pillars.

"That you wouldn't want to just blow him away, throw a gun down, take care of things that way. You've been telling me all along you know he's guilty."

"I want this guy so bad I can taste it," Driscoll said. "I know he's guilty, but I'm not the judge, and I'm sure as shit not the executioner." He drove another hundred yards down the tree-shrouded road, made a U-turn, pulled off in the shadow of a huge banyan tree. A screen of tendrils hung down from the limbs, draping over the windshield like a veil of tiny roots flourishing in the air. In the fading light, the Ford would be hidden from anyone approaching the gates.

Driscoll killed the engine and turned, giving him an uncharacteristically harsh stare. "That's one thing too many of my compadres down at City-County forgot about. We're supposed to *catch* the bad guys, that's all." He stared off, a forlorn expression on his face. "I dunno what makes some cops do the kinds of things you were talking about. Maybe it's the heat. You stay around too long, it finally fries all the good sense out of you."

"Well, I'm with you, Vernon," Deal said. "Let's catch a bad guy, then."

Driscoll nodded. "There's just one thing, though."

"What's that?"

"I'm still wondering why it took you so long to see this scumbag for what he is."

Deal stared at him. He wanted to say "Because you're the detective, Driscoll. Because you're used to seeing murderous intent behind the appearance of simple tragedy. I'm just a citizen." But Deal didn't say that because he knew it wasn't true. Instead, he took a deep breath.

"My old man was a crook, Driscoll. You've been around this town long enough to know."

"Hey . . . " Driscoll started to protest, but Deal cut him off.

"He called himself a builder, but he was really a crook. A crook, and a boozer, and a ladies' man. He was a wonderful character, my mother loved him, everybody loved him, even I loved him, but that doesn't change the facts."

Driscoll shifted in his seat, clearly sorry he'd started this.

"The point is," Deal said, "I saw how he threw his whole life away, how he had an excuse for every bad break he ever got, how that ruined him. What I think is"—Deal drew himself up—"I think I've spent my whole life trying to do just the opposite. Make your choices, put your head down, do your work, take what comes." He stared hard at Driscoll. "When my place burned down, I had no choice but to take the blame for it. I *wanted* to take the blame for it."

Driscoll stared back at him for a moment, finally nodded.

"So how's it feel, now you decided to stop whipping yourself?"

Deal smiled and shrugged. "Of course we don't know I've stopped, do we?"

Driscoll grunted in amusement, was about to respond when he seemed to notice something out of the corner of his eye. He sat up in his seat, pointing tensely out over the hood of the Ford.

Deal followed his gesture, saw a white limousine, its headlights glowing softly in the twilight as it approached in the distance. The limo slowed, turned into the graveled entryway. The driver's window slid down and a man in a visored cap leaned out, spoke into a speaker box mounted by the drive. After a moment the big gates swung open and the limo eased on inside.

"Sure, let's do it," Driscoll echoed, and eased the Ford out toward the gates.

Deal and Driscoll stood in the marble foyer of the main house while the servant who'd admitted them, a wizened Hispanic man who might have been seventy or eighty or one hundred, limped off down a hallway, his footsteps echoing arrhythmically off the stone floor toward the lofty ceiling above.

Deal gazed up at the stained-glass rotunda that capped the immense entryway. The thing was either backlit, or was catching the last rays of the sun: It depicted a scene that looked suspiciously like Washington's crossing of the Delaware, only this showed a dashing Hispanic man at the prow of the boat, a sword in hand, pointing the way into a tropical harbor.

Deal shook his head. It was like standing in a mock-up of some public building. He'd built entire houses you could fit into the space this guy used for stepping in out of the weather. "Where in the hell do you go from here?" he found himself wondering.

"What's that?" Driscoll asked. He'd been examining an elephant's-foot umbrella stand near the doorway.

"To have all this, and still want more," Deal said. "I can't figure it out."

"It's all relative, isn't it?" Driscoll shrugged. "A guy who lived on the street might see your place, say the same thing."

"Who said I wasn't happy where I was?" Deal said, an edge in his voice. "I don't recall asking to leave."

"You got a point," Driscoll said. He nodded down the hallway where the old servant had reappeared, hobbling as briskly as he could toward them.

"He's not aiming a gun at us," Driscoll said cheerily.

"So far, so good," Deal said.

"This way, *señores*," the servant said, and they followed.

Deal had the manuscript tucked under his arm as he leaned across the gleaming amber desk, handed Torreno his card. "James Ferrington," he said. "Department of State." Torreno inspected the card, his eyes flicking neutrally from it to Deal to Driscoll, who stood at military ease, his hands behind his back, the model of a disciplined goon. Deal had to marvel—he'd never seen the ex-cop in an erect posture before.

Osvaldo had pulled the design out of the State Department's computer. A half-hour later, Deal was holding half a dozen business cards, the gold seal embossed, the lettering raised. "This is Agent Dowd," Deal added. He watched, aghast, as Driscoll nodded, reached in his pocket, flashed his phony shield.

Torreno had barely noticed. His gaze was fixed on Deal. Deal had slicked his hair back in the men's room of the clothing store, borrowed a spritz from the bottle of styling gel there. At the time he'd thought he looked lawyerly, but under Torreno's scrutiny, he felt more like a clown. The man's suit was impeccably tailored, his nails glistened from a recent manicure, his skin glowed with health.

Deal was conscious of the hundred little construction man's nicks on his own hands, the telltale ring of a working man's tan at his neckline. They'd hemmed his pants with duct tape. Any second now, Vicente Luis Torreno was going to lean forward, press a button, and send them to oblivion. What had ever made him think this would work, he wondered. The whole thing was madness. But there wasn't much point in second-guessing himself at this pass.

"You received our fax," Deal heard himself saying. His voice sounded surprisingly confident in his own ears.

Torreno glanced at the machine on a credenza behind him. A secure, unidentified line. It had taken Osvaldo nearly an hour to find it in the Southern Bell records, distinguish it from the several other phone lines in the house by dint of the usage patterns: "A few hundred one-minute toll calls a month? Gotta be a fax line." It had seemed a reasonable guess, but the receiving tray was empty.

Torreno turned back to Deal, impatient. "Who *are* you, Mr. Ferrington?"

Deal felt sweat slick in his armpits, his groin. He'd forgotten how miserable it was to wear a suit.

He stared back at Torreno, who was clearly jacking himself into his intimidation mode. He'd encountered it before, from prime suppliers threatening to hold up delivery unless he'd agree to a kickback, from major developers trying to squeeze him into a lowball bid: "We've got a half-dozen outfits want to build homes on our properties, Mr. Deal. Every one of them twenty percent under your prices. Why would we want to do business with you?"

And how had he handled it all his workday life? What other choice was there? He'd simply had to trump them.

"Who I am is not important," he said to Torreno. "*This* is what's important." He took a breath, pulled the banded manuscript from the envelope under his arm, tossed it onto the burled walnut surface between them. It landed with a thud that sent a desk pen rattling out of its tortoiseshell holder.

Torreno gave him an uncertain look, then glanced down at the cover sheet, the very one they'd pulled from the water near the Marquez gallery. Deal could see a muscle begin to twitch in Torreno's jaw.

Let the sight of that rumpled cover be enough, he prayed. If he opened it up, Torreno would find himself reading volume A of the *Encyclopaedia Britannica*, courtesy of Osvaldo's CD-ROM library. At least he might have had the foresight to suggest printing out the S's, Deal was thinking. At least there would have been something about sugar inside . . .

Torreno pushed himself away from the desk, as if that would distance him from what the manuscript might contain. "What do you mean by this?" he said, indignant. "What do you intend, bringing this into my house?"

Torreno was good, but Deal had seen that momentary look of fear in the man's eyes, and now he could feel it, the tiniest tilt of balance.

And then, as if it was a sign, the fax machine chirped, then stuttered into life. Deal folded his hands behind his back and gave a meaningful look at the document that was unfolding from the green-haloed slot. Just let it be the one, he prayed. The machine gave a final chatter and clipped the sheet into the tray.

Torreno reached for the message, his eyes still on Deal, then bent to read the type. After a moment, his eyes flicked back to the manuscript that still lay untouched on the desk. Finally he looked up at Deal. "Why did you not say this to begin with?" he said. Deal felt relief flood over him. Torreno's voice was still gruff, but the suspicion seemed to have vanished.

"I was about to," Deal replied. *And thank God for Osvaldo*, he thought.

"Then let us go outside and talk," Torreno said with a magnanimous gesture. "The grounds are much more congenial."

Deal signaled his agreement with a nod, scooping the manuscript up in the same smooth motion, then followed Torreno out into the night.

Coco Morales had hesitated upon leaving the hospital. It was a puzzling sensation, hesitating, feeling the willingness to waste time. He had stood outside on the curb in the balmy evening, watching the visitors stream into the hospital, carrying bunches of flowers, boxes of candy, tightly rolled coils of magazines and newspapers.

He tried to discern from the looks on the faces of those entering how severe were the cases of those they had come to visit, but it was a difficult task. Most of them seemed inordinately cheery, given their destination. Then again, they were not the ones lying ill or dying.

He left off these thoughts, reminding himself that he should not be lingering. This normal world was not his arena. He had already seen a few uncertain glances come his way. He functioned here well enough when there was work to be completed. After that, it was best to retire to his domain, to his tiny TV set, and the quarters where he had learned to be comfortable, where he knew he had a place.

And yet this night he hesitated, drawn by the sight of all those cheery people rushing to comfort those whom they loved, or professed to love, perhaps a bit saddened by his realization that his work was in fact nearly completed. Of course, there would be a mission here and there, surely. But soon, whether in a few weeks or months, a year or two at most, his employer would realize his dream, and they would return. . . .

And Coco knew he would not go. Could not return, no matter what it might mean. For his employer had been correct. Home, for Coco, was where he hung his hat. Whatever he had become, he had become that by doing what he had done and going where he had gone, and it did not seem to him possible to transport this self back again.

To touch his foot upon that soil would be fatal. He could not survive it. He could not explain the reason for it, but he knew it to be true, just as he knew that a witch would die when plunged into water, just as he knew that his employer would return and thrive, thrive and flourish like some strange jungle creature taken to a place where nothing existed to prey upon it.

It would be difficult to remain behind, of course. As it was difficult to imagine an existence apart from his employer, after all this time, after all the deeds he had done in his service. But he could not go back, that much he knew. Coco could not go back.

"Look at the man, Mommy," a distant voice said.

Coco blinked, came back from his thoughts, saw a little girl in a sailor's dress being dragged over the curb by her embarrassed mother. The mother had averted her face and hissed something at her, but the mask of concern on the little girl's face was not affected.

"What's wrong with that *man*?" Coco heard her insist as they disappeared inside the hospital doors.

A perfectly acceptable question, he was thinking. And turned to make his way home.

"This rum is more than a century old," Torreno was saying. He stood at the railing of his lakeside pavilion, his back to the water, raising his glass. "You can taste the very essence of our land in it. The strength. The beauty."

Deal saw a strange rippling movement break the reflection of the moon on the surface of the water nearby. *Something's hungry*, he thought. He had a vision of driving his shoulder into Torreno's chest, sending him into the water. The thought made him giddy, and he fought to return his attention to the matter at hand.

An impassive young man in a white coat stood behind the bar. He'd poured drinks for Driscoll and Deal, but they remained untouched.

"I'm sure you can," Deal said. "Another time, maybe."

Torreno raised an eyebrow. "In any case, I am honored to welcome a personal representative of our President to my home," he said, then tossed his drink down.

After a moment, he pointed at the manuscript that Deal held. "Garbage," he repeated. "An embarrassment to us all. It is unfortunate that a man in my position must suffer such unfounded outrage . . . "

Deal, forced himself to cut Torreno off. He gave a curt gesture. "We really don't care what you've done, Mr. Torreno." He hesitated, suppressing the urge to snatch up his own drink. "You've read the fax. We're only concerned with what might be proven."

He gestured back at the house and uttered another unspoken prayer of thanks to Osvaldo. "This is a matter of utmost concern, a concern that extends to the highest levels."

Torreno stared at him darkly. "*None* of it can be proven."

Driscoll finally broke his silence then. "I'm sure that's true, Mr. Torreno." He was staring down, his hands clasped in a thoughtful manner. When he glanced up at Torreno, his face seemed avuncular, reassuringly wise. "But, you see, we're here to help you, and unless you're willing to speak frankly with us, we're not going to be able to accomplish what's necessary."

"And what is that?" Torreno asked. It was less a demand than a question. *Please, let this work*, Deal found himself praying. He waited, almost afraid to breathe, for Driscoll's reply.

Driscoll waved his hands in a placating gesture. "Mr. Torreno, I deal in security." He gave him a reassuring smile. "There are none of us, all the way to the top, who are exactly what you'd call naive. We understand what's involved in achieving a position of power, and in maintaining that position." He glanced over at Deal. "We also understand that people in a desperate situation may be forced into actions that those in more comfortable positions find it easy to criticize."

Deal tried not to stare. He'd never heard Driscoll approach articulate status before. "But what's most important to us," he cut in, "is that there be a smooth transition in your country once Castro is gone. Given your position within the exile community, you can be of tremendous help to us. You'll control the most important cash resource in the country. You'll lend stability to the political process."

Torreno watched them carefully, his eyes going back and forth from Deal to Driscoll, his expression beginning to soften as Deal larded it on.

Driscoll nodded in tune to Deal's speech, stepped in adroitly on his pause. "But you know all this, Mr. Torreno. What we need to know is what you've actually done. So we can make sure nothing—I mean *nothing*—ever sees the light of day. You're our man. We want you to be absolutely safe."

His moon-shaped face was absolutely benign as he stared into Torreno's eyes. Here was the protector everyone dreamed of, Deal thought, the wise and kindly uncle who only wanted the best for you, the man with the thick fingers to chuck under your chin . . . and the strength to kick the living shit out of the baddest bully on the block, reach into his chest and tear his heart out bare-handed, if it came to that.

Driscoll's whole being seemed to radiate that promise: *Come on in close, let me put my great big arm around you, you won't have to worry about a thing.* Deal marveled at the transformation. Every fiber in the big cop's body had to be steeped in loathing for the man in front of them, and yet somehow he'd transformed that energy into a beam of radiant goodwill.

"We can discount much of what's in here," Deal said, indicating the manuscript. "But if there are records that support the charges of financial irregularities . . . "

Torreno broke in. "I destroyed them myself."

Deal stared, feeling a wave of relief wash over him. He forced himself not to look at Driscoll.

But then Torreno gathered himself. "They were forgeries, of course. The foundation had employed an accountant, a traitor. He came to me with documents he'd created, accused me of embezzling funds meant for *la revolución*."

"What did you do?" Driscoll asked. Something splashed in the water behind them. Deal heard a sucking sound, like something being pulled down a clogging drain.

"I paid him," Torreno said. "A foolish mistake. He delivered what he said were the only copies of these documents, disappeared, and then, later"—he waved his hand dismissively at the manuscript under Deal's arm—"*this* assemblage of lies came to my attention."

He was either incapable of telling the truth or was determined to protect himself to the bitter end, Deal thought. Whichever it was, he was like some slithering creature it was impossible to catch. The moment you thought you had him, he twisted away.

"There's another problem," Driscoll said. "There's an intelligence operative who's mentioned in the book; he makes allegations that you actually cut a deal with Castro . . . "

"Outrageous lies." Torreno's eyes were flashing. "There is no such operative. He's a figment of a madman's imagination . . . "

"His name is Anthony Everett," Driscoll said. "At least that's the name he used when he worked with you." Driscoll's demeanor had shifted suddenly. He'd gone from good cop to bad cop in an instant.

"Don't bullshit us, Mr. Torreno. We know who Anthony Everett is, for Chrissakes. We sent him to you. The question is, where is he now? If you know the slightest goddamned thing, you better speak up now."

He gestured at Deal, who held his breath as he listened to Driscoll running their bluff. "This man here says the word back in Washington, you're history. You understand me? Your whole frigging deal is history."

The two men stared at one another for a moment. Deal heard an unearthly howl from somewhere deep in the forest that stretched out beyond the lake.

"He is dead," Torreno said finally.

Deal flinched at the words. He was finding it hard to concentrate as Torreno continued.

"He died off the coast of Cuba, assisting the valiant efforts of a band of freedom fighters."

"Excuse my French, Mr. Torreno, but you're full of more shit than a Christmas turkey," Driscoll said. "We have it on good authority that this Anthony Everett's right here in South Florida, ready to blow the whistle on your whole operation."

It stopped him, all right. Driscoll had played their last card, and it had stopped him. But the question was, would it carry? Torreno had turned to stare off over the water in the direction of the echoing howl.

"What did this man know about you, Mr. Torreno?" Deal persisted. "Tell us what he's got, so we can make a proper evaluation. Otherwise"—Deal shook his head—"I'm afraid . . . "

Torreno turned upon him, his face composed. "What this man knew is of no consequence, Mr. Ferrington." He glanced bitterly at Driscoll. "In fact, he *was* here, threatening me, threatening all of us. But now he is dead."

"He's in a hospital . . . " Deal heard himself say.

"No, Mr. Ferrington," Torreno said flatly. "He is dead. Trust me."

Deal swung his gaze to Driscoll. Driscoll ignored him, his own eyes on Torreno.

"How do you know this?" Driscoll said, his voice thick, resolute.

"It is done," Torreno said. "You must trust me."

Deal stared at Driscoll, waiting for some sign of confirmation. Was it enough? Had the man said enough?

273

Torreno picked up a phone mounted near the bar, punched a few buttons. "Coco," he said into the receiver.

"Is he returned?" He paused, staring at Driscoll. "Good," he said finally. "Send him to me."

As Driscoll turned to him, Deal could see the old self mustering itself, ready to burst through the facade of their playacting. Deal's mind was reeling. Tommy. They'd left him lying there in a hospital bed, helpless. . . . Deal felt himself swinging between rage and guilt, his hands knotting as he stared at Torreno.

He heard a door close softly somewhere behind them, then the sound of footsteps moving along a gravel path. He turned as the man stepped out of the shadows and came toward them. He was tall and gaunt, moving with the lope of a rangy animal, like a dog that had been beaten into a permanent cower. *And those are the dangerous ones,* Deal found himself thinking as the man moved into the circle of light that the flickering lanterns threw.

When he saw the ruined face, he knew his thought was true: It was a ruin, unsightly enough in its cadaverousness, made worse by the years of disdain the world must have reflected back at it. And the eyes. The eyes were the worst. They stared at Deal with the same impersonal calculation an animal might cast on its prey. Deal had seen bigger men. He had seen violent men. He had never seen a more frightening man.

"The man who would not die, Coco," Torreno said. "Tell them what has happened to him."

Coco had not taken his eyes off Deal.

"It is all right, Coco," Torreno said. "We are among friends."

Coco still did not answer. He lifted his hand, pointing a long finger at Deal. "I know this man," he said.

And then Deal knew they were lost.

"Excuse me," Torreno said, sudden concern on his face.

"It was his building," Coco said. "The apartment building . . . "

Torreno turned, astonished. "Deal?" he said. "Your name is Deal . . . ?"

He lunged toward the bar, and Driscoll's hand went into his jacket. In the same instant, Coco spun toward Driscoll, a blade flashing in his hand.

Without thinking, Deal snatched up one of the flickering kerosene lanterns from the bar and heaved it at Coco. The glass shade shattered and flames exploded, flames that rolled down the length of Coco's back.

Coco straightened, a man suddenly bathed in fire, his hands flaring straight upward, his fingertips spitting molten blue light. He stood there, wavering, a beacon, a pillar of fire. Flames leapt from his outstretched fingers into the dry palm leaves that formed the low thatched roof of the pavilion.

Driscoll had his pistol out now, was backpedaling from the flaming creature that staggered toward him. He turned back to the bar just as a shot rang out. The ex-cop clutched at his chest, firing a shot from his own pistol. He gave Deal an instant's hopeless look and went over backward.

To Deal, it all seemed to happen in slow motion. Coco tottered in an agonized circle, his hands waving out some semaphore message from Hell. Driscoll's legs struggled, drew themselves up under him as if he might somehow rise, then fell slack. The servant who'd been behind the bar stared down at a widening circle of blood in the middle of his white vest, then slumped over.

Torreno stared from behind the bar, pistol upraised, as if he had turned to stone himself.

And that was the moment, Deal sensed. The moment where he might have acted. Might have vaulted over the bar in some hero's leap, wrested the pistol from Torreno, ended things the way they should have been ended.

It wasn't that he lacked the will. He would have done it, taken a bullet on the way, if that's what it would have meant. But it was like being in a car skidding out of control, one part of yourself perched on your own shoulder, offering advice to a body that has gone as dumb as death itself.

As quickly as he had sensed it, the moment had passed him by. Torreno turned toward him then, bringing the pistol up, pointing it toward him, firing in the same motion . . .

Only the man's urgency to kill, to shoot without aiming, had saved Deal's life. Deal heard the explosion as he dove behind one of the tables. He slid across the cobbled floor of the pavilion, past Driscoll's feet, another shot tearing a gouge in the pavement by his face. Fragments of tile tore into his cheek like buckshot. The flames were racing through the dry thatched roof now.

He saw Driscoll's .38 on the rough stones a yard away and

lunged out for it. Another shot rang out, and another, and he heard a groan above the roar of the flames. The shots, intended for Deal, took Coco squarely as he reeled blindly across the room. His back and head were still a mass of flames, the front of his shirt now soaked in blood. His feet stuttered aimlessly past Deal's outstretched hand, kicked the .38 across the tiles toward the water.

Deal scrambled to his knees and dove for the pistol as it slid over the edge. He got his hand on it, fumbled at its stubby barrel. He felt its cold weight in his fingers, and for one brief second thought it was his. Then it slipped from his grasp and fell into the dark water.

Coco staggered past him, so tall he hit the wooden railing at thigh level. Out of balance now, he flipped on over in an acrobat's move, disappearing in a whirl of fire. There was a hissing sound as his body hit the water. Then there was a frenzy as the lake's surface came alive with thrashing fins and that terrible sucking sound.

Coco's arm raised once, clawing toward the sky, then sank beneath the boiling water. Deal felt a searing pain in the back of his leg, felt his flesh erupt even before the sound of the shot echoed in his ears. For a moment he thought he would lose consciousness. He felt an iciness race through him, saw nothing but bright pinging lights and blackness.

Then he was on his side, his vision coming back, but bleary. Two Torrenos seemed to be coming at him: one tiny man who appeared very far away, along with another mirroring the tiny one's movements. This second Torreno was huge, looming, and the pistol he was pointing at Deal seemed as big as a cannon.

Torreno was careful this time, planting his feet squarely, bracing his back against the railing, bringing his other hand to steady the pistol so there would be no mistake. Deal struggled to get his feet under him, but one leg stuck out at an odd angle, refusing to cooperate.

So this was how it would end, Deal thought. He wondered how it would all be explained. Janice and Isabel. What would they be told? Some lie that would make it seem like Deal and Driscoll were the true criminals? Or were they even worthy of any explanation? Maybe they would simply disappear, buried in the bowels of the Everglades forever?

Deal had drawn his good leg under him now, had struggled to one knee. He stared up, his vision wavering. The two Torrenos swirled farther apart momentarily, then rushed together into one.

And that one was smiling, enjoying Deal's efforts. He waited for Deal to bring his face up into the light, thrust the pistol forward, and pulled the trigger.

Pulled again. And again. He turned the weapon over, staring stupidly at it, wondering. He was still staring at the gun when Deal came up off the floor, ignoring the pain in his ruined leg, taking Torreno with his shoulder.

The blow caught Torreno by surprise, striking him solidly on the chest. He staggered back against the railing, the empty pistol skittering away as his hands fought for purchase. He balanced there for an instant, his face a mask of panic as he willed his weight back toward land.

Deal caught hold of the railing, threw himself forward with his last fragment of will. His fist caught Torreno's cheek flush, just as he was coming forward, back toward safety.

Maximum resistance, Deal was thinking . . . and then he fell back, his own face cracking off the decking. He'd hit a golf ball like that once. One perfect shot. That seemed good enough for a lifetime. What were the chances of two?

Deal was prone now, sinking toward the darkness. Out of the corner of his eye, he saw Torreno go over the rail, hit the water with a cry. The man flailed about, seemed to propel himself upward for an instant, headed desperately back toward the overhang of the deck. If he made it, Deal thought, there'd be nothing he could do. Already his senses were closing down. The heat of the blazing roof was fading, the sounds of Torreno's struggles had gone dim, his own shattered leg was a numb memory.

Torreno had one hand at the railing now, was hauling himself up onto the deck, some awful eel-like creature thrashing at his face, its teeth locked into his flesh like something out of a nightmare. . . .

Goodbye and so long, the old college try, Deal was thinking, his vision going in and out . . .

And then he saw it—thinking it might be a dream at first—a hand rising impossibly up from the water. Coco's grisly hand, Deal realized, a charred ruin risen up from the deep, and now there would be two men to finish him . . .

. . . when the charred fingers locked at Torreno's throat, locked and squeezed and pulled Torreno over backward. And then there was nothing but frenzied water and darkness.

"There's somebody here to see you," a voice said.

Deal blinked awake. He saw the smiling face of the nurse wavering into focus above him. She had the bed control in hand, her finger on the button that was cranking him to a sitting position, never mind if he'd said whether it was okay or not. For a moment he thought it might be the middle of the night, then saw a square of sunlight on the wall beside his bed.

"Who is it?" he managed, drawing a breath as a jolt of pain took him. They had cast his leg all the way from his toes to his hip, leaving cutouts for bolts at his knee and his ankle. A series of cables connected him to a traction machine that looked like it had come from a medieval dungeon. Sleep came rarely these days, and he was not happy to have it snatched from him.

"You'll see," the nurse said, cheerily disregarding his mood.

Deal stared out past the network of cables. There was a muffled clanking sound as a pair of hands clutching a walker appeared in the doorway . . . and then he saw her.

Janice stood in the doorway staring back at him, the bandages gone from her face. Her hair had become a bona fide crew cut by now, even edging over the bandages that still covered her ears. Her eyes, bright with fear, with anticipation, followed his gaze.

"They take a while, Deal," she said. Her voice faltered. "The ears,

I mean. The doctor says they'll be fine, though. He's going to do them like Debra Winger's. She's got the greatest ears, don't you think?"

Deal swallowed. "Could you come over here?" he said.

She moved toward him hesitantly, the walker making skittish little sounds on the polished floor. She stood above him now, tears streaking her still swollen cheeks.

"This eye," she said, pointing. "It has this little droop. I think it's there to stay."

"You're beautiful," he said, fighting the raspiness in his throat. "You're the most beautiful person I've ever seen."

She stared at him silently.

"I've been doing a lot of thinking, lying here," he said.

She nodded uncertainly.

"Did I ever tell you about my old man?" he said.

She looked at him strangely. "A million stories," she said. "He was that kind of guy."

"This is a different one," he said. "Actually, it's more about me. About us."

She shook her head, still unsure. Her hand went absently to her face, traced the new skin there.

"But it can wait," he said, struggling to raise himself. "I love you, Janice. That's the important thing."

"Oh Deal," she said. Her tears were flowing freely now.

"I can't get up," he said. "I want to kiss you and I can't get up."

She shook her head. "I can't bend over," she said helplessly. She glanced down at the walker. "I can't let go of this damned thing. I made them let me walk in here, but I can't let go of this thing."

But he wasn't listening. He was fighting up off his pillows as she spoke, she was flinging the walker aside as he did. Her embrace was the promise of life itself.

"What's that thing on the wall?" the woman asked. She was sitting across from him in the new office, rearranging herself on the chair he'd had delivered yesterday from Office Mart. He hadn't bothered to try it out. If it was as uncomfortable as the number he was on, he didn't want to know about it.

She'd dried her sniffles, had gotten her voice under control finally. She was fifty trying to look thirty. Too bad, he thought. She'd be a drop-dead fifty.

It had taken her a while to get through the story. Some sleazewad who couldn't appreciate it had hooked up with her, run off with her car and the cash he hadn't talked her into spending yet. The cops had been sympathetic. The guy had done the same thing to a couple of other nice ladies in town. But they doubted they'd ever catch the guy. The question on the table was whether *he* could—this private detective, who if the truth were known was meeting with his very first client. Take a note, he thought, speaking to an imaginary secretary: Thank Berto and the boys down at Metro for this referral.

"It's just a memento," he said finally.

"That's an odd memento," she said. She was quiet for a moment, studying the arrangement.

"I would think you'd have something to advertise how you uncovered that Torreno scandal," she said. "What you two men went through . . . " She broke off and turned to him, shaking her head, her eyes wide.

Driscoll turned away, reddening. "Just a public service," he mumbled. They had nailed Torreno, of course, uncovered his embezzlements, even connected him to the museum bombing and the murder of the Valles brothers. Driscoll had, in fact, received a letter of thanks from Jorge Vas, the chairman of the Patriots' Foundation himself, expressing gratitude for Driscoll's efforts on their behalf. He supposed he could frame that letter, but the irony seemed a bit rich.

What still galled him was that the subsequent search of Torreno's property, delayed by the department for reasons never made clear to Driscoll, had not yielded the biggest prize. No notes, no documents, no letter from the President. Any chance of proving the deal Torreno had cut with the government had gone to the grave with Tommy Holsum. Half a loaf, Driscoll told himself. Half a loaf.

He shook his head to clear it and glanced up at the thing his new client had pointed out. Actually it looked like a piece of art, some kind of weird collage, framed and matted behind glass like it was: a spray of gears, spindles, a metal case. There were two mangled batteries and a tiny notebook, its leather cover pierced by a neat hole. A bird's-nest swirl of micro Mylar tape held it all together. His partner's wife's idea, framing the shattered tape recorder that had saved his life.

He rubbed his chest absently, remembering the night the bullet had struck him—and how could he not, the only time in his life he'd ever been shot. If he pressed down hard, he believed, he could feel the knot of the slug they'd left inside him, even though the doctors claimed it was impossible.

The whine of the tattoo needle from the shop next door started up, bringing him out of his reverie. He wondered if the woman heard it too. He worried about how the sound carried in the cheap offices, but what the hey, he was just starting out. "My partner gave that to me," he said finally. "I call it 'Shape of a Fat Man's Luck.'"

"You don't look so fat," she said, giving him an appraising look. He felt the color rising in his cheeks. She *was* a lovely woman.

"Which one are you again?" she asked, studying the card he'd given her. "Driscoll? Or Deal?"

He laughed then. "Oh, I'm Driscoll," he said. "The other guy builds houses."

She stared at him, puzzled. "He's not a detective? Then why is his name on the agency?"

Driscoll laughed again, felt a twinge in his ribs. "It's a long story, ma'am," he said.

Behind the puzzlement in her eyes was the pain that had brought her into his office. He had a sudden flash then, of all the people who'd been drawn to this oddest of cities, of all the bewilderment and sadness out there. And then he found himself thinking of dark water. Of creatures feeding upon one another, of the snake that eats its tail. He'd found himself thinking about a lot of things lately, and he thought that was good.

He smiled at the puzzled, pain-filled lady, pointed at the card she held. "But trust me. I wouldn't have it any other way."